# A DYSTOPIAN SCIENCE FICTION ACTION THRILLER

# THE ROSE

## VOL. 1

# PD ALLEVA

QUILL AND BIRCH

*Published by:*

## QUILL AND BIRCH
TREASURE COAST, FLORIDA
quillandbirch.com

Website/Newsletter www.pdalleva.com
Facebook Page: @pdallevaauthor
Twitter: @PdallevaAuthor
Instagram: pdalleva_author

ISBNs:
978-1-7351686-0-9  (Ebook)
978-1-7351686-1-6  (Paperback)
978-1-7351686-2-3  (Hardcover)

Edited by Judy at GoddessFish Promotions
Cover design by Cherie Fox
Interior design by Gary A. Rosenberg

Printed in the United States of America

*For Dominick*
*All is as it should be.*
*Keep your wits about you.*

*"Sit with elders of the gentle race*
*This world has seldom seen*
*They talk of days for which they sit and wait*
*All will be revealed"*

~LED ZEPPELIN ("KASHMIR")


*"I must not fear.*
*Fear is the mind-killer.*
*Fear is the little-death*
*that brings total obliteration."*

~FRANK HERBERT (*DUNE*)


*"I have come here to chew bubble gum and kick ass.*
*And I'm all out of bubble gum."*

~JOHN CARPENTER'S *THEY LIVE*

# PART ONE

# YOUR DEATH WILL NOT BE IN VAIN!

# 1

TO SANDY COX, FORTY-EIGHT HOURS AGO seemed like a different world. A
sadistic galaxy. An alternate universe. Not that the now was any different, like waking from one nightmare to learn you're in another,
even worse than the one before. Forty-eight hours ago she was
with her husband, Ben. She had some sense of hope, a semblance of
order. Forty-eight hours ago she was a prisoner, although she didn't
know it at the time.

She looked over from the window where she'd been standing
for more hours than she'd like to think of. Her throat burning,
swollen, she forced a swallow and her face winced, watching the
stranger, Phil, meticulously count his weaponry. She looked down
to her stomach, her hand drifting to her navel, staring. Her thick
paunch revealed through the tight dark brown tank top turned
even darker by sweat and soot. She breathed deeply then crossed
her arms and leaned her head against the windowsill, exhausted,
scared to all bloody hell, and overwhelmed. Caught her reflection
in the window, noticed how tired and drawn she appeared. The
skin beneath those dry brown eyes thick and dark. She hadn't had
much sleep, too many thoughts and concerns swimming through
her mind, refusing the body rest. Noticed how her shoulder length
hair was matted and nappy. Sandy looked through her reflection to
what was happening outside the hotel.

The scene outside was surreal, outlandish and disheartening.
But she had to watch. Proof that the world continued to spiral into
peril. Watched and listened. Except when the killings happened as
they had been all morning. No. Sandy refused to watch the firing
squad drop dead bodies to the concrete. Instead, she'd clamp her
eyes shut, held her ears as tight as possible, wishing gunfire wasn't
so loud.

*This isn't going to end well.* Sandy's thought kept looping back like a freight train colliding with a brick wall.

Forty-eight hours ago World War Three was over. As far as she was concerned, none of this should be happening. None of it made any sense.

Now, they were holed up in a small hotel. Two strangers waiting for the exact right moment to move forward. The room was dark. Electricity had gone out in this area more than a few years ago with no reprieve expected to ever arrive. And they had to be quiet, whispering to each other every so often, and mostly out of necessity when hand gestures and lip movements were unsatisfactory to the message either needed to send. The need for quiet was paramount. There were soldiers outside.

"When can we leave?" Sandy whispered, still staring out the window, watching the men outside placed in rows waiting for the firing squad to begin. A defeated disbelieving stare gripped their countenance. Disbelieving, Sandy thought, because this is how their lives were ending. After all they'd been through, all they had survived, the end for them was now, under the declaration of peace, staring down the black hole of an AR15.

The compound, roughly fifty yards from the hotel had been barren when they arrived. Why did they stop? Because of the questions. Sandy had lots of questions for Phil. Plus she needed to rest. Pregnancy often comes with an overwhelming need for rest, and they'd been travelling for more than a day when she broke down. Her questions always received an answer, although those answers brought on more questions. The biggest question is always "Why?"

The hotel upon arrival seemed like the best place to rest the back and try, try as much as possible to close those eyes and dip into a few winks of sleep and rest. That had been in the dark hours before dawn. Sandy had dropped into sleep, exhausted, frightened and confused; however, sleep was needed, the baby told her so. And then the compound became teemed with life once dawn arrived. Military vehicles, military personnel including American, Chinese, and Russian soldiers escorting American civilians into the compound — male adults and children — by gunpoint. The commotion stirred Sandy awake. Squealing tires. Humming engines. Shouting and sometimes even laughter. And then electricity. How did they have electricity when the hotel was still without? Another question with an answer resulting in another question.

And all too quickly, as if to cease the onslaught of questions and answers, the killings began.

Sandy turned to Phil, who rifled through his bag laying out on a small round table his weaponry and supplies. A metal belt, at least it looked like metal, vials and two handles she assumed fit neatly and firmly in his palms, for what reason she did not know, never asked either. And the armor he wore, faded white, snug, and tight around his shoulders and torso, made him appear a bit broader than she assumed he was. His bare arms toned, muscular with thick forearms and strong massive hands. Phil had to cut off the sleeves to his armor, the result of taking too many bullets, knives and hits during the rescue. The sleeves had dangled on a thread from the shoulders until Phil removed them, revealing a sleeveless Kevlar shirt beneath. Staring, Sandy thought he must be mulling over for the gazillionth time their escape plan and justifying the reasons he'd chosen to occupy the hotel room instead of moving forward like they were supposed to. He had said his justification for the decision was instinct, sensing in his gut something had gone wrong with the larger plan. She wanted to believe him, although she suspected there was something he wasn't letting on to. But she had no reason not to trust him, not after what he did for her. Plus, the pregnant Sandy needed rest. Atlanta was at least another two days away by foot. Of course, Phil could requisition one of the many vehicles left on the side of the road but that could result in unwanted attention. It was best to go by foot, Sandy had agreed.

"Soon," he said. "We can leave within a day."

Sandy bowed her head and sighed, feeling her stomach and the child growing within. Hoping and praying for a sign her unborn was simply a quiet baby, resting in the womb, content.

"Are you hungry?" Phil asked.

"Always!"

"Come eat something. You'll need your strength."

"Something?" she said. She sat on the couch. "That word implies there's more than one choice." She forced a smile taking the bread Phil handed her.

"What about you?" asked Sandy.

"We haven't enough. I'll eat before we go."

Machine gun fire exploded beyond the hotel, followed by the heavy thud of bodies falling to the concrete. They both paused and Sandy felt her blood cringe. Voices now from outside the room, on the street, were muddled and fast spoken, but Sandy couldn't understand what the soldiers were saying.

She tore off a piece of bread, chewed, and swallowed.

"I wish I knew Chinese…or Russian," she said, staring at the scene outside the window. The line of dead bodies. Soldiers talking and laughing, smoking cigarettes. "I'll make sure she knows these languages…" Sandy touched her stomach. "Going to need to know a lot more in the new world…. if we make it."

"We will," Phil said. Sandy noted how calm he was. "We need to be cautious, but we will make it."

"To Atlanta?"

"Yes."

She paused biting off another piece of bread, forcing herself to look away from the dead.

Her nerves were shot to all hell, she was sure, the tightness she felt in her jaw, reaching to her temples confirmed her assumption. Plus, the nagging nausea she was hopeful had nothing to do with the baby was another telltale sign of high anxiety. Her heart racing as if sprinting towards a finality she refused to acknowledge.

She turned to the window, staring at the line of dead bodies on the street as a dump truck stopped outside, its wheels whistling and hissing to a stop. The soldiers escorted a group of young men by gunpoint, shouting in Chinese and Russian to pick up the dead and throw the bodies in the truck.

Sandy asked, "Why do they only kill the old?"

Phil paused, his eyes wide, staring at the carnage on the street. "Because they have no use for them." His voice just above a whisper.

She started to cry, her jaw quivered. She held in the whining noise that crying so often brings.

"Come," Phil said. "Let's continue your training."

"I don't want to. Not right now."

Phil paused. "I know this is difficult, but if something does happen to me, you'll need it to get you to Atlanta."

"How could anything happen to you if you have the same training?"

"Circumstance," was his reply. "There is always circumstance that drives us to make choices."

"Like when you left my husband?"

Phil paused before answering. "I couldn't save him. I had a choice to make and I'm more than positive if he were here with us, he would agree with what I did. We're at the tail end of World War Three, and life as we know it has changed."

Staring at the floor now, moving her head back and forth. "That's what I don't understand...we were safe in the camp, that's why we all went there during the war. To be safe. And when we signed the treaty, we thought it was all over." She turned to Phil. "Why did our own soldiers allow them to come in and take so many? Why were other people not even touched or even looked at? None of this makes sense. The treaty was signed, it should all be over, but it's not...it's..."

Her thoughts trailed off. What she couldn't speak about—or what she didn't want to talk about—were the children. And the pregnant women in the camp. After the treaty the children were taken and the pregnant with them. Sandy had been spared because her belly showed no signs of pregnancy. She did all she could to conceal what did show and then it came. She woke up the day after the treaty and that baby bump was there, too large to hide. She talked with Ben and the plan was to conceal the pregnancy for as long as possible. Until they were allowed to leave the camp. But that reprieve was never meant to arrive.

Instead a Chinese soldier identified her growing stomach. Taken by gunpoint, they were escorting Sandy and Ben when Phil arrived. And that's when all hell broke loose. Phil, the sole survivor, lost eight men during the rescue. Ben had been captured, and Sandy knew she had to go with Phil then. The rumors had surfaced a day before, stories of torture and mind manipulation. Genetic testing on the unborn! Whoever this stranger, Phil, was he went to great lengths and sacrifices to find her, and there did not seem to be anything off with the man, or boy for that matter. He looked like a baby, no more than twenty, compared to Sandy's age of twenty-six. Although strange...*odd is more like it, like he grew up in a different world*...his heart seemed genuine. The result had brought them here, to this hotel, with a horde of questions to be answered.

"I don't know about the terms of the treaty. I don't know what was discussed or agreed to. But the 'why' doesn't matter. Look with your own eyes at what's happening, not with what you wish or think."

Her eyes were downtrodden. "We were safe in the camp," she said softly, as if to herself. "We were told to go there...they turned on us, our own people...turned on us. And now this and what's happening out there, on the street. None of it makes any sense...." She felt her face heat up, blood rushing to her forehead. "Why couldn't you save my husband? I want him here with me, with our baby."

"We can't be irrational or make decisions in haste. My mission was to secure the target and bring you to Atlanta to train under him, not to rescue your husband."

"Why me, what have I got to do with any of this?"

"Because of what *will* happen," Phil said. "Not what has happened."

She shook her head. "This is crazy. How could anyone know the future?"

"Because *he* does know the future. The things I've seen him do and predict have been one hundred percent on point." He pointed to her stomach. "If it weren't for him you would also be under their control. Have a bit of faith, please."

"Robyn Winter?" she scoffed.

"Yes," Phil replied.

"How does he know so much about the future?"

"The record," Phil said. "Everything exists inside the record.

In codes not yet discovered by human intellect past, present, and future exist."

"That's right, human evolution will manifest through *the rose*, according to the record, to usher in utopia for those who are left on earth." Her voice sarcastic, unbelieving. She rolled her eyes with a quick shake of her head. "Any idea when that's happening because if you've looked around for the last ten years we are far away from peace on earth." She wiped her eyes, her jaw tight and quivering. "What is the rose?" she asked. "And if human beings can't access this record, how does Robyn Winter know it?"

Phil's answer came quickly, subtle, and poised. "Robyn was taught how to access the record. The *Akashic Record* and the rose are two very different things. The record is a recording of all events, past, present and future. The rose is for protection. It is a meditative practice."

"You know how to do it?"

Phil stiffened. "Robyn started teaching me before I left to secure you."

"So, you don't know how to do it?" She turned away, eyes darted to the wall.

"You'll be ok," Phil reassured. "I have many skills to protect you. My experience with the rose may be limited, but what I've learned so far, Robyn has asked me to teach to you."

"Why?" She shook her head.

Phil paused before answering. "Because he said you will need it."

Sandy swallowed the last bite of bread; her tears now dry beneath the eyes.

"I don't want to," she said looking down to the floor.

"I've lost people close to me too," he said. "But if we give in there is no more hope. There is only fear and death." He offered his hand.

She paused not giving him audience.

Phil waited a few moments before retracting.

"Maybe a little later," he said and went to the window, watching as the dead were thrown into the truck. "Try to sleep."

But she couldn't sleep. Lying on that dusty mildewed bed with thoughts racing like a conveyer belt turned on high, she heard more shooting. And all Sandy could think about was what if? What if they find her? What would they do to her and her baby?

\* \* \*

The hotel started to shake and rumble with a deafening thunderous rattle. Phil looked to the ceiling, the door, and the walls.

"What is it?" Sandy hollered over the rumbling. She was sitting on the bed. Phil caught her stare, her eyes darting from one end of the room to the other, watching the walls tremble.

He held his finger to his lips. "Shhh!" His eyes fixated on the trembling ceiling.

"Helicopters? Jets?" Sandy shouted.

"Shh," Phil ordered. "That's neither helicopter nor jet."

Phil surveyed the ceiling, moved his head to the window where he watched the road outside shaking as if an earthquake rattled beneath. Watched as the shaking snaked toward the compound. The rumbling in the hotel ceased. The compound rattling and quaking abruptly stopped. Beyond the compound the sun began its decent from the world, night on its heels.

"Another drop off?" Sandy, her voice rushed, loud.

"I don't think so."

"My husband could be in there."

"Not likely."

"How do you know?" She stood up. Her hands were shaking. "He could be in there. I…"

"You don't know that. It could be nothing."

She went to the door. "I've got to know."

Phil took large strides to the door. He was quick on his feet, gripping the doorknob before Sandy.

"Let me go!" she demanded.

"I understand you want to go but it's foolish. Think about your child!"

She stiffened, giving up on leaving.

Phil stood by the door and Sandy walked away, clasping her hands together, rubbing her palms. She started to cry, fell to her knees.

"Listen," he said in a soft voice. "I understand what you're going through."

"Sure you do," she said through streaming tears.

Phil dropped his head, staring at the floor. "I have my own children and a wife." He went to her, kneeled beside her and put his hand on her shoulder. "Let's resume your training."

"Get your hand off me!" she demanded, shrugging him off.

He withdrew and stood up.

"I need to be alone."

"Where do you wish for me to go?"

"I don't care."

"Sandy..."

"Go!" she hollered.

Phil looked through the window. None of the soldiers stirred.

"I'll be right outside the door," he said and walked softy to the door. His hand on the doorknob he took one last look at Sandy, pursed his lips, tightened his jaw then opened the door. He could hear Sandy, crying.

Phil thought, *She'll come to her senses once the emotions are processed.* He closed the door. *I can't imagine what this must be like for her. For...all of them. Completely taken off guard, unknowing the truth that has been hiding in plain sight for so long.*

He sat cross-legged, leaning against the door, ran his hand through his thick sandy blonde locks.

Closed his eyes, listening to the voice of Robyn Winter, his training of the rose.

*Find the center of your mind, feel it, sense it, be within it. Now reach out your hand, see the rose at the edge of your fingertips. The calm red lines. The stem, strong, its roots in the earth. Let your hand down. See the rose in front of you. An extension of the center of your mind. In between you and the rose, this is your space, and nothing can come between yourself and the rose. Nothing! Only what you allow in. Allow nothing to enter that is dark. Allow only white light.*

Surrounding Phil was the white light, so bright the once dark hallway shined with light.

*Now look through the rose. Extend the light through its calm vibration. This light is the color of gold. You choose what can enter. Be one with the light. The light is an extension of you, of your heart. You can move freely within this light, untouched by fear, immune to hate. There is only your essence. The essence of the light of your cells, your calm vibration through the rose. It is protection, a shield where anything that enters your sacred space is yours to bend and manipulate. Suspend gravity. Move objects with a thought.*

The gold light stretched like a mushroom cloud billowing off the edges of white light. More than double the size, the gold light carried a thickness to it, as if it were a shield, manipulating the atoms in close proximity, creating a solid substance.

Phil drew breath into his nose, slow and steady. The light mirrored his breath, contracting upon inhale, expanding and loosening with the exhale. He opened his eyes, seeing the light and holding it. He practiced dissipating the doors and walls around him, turning what was once solid matter into light, except for the room where Sandy remained. He thought of her then, hoping she could gather the strength to move forward. He knew she had the ability. Not only did Robyn assure him she did, Phil felt it himself. The sensation brought him peace, knowing this would be a successful mission. Sandy will be delivered to Robyn Winter as predicted.

*Robyn*, Phil thought. He was pure calm and peace, pure commitment to the cause of saving lives and fostering human evolution. As Robyn had told him, the evolution of the human heart is bliss in the boundaries of a grand utopia. It is inevitable.

Robyn's predictions were always spot on. He knew Phil would have to leave Sandy's husband. Knew they would come to this hotel and that a truth would be revealed to Phil during this mission. A truth that would lead to a choice.

*The Gods manipulate the scene for what is needed to bring the final judgment! The record shimmers within manipulation, unfolding a new reality.*

And somewhere in the in-between, Phil could sense it, a place inside the rose where he wouldn't allow himself to fully invest. Beneath the rose there was a rumble, a vibrating thunder under his control. With it the fear of letting go, or losing control. Phil dropped his head, staring at the floor. His light dissipated. The hallway turned to normal. He waited for Sandy's escape, knowing his choice was spiraling towards him.

* * *

Sandy's jaw trembled, her mind numb, racing with possibilities, rationale, and irritation. There was so much to accept, but some situations were unacceptable. This guy Phil was strange. Strange indeed, she thought, as if he'd come from another planet. Another reality. But he *was* human, from what she'd seen so far. And he did save her. He did get her out of the camp, so she owed him that much, considering the rumors that had infected the camp like a plague. Mind manipulation and genetic experimentation. That's what they were doing with the children and pregnant women. Taking them away to places unknown, maybe to camps like this one, the one outside the hotel. Even though she hadn't seen even one woman in the camp, only men and male children, perhaps they were hiding them like a dirty little secret. Kept in the dark, away from the eyes of men.

Shouting out on the street now, beyond the window. Fast-talking gibberish she did not comprehend. Soldiers surrounded a young man, their guns drawn, his hands up. Whatever had happened was over. The soldiers did not hesitate. One bullet straight through the skull. The boy's body dropped with a thud. And then laughter; laughter from the soldier who wedged his Glock 9mm in the holster on his hip.

Sandy clenched her jaw, turning her eyes away from the boy's body now lying in a pool of his own blood. She saw her husband, standing in line, in between soldiers, on the opposite side where the dead boy lay. Ben's face filled with absolute fear and dismay. He was holding thick bed linens, the same as the others in line with him. The soldier leading them shouted an order in Russian, and the line started moving, through a tall chain link fence that housed hundreds of prisoners.

She couldn't help what happened next. Maybe it was the shooting, or the rumors that continued to wriggle into her thoughts. Or perhaps it was simple, scared and frightened, lonely. A stranger in an even stranger situation.

"*Beeeeennn!*" she hollered, covering her mouth the moment her voice reached the street. The soldiers stiffened, started yelling and screaming orders. Guns drawn as they approached the hotel. She saw Ben; still wearing a stare of dismay and fear, stop abruptly.

Sandy stepped away. She touched her stomach. Her heart sank. She saw Phil's reflection in the window.

* * *

"Time to go." Phil gripped Sandy's hand, watching the soldiers approaching the hotel. One soldier lifted his grenade launcher, aiming at the room. "NOW!" Phil demanded and took off running with Sandy in tow when the grenade ripped through the hotel with an explosion that tore the wall opposite to the window, knocking Phil and Sandy to the floor.

A shout in Chinese erupted in bullets sprayed into the hotel. Another grenade resulting in an explosion that tore through the walls. Bullets ripped through the hotel. Phil dropped to his stomach pulling Sandy down with him. She was screaming, loud and frightened. Another explosion and the wall started to fall over them. Phil jumped up cradling Sandy as his light appeared, the white light reached into gold and the wall dissipated, the bullets too, disintegrating within the gold light.

A second shout in Russian stopped the onslaught of bullets and grenades. Phil felt that thunder within the light, roaring pulsating waves and he could see the soldiers in the corner of his eye. Their jaws wide. Standing, unmoving like plastic soldiers, mesmerized, watching as the battered walls were manipulated into light.

*They must see us.* Sandy in his arms, Phil watched his light illuminate the hotel, the street, and the compound, turning night into day. He could see the Americans inside the fence, their heads turned up, mouths open observing the light. And beneath the fence, under the earth an underground compound with multiple floors.

Sandy's screams carried on the thunderous waves of light and he held her close, tight against him.

*This is it,* Phil thought. He felt elation writhe in his bones. The gold light extended into indigo, covering the whole of what had been the hotel, reaching onto the street. Pure concentration, Phil looked at the soldiers who were tossed backward, skimming across the ground, moved by Phil's thought.

And then the in-between, the place Phil had refused to go, like a brick wall he couldn't budge. A sensation like a thick impression, heavy and impinging on his heart, in his mind, slithered into his thoughts. It wore him down. He never felt anything like it.

*LET GO!* he screamed in his head, clamping his eyes shut. But the sensation pushed down on him, tossing into his mind thoughts of fear and frustration. Like drifting in open space, being dropped from a plane without a parachute, realizing he'd let go of Sandy. His light weakened. When he opened his eyes, he saw the wall come roaring down. He jumped to his feet, tossing Sandy out of harm's way and taking the full brunt of the wall, falling unconscious as more debris and concrete dropped on top of him.

* * *

Sandy stood in the clearing, wide eyed and trembling as guns were drawn in her direction. The soldiers moved cautiously. An order was shouted. She closed her eyes. The next voice was softer, like a discovery was made. No bullets were fired. She opened her eyes and a soldier was pointing at her stomach. The others laughed. Orders given in Chinese, with gestures to move forward, towards the compound. Sandy looked over the decimation at her feet. The hotel in pieces all around her. She opened her mouth to speak but not words came. More shouting from Chinese soldiers, voices hurried, angry.

"Ok." She raised her hands, stepped cautiously from the decimation, surrounded by soldiers.

*I'm so sorry Phil.* She gritted her teeth, tightened her jaw. A soldier pushed her forward, toward the compound. Their laughter stung her ears.

She caught Ben's eye, standing motionless.

He was ordered to move, to fall in line with the others. But he couldn't take his eyes off Sandy, and the soldiers noticed. Noticed how she looked at him too. One of those soldiers smiled, shouted an order at Ben who had no understanding of what he was told. The soldier pushed his shoulder, keeping his rifle drawn. Ben looked at him and the soldier pushed a second time. Ben started walking towards his wife, escorted by gunpoint. Sandy saw him approaching, she stopped, froze, waiting for Ben who ran to her, dropping those bed linens with his approach.

"My God," Ben said. "I thought you were gone."

"I thought the same." Sandy rested in Ben's arms.

"Is the baby ok? Who was that person who took you? How did you end up here?"

"I…" Sandy was interrupted with a poke in her back. The same soldier escorting Ben pushed his rifle between her shoulder blades. His order was apparent, 'move along.'

They moved together, through a makeshift hallway that separated two large areas. On one side the clearing was lit with large industrial lights affixed to the top of the fence. The opposite side, dark and black as the night itself and surrounded by an incomplete concrete wall. Ahead was what would have been a warehouse before the war, about ten yards away. Double doors waited for them to approach.

"What is this place?" Sandy whispered.

"I don't know…I was brought here on a convoy truck with so many other men. Packed together on top of each other. Some of them said the treaty was a farce. That the war isn't over. They said it was to get us to drop our guard and…"

The soldier smacked the back of Ben's head with his open hand.

"Be quiet," Sandy whispered. "They don't want us to talk."

"How does he know what we're talking about? I can't understand a damn thing they're saying."

Another whack across his skull. Ben scowled at the soldier, his hand on the back of his head. As they neared the warehouse doors they hesitated to enter. The soldier pushed his rifle into their backs, shouting.

Ben reached for the door handle, but the soldier smacked his hand away, cautiously moving to the door, his gun still drawn. The soldier reached out and pulled the door until it popped into place to remain open and the soldier took the gun into his hands, shouting at them, gesturing with his gun for them to enter.

The room was dark, a dull purple fluorescent lamp the only light. The air cold from industrial fans Sandy was sure came from the open room to their left. At one time this room had been an office for whatever business had occupied the space. The office was large and open. A metal desk sat in the room's center. Ahead was an elevator. To their left an open door that led to a large open room occupied with rows and rows of cots where soldiers slept, sat, talked, played cards, and smoked cigarettes. But they all stopped to look at Ben and Sandy. Sandy turned away. On the right were blacked out windows as if whatever was inside the incomplete wall beyond the office was not to be seen. Or didn't want to be seen.

Sandy's belly jumped and bumped, the baby erupted into a frenzy, as if frightened over the current predicament. Or sensing Sandy's fear. She wanted to touch her stomach, to feel her child and give the baby a sense of relief that the mother was there for protection. That both parents were there to protect.

Its ok my love, Sandy thought. Momma's here, baby…momma's here!

The baby continued to jump, push and kick. Sandy eyes filled with tears.

"*Close the door!*" a voice from the cot area hollered. "You're letting the heat in."

Sandy and Ben shared perplexed stares. This was the first time they heard an American voice, the English language. Sandy heard the door behind them close with a metal bang.

"Help!" Ben hollered. "You're American, please help us. My wi-- the lady is pregnant, please help her."

His plea brought laughter from the soldiers.

"My man," said the American. "In ten minutes, you won't give a damn about anything. Shut up and follow orders."

The couple froze, tense, but the baby jumped in the womb. The hum of ascending, scraping metal filled the room.

"Sorry, more like ten seconds," the American said, his voice now faint, compassionate.

Elevator doors scraped opened from the far end of the room, shimmering from within with a distinct but faint white light that reached from the doors but faded quickly into the purple dark of the room.

Emerging from the elevator was a petite and thin older woman. No taller than four feet with arms abnormally long for such a short stature, her knuckles close to scraping the floor as she ambled towards them. Bones so thin they resembled toothpicks, all skin and bones. As she approached, the elevator doors scraped to a close. Her eyes and skin in the purple light reflected large bulging slanted brown eyes, skin like leather, and a large elongated bony skull with no hair. The glint in her eye revealed an excitement and sense of urgency.

She didn't look at them. Her eyes fixed on Sandy's stomach, growing wider with every step.

Sandy watched the woman approach. She closed her eyes then snapped them open, her brow furrowed watching the woman who moved with a peculiar stride as if the molecules between them were bent and raging fast. With every step Sandy felt her body constrict. All she could see was this tiny woman, approaching with mesmerized eyes and a stare that cut straight through Sandy's stomach. She seemed to float across the floor. The woman stopped in front of them, her arms stretched to Sandy's stomach with tiny hands that hovered over the abdomen.

"Don't touch her!" Ben ordered, voice constricted.

But she ignored his order. The baby jumped, clawing inside Sandy's stomach, as if trying to get away. Attempting to run. Sandy felt a tightness across her throat, unable to speak or move.

Ben's voice stuttered. "I sa--sa--sa--said get away..."

Sandy forced her eyes to move, to look at Ben, seeing blood spilling from his nose.

"Shut up," a second American soldier ordered. His voice frustrated and fearful. "Can't you see? Just shut up."

"Leave it alone, Cameron," the first American soldier said.

Ben fell to the floor, convulsing, flapping on the ground.

Sandy watched him in the corner of her eye. Her throat constricted, her body paralyzed, as the open door to the soldiers was slammed shut. She heard the elevator doors scrape open. The woman reached her hand to Sandy's forehead. And all Sandy could see was white. Blinding white light with a sensation that she was moving. Or being moved.

In the elevator.

White light.

Heat so immense the air was stained dark red. Beneath the earth, corridors everywhere!

White light.

Screams, echoed through the corridors, bounced off concrete walls, reverberated in Sandy's ears. She's on a gurney now; her feet flopped to the side, being wheeled through the hall. Short beings, the backs of their heads, grey, thick and wide, long arms with tiny hands pulling the gurney.

White light.

White light.

White light.

# 2

**BEN'S EYES ROLLED OPEN TO A STRIKING LIGHT.** A sharp pain squeezed from his eyeballs to the center of his brain. He pinched the bridge of his nose. Eyelids fluttered open. His head was heavy and weary. He lay on a bed in an otherwise empty room. No windows, only painted white concrete walls that exuded heat igniting a burning sensation that formed beads of sweat across Ben's forehead, torso, arms and legs. His head and thoughts groggy, realizing he had no clue where he was. He forced himself to a sitting position, recognizing he was naked.

*Where am I?*

Of course, the first question concerned location.

*What happened? Sandy?*

He held his head, feeling a painful twitch in his abdomen and right forearm that dropped his left hand to his navel and his shoulders to arch and constrict. His face flinched in pain, squinting his eyes. The pain squirmed from his navel to his chest and throat, igniting a burning in the back of his brain.

*What…?*

Eyes wide now, studying his forearm and a tattoo of four symbols like hieroglyphics, running from his wrist to his elbow that had not been there before. The skin was irritated around the tattoo, and Ben ran his fingers across the symbols, hoping it would have been no more than a marker drawn symbol than a permanent design, with no such luck. He'd been branded by…

*That lady?*

The thought of the short, thin woman shrieked in his memory, her hands over Sandy's stomach. His thoughts interrupted by a click at the door, eyes fixed on the turning doorknob. The door opened and in came an older man, an American, dressed in scrubs and white doctor's coat. Short in stature, his sandy blonde hair was worn like a disheveled mop that hung over his forehead just above his blue eyes.

"Mr. Cox," he said, offering his hand. "Dr. Blum."

Ben ignored the offering. "What the hell is going on here?"

Dr. Blum paused. A gruff smile curled the corner of his mouth. "Mr. Cox, your behavior was witnessed to be rather erratic and rebellious…"

"By who?" Ben's voice was abrupt.

Dr. Blum sighed, shook his head, and cocked his eyebrows. "By those in charge, Mr. Cox, and you were brought to me…"

"Who's in charge? What behavior? All I did was obey what I was told. I never behaved with any resistance."

"Brought to me to prepare you for reconditioning."

Ben shook his head. *"Reconditioning for what?"*

*"Of* your behavior, Mr. Cox. *For,* those that are in charge. They…" Dr. Blum paused as if searching for the appropriate words. Cocked his head, eyes squinted. "…delight in people like yourself."

"Delight?"

"Well, we ran tests. You're in perfect health, no diseases, no signs of any hormonal imbalances, and you're obviously potent… considering your wife is pregnant."

"What's that got to do with any of this? Where is my wife? Where's Sandy? How's the baby?"

"Perfectly fine, Mr. Cox, there is no cause for concern with those two; they'll be taken care of better than we are, that's for sure."

"I want to see them. Where are they?"

"Your second child, correct?"

Ben shot Dr. Blum a baffled stare. His eyes narrowed. His body tensed.

*How does he know about Ares?* During the chaos and carnage of the war, under the guise of safety for the children, the parents had given their children over to the American government who loaded the children onto buses to be brought to the safety camps with the hope they would survive. Unfortunately, Ben and Sandy were provided with an update once they arrived at the safety camp six months after. Their son had been kidnapped, along with the other children, after a military convoy laid siege to the blue bus they had been riding on.

A pause as Ben sized up the doctor.

"I want to see my wife. NOW!"

Dr. Blum shook his head. "Not gonna happen, Mr. Cox. It's better if you fall in line and follow orders like the others."

"What others?" He looked back and forth over the room. "There's no one else here."

"Not in the room, Mr. Cox, but there are many here, and many more to come."

Ben jumped off the bed, nose to nose with Dr. Blum. "I'm leaving, gonna find my wife, and we are out of here. The war's over. You can't keep us here."

Dr. Blum laughed. "Where do you think you'll be going?"

"Out of here for sure."

He pushed through the doctor, who rolled his eyes.

"Do you have any idea where you are?" Dr. Blum sighed. He took a tiny round device from his pocket. Ben pushed through the door. "Mr. Cox is in the hallway," he said into the device.

Ben ignored the doctor.

"Sandy!" he called. The hallway consisted of clean, well-lit concrete walls and floors that stretched endlessly in both directions with numerous doors, one every few feet, like jail cells with no bars. Double doors at the end in both directions, but so far away they were tiny to the eye.

"SANDY!" he hollered.

The doctor stood in the doorway. "It's useless, Mr. Cox, all you're doing is making the situation worse. Come back in the room."

Ben checked doorknobs. All were locked. Turned up the hallway, checked them all.

"Sandy!"

"You don't get it, Mr. Cox!"

"SANDY!" Ben tried another door, there were so many to check.

"Look at you, naked and screaming down the hall. You look ridiculous, and your behavior is erratic."

"Sandy!"

"Come back in the room, Mr. Cox. I'll explain more. At least with proper information you can make an informed decision on whether or not you want to continue this search ..."

"Sandy!" Ben's fear manifested in the doorknob snapping in his hand.

"Mr. Cox!"

He threw the door open. Inside an adult male was stretched on a bed much like Ben had been. A needle in his navel, being guided by...

Ben's jaw dropped.

The hallway double doors swung open at the end of the hall. Ben did not notice who was coming.

"Probably not the best idea, Mr. Cox, but at least you know now...well, you know part of it. But not the part that concerns you. What you're seeing is merely a necessary procedure for appropriate preparation."

Ben witnessed the grey alien, extracting fluid through a needle wedged into the man's navel. The alien continued without distraction. Ben stood, unmoving, confounded. His mouth agape, mesmerized, his brain twisting with a sharp pain and then...darkness.

*  *  *

In her dream, Sandy returned to the safety camp, a few days before word of the treaty would arrive. The sun hid behind a veil of grey clouds, the grand star descending, signaling an end to the day's work of farming duties, sifting through rice and wheat. On this day she hadn't seen Ben in over a week, standard protocol during her time in the camp: men and women were separated. She ran her hands through her hair, brunette locks made even darker by matted sweat and grime. She gripped her hair in her hands to cool off the nape of her neck while listening to the moans and groans from the throats of cohorts, when the soldier standing guard took her attention.

The camp occupied a small town in the northeast, a wall had been constructed surrounding the camp under the guise of safety from their enemies: Chinese and Russian military. A soldier had taken his post on top of the wall. Over the years Sandy made it a point to keep the soldiers in sight. Her reasoning was simple, should the soldiers begin to stir she could prepare herself quickly for any possible battle or siege that was on the way. Nonetheless the practice had turned skeptical. Sandy noticed a shift a week prior, like a flick of a light switch when electricity ceased pumping power. A change in the wind that carried an uneasy sensation on its heels.

At first, she paid it no mind, thinking the pregnancy created a false narrative with all the hormones competing for a place in her mind. Except that nagging instinct that something was truly wrong stayed with her. And here, on this day, oddly peculiar, the soldier had no interest in what was happening outside the wall. No, on this day he turned his attention on them, to those inside the wall.

And he seemed to be searching, devouring each and every one of them with apt focus. Like sizing up an enemy, searching for any possible threats or insurgencies.

Her stomach bumped and her hand went to it, instinctive, grateful the pregnancy continued to be kept a secret.

"It's in the blood, dear," said Ellen, one of the women Sandy shared time and space with, her skin worn by age, hard labor, and days spent under the sun. Blotches, liver spots and creases led the observer to the eyes. One dark, the other a cataract milky white and she always wore a dark shawl draped over the head and shoulders. Sandy was afraid of Ellen, she reminded Sandy of a gypsy or witch from a fairy-tale.

"Come again?" said Sandy, her eyes shifting from soldier to Ellen to soldier then back to Ellen.

Ellen had cut herself transferring a wood bucket filled with rice to add to an already large trough of buckets. A thick wood splinter pinned in the bottom of her palm dripping with a thick stream of blood. She turned to Sandy raising the bloodied palm and caught a drop of blood in her unwounded hand.

"The blood dear," said Ellen. "All magic comes from the blood."

Sandy cringed at the sight; she'd always been squeamish. Her stomach bumped, blood curled. Magic, Sandy thought. If only magic *was* real. How wonderful would that be? Sandy understood she was naïve, the result of an isolated childhood and her parents' death when she was ten years old. Not that they had taught the young Sandy about the world she lived in either. They'd kept her under lock and key, never so much as offering a glimpse or advice on the outside world. They were always so cryptic with their explanations, living in an abundant and overgrown mansion as if luxury were a childhood friend. Sure, there were plenty of rooms for a child to explore but as time went by those rooms seemed more like a prison than a home.

Years of neglect, isolation and secrets were as torturous as physical suffering. And she was tired of secrets. She wanted to know truth. Truth was like a blanket that keeps you warm in the coldest winter.

"The blood, Sandy," said Ellen who clenched her fist around those crimson droplets, shaking her hand in front of her face. "All is in the blood."

The dream dissipated and Sandy could see, and feel, a white bulbous light move through her brain with a soft fluttering that graced the back of her eyes. And her ears pricked to the sound of bleep, bleep, bleep, kindling a sensation equaled to hollow pain, knowing...

*Something's different!*

*Something's very, very different. Something's wrong.*

Sandy drifted awake to the sound of bleep...bleep...bleep. Her thoughts floated into existence.

*Something's very...very wrong.*

Her body paralyzed, incapable of feeling her limbs or even sense they still existed. Blurred vision beginning to focus and she could see her surroundings. White concrete walls, herself on a bed with a heart monitor by her side. The steady bleep ringing in her eardrums when she noticed the wires and electrodes stuck to her skin beneath a white gown she didn't remember putting on.

The room was quiet, the air stuffy and hot, burning hot like standing near an open oven, the flow of heated air thickened in the room. Her mouth dry, she pursed her lips attempting to swallow as a rush of heat was forced down her throat. A throat that felt sore and swollen.

*What is this?*

She strained to think and remember. Remember something, anything that would provide a clue to where she was and how she got here. But the memories refused to indulge her want and need, evading consciousness as if the memories desired to be kept a secret. Sandy lifted her head, looking down the length of her body. Yes, her arms were there, lying limp by her side, her body and legs too, wrapped tightly in the gown.

"*Hello,*" she called through a cracked voice. The bleep, bleep, bleep jumped. Sandy cleared her throat. "Hello!" she hollered, forcing the word through labored breath. "Help."

Her heart racing. Bleep bleep bleep bleep.

"Somebody? Anybody? *P-L-E-A-S-E!*"

She tried to move her arms, her body, her legs, but with zero result. Tried again, pushing, forcing her body to move and lifting her head as if the rest of her would follow. Nothing!

"Jesus, please!"

She started to cry. "Please, please, please." She slammed the back of her head against the bed. Trying, forcing, doing everything to get her body to move.

"H-E-L-P!" she screamed. "Oh, God, help me, please."

Sandy wept, tears cascading from the corners of her eyes, saturating her dark hair. And then the thought came; perhaps a memory but she couldn't remember the actual incident. She saw the tiny woman at her side as three more beings surrounded her, working, performing a surgery. She saw the baby, *her* baby, lifted from her stomach in tears and wailing cries. The beings surrounding her, holding her baby, clipping the umbilical cord, placing the baby on a table and rushing it out of the room. The baby's cries wailing down the hallway, softened the further the baby was taken.

Sandy saw herself on that surgery table. Her eyes drifting to the being that took her baby. Slightly taller than the tiny woman by her side, but not by much. And the skin was lighter, not as dark as the other who stood beside her. The being gazed into her eyes as if seeing inside her soul. Sandy could see this thing, this unidentified being consumed by the work being performed; shoot her a stare that tore through Sandy's mind.

Sandy screamed, hollered, and wailed.

The being spoke telepathically. *Your child is safe. He is with us now.*

She heard the voice, repeating like an echo rattling in her skull. Her labored breath calming to short and quick shallow huffs. Sandy's eyes stared wide, the memory stained on the back of her eyes, trying, struggling to push through it, to somewhere she could find help.

One name forced itself over her lips.

"Ben."

* * *

Dr. Blum escorted an alien vampire, a Drac, down the pristine hallway. This Drac was tall, standing well above six feet. He wore thick black armor that shined under the light, covering his torso, neck to navel, all the way down his arms, locked at the wrists. Standard armor for Drac soldiers. His skin was pale, at least as pale as a scaly brownish auburn flesh could allow. His skull was smooth and large, and his neck bones stood on his shoulders protruding from the skin and skull like two thick stints up to the top of his head. The bones swelled then retracted, in unison with his breathing. The skin beneath his eyes was a pale red circling dry yellowish eyeballs with emerald pupils. His fingers were long and thick with sharp nails. Part of the Drac species, he wore his people's badge of honor proud on his sleeve.

"He's the first to receive the new pills," Dr. Blum explained. "He's still coherent though, seems his strength and adrenaline are fighting off the effects, but at least he's calm. Shock to the system if you know what I mean, Sanos?"

"Indeed," replied Sanos, his voice a thick and heavy baritone. "He's had all the necessary tests completed?"

"Of course," Dr. Blum replied.

"Good...I'm starved."

Dr. Blum bowed. "Of course."

They stopped in front of the door leading to Ben's chamber.

"This is it," said Dr. Blum, sliding a panel from the small window. He looked inside seeing Ben sitting on the floor, his back against the wall. Ben's pupils circled beneath half closed eyelids. His body jerked. The back of his head smacked against the wall. "Hmm, see, much more calm."

"Delightful," breathed Sanos. "May I?"

"Naturally."

Sanos commanded perfection in his food. His eyes widened, delighted in observing Ben.

"Have we done well?"

Sanos licked his lips

"*Very* well...very well indeed."

"I'll leave you to it then." Dr. Blum stepped away, turning down the hall, but stopped abruptly. "Almost forgot. He's the father of the child we secured this morning. Quite potent he is, this being his second child."

Sanos's eyes widened. His grin revealed a mouth of razor-sharp teeth. "Truly remarkable."

"Enjoy, Sanos." Dr. Blum continued his retreat down the hall.

Sanos gripped the doorknob, entering Ben's chamber, with a hurried anticipation.

# 3

**EVERYTHING WAS DARK.**

There was debris and concrete blocks pinning Phil to the ground. He tried to move but his arms were confined. His left arm trapped beneath his body. Pain jolted to his brain, a thick wallop of hurt that rang in his skull creating a nauseous stomach. It was difficult to think, to put together thoughts and memories.

*What happened to the Rose? It was working. I was doing it right. Everything Robyn taught me I did. Why didn't it work?*

He breathed deeply; his nose and throat drew in concrete air.

His heart remained calm.

*Sandy? Is she lying dead in this mess?*

His body jumped and pain rushed to every part of his body. Phil felt the concrete wall lying on top of him.

*I must get out of here. Find Sandy and make sure she's still among the living.*

He used his healthy arm to try to push through the wreckage.

*Stay calm. It's too heavy. Too heavy to push physically.*

His heart jumped, started thumping.

*No! Breathe deeply. This concrete is not here, not really touching any part of me. Go to the center, the center of the brain, to the pineal gland. The seat of consciousness. See the rose. Focus!*

*Let go.*

Phil breathed through his nose, drawing in his navel with the inhale, letting go of the exhale.

*Let your lungs do the work.* Robyn's words in Phil's mind.

*No matter how close any object or person is…even if it feels like it's touching your skin…your bones…the rose is between you and it…expand the ether. Manipulate the cells and atoms outside of the ether, through the rose…*

Phil saw the rose, felt its calm vibration rooted in the earth as the light emanated from his core, beginning to expand, drawing the concrete into the light and manipulating the constricted atoms into a frenzy changing the concrete into vapor.

And he was able to move.

*It's not about believing, Phil, it's about knowing. Don't believe it can happen!*

*Know that it will happen!*

\* \* \*

Sanos stretched his arms, his footsteps tapping against the concrete. Ben's chest jumped, his head drifting from one side to the other. Sanos cracked his neck, stretching his chin left then right, standing in the middle of the room.

Ben attempted to open his eyes. "Who…who's there?" His eyes dripping with tears as his head flopped back to the wall.

Sanos's eyes narrowed. "Can you not see me?"

No response other than Ben's shallow breathing. Sanos moved his head and shoulders left and then right, eyeing Ben. His tongue jutted over his lips like a snake then recoiled.

"I…I…" Ben whispered. His eyes fluttered beneath his eyelids.

Sanos clenched his fists. Looked to the right while shaking his head. "Disappointing," he snarled then stared at Ben, shouting, *"DO YOU NOT SEE ME?"*

Ben shuddered against the wall as if Sanos's voice had attacked him. But briefly, he returned to his sedated state a moment after. His head swayed gently back and forth.

"Wh…where…where's Sandy?" Ben's head flopped back against the wall. His eyes rolled behind falling eyelids.

Sanos stared at Ben, sizing him up, a snarl across his lips. "Somewhere," he said. "In here with the rest of us, beneath the earth."

Ben swallowed his labored breath. "I…want…to see…her… *Now!*" He clenched his fists as if to strike but they fell to his sides like heavy anvils he had no strength to hold.

Sanos laughed. "Good Ben," he said. "Bring rage to the forefront of consciousness. I enjoy it more when the food is resistant. There's no sport with a submissive animal."

Ben's brow furrowed. His right eyelid fluttered as if attempting to see. To see what or who was in front of him.

"Yes, see me, Ben. I want you to see me." Sanos dipped his shoulders down, leaning his head closer to Ben.

Ben forced his eyes open. Sanos could see his reflection in those eyes. Sanos's countenance resembled a cobra, his neck bones swelled with the anticipatory feeding, resembling the cobra's trademark hood. Also, a common occurrence prior to a Drac feeding, the stretched bones effected the eyes, changing the otherwise elongated emerald pupils into dark pins, as if the soul retreated into darkness. Ben flopped to the floor on his side, limp and futile.

Sanos shook his head. "Dr. Blum, I'm very disappointed. Look at you, Ben, you can't even see. There's no indulgence in this, keeping food in cages is all too…human." He rolled his eyes, standing stiff and frustrated, releasing a growl from the bottom of his throat. "This is what we've come to? Making deals with a species clearly primitive to our own." He went to Ben, crouched in front of him. "I miss the days, Ben, when we'd hunt and prey on our food. Not this…wretched, fiendish way of feasting." He tapped Ben's head with a thick finger, sharp at its tip.

"But I am hungry, Ben…oh Ben, I'm so frustrated. I wish for you to be awake, to pace with fear…to fight and fight with all your strength and might." He slapped Ben's head. "Wake up!"

No response.

"Can you hear me, Ben?" He slapped Ben again. "Can you even hear me at all?" Another slap. Followed by another and another. Each slap thrown with a stronger force, the last crushing Ben's nose spewing blood on the floor, and Sanos widened his eyes.

"I'm so hungry," moaned Sanos, staring at the blood that crawled across the floor. Sanos dipped his finger in, touched the blood to his tongue and his insides shivered. His lips turned numb.

"Haven't had blood like that before," said Sanos. His body quivered as he stretched his neck. The pills in Ben's blood were now coursing through Sanos's veins. He ground his teeth, parting his lips. His body shook, jaw tight, wide eyes filled with rage. He grabbed a handful of Ben's hair snatching him up and slamming his body against the wall. His teeth tore into Ben's neck, gulping blood.

Ripped into Ben's skull, tearing at the bone. Ate his ear in one swallow. Growling as he tore Ben's windpipe from his neck, which he spit to the floor then wrapped his lips across the open cavity, bending Ben's head, drinking with frenzied indulgence.

Sanos snapped his head back. "MAGNIFICIENT," he hollered, holding Ben's body. His tongue lapped across his bloodied teeth. His head swayed side to side violently. His whole body shook as he thrust his fist into Ben's chest and tore out his heart. As he took the organ into both hands, Ben's body dropped with a thud. Sanos tore into the heart, devouring the organ. His jaw tight, mouth open wide, as a low roar erupted from his throat. His hands shaking in front of him.

He stood, feeling the hypnotic sedation turning his mind into a raging fury, swallowing the moment of pure elation. When he opened his eyes, he had one word on the tip of his tongue,

"More," he breathed. "*I need more.*"

# 4

CAMERON PATROLLED OUTSIDE THE QUARRY ALONE, his AR-15 holstered over his shoulder. He observed the people behind the fence with eyes and faces that bore a frightened and confused stare. They were Americans, like him, brought to this prison against their will. Brought for experimentation, prodding, and innovation.

His platoon's orders were simple. After the treaty was signed, they were ordered to provide support to the Chinese and Russian soldiers and obey their orders, to follow and fall in line when told. To take up arms against their American brothers and report any extravagant circumstances or special gifts the prisoners displayed. In return the soldiers would receive special accolades, usually an extended rest.

And to not interfere when the elderly were put in front of the firing squad, an act of desecration that turned his gut.

*Can't believe this is what we've come to.*

His rage over seeing the people he was protecting during the war being torn to shreds then dropped in a truck to be buried in a hole a few miles away like they were pieces of garbage boiled acid into his throat.

He stiffened staring into the quarry. A father sat beside his son.

*They'll take that kid too; it's just a matter of time. Take him and...*

Cam refused to think about it. Refused to allow his thoughts to go there, to that unknown place concerning what they were doing with the children. Old men and adults were one thing; the children were a different story. He'd seen so many brought below. None had come back. Not alive anyway. And when they did their bodies were torn, ripped to shreds as if they'd been eaten. Not the kids that is, only the adults. The kids he never saw again.

A Chinese soldier blew a whistle inside the fence.

"Time for the pills," Cam whispered, shaking his head.

The prisoners obeyed the whistle, falling in line by the rows of tables where American soldiers sat handing out pills. Pills that kept the prisoners sedated.

*Easier to control. Less apt to cause trouble.*

The pills created that blank stare, as if they dismantled all ability for rationale thought.

"Zombies," Cam said. "So they don't care what happens to them."

Dr. Blum entered the quarry, carrying a large box.

"What're you doing up here?" Cam said to himself. "You never come up here."

He strained to hear what Dr. Blum was saying to the soldier in charge, focusing on his lip movements. Cam was taught to read lips during the war in an effort to gather intel.

"They're new. A different formula." Dr. Blum said. "Stronger effect."

The soldier stared at the box, taking it from Dr. Blum while calling out an order to his subordinates.

"Replace the medicine with these," the soldier said, handing the box over, which was brought to the table and provided to the soldiers to distribute.

Cam shook his head. "Jesus Christ," he said. "How fucked up do you want them?"

Dr. Blum grinned watching the prisoners take the pills. He bowed to the soldier in charge before retreating into the building. The prisoners who'd already taken the first pills were ordered to take the second. Within minutes they fell convulsing to the floor, their heads snapping back and forth, foaming at the mouth.

The soldiers looked on, laughing.

Cam looked away.

*I can't take this.*

He sat, crouched on the ground, holding his stomach. He wanted to puke.

*Can't sit here and do nothing. I can't. Where the fuck is my dignity? We're supposed to help these people not deliver them into bondage.*

He vomited bile and acid. His head spinning and eyes wet with tears.

"Jesus Christ, please help me."

He closed his eyes trying to ward off that spinning, nauseous sensation.

"But what can I do?" he said. "There's got to be something I can do."

* * *

Sandy tried to remember what Phil had taught her about the rose. Even in Sandy's desperate resistance, Phil had explained the rose and Sandy *was* listening, although at the time she displayed no interest.

*Keep the rose at the tip of your fingers. See the rose, its gentle vibration rooted in the earth. Nothing can exist in between you and the rose that you don't choose to exist.*

Except the mounting frustration, the inability to move, and that God forsaken bleep bleep bleep kept intruding on her concentration. And the memory of those *things* taking the baby from her womb, consistently crept into her thoughts, summoned an empty sensation, a tingling sting in her navel.

*It's just in my mind,* she thought. *I can't feel anything…I can't…it's all in my mind.*

Her eyes dropped to a blank stare.

*But I know the baby's gone. I can see them, maybe they aren't real. Maybe it was just a nightmare…aliens don't exist. Even if they did why would they want my baby?*

Sandy saw the alien's eyes, green with a glint of champagne in the iris. Pupils not round but elongated. Yellow eyeballs. Those eyes saw straight through her. She could feel them looking into her heart, sensing the slow, thick beat in her chest. The alien lifted the wailing baby onto a bassinet then ran its fingernails over the baby's skin, caressing the forehead. And the baby's cries ceased. Sandy's breath constricted, in the dream and in the moment, dulled to a thick intermittent huff.

Her thoughts drifted, the scene bending and dissipating into the past. Sandy's eyes rolled, and that bleep bleep bleep returned to consciousness. She saw the rose then. An arm's reach from the eyes, unwavering, solid as if it were real and she traced every curve, every silken smooth petal, circling to its center. The core where the stem carried the flower's vibration down into the roots she could see was firmly held by the earth.

Sandy sensed calm writhe through her body. Felt sensation return to her toes, legs, torso and fingers.

*Hold the image!* Phil's words. *Let your thoughts go. Don't force it, allow the vibration to flow, allow the rose to guide. Be one with the vibration, see it, sense it...feel it. It will obey your command because it knows your desire. There is no need to force it with thought.*

*Be one with the rose!*

She wiggled her big toe, felt a rush of vibration course through her bones that lifted the pelvis and jolted her chest and shoulders.

She felt free. Started moving her legs back and forth feeling sensation return. Feeling good and vibrant and elated. She pulled the IV from her arm and tore electrodes from her chest and temples, igniting a fury of bleep bleep bleep as she jumped off the bed. The cold sting of concrete beneath her feet jolted up the ankles. Sandy stood erect with thoughts rattling in her skull.

*Is it true?* She touched her stomach. An empty feeling like nausea writhed into her throat. She lifted her gown and surveyed her flat stomach. A small incision below the navel was prominent. She ran her fingers over the incision.

*They took my baby.*

She wanted to cry but turned those tears into anger.

*Get it together, Sandy. Keep it together. The baby is here, somewhere in here. They wouldn't have taken the baby without cause.*

Grinding her teeth she dropped the gown. Interrupted by a click of the doorknob. Her gaze jumped to the door, watching as the handle moved.

# 5

SANOS RESTED ON SILK SHEETS covering a large round bed. His place for rest was luxurious, given freely to Sanos because of his high rank in the Drac government. He gazed through slitted eyes at the ceiling. His stomach twisting with a hollow pain and his bones, muscles, and organs wrenched with a heavy and thick pounding. And the voice that surfaced after the effects of new blood waned, dropped in the center of his mind as if the new blood had a voice all its own, kept creeping between the ears.

The voice was raspy, sinister and controlling. (*Exquisite, isn't it? More blood will help alleviate the pain you're going through. There's no need to suffer the way you are.*)

He heard the door open and close as footsteps clambered across the concrete.

"Sanos?" said Telas, Sanos's right hand.

She'd been with him for decades, since before the war when they gathered intel on human genomes and human DNA. They carried a mutual respect although disagreeing on a major issue, behind closed doors of course. Sanos had become disenchanted with the human race, an inquiry that had first been met with wondrous possibilities when he was ordered to study the human species. But the more time he spent with humans, and the higher he climbed the provincial ranking ladder receiving information on the human tie with his Drac brothers and sisters, the more he regarded humans as a species not worth the food they offered. Any race that treated each other with such disregard deserved to be subjugated. How could a species survive who consistently caused each other harm with malicious intent? Sanos's conclusion on the human race was to take what they needed from humans and eradicate their existence from the earth. Don't make deals with food. It may come back to haunt the future.

Of course, the optimistic gathering of scientists and sophisticated branch of the Drac government, a sect referred to as the Commission of Ra, disagreed with Sanos's philosophy, as did Telas. It was best practice to work with the humans in charge. The species had evolved with promise and power requiring an alliance with humans to maintain a continued and controlled arm on the planet. And the humans offered an even more promising solution to interstellar concerns that plagued the Dracs and their ancestors for millenniums. Cooperation between the two species had become a necessity.

"Sanos, what happened to you?"

Sanos sat up slowly, pinching the bridge of his nose.

"Sanos?"

He glared at Telas through watery eyes. Quickly his lips curled into a grin.

"What's gotten into you?" Telas's voice was sharp in tone, almost scolding.

Sanos stood, eyeing Telas. "What got into me? Dr. Blum is not playing by the rules. This new concoction drives Dracs into a frenzy, raging and mad."

Her eyes narrowed. "What? Dr. Blum has been our most trusted advisor throughout the war. What are you insinuating?"

"He's human, Telas, don't ever forget that. He can never be trusted."

"Sanos, you talk nonsense. Be specific."

"The new drug, Telas, he gave it to a human I fed on and it...it drove me insane. Turned me into a true monster."

Telas laughed. "You are a monster!"

Sanos returned a grin. "Not like this," he said, moving his head side to side. "This is different. If the humans we herd carry this drug inside them it'll turn us against each other. We can't take them home like this, and Dr. Blum knows it. He is not to be trusted."

Telas sighed. "Sanos, he's doing what he's ordered to do. Create a drug that weakens human will and human minds. Maybe you shouldn't have fed so eagerly."

Sanos chuckled through his smile, his body stiff. He stepped away from Telas, with his hands folded behind his back.

"Even so, I want none of the seven to feed on humans who've taken Dr. Blum's concoction. Not until we can assess completely the drug's effect." The seven Sanos referred to were the consortium of soldiers under his direct command. Every high-ranking official was provided with a team of seven to carry out commands. Each team consisted of seven soldiers, a right hand consultant, and the leader, forming the ninth order with a chain of command that spiraled down, each member a rank above the next.

Telas looked at Sanos. "That's going to be difficult."

Sanos froze. "Why?"

"Because the new drug was just given to the humans. They all have it in their system, and the seven wait to feed. Especially when they awaken from hibernation, which will be all too soon."

Sanos stretched his neck turning to face Telas. "Even so, they are ordered not to feed until I give the order. Being dependent on human blood for food turns my stomach to begin with. In the old world…"

"Food was plentiful, I know, Sanos, but that's not how it is today. Human blood gives us the antibodies and nutrients we need to survive. Plus, the taste is exquisite."

"Indeed." His pupils gleamed. The thought of Ben raced through his mind. He saw himself feeding on Ben's throat. Remembering the sensation that writhed through his body.

Telas bent her head, eyeing him. "Sanos?" Her voice just above a whisper.

Sanos shook his head, wiping his thoughts clean. "Yes," he said. "What was your reason for entering, Telas?"

She paused, looking him over before answering. "Update on the baby,"

"Another disgusting tyranny against our people. Mixing our DNA with a human. It's sacrilege."

"What's gotten into you? This is the main reason we've been working with humans. You know this is COR's main agenda, delivered to them from the highest Draconian order. We have to experiment to get it right."

Sanos checked himself. *What has gotten into me?*

*(Just a newfound curiosity. A different perspective.)*

He breathed deeply. "I'm ok," he said. "Must be an after effect of the new drug." He arched his shoulders and rubbed the back of his head. "What is the update?"

Telas glared at him. "The baby is secure, breathing on its own already. It survived the DNA transfer and so far, is accepting the procedure."

"Good," said Sanos. "What is the next phase?"

"Re-introducing the mother to provide necessary food."

"And the concern?"

"We are not sure of the baby's reaction. If our DNA has proven anything in the past, the baby could…over-indulge on the mother."

"Not much we can do in such a situation."

"It would be unfortunate to lose such a prize sample."

"Understood." Sanos stepped closer to Telas. "What is your suggestion?"

"If the mother dies, it will mean the baby needs food, our food. I came to request permission to feed the baby in such an event."

He lifted his chin looking to the ceiling. "A human child feeding on human blood." His lips turned to a grin, returning his stare to Telas. "Absolutely outstanding."

"Which brings up your current concern with Dr. Blum's new drug. If the drug works as you say it does, the baby may react adversely. Where do you suggest we secure untainted blood?"

"Telas, choose a soldier. They're all over—just pick one. It's as simple as taking blood from their arm; the nominee wouldn't be any more the wise to what we're doing."

She pursed her lips. Shook her head. "Such blood runs cold too quickly. By the time the baby would begin feeding the blood would be sour. You know more than any of us how feeding on a fresh human is paramount, especially for a baby. Additionally, the baby may not take cold blood. It doesn't have anywhere close to the understanding of what it's taking. It will need fresh blood. We will need to secure a human specifically for this purpose. Once the baby is healthy that human will need to go."

"Understood. Telas, I'm impressed, you're compromising for the sake of our race and greater good. Understanding sacrifice leads to taking the steps necessary to allow us to thrive. Very impressed, Telas, very impressed indeed. Proceed as you wish, but keep Dr. Blum in the dark; our orders are very specific on this. Allow him to believe he is still in charge."

"Of course, but who do we use?"

"Someone will rise to the occasion, someone always does."

"And if we're found out?"

Sanos smiled. "Then we do as we always have...burn the whole damn compound down. No survivors, no evidence, completely scorched earth."

Telas paused. "Hopefully the baby takes the mother's milk."

Sanos rolled his eyes. "Hopefully. Is there anything more, Telas?"

"No, Sanos. I'll keep you updated."

She bowed before turning, ambling to the door.

Sanos eyed her movements. "Oh, Telas, I almost forgot."

Telas stopped, turned slowly towards Sanos.

"Bring me three humans from the yard."

Telas cringed. "But you said..."

"I know what I said, Telas. As the highest-ranking official on this base, I must hold my own research on Dr. Blum's drug and its effect on our species. Such research requires a greater...*will*...than subordinates. I will assess the effects for any additional adversity. If it is how you say and this drug turns humans into the passive cattle as required, then we will need to know all the effects on our bodies and our minds. Do you agree?"

She paused, glaring at Sanos. Her eyes narrowed.

"Telas, do you agree?" he growled.

"Yes," she huffed. Sanos looked her over, surveying her reaction. Telas looked away.

(*She doesn't agree. She hasn't tasted how profound the new blood is. Why don't you show her? Allow her to feast as you have?*)

Sanos breathed, pursing his lips, tightening his jaw, eyeing Telas.

*Foolish.* He thought of new blood then, tasted it on the back of his tongue.

"Good then bring me three. To my chambers sooner rather than later."

"As you wish." Telas bowed again, turned and scuttled to the door.

Sanos hollered as she was leaving, "And do tell Dr. Blum I'll be meeting with him soon."

Telas froze, standing in the doorway. She cleared her throat. "Of course," she said.

Sanos heard the door close with a slow almost hesitating click. He stood, head down, arms folded behind his back. Again he saw himself feeding on Ben, gulping down his blood. Sanos constricted then shivered.

(*She'll go to Dr. Blum. She'll eradicate the pills and new blood will be no more. Something must be done.*)

His blood curled with a strange, hollow pain he hadn't experienced before.

(*New blood is too precious. For the sake of your species, your own mind, something must be done with her.*)

* * *

Telas stood outside Sanos's door.

*He's gone mad. He's more out of sorts than usual.* She was concerned Sanos would act against the baby. Giving his vehement stand against DNA experimentation that included Drac and human pairing, coupled with his historic disregard for COR values in the heat of battle, Sanos was indeed a threat to current progress. *Something must be done. This baby is what we've been working for. I can feel it.* But she would never go over his head, not ever. In all the time she was under his command, no matter how much she disagreed with him and his antics and methods, Telas always obeyed the chain of command.

*But we're so close. The baby is a gift that landed on our doorstep. We aren't even here for such an experiment.* She leaned against the door, planning a course of action, mulling over the different possibilities and outcomes.

*If I go over his head they'll investigate. They'll send a team here and take the baby. We'll all be detained until the investigation is complete. I can't do that. I can't risk it. We're so close, the solution is right in front of us. We just have to reach out and grab it.*

She started down the hallway. The greys were in the process of securing the baby's mother and delivering her to the baby. She had little time. Telas took a receiver strapped to her hip.

"Admiral Lao receive," she said in a thick Chinese accent. Admiral Lao was in command of the troops above ground. She'd always found it humorous giving orders to humans without their knowing she was a Drac.

A second later a voice rattled in on the other end.

*Admiral Lao receiving…*

The hesitation lasted less than a second but the thoughts that surfaced seemed to last forever. A vision. Sanos with mad eyes and an insatiable appetite. Everyone in the camp dead. And an explosion that tore through and desecrated the compound.

*Admiral Lao receiving…*

She breathed deeply. Started walking again. "Admiral Lao, secure three prisoners to chamber A1 immediately."

*Admiral Lao received. Chamber A1 confirmed.*

Telas secured the receiver to her hip.

*Keep your wit in check, Telas.*

*Proceed with extreme caution.*

* * *

*Your baby needs to feed.*

These words kept looping through Sandy's thoughts. She was being pushed in a wheelchair by one of those *things*, as she referred to them. The things that took her baby and Sandy was sure this thing pushing the wheelchair was the same woman who'd come up from the elevator when she was with Ben. Although she appeared different then, the energy was the same. The essence and the demeanor. She'd been sure a human woman greeted them at the elevator, only the person, the thing, pushing the wheelchair was an alien. A grey alien. Sandy knew about aliens, having an interest in the conspiracy theories most of her life. This surreal scene seemed like a waking nightmare. Sandy had jumped back onto the bed before the alien had entered the room. Despite Sandy's continued protesting over how all the wires detached from her head and body, she sensed the alien hadn't a care for such things. The alien lifted her onto the wheelchair with surprising ease as Sandy pretended to be unable to move.

Now she was being wheeled through the hallway, past rows of doors and rooms. *Is Ben in one of these rooms?* Her thoughts flashed with possibilities of torture and sadistic experiments. She stopped her hand from moving to her mouth, remembering that she had to play the unable to move game. Her eyes filled with tears, thinking about Ben.

*He'd want me to take care of the baby.*

*Yes, he does,* the alien answered, a voice in Sandy's mind. But it was Sandy's voice. Sandy's voice mimicked by the grey alien driving the wheelchair. Sandy was sure of it.

*I can hear your thoughts,* the grey said. *So can most of us. Be selective with what you allow to be heard.*

*Is my baby safe?* Sandy thought.

*Yes, he is in good hands. Breathing on his own already.*

Sandy's jaw dropped. *A boy! Breathing on his own? How is it possible, I was only six months pregnant?*

*We have our ways,* the alien answered. *And we are highly efficient at what we do.*

Sandy sensed the alien's pride click in her stomach. An uneasy sensation and she shifted in the wheelchair.

*No longer unmoving,* the alien said. *No worries I won't tell. But I wonder how you are able to do so?*

Sandy stiffened, controlling her thoughts. *I don't know, I focused on moving my big toe and everything started to move.*

Quiet. It seemed as if the walls breathed with a constricted stutter. Sandy saw the alien grin knowingly in her mind's eye as they stopped in front of a door. The alien reached for the doorknob, holding her hand above the handle. A second later the door clicked open. The room was large, reaching to depths that appeared to go on forever. Rows and rows contained a cross between a hospital nursery and emergency room. The alien wheeled her into the room, passing incubators, beds and machines. Although there wasn't many people in the room every so often Sandy witnessed a child laying on one of the beds, unmoving and connected to heart monitors and IV's. They continued, down the corridor and Sandy's heart started to pound.

*Don't be so nervous, dear; of all the humans here, you are the one with the least to be concerned with.*

*Why am I so important?*

*Not you, dear, the baby. Since you are the mother of such a young infant, the baby needs its mother; the bond is strong and everlasting. The baby needs you.*

They turned down a long hallway that led to an opening. The hallway was dark, but the room was filled with light. Sandy heard bleeps coming from that room. When they entered Sandy saw two aliens of the same stature and presence as the one who had wheeled Sandy here, and a tall female who was engaged with the other two occupants. Sandy cringed when she saw this woman. She was tall with a smooth skull; scaly skin and Sandy could see she had a row of sharp teeth. A hospital bed occupied the room's center and behind the occupants was an incubator. Sandy moved her head side to side hoping to catch a glimpse of the baby she was sure was in there.

*She can hear!* the alien who wheeled her in said to the others. Her words hurried as if to catch her associates before they revealed anything too sinister.

Telas cocked her head, surveying Sandy. Telas introduced herself then asked, "How do you know telepathy?"

Sandy gawked at Telas with a mix of anger and relief that someone was actually speaking. Telas smiled, revealing her sharp teeth. Sandy cringed following those teeth up to Telas's eyes and the elongated green iris that stared back at her.

"I...I don't," Sandy said. "I mean she started using it and I...I didn't even realize I was doing it."

"This must be a lot to take in."

"Take in?" Sandy said. "You couldn't possibly fathom how

hard this is to take in. It seems like a bad dream I can't wake from. My thoughts, my private thoughts aren't even safe." She shook her head. "I just want my baby."

"Of course," Telas said as an alien connected electrodes to Sandy's chest and head. Telas went to the incubator, sliding the small plastic door open.

The room was quiet as if they too were waiting with bated breath for this moment. Telas removed the baby, holding the infant close to her chest. Sandy's eyes widened, seeing her baby for the first time.

"He's beautiful," she said, her eyes filling with tears. The baby was unmoving in Telas's embrace. No cries, no wails. Telas handed Sandy the baby, sensing something was out of place.

"Oh, my dear," said Sandy, gently embracing the baby whose head moved close to her throat.

Telas eyed the others.

Sandy showered the baby with kisses. "Momma's here," she said. "No need to worry, Momma's here now."

She looked to Telas. "Why doesn't he cry?"

Telas looked on mother and child fervently. Her eyes wide. "He needs to feed, Sandy. Are you able to accommodate?"

Sandy's heart jumped. Again, those *bleep bleep bleeps* rang through the room. She rocked the baby back and forth, hoping to get a sign of life from her baby, a cry a whimper, anything.

"What's wrong with him?" Sandy demanded.

Telas turned to the grey standing behind Sandy. *Mono?*

Mono touched Sandy's shoulder. Mono said, "Best to feed the baby. He is starving." Her voice low, solemn, with a soft echo that hung in the room.

"If he's starving, why doesn't he cry?" Sandy's throat swelled with desperate emotion.

One of the aliens who had connected Sandy's electrodes scowled at Mono.

"Because alien babies do not cry. Your baby, Sandy, has been altered with alien DNA."

Sandy's body twitched with disgust. She didn't know whether to give up or squeeze the baby tight. She started to cry.

*But he is still your baby. A baby needs its mother, remember?* said Mono telepathically.

"And he is hungry." Telas's voice was stern, impatient.

Sandy cringed. "How do you know that? Human babies cry when they're hungry. How could you possibly know he's hungry?"

Telas glared at Sandy. "Because I, too, know my child."

Sandy felt her heart sink.

"You...you're a monster, how could you do this? How could you do this to him?"

Sandy cradled the baby, needing to see and examine every part of him. "He looks normal to me; I don't see anything that resembles you."

*Lift the eyelids dear, part the lips,* instructed Mono.

Sandy froze. She could hear her breathing and everything in the room seemed to stop. She hesitatingly raised the baby's eyelids. Staring back at her were Telas's eyes. Sandy wailed and cried. She parted the lips witnessing the jagged tiny teeth.

"This isn't my baby," Sandy cried. "This isn't my baby, it can't be." Yet she felt a kinship to the child, felt it in her gut and in her heart.

Telas crouched beside Sandy, touching the baby's head. "You will be celebrated for this, Sandy. Your baby is the first of its kind, born of two species. Human and Drac."

"Don't touch him," Sandy yelled. "Get away from him." Sandy pulled the baby from Telas's hand.

"You're all evil. Pure evil!" She shifted the baby to her shoulder. "I hate you! I hate you all." Her jaw quivered. Tears streamed from her eyes.

The baby squirmed in her arms. Sank its teeth into her neck. And Sandy screamed like no other had ever screamed before.

## 6

**PHIL HID BEHIND ONE OF THE FEW HOTEL WALLS** still standing. He was looking for a sign telling him where Sandy was; concluding she was taken inside the compound. Had to be, there was no sign of her anywhere.

*It's full of men and boys. I don't see a single woman.*

He tried to maintain focus, to keep calm under duress, scanning the camp for the hundredth time.

I can walk up and go right in if I choose. But what would that do other than alert them to my presence and then Sandy…whatever they are doing with her will lead to…

He bit his lip not allowing himself to go there. Not wanting the thought to escape and manifest into a possible reality.

Robyn was right. Knowing I would make a mistake and come here. Knowing Sandy would be taken.

He could hear Robyn's voice, the warning and insight he'd given Phil before Phil ventured off on his mission to secure Sandy.

*You lack faith in yourself,* Robyn had told him. *Faith in your ability. You keep trying to force it instead of allowing it to be. To manifest on its own. The rose is a special power with great responsibility few are able to master.*

He was right, and Phil knew it. He failed under duress. Had the power moving at his will and he failed. Lost concentration and they took Sandy because of it. Now everything was compromised.

Phil scanned the perimeter, studying the wall on the opposite side of the building. It was all dark, pitch black, and impossible to see into. Even the opening in the incomplete wall revealed nothing more than darkness within the perimeter.

*What's hiding in there? Why is everyone kept on one side and the other in total darkness?*

He searched for a path to bring him to the other side of the camp. Surveyed the wall that was covered in darkness and located a path where he could sneak in unseen.

*I'll have to duck down, crawl on my stomach but I'll get there. There's no other way...and I'm losing time.*

He turned around and squatted.

*I'll need my blades.*

The blades he referred to were part of an ancient martial arts practice. Kobudo Tonfa matched weaponry with martial art skill. Normally practiced with wood, the blades were a step up from mere practice. They were used in combat and in sport. In Phil's inner circle, they referred to this weapon as the blades. He remembered what Robyn had said when his training had begun. Phil was no more than seven at that time. A time when he was unaware of the alien species.

Again, he could hear Robyn's voice. *You will face enemies who know Kobudo Tonfa. These enemies are keen to hand to hand combat. They will have the blades too. Hand to hand combat is their sport. Their heroes are cheered when the blades are mastered. A practice they've indulged in for millenniums.*

Phil looked over mounds of broken concrete, searching, eyes darting over the debris.

*Where's my bag? I kept the blades in there. My medical belt too.*

He recalled putting the backpack on the table before leaving the room when Sandy had demanded he leave. The table would have been a few feet away from where he was now, buried beneath debris. Phil closed his eyes and the rose beamed with light, manipulating broken rock and cement to move and part way.

*Quickly. Before they see.*

It was there and, despite being covered in debris the bag was unscathed. He released the rose and the dark returned. He quickly took up his bag, zipping it open.

The blades were unharmed. The blades are a unique contraption with thin handles held in the palms, clamps that wrapped around the wrist and just above the elbow, connected by a thin, almost string like plastic. The metal blade descended from the handles down across the arm bone to the elbow clamp and locked into place. The metal they were made from was not of this earth and was able to collapse inside the handles and wrist clamp like tin foil crumples inside a fist. But this metal was strong and solid and unmatched to any substance on earth. The handles when pressed by the index finger would ignite the blades down the arm, locking in place. Another unique feature were the handles, fitted comfortably in the palm, when pressed with the thumbs would ignite claws of steel. A useful tool when needing to climb walls. Robyn had spent years teaching Phil the art of Kobudo Tonfa. An art he'd become supremely confident with.

Phil's stare drifted to the full blood moon rising over the compound. Eyes wide, thinking: *You know what that means. There's more under the moon tonight than just alien vampires. And they come with teeth.* The moon's red glow crept across the landscape as Phil dipped his chin to his chest, grinding his teeth. Four simple words on the tip of his tongue…

"Get ready to bleed."

Phil quietly moved through the hotel rubble. His thoughts returned to Robyn.

*How do you know all this?* Phil had asked over the years. *How do you know so much about the enemy?*

To which Robyn would respond,

"I've been around for a *very* long time."

* * *

An order had been given to escort three men to the tunnels. To deliver them to chamber A1, allow them to enter then quickly and quietly leave. Cam volunteered for the assignment. The way he saw it, everyone in the camp was dead already; it didn't matter what happened to them or how they died. Soon the camp would be wiped off the map, leaving nothing to tell they existed. His plan was simple, having been an explosives expert during the war; Cam was going to blow the compound to all hell. But to do so, he needed to get into the tunnels where he'd seen the equipment he needed to bring his plan to fruition.

*Blow this place to hell. Whatever they're doing must end.*

He looked on his countrymen, the American prisoners, as he escorted them into the elevator. Their blank stares revealed there was nothing going on behind those eyes. They seemed simplistic, like something had snapped in the brain that derailed rational thought. They followed orders without hesitation or question, devoid of all emotion. Leaning against the elevator walls for support, their eyelids blinked every so often, revealing eyes rolling to the back of the head. One man was drooling, his jaw hung open.

"Wipe your mouth," Cam said but received no response. The man remained, standing, unmoving, staring, unaware or not caring about the drool that dripped off his lip. Cam's anger burned his gut. The scene confirmed that he should follow through with his plan.

The elevator opened with a metal scrape, and a rush of heat walloped into the elevator.

"Fall in line," Cam said. "Single file." They did as he ordered shuffling one behind the other.

*They're like zombies. What are they putting in those pills?*

"To the end of the hall," Cam said, following behind.

He'd been down here before, when he was first brought to the camp, before Dr. Blum arrived with his team of medical professionals. Before the treaty was signed, Cam and four additional soldiers arrived at the compound to secure the tunnels and the quarry in anticipation for the others to arrive. He'd spent a long day in those tunnels prior to receiving the order for all soldiers to vacate and remain above ground. He knew this place and the corridors and hallways. Knew where the supplies and weaponry were kept. And the explosives. He hoped they were in the same place and hadn't been moved.

A loud groan erupted from one of the rooms. The three men stopped as if on cue with the groan. Cam stopped too. They were in front of the room where the groan had come from. Another groan, louder than the first.

"Continue," Cam ordered, and the men obeyed.

He was in front of the door. He could hear movement inside the room.

*Just keep moving. Doesn't matter what's going on down here.*

Watching as the men continued down the hall, to the double doors.

*We're all dead anyway.*

Now a scream rattled the walls, a high-pitched squeal that was quickly and suddenly silenced. He wanted to open the window flap to see what was happening. To know exactly what they were doing with the men brought down here. They never returned, none of them, except as body parts and limbs to be tossed away like garbage and brought to the hole with the rest of the dead.

The men stopped in front of a double door. Cam eyed them, standing idle, waiting for his command. He could hear labored breath, not from the men but from the room. He reached his shaking hand to the window flap. Pushed the flap open a smidge but retracted.

*I don't wanna know. Less is better.*

Swallowing his breath, Cam ordered, "Keep going, through the door."

But they remained still.

"I said…"

Something slammed against the door. Cam heard breathing, heavy and labored. Felt like being watched. Whatever was behind the door was listening to him.

*Don't fool yourself keep going.*

He followed down the hall, opened the doors and the men walked through. The hallway emptied into a large open room with hallways sprouted in five different directions. Cam remembered the layout, the explosives were down the hall on the right, but his orders were to take these men to chamber A1 far down the second hall on the left.

"Follow along," he ordered leading the way down the hall where the lights dimmed, reflecting the concrete walls with a faint yellow glow. Cam's heart started pounding, flushed skin wet with beads of sweat. He felt sick and his body cringed as if something had come over him. A fearful energy leaving an impression in his heart.

*Is someone following us?*

He shot a look back down the hall. The men stopped. Cam searched the hall.

"Hello," he called. "Someone there?"

Silence! But he still felt that sting, the churning burning in the back of his throat rising to his brain. He looked up and down and back down the hall but there was nothing. No sound, no movement.

He swallowed his breath. "Alright, keep moving." Giving up his search he led the men down the hall to chamber A1. Before he opened the door, he searched the hall again. Nothing! He looked at the men, standing, and waiting.

He understood that whatever waited in A1 intended the end of these men's lives. Whatever horror waited for them he knew was no way for a life to end. His hesitation seemed to last a lifetime, eroding every moral he'd ever held sacred.

*If I'm caught, this will all continue. They'll keep destroying us. I've got to send a message to whomever is pulling the strings on this camp.*

He looked over the men. "I'm sorry," he whispered and opened the door.

"Enter," he said. "And wait for further instruction." He swallowed the lump in his throat as the men filed into the room. "Someone will be along to assist."

He took one last look at them, standing still and unknowing. One of them turned to Cam before the door closed. His eyes were blank as if the light had gone from the soul. The stare a stab to Cam's heart.

*I'm so, so sorry!*

Cam leaned against the closed door, catching his breath.

*Don't cry. Don't let one single tear fall.*

He pinched the bridge of his nose as that eerie sensation crept into his heart. He searched the hall again, looking for cameras or any possible sign that someone was following him, watching him, listening to him, but still there was nothing. He never heard that cameras were down here, although he couldn't dismiss the idea. There was so much he didn't know, so much he and all the other soldiers were kept in the dark about.

*Wish there was a different way.* He thought about the men, that blank stare, delivered to what he was sure was certain death. He started down the hall, calculating his next move and trying to forget about them, rationalizing his plan.

*They're all dead already. Me too, all of us. No matter what, we are all dead in this camp.*

*I don't see any other way.*

Cam watched for any sign of life coming in and out of the rooms. If he were caught, he would say he was lost. That was his plan. Play stupid. He touched the knife sheathed on his right hip. Gunfire would alert them to his presence, destroying any possibility of setting off the bomb. A knife fight would not be expected. Aim for the lungs so they can't scream.

*Be ready for anything.*

He passed the open area where they came in, paused a moment, listening. Then started moving down the hall.

*ANYTHING!*

* * *

Titus, the Drac vampire watching Cameron stepped out from the darkness at the end of the hall. He felt strong after feeding, his senses on high alert, thinking clear. The taste of the human remained on his tongue, he felt the human's blood in his veins. Blood brought strength, fuel for heightened senses. He knew he should have reported to Sanos before feeding, but he felt weary and depleted upon awakening. And the scent of the human made his stomach growl. It was clean blood, the human he fed on hadn't been given any pills or medicine and Titus had waited so long to feed on a clean human he refused to allow the opportunity to pass. And his appetite may have delivered a bonus. Titus, number one on the list of the nine, the lowest in command, was feeling ambitious, watching Cam, listening to his thoughts. Titus knew capturing Cam would help his title, possibly result in a transfer to another facility where he could be number two or three, moving up the ranks in his government.

But what this human's actual plan was he did not know. Capturing a soldier, an American soldier, would give him credibility, and Sanos would be pleased with his work. Depending on how far this human was willing to go, Titus would require as much proof of Cam's plan as possible. COR would require evidence when considering his promotion and the depths for which Cam's plan reached would reflect how high his climb in the ranks would be.

Quietly, he followed Cam down the hall.

## 7

TELAS ENTERED THE CHEMICAL LAB where Dr. Blum spent most of his days and nights. He sat in front of a computer, a three-dimensional chemical compound glowed on the monitor. His team of three grey aliens actively creating more pills under his direction and chemical structure. They worked quietly and efficiently without distraction.

Swiveling his chair to the left to see Telas, he asked, "How are mom and baby?"

"Mom and baby are both sleeping," Telas said.

Dr. Blum shook his head. "I was referring to you, Telas."

Telas bowed. "I am good."

"Excellent," responded Dr. Blum, returning to his computer. "What can I do for you, Telas? Been a while since you came in here."

"Indeed. Honestly, doctor, I'm concerned with the strength of the new pills. Seems some of the humans are not reacting well."

Dr. Blum stiffened. "All is well," he said. "The few we've lost were given too heavy a dose." He shrugged. "Happens, you know what they say about making omelets. What we're doing is not an exact science."

Telas glared at Dr. Blum. "What's the base chemistry?"

Dr. Blum paused and cocked his head to the right. He punched a key on his keyboard then turned to Telas. "It's an opiate base. Same that was used in the opiate epidemic, but much stronger. The drug reduces gray matter in the brain and the medulla oblongata, essentially destroying empathy and aggression. These pills will have the required effect both species are looking for. Only question I have is how many doses will render the effect permanent, and if that permanent effect will transfer during pregnancy. But what is your concern?" His eyes narrowed.

"My concern, doctor, is the effect these pills will have on our species. I'm aware Sanos has tasted the new medication. Have you seen him? He seems different."

Dr. Blum shifted in his chair. "Different how?"

"Difficult to explain...more aggressive and yet distracted. There's a look behind the eyes that wasn't there before."

"A look?"

"Yes, as if something changed inside, possibly responding to internal stimuli. He wants to speak with you about it."

Dr. Blum shook his head. "Speak to me? Telas, he just ordered three subordinates to his private chambers. If he's so concerned, why the order?"

Telas looked over the lab assistants. She felt weak. She pursed her lips, swallowed, then clenched her jaw.

Blum looked her over, leaned his head to the right to gain her attention. "When was the last time *you* fed?"

She cleared her throat. "Four days," she whispered.

"Four days!" Dr. Blum raised his voice. "Look at you, you're depleted, and it's affecting your work. You're being irrational. We've studied the effect prior pills have had on your species and there have been no adverse reactions. There's no reason the new chemistry would be any different. I see no reason to cease our work when we're so close; we have it right at our fingertips. A few tweaks aside and both sides are in the clear to begin the final phase."

No response.

"Telas?" Dr. Blum shifted, staring at her. "Don't lose sight of the larger plan. The work we're doing benefits both our species." He sighed. "Listen, taste the new blood for yourself, give me your honest opinion, and I'll tweak the chemical structure if necessary. But I am sure you will be satisfied with the result."

"Yes, Telas," said Sanos. He had slipped into the room unnoticed. "Taste the new blood for yourself."

"Sanos," Dr. Blum said. "Good you are here." Dr. Blum shifted his seat to face him. "Can you please give me your opinion on the new blood? The prisoner, Ben, he was given the pills prior to your feeding. Did you notice any adverse reactions?"

Sanos glared at Telas who returned his stare, anticipating Sanos's reaction.

"The pills are fine, doctor. No adverse reaction other than the initial lethargy. A small price to pay for the larger accomplishment."

"Well," Dr. Blum said. "There you have it, Telas. Sanos gives his stamp of approval." The doctor was excited. He addressed Sanos. "And you'll inform the nine of our accomplishments? You will sign the decree that the pills are safe?"

"Of course."

"That is not what you said, Sanos," Telas intervened. "You said the pills were not safe. Why the change?"

"I was wrong. My initial disposition was not accurate. In retrospect, the pills are fine. I am fine." Sanos pursed his lips. "Try it for yourself, Telas. I feel wonderful!" His eyes glinted with a strange devious satisfaction.

"I will not," she said. "There is something different about you, Sanos. Something you're not telling us. It's our species safety; do you not care about that? You said, in your own words, there was something wrong with the new blood and ordered us not to feed on them…"

"QUIET!" Sanos raged. "I will not accept insubordination. Your orders are simple, you must feed and so must the seven. You will give that order immediately."

"I will not."

Sanos leaped at her, taking hold of her throat. "How dare you question me!"

"I question your judgment, yes, the new blood has done something to you. It is not safe."

Sanos squeezed the air from her throat.

"You are stripped of your command, Telas. The nine will deal with you." Sanos released her throat throwing Telas to the floor. "You will spend the rest of your time here under lock and key."

Telas coughed and gasped for air. "I will not," she said, forcing the words over her lips. "I'm informing the nine of my suspicions. We will both be held under judgment."

"Insolent bitch." He gripped the back of her neck, forcing her forward. "I should kill you now, Telas."

"She needs to feed," Dr. Blum shouted.

Telas punched Sanos in the gut, trying to pry his hand off her neck with no avail. His grip was like an iron vice she couldn't budge.

"Unlock the chamber," Sanos ordered Dr. Blum who jumped off his seat, fumbling his keys, stomping to the chamber door in the front of the room.

"Now, doctor!" Sanos hollered.

Blum unlocked the door, opening it quickly. Sanos tossed Telas into the room. She slid across the floor crashing into the wall, and Blum closed the door locking her in. Telas jumped at the door, kicking and clawing.

"You can't do this, Sanos," Telas raged. "Dr. Blum, unlock this door immediately."

"She can't get out," Blum said.

"Good," Sanos replied. "Then she can't cause any more trouble."

"She hasn't fed in four days. This could explain her rebellious behavior."

Sanos nodded. "Get her to feed, doctor. She will feel so much better after she's fed."

Dr. Blum placed his keys in his pocket. "Consider it done." Dr. Blum stared at Telas, pleading through the window to be let out. "Unfortunate this is… Telas has been ideal to work with, I do hope she comes back to herself."

Sanos sighed. "She will," he said. "If not we will need to dispose of her. Perhaps this new-found child of hers has derailed rational thought."

Dr. Blum cocked his head. "Perhaps. Motherhood does something to all of them, why would she be the exception?"

Sanos turned, walking to the door, holding his hands behind his back.

Dr. Blum eyed him. "Sanos?"

Sanos paused, then turned, hesitant.

"What was your reason for visiting? Surely it wasn't concerning Telas. Something must have brought you here."

Sanos cocked his head, staring with a blunt affect. Shook his head then widened his eyes, breathing deeply then cleared his throat. "To congratulate your efforts. You and your team. A truly incredible accomplishment. In a few months we can all leave this place. Your efforts are duly noted."

Dr. Blum bowed. "We thank you."

Sanos returned the bow, hesitating.

"Something more, Sanos?" Dr. Blum's eyes narrowed.

Sanos paused, thinking. "Are we continuing with genetic testing?"

Dr. Blum cocked his eyebrows. "Of course. We've deposited a group in the dark area, and they wait for sunrise. A bit lethargic but hopefully this round will receive the sun without desecration. We've had difficulty isolating the appropriate gene. Definitely a trial and error study." Dr. Blum laughed. "But the baby is doing well. I understand he fed today without adverse reaction. We will initiate tests prior to a daytime experiment. If we have to grow a new species to isolate the gene so be it. We have nothing but time, Sanos. As your species is fully aware of."

"That I am, doctor." Sanos returned to leaving. "That I am."

"And no need to be concerned with Telas, we will be sure to take care of her."

Sanos exited the room with a hurried step. Dr. Blum looked on Telas through the window. She sat against the far wall.

"You need to feed, Telas. You will be better once you've fed. I'll bring someone down for you, and then you will know the new blood is good and sweet, and I'll let you out."

She did not respond but looked on Dr. Blum with a tired stare.

"Telas, it's for your own good. Your hunger is getting the best of you, and you're not thinking rationally."

She turned away.

"Very well then. No need to answer. I'll have someone to you soon."

She could sense the doctor's blood. Heard the stream running through his veins. The scent so effervescent and sweet. She knew she needed to feed, feeling depleted and weary. But the new blood was not good, not good in any way and she had to inform the nine about her suspicions. If the blood is given to her people, it could end in catastrophe. Sitting hungry and tired, she thought of her next move.

PHIL SCURRIED BEHIND THE WALL under the cover of darkness, unseen. Preoccupied with falling, convulsing prisoners, the soldiers tasked with securing the perimeter (perhaps out of boredom) focused their attention on the happenings inside the fence, paying no mind to the perimeter or the wall. Phil could hear mumbling and fumbling from the other side of the fence where the prisoners were held, mostly from soldiers who laughed every so often. And then the groans, soft and labored as if struggling to breathe. Phil used his handles, now metal claws, to scale the wall. He ascended quickly, thirty feet up.

But the moans and groans seemed closer as if they were in the same vicinity. Phil peeked over the wall, surveying the surroundings. Sprawled on the ground inside the wall were four people, sleeping.

*Why are they here?* Phil pondered the odd situation. *What have they done to them?*

He dropped down inside the wall. None stirred. All was quiet except the occasional laugh outside the wall. He scanned the surroundings, listening to the chirp of crickets wedged inside the quiet of the night. Peered through the opening, through the fence, where the wall had not been completed. Listened carefully for any possibility of his discovery. Nothing. No one, except the four lying helpless. Phil surveyed the four, his head turned to the side, observing, listening to their struggled breath and occasional groan. He went over, kneeling beside them. All were breathing heavy, their bodies constricting as if something within was suffocating their insides.

"My god," Phil said. "They're children. Can't be any more than teenagers."

He felt a forehead; the skin was warm and moist with perspiration as were all of them.

*This isn't the mission and you're running out of time. You've got to find Sandy and get out of here.*

He felt a driving sting hit his heart.

*I hate this!*

He understood he couldn't compromise his purpose. Not for them or anyone else. The baby and Sandy are his mission, and he couldn't jeopardize it any more than he already had.

He touched a child's head. "I'll be back," he told him. "I promise, I'll be back." Phil turned his attention to the building. Although the windows were blacked out, he could see shadows within. Probably soldiers moving about.

*There's got to be a door somewhere. They got them out here, didn't they?*

He went quietly and quickly to the wall, finding the door that, from a distance, was hidden from plain view. He gripped the doorknob.

Locked.

*Locked... Why? So, they can't get back in?*

He cut the knob with a swipe of his blade and slipped through the door. A long concrete stairwell led down, way down. Phil took the stairs, at first cautiously then fast. The air thickened with a hot constricting wallop. Apt focus, listening for a sign of life, for soldiers or guards or...but all was quiet.

*It's like a ghost town.*

At the bottom stairs he glanced around the corner. Two directions led into dim lights.

*Right or left? Trust your instincts. Trust your gut. Go right.*

Phil took off down the hall, moving swiftly and on guard. Ready for anything that may creep out of the hall and confront him.

*Stay on point. Be ready for anything. Anything! Just like Robyn said. The enemy will come with fangs and immense strength. But not invincible. They die like we do.*

The walls went by in a flash. Phil paid mind to his breathing, maintaining easy breaths, running in strides.

*They will have the same weapons.* Robyn's voice. *The rose and the blades. Some more powerful than others, and some more powerful than yourself. But this does not mean you cannot defeat them. Use your mind. Trust your instincts. Do what is necessary.*

He saw the end of the hall and quickened his pace, remembering that burning question he had asked Robyn.

*How do they know the rose? How do they know the art of the blades? If these are secret teachings, how do they have the same discipline?*

Phil slid to the end of the hall, crouched down against the wall, and drew in a deep breath. Peeked around the corner, again two ways to go, two choices and he caught a glimpse of a shadow, a silhouette that disappeared down the hall moving away from him.

*That's the play. Where there's one there's more.*

He tensed his arms, getting ready for what lay ahead. Took another look down the hall. The silhouette was gone. Phil took off in the same direction in a hurried yet smooth stride. His thought returned to Robyn and the answer he'd received.

*Because I learned it from them.*

\* \* \*

Sanos's chambers had two entrances, the second hidden from view so he could sneak up on any prey brought to him. He loved to toy with the humans. Loved to savor the moment before he took their blood. But this new blood turned a rage inside of him, a turn of the mind revealing primal instincts and savage debauchery. He couldn't wait to feed on them; they were all he thought about. The new blood was not only good it was Godly, the euphoria pure elation; he could taste it on his lips and tongue and sensed the rush writhing through his veins.

He wanted to devour all of them, every single prisoner who'd been given the new pills. Wanted to tell everyone about it, how it made him feel, awakening his senses like he'd never experienced.

Except this sensation was exactly what the nine had warned against. A false euphoria. But if his team would all have the same story, the same conclusion, the nine would have to concur with his findings. Knowing he was about to feed again brought back that euphoric sensation. The anticipation was almost equal to the feeding itself. Sanos looked through the chamber door, seeing the three men standing, swaying back and forth, and cradling their arms against their chests. His hands shook with excitement as he turned out the lights so he could sneak up on his prey, take them one by one and devour and tear at them.

*What if the nine do not concur? I'll lose my rank. I'll be disgraced.*

He leaned against the wall, flopping his head back and closing his eyes.

(*The nine will concur. They will have no choice. Sense how sweet the blood is, like nothing you've ever tasted before.*)

He could smell their blood, like a sweet fragrance captivating his senses. His mouth salivated with the thought.

*Perhaps they will listen, take my word for it. And the seven. After they've fed, they, too will know how good it is and will reach the same conclusion.*

(*Exactly right. All Dracs will know how good it is. How powerful.*)

His breathing turned heavy. He could no longer resist. Sanos went into the room, hiding within the darkness, taking them one by one. Tearing at them, drinking, gnawing on their flesh. Each tasting better than the previous.

Once he finished, his eyes fluttered, the sensation of the blood jutted up his chest to his brain. His eyes rolled falling on his back. His body convulsing, falling unconscious.

* * *

Telas could feel her body weaken. The blood thinning in her veins depleted the oxygen to her brain and caused an immense headache. *Four days*, she thought. *Four days is much too long.*

Now she was locked away, and Sanos was clearly out of his mind. The new blood would be the scourge of her people, a plague she couldn't allow to happen. Sanos's first reaction was accurate, the pills caused his change, and now he acted like a monster. He never turned on her before, no matter how they argued or differed in opinion, they always held each other in high regard. The pills, the new blood, had destroyed his rational thought.

*The drug reduces gray matter in the brain and the medulla oblongata, essentially destroying empathy and aggression.*

She repeated Dr. Blum's description.

*For us it is the opposite effect. One of rage and no control.*

With obvious apparent differences her species was similar to the humans in many ways. Like a chimpanzee to a human. And she'd come to respect the humans, an intelligent race whose ambition was equaled by catastrophe. The horrors they put themselves through was enough to declare the species subordinate. Only time and evolution could save them, deliverance into a higher understanding, a realm consisting of science of mind, logic and rationale.

*If they make it.*

Telas was a student of history. She'd read about the numerous species across the universe who never learned to balance their eager insatiable appetites for power with the understanding of connection. Species' whose actions rendered them extinct in the universe, blown into dust particles only to resurface in a different form some millenniums later, to begin again. Not that she had ever been concerned with her own species extinction. Earth provided them food and their ability to walk on the surface, even if only after dusk — the sun caused a chemical reaction that degenerated their cells — rendered them capable of providing the research their Drac ancestors required. Except there was more happening than she was aware of, and that lurking sensation that there is something more to their ancestor's interest in humans remained a constant in the back of her thoughts. And to many other Dracs outside of COR.

Always hiding in the shadows, snaking around the prime directive with a hasty and devious iron fist, the Drac ancestors required domination over the planet earth. For this to happen it was required for them to work with the humans in charge while continuing to live in the shadows to ward off any possibility of the larger mass of humans uncovering the truth. If they all knew, there was a large possibility the humans would declare independence and initiate their right to the planet.

And then there was the directive handed down by the ancestors: DNA manipulation would secure their hold on the planet. Of course, there was more, so much more, from what she surmised — subordinates like Telas were never informed of the larger plan and were always on a need to know basis. Interstellar domination being one. Why stop with one planet when you can have the galaxy? But a threat had surfaced. A threat that would render the larger plan ineffective if not dealt with in the harshest manner. Alternatively, this same threat also threatened the humans in charge. A threat that kept her people and the humans in power in a frenzy. She was sure of it. Although she was kept out of the need to know on this threat, an intelligent creature could still add two plus two. The word *indigo* had surfaced over the years, and Telas had concluded this word had something to do with the threat.

For more than a century they attempted to stamp out the threat, using all means necessary. Programming. Pills. Drugs. War. Illness. All initiated with the ultimate goal to rid themselves of the threat to the dominant order. The effort had succeeded on a large scale, although few remained. The threat was human, this she did know. It was the answer to two plus two, because it could only be human. Handed down from the human God from the very beginning of their existence. It was why the war had been declared. The effort was to isolate the potential human threat. Study them and decipher a means to eradicate.

*For the benefit of our people.*

And now her species was on the verge of annihilation should the new blood be promoted and approved. She knew she could not allow this to happen.

*I have to stop Sanos. No matter what, I have to stop him.*

She pushed herself to her feet, leaning against the wall. If she didn't feed soon, she'd go into slumber, an alien coma, and would be rendered powerless. She thought of synthetic blood, or finding a horde of rats, but such blood was for survival and did not offer the same nutrients as live human blood. After four days of not feeding she required the nourishment live human blood would provide.

*And yet how do I feed on blood not tainted with new pills? Dr. Blum insisted on the new pills. Any one he brings will have them in their blood.*

She thought of the soldiers. Thought of Dr. Blum.

*All protected. Feeding on them would be against the treaty and a direct violation of COR.*

Telas looked through the window, seeing the greys working diligently on the new pills. Dr. Blum was not in the room. She searched for him everywhere with no avail. But Mono was, overseeing Dr. Blum's work. Mono was a different story. Telas did not trust her in any way possible. There was something sinister about Mono. Telas sensed it when the baby was born. A shift in consciousness, a change in energy, and Telas was sure Mono had blocked Telas from her thoughts. But trust with Mono took second place to her need to feed. Telas closed her eyes, locking in on Mono, using telepathy to reach her.

*Mono, Dr. Blum was right. I need to feed. Please let me out.*

But Mono did not respond. She kept working.

"Too weak," Telas said. "Too far away." She put her hand on the door, the other to her heart.

*Use the rose. Talk through the rose and you will reach her.*

An effort she feared she was too weak to accomplish.

## 9

CAM FOUND THE EXPLOSIVES, IN THE weapons supply closet as he remembered. He worked quickly, his training providing the necessary knowledge to construct the bomb. The wires and the C4 were all at his disposal. Scenes and scenarios played through his consciousness.

*Can I get them out?*

His change of heart to destroy them all came after he delivered the men to Sanos's chambers. *They are Americans and I've got to at least try to get them out.* They were worth the risk he would endure.

He decided to schedule the bomb to explode after dawn. He always noticed how everything seemed to stop after daylight, the orders, and the doctor coming up to camp. Everything worked at night.

*And if I can't do it?*

Cam hesitated. There was one last element to the bomb he needed to secure—turning the explosive on by setting the timer on the detonator.

*Doesn't matter, at least I can try. If this camp continues to exist there's no life to live anyway.*

He also knew he had to return to camp.

*They may be looking for me already.*

His finger hesitated over the remote detonator. He ran through the possibilities. *How much time do I need?* Measuring the time it would take to create a distraction, get them all out, and reach a safe distance…no, *we will be followed. They're like zombies; they won't move that fast and we will be caught. It has to happen quickly.*

*That's the chance I'm willing to take.*

If he could get them down into the tunnels, Cam knew the pace could happen faster, perhaps go unnoticed under the guise he received orders, after sunrise, to bring them into the tunnels. He knew where the tunnels led, flowing to the river a few miles away.

*I'll need an hour.*

He reset the timer for an hour after sunrise. One last thing to do, set the bomb and go. Cam held his finger over the trigger.

*If I fail?*

He saw his countrymen, heard the soldiers speaking in foreign languages and laughing, heard the firing squad killing the elderly and dumping bodies into trucks to be brought to a shallow nameless grave.

*Insignificant! It's worth it. The only possible chance for...*

Something flashed in the corner of his eye. Cam jolted to his right. The figure was rushing at him. Long talon hands gripped his shirt.

"Insolent human!" The voice was clear with a thick growling edge. And the hands were strong, like an iron vice. He was thrown against the wall. The back of his head smacked concrete. The detonator dropped to the floor. Cam winced, his vision blurred as he hunched over. Pain snared into his brain. He backed up holding his hand out. Part peace offering. Part pause to collect himself.

"No," he shook his head, pleading, "I'm a sol..." He snapped his head back and his eyes widened with disbelief. This thing rushing at him was like a cobra with legs. Pulsating flaps on the side of its skull and its eyes turned instantly from green to black pins.

"What the FUCK!" He tried to back up. Back into the wall if he could. Through the wall would have been better. The cobra bared its teeth, revealing a row of fangs like thick daggers. He caught the eyes then and lost all recollection of time and space. Staring into those dark black pins was captivating. They held Cam frozen against the wall, as if they held some mystic cosmic power of their own. Everything surrounding those eyes disappeared. His body disappeared with it. All he saw were the eyes. And then the pain erupted as those teeth popped into his neck and veins. He felt the pain wrench into his brain.

It was as if he was outside himself. Had drifted out of his body and was watching this cobra, this vampire, feeding on him. Saw himself wriggle in its embrace, giving no fight against it. His body fell limp. His arms dropped to his sides as his heartbeat slowed.

Cam heard the slow thick beat of his own heart as if it pounded in his throat like a signal to end his life. The cobra pulled its fangs from Cam's neck. Blood stained its teeth. Dripped off its lips and chin. The cobra breathed and his body shivered. Breaths, putrid and foul, like the stench off a rotting corpse.

"I think I'll keep you," it said. "Give you to Sanos. We can all feed on you, our little pet."

Cam's eyes fell lazy behind sagging eyelids, drifting to a silhouette behind the cobra. He saw a flash of light, the silhouette's left arm swipe up the length of the Cobra's back followed by the right arm across the neck. The cobra's head spun off the shoulders, spouting blood from the neck. The sandy blonde shadow kicked the decapitated body as Cam slid to the floor, flopping forward. His heart thumped between his ears like an echo, sensing life leaving. Looking, staring and seeing the detonator he reached for it. Before losing consciousness, he triggered the bomb.

* * *

Six of the seven soldiers under Sanos's command entered his chambers.

"Sanos," called Orion, the third in command directly under Telas.

They filed into Sanos's chambers surveying the apparent massacre of three human bodies torn to pieces and scattered across the room.

Orion, Cade, Rygel, Jubal, Kaidan and Moya, the remaining six of the ranking seven soldiers had been resting for the last twenty-four hours, on strict orders from Telas. They awakened and immediately went to receive orders. They had questions and an alert to provide Sanos. Titus was missing. Was he given a command, or had he defected like so many others over the years they'd been together? The scene in Sanos's chambers was surreal, to see humans ripped to shreds brought back the old days before the treaty, when desecration of human existence was not only allowed it was encouraged. The revelation excited them with a hope that Sanos had had enough with all the civil bull shit between the two species, declaring open season on humans.

"Sanos?" Orion hollered and slapped his hands together.

Sanos was sprawled out in a pool of dried blood from one of the torn bodies, its head decapitated, lying on the floor beside him. Sanos's eyes were open wide, staring at the ceiling.

"Does this mean we are free to feed?" Cade, the fourth in command.

"No, it does not," Orion answered. "Sanos!" he called again, touching Sanos's forehead. He turned to Jubal. "Help me get him up. Take him by the arm." They lifted Sanos to the bed, sitting him up and holding him there. Sanos's body shivered.

Jubal laughed. "He's drunk on blood," he said. "I'm jealous."

"He'll be fine." Orion slapped his hands in front of Sanos's eyes.

Cade bent down staring at Sanos. "He's much more than drunk; maybe Dr. Blum finally got the pills right." He stood up, looking around the room. "I mean, look at this place, he tore them apart."

"Must be some damn good blood," said Rygel.

"Ex…exquisite blood," Sanos said, widening his eyes. He shook his head.

"Are you sure?" Orion's eyes narrowed. "You're completely out of it."

Sanos breathed. "It doesn't last. I'll be fully awake in a minute or two with heightened senses. Fatigue is a simple side effect." He touched his hand to his head closing his eyes His stomach turned, wrenching with a painful hollow sensation.

"Perhaps you had too much?" Orion put his hand on Sanos's shoulder.

Sanos tipped his head, that fuzzy feeling beginning to subside. "Perhaps." He smiled.

Orion stood. "How do we clean up this mess? This isn't the normal drain the blood with a simple bite that can be covered up. You literally tore them to pieces. How do we account for the massacre?"

"Simply get another human to clean it up!" Sanos's voice was stern with an edge behind it, raised with anger.

The six stiffened looking at each other.

"Is Telas aware of the effect?" Cade asked.

"No doubt she is."

"She tasted this blood? Did it have the same effect?"

"No." Sanos shook his head. "I've placed Telas under arrest for insubordination. She remains under lock and key to face the council for her actions. She is no longer in command and none of you are to visit her unless I give the order."

"What did we miss?" Orion said. "New blood, insubordination, Telas under arrest. What happened?"

Sanos stood abruptly glaring at Orion. "You dare to pose a challenge to me?"

Orion shook his head. "Never, Sanos." He swallowed his breath. "What happened is between you two. I have no qualms. I obey your command."

Sanos scowled at Orion.

"What *are* your commands?" Cade intervened.

"Simple," Sanos began. "You are all to feed on the new blood and report your finding to Dr. Blum. You are not to seek out Telas... let her rot where she is. And..." he noticed there were only six in his chambers. "Where is Titus?"

"We do not know," Orion answered. "We were hoping you'd be able to shed light on his whereabouts. He must have awakened before us. Perhaps he went to feed."

"Perhaps?" Sanos raged. "How are you not aware of his location?"

"He awak..."

"Yes, I heard you, but you are in charge of him, he is under your command and should have reported before taking leave, whether to feed or not."

Orion bowed. "Understood!"

"Don't understand, find him. If he has taken up with Telas I will hold you responsible and strip you of your command. You will do this NOW!"

"Yes, sir." Orion shot up, stiffened his shoulders. "Kaidan, Moya, follow in line. We..."

"I said *you* find him. Leave them to my command."

"Yes, sir!" Orion answered turning to leave.

"And do not come back to me unless he is located, then bring him to me. He will be disciplined accordingly for not following the chain of direct command."

Orion bowed once again. "As you wish." Orion opened the door finding Dr. Blum with his hand about to knock. The two shared perplexed stares before Orion moved past the doctor who strolled into Sanos's chambers, taking in the scene of carnage.

Blum said, "It seems the blood is a lot more potent than I expected."

"Yes, doctor. What brings you here?" said Sanos, his tone soft.

"I came to hear your thoughts on the pills after such an...extravagant feeding." He looked around the room. "Guess I don't have to ask. The new blood is obviously delectable."

Sanos stiffened in the doctor's presence. "It is," he said clearing his throat.

Blum crinkled his nose, eyes roaming from one body part to the next. "Kinda stink, don't they? I suggest cleaning this mess as soon as possible. The dead rot so quickly, especially when they're opened as they are here."

"We don't mind the stink, doctor. It's a scent we're accustomed to. But albeit, orders have been placed to retrieve a human to clean up. Rest assured doctor we are on top of it."

"Another human? Not a soldier I hope, such a site would incite further inquiry. Whether American or not." He kicked a severed head lying at his feet. "Perhaps Telas's observation is accurate."

Sanos turned from the doctor, hiding his cringing scowl. "Has she fed, doctor?"

"Not yet. I've instructed a human be brought to her, but there is another concern that sprang in the interim. An American soldier has gone AWOL. We have reason to believe he is making his way through the tunnels. I plan to dispatch a team of six to find him. The Russians namely, they love the satisfaction of capturing American soldiers, especially when given shoot to kill orders."

"Six men for one soldier?" Sanos turned to face Dr. Blum.

"That's a waste of power, doctor. Why waste the time, and why are you giving orders you are clearly incapable of giving? Such orders are to come from me doctor, not you. I'm in charge of military operations." He paused searching the doctor, listening to his heart and sensing the vibration writhing off the doctor's body. He was calm and calculated, his heart not skipping a single beat.

"The soldiers are bored and tired, Sanos. This kind of assignment gets the juices flowing again. They are men of action, sitting around babysitting a horde of zombified Americans taking pills and convulsing is not up to par with their usual play. They yearn for action. Much like your own men. Boredom creates inquiries and chances to think on their own. To find slivers of wrongdoings they can report and exploit. Remember, Sanos, we are not ready to introduce your race to the masses. Not yet. We are far from exposing this revelation. Men are more apt to question orders if they are aware of a direct threat to their existence, especially when those orders follow a connection to the same threat. It is required by all parties to continue your exclusion."

"My men and I are tired of hiding. These walls and tunnels are a prison. We want to rush out into the night and hunt, not be contained and not be fed like we are animals in a zoo."

Dr. Blum cocked his head, glaring at Sanos. He curled his brow. "Perhaps you should relieve your men?"

Sanos's body constricted. His eyes scowled with anger. He lifted his chin, gesturing to his men. "Leave us," he ordered.

The remaining five stiffened their shoulders. "Yes, sir," they shouted, crossing their right hands over their left shoulder, stretching the arm towards Sanos.

Cade ordered, "Fall in," and led the men out. Sanos and Dr. Blum waited as they filed into the hall, closing the door behind them.

"Sit," Dr. Blum said, gesturing to Sanos's bed. "You appear tired. I think the blood is having an adverse effect. I'd like to offer a brief examination."

Sanos looked away.

"I said sit!"

Sanos obeyed. The doctor's order enraged Sanos. Under any other circumstance he'd tear the good doctor apart. But the Drac nine had handed down orders that Dr. Blum was not to be touched. Indeed, he was protected, and any harm that came to Dr. Blum by Dracs would be dealt with in the harshest manner. Even more, only Sanos and Telas were allowed this information. To the remaining seven, order needed to appear as normal, with Drac's completely in charge. Another order that brought shame to Sanos's command.

Dr. Blum observed Sanos whose body trembled and quivered. He pulled a seat close to the bed, whacked a severed hand off the chair and sat facing Sanos. He felt Sanos's throat, his head, raised his arms, and placed his hand to his heart.

"You tremble," he said, raising his eyelid. "Pupil dilation too."

"I am fine," Sanos replied.

"You're not yourself. This rage is unbecoming, a direct behavior change. And the trembling is a concern."

Sanos cringed, hating being so close to the doctor.

"I have to concur with Telas, the pills have an adverse effect on the blood. I will need to inform COR. The chemistry will need to be tweaked."

"We are not pin cushions, doctor. Another round of chemistry? We're dying here. My men and I…"

"Your men?" Dr. Blum laughed. "Your men are losing faith in your leadership. Where did you send Orion? Where is Titus? Telas is locked away by your own hand, your men Sanos, are on the brink of mutiny and they've every right. I apologize for the chemistry; perhaps my eagerness to be gone from this place affected my judgment. The pills are too strong. I will need to alter the potency."

"But you've done it. Look at the results, the Americans are mindless and easily controlled. What you've created is exactly what all want."

Dr. Blum shook his head. "The cost is too much. Until a different chemistry can be found we will need to continue testing." He sat up, staring at Sanos who looked away. "Order your men not to feed."

Sanos was quiet. He despised taking orders from a human.

Dr. Blum persisted. "If you disobey me, Sanos, I will inform COR and both my people and yours will remove you of your duty. You'll end up shoveling feces and body parts in a ditch. None of this works if we don't have full cooperation. You are aware of the order, Sanos; I am in charge here. Your command is for show to keep your people in line for experimentation. That is your one and only true order, acknowledge it."

Sanos remained quiet.

"Acknowledge or the next call I make is to COR."

Sanos turned to the doctor, eyeing him with disgust. "Acknowledged, *doctor*."

Dr. Blum smiled. "Good," he said, walking to the door. "I'll release Telas immediately and let her know you've come to your senses and ordered your men not to feed. Understandably she's become a bit sentimental since the baby arrived. I'll allow her to continue her diligence with that product and order her to feed once the new rations arrive. I expect you to do the same. Indulging on common blood may restore your senses and logic. Alternatively, I suggest you sleep a few days and allow your body to reset."

He turned in the doorway. "Also, report any other adverse effects please. I'd like to have a complete case study to provide to COR."

He waited for a response. "Sanos?"

Sanos turned to him. "Of course," he said.

"Very well then." Dr. Blum bowed before leaving.

Sanos felt his blood turn cold, his body shivered, staring, glaring, sensing his heart thump in his chest.

"I should have torn you apart," he whispered.

# 10

CAM'S NECK AND SKULL THROBBED with a pulsating sharp pain as he regained consciousness. His blurred vision started to focus, and he saw Phil kneeling beside the bomb. Cam, lying on the floor, started coughing. Choking, he sat up, bent over, gagging and hacking, and noticed he was in a pool of blood. He searched the room and locked eyes on Titus' severed head. The stale dark eyes leapt out at him. Cam jumped, startled and shivering and slammed back against the wall.

Phil raised his eyebrows. "You ok?"

Cam nodded. Started another coughing fit. "Yes," he said holding his fist to his mouth.

"You sure?"

"Yeah…" he coughed again. "Yeah."

Phil watched him, eyeing his movements.

"Can you tell me what the hell is that?" Cam pointed to Titus.

Phil looked at the decapitated head. "*That* would be a vampire. An alien vampire. A *Drac* to be accurate."

Cam paused, his eyes wide. Looked to Titus then Phil then Titus again. So many thoughts and questions raced through his mind. He couldn't deny what was lying on the floor nor that he'd been bitten. And at the moment he wished he'd never come down into the tunnels. Wished he had gone back above ground like he was supposed to.

"How's your neck?" Phil pointed to the puncture holes and the large bruise surrounding them.

"Hurts like a sonofabitch." He cringed when he touched the puncture wounds.

"I'm sure. That was a nasty bite."

Cam touched his neck, stretching his head as his neck bones cracked and popped.

"Mother fucker bit me." He kicked the head. "Stop looking at me." The head rolled closer to Phil who watched as the head stopped a foot in front of him.

Phil cocked his eyes. "I don't think he's looking at you. He's dead."

"Yea, well, who the hell knows?"

"True, but I think you're ok."

A thought rattled in Cam's mind. "My God, am I going to turn into one of them?"

"No," Phil laughed. "That's fiction. They're aliens, not demons from hell. They're not diseased, just living creatures that feed on human blood."

Cam shot a look at Phil, noticing he was covered in blood. "Did he get you too?"

Phil looked puzzled. "Come again?"

"You've got blood all over you..."

Phil looked himself over.

"Did he bite you too?"

"Not at all." He locked eyes with Cam. "Cut off a head, and a lot of blood spills." Phil showed his forearm and the blade attached to it.

Cam shook his head. "Who are you?"

"Really insignificant, isn't it. At least you know you can trust me."

"For now, yes, but..."

"What is significant is how to turn off this bomb? I don't have any expertise with bombs."

Cam coughed once more, still touching his neck. "Why would you want to turn it off? This place is worse than any level in hell. Fucking alien vampires, evil doctors and pills turning Americans into slaves. This whole damn camp needs to be blown off the planet." Cam eyed the bomb, watching as the timer continued to race down in time.

"What's happening here is not my concern, but the woman brought down here, Sandy, is my concern."

Cam released his neck. "Why?" He pushed himself to his feet.

"Because she means a lot to my people." He kept staring at the bomb, looking for a way to shut it down.

"Mister?" Cam said. "Are you an alien too?"

Phil laughed. "Definitely not."

"Good. Then I don't have to kill you."

Phil rolled his eyes. "Sure," he said. "Now back to the bomb. Can you shut..."

"It can't be stopped, not by me or anyone else. I set it that way. In case something happened to me I wanted to be sure this place would blow sky high."

Phil stared at Cam. "Yourself included?"

Cam nodded and Phil dropped his head. "Shit!"

"Doesn't leave you a lot of time?"

"Not at all. I don't even know where she is."

"Best advice I have is to find Dr. Blum; he seems to run things around here. Stocky guy with a mop of blonde hair. If she's still alive, he would know it and where to find her."

Phil stood. "Thank you. I suggest you leave. It's only a matter of time before they come snooping around to find him." He gestured to Titus. "I don't think you want that kind of wrath before death comes."

Cam nodded looking over the floor then to Titus, lying stiff and surrounded by a pool of blood.

"Can you point me in a direction to Dr. Blum?"

"What about the people?"

"The people?" Phil cocked an eyebrow.

"Yes, the Americans they're experimenting on."

"I'm not following?"

"Your people? You said you have...people. It's obvious you have a safe place to go. If I can get the Americans upstairs out of here can we come with? It may be the only chance we have. Considering we're all about to die, saving as many as possible is better than nothing. Especially if there's a safe place to go. Away from all this..." He shook his head. "Carnage."

Phil paused, studying Cam, locking eyes with him. He swallowed his breath.

"Atlanta," Phil said. "Outside the city, southeast quadrant. Find a man by the name of Robyn Winter. If for some reason I don't make it, he'll take you in. All of you."

Cam nodded and said, "Down the corridor take the first left. It's a hike but you'll come into an open area; go right, and you'll come to a door. It's like a medical room and lab. I was there when I first arrived. If you find her, there are tunnels throughout this bunker; they lead to the river a few miles away. That's your best chance to get her out. Just be out of the tunnel before the bomb goes off. If you're not, you'll both be incinerated. Those tunnels will turn into a nuclear holocaust once the bomb explodes."

"Understood." Phil went to leave.

"Mister?" Cam said. Phil stopped and turned back. "Was the war bull shit?" he asked, his eyes down staring at the bomb. "Did so many die for nothing?"

Phil swallowed, cleared the lump in his throat.

"No answer," Cam said. He turned to Phil. "What was the point?"

"Wars are fought between enemies. An enemy is not someone we've been allies with. The war was a farce to drive people into camps. Weeding out any unnecessary rogues that could cause trouble. It was part of the plan for a long time. An inevitable contingency for the larger design."

"Is that why we never used nukes?"

"Yes," Phil said. "They are for something else."

"What?"

Phil bowed. "Look...I know this is a lot to take in, but we haven't time. Get out of here, find Robyn, and you'll have your answers."

"Understood."

Phil went to leave but stopped abruptly. "Oh, there is one favor I need to ask?"

"Shoot."

"The kids."

"What kids?"

"I came in through the wall. There's a group of kids there. Can you promise me you'll do all you can to get them out?"

"You have my word."

Phil paused, gave a quick nod. "My name's Phil by the way."

"Cameron. My friends call me Cam."

"Cam," Phil repeated. "You can get out through there too. There's a fence outlining the wall, you can climb over. May be a good way for you to slip in unnoticed."

Cam nodded. "Go," he said.

Phil gave a quick nod then was gone. Cam stood looking at the bomb.

"I'm sorry," he breathed.

For the first time in a long while, he sensed a sliver of hope. He surveyed the room. The blood and carnage, severed head and decapitated body. Phil was right, they will be looking for Titus and when they find him, they'll find the bomb too.

*But they can't disarm it. Not without the detonator and even then, they'll trip the wire.*

"No, but they can take it out of here. If they find it with enough time, they can take it somewhere. Use it against more Ameri..." He paused, thinking. "More humans." The thought stung like a knife twisting in his skull.

*Aliens do exist. Vampires too. For God's sake, friggin alien vampires exist!*

The proof was lying dead at his feet. He bent down, looking at the detonator

"Where can I hide it?" He searched the room, corner to corner, every crevice, every inch. Clucked his tongue.

"Got it," he whispered and carefully picked up the detonator.

* * *

When Sandy awakened, Mono was at her bedside.

*All is well, child,* Mono's words in Sandy's mind. *The baby is healthy. He took to the food without incident.*

Sandy turned from Mono. A painful sting jolted up her neck. She immediately touched the wound where she'd been bitten. Fed on by her baby.

*This is a nightmare.*

*No, no, dear,* responded Mono. *It is all for the best.*

Sandy turned to Mono. Saw her own reflection in Mono's dark, metallic eyes. How disheveled and drawn she appeared. Pale and defeated. She snapped her eyes shut, shook her head, pursing her lips, holding back her tears.

*None of this is possible. It can't be...*

*It is possible.*

She kept her eyes closed. *It's not happening. I'm dead that's what it is. I died when the soldiers shot up the hotel. That's what this is, it's death. It's...*

*Come now dear, no need to dilute yourself with crazy notions.*

"Get out of my fucking head!" Sandy screamed through a wail of cries and tears.

Mono stood erect, shoulders back, chin up.

Sandy opened her eyes, not looking at Mono, moving her head feverishly back and forth. *Stay with the hotel. You're lying in bed in the hotel, ready to wake up.* As strange as it had been hiding in the hotel, life was still somewhat normal. She'd become used to the trappings of war over the last decade. It was all she knew. But these latest incidents, there was nothing normal about them. And her baby...what they did to her baby? Not to mention an alien was at her bedside, now examining the wound on Sandy's neck. Definitely not how she pictured the birth of her baby. Not at all, she'd always pictured sharing such a miraculous event with...

*Ben...where is Ben?* A picture of the firing squad raced into her mind.

Mono worked effortlessly, examining Sandy's neck, checking her heart rate and pupil dilation.

*Where is Ben?*

Mono paused, staring at Sandy. Her thought crept into Sandy's consciousness. *Ben is no more.* Mono's words rifled into Sandy's brain, stabbing at her heart, and closing her throat. She turned from Mono with tears in her eyes.

She didn't want to believe it but she felt it, knowing he was gone, and there was nothing left of him. Not even a part of him remained in their baby. Not at all, they took that from her too.

"No time for tears," said Mono in that soft echoing voice. "Your baby needs you to survive." She continued telepathically, *A boy needs his mother.*

Sandy sniffled, sucking back a stifled cry. Her bottom lip quivered. "Of course he needs me. A mother protects her child from..."

"Not exactly what I meant, dear."

Sandy's eyes narrowed, perplexed. She forced herself to look at Mono.

Mono bent her head, eyeing Sandy, speaking telepathically. *What I was referring to is how Drac babies feed on the mother. Not like mother's milk for humans. Drac's require the mother's blood. Not just for nutrients, the sharing of blood develops a psychic connection Drac's require for intelligent and emotional thought. There is a unique connection within the species between mother and child, even into adulthood. A mother's blood could cure most illness, helping to sustain the species for centuries. In turn Drac women are stronger than Drac men, both physically and mentally, sharing a psychic connection and foresight even across time and space. As a scientist, I am deeply intrigued over this newest experiment. I wonder if these traits will pass to you, Sandy. But your cooperation is paramount.* She touched Sandy's forehead. *Think of your baby. Try to hear his heart.*

Sandy turned to Mono, staring at her with disgust. *Get away from me!*

Mono provided no response. Her countenance was calm, as if this were all normal. Sandy moved away from her hand, closing her eyes, hoping Mono would leave.

"Very well, dear, but you must come to a single conclusion. If you don't help us, we have no reason to keep you alive. You'll be thrown to the wolves and trust me, they will not be as kind as your baby when feeding on you."

Her words struck Sandy.

"Your baby is the only reason you're still alive. Be it as it is, that baby is your lifeline."

But Sandy did not move.

"I'll give you a bit of time," said Mono. "Understanding how all this may seem to you, I'll give it a bit of time to sink in. But do know there is nothing you can do about what has been done. All you have is your baby, without you he will die and then there is no need for you. I will be back, Sandy. And when I return, I expect your full cooperation."

Mono left the room. Sandy pictured her baby. The thought was powerful, seeing the baby lying safe and secure. She could hear his heartbeat. Hear his blood flowing through his veins. Sleeping soundly and peacefully. Her brow furrowed. Now she felt hunger, neither from herself nor the baby. Instinctively she knew the baby was fine. She thought of his heart, beating calmly, the red organ changing into a picture of the rose surrounded in white light. The picture was clear, sitting in the center of her mind. And through the rose she saw Telas. Sandy's heart was calm, her body relaxed with a profound relief she hadn't expected. She could see Telas was trapped in a room sick and weak.

*I must feed!*

Telas's voice in Sandy's mind. But she was sure Telas was not referring to Sandy or that her words were meant for Sandy's ears. There was an air of desperation in Telas's voice. And with it an odd kinship clicked in Sandy's stomach. She turned her head, staring through the wall, seeing Telas's heart where she travelled within the heart rising to Telas's thoughts. Again, that click. A sensation like confidence, a certainty, compassion, clicked inside Sandy.

*Telas is safe.*

She couldn't tell if she said this herself or if someone had provided the declaration, although it mattered not.

*It is true, I know it. I can feel it.*

Telas would die before allowing the baby to be hurt.

Sandy allowed her thoughts to find Telas. Unknowing where any of this all came from, nor what she was about to do or why, but she said the words, dropping them into Telas's mind like a stone thrown into water.

*Come and feed, Telas.*

*Come and feed!*

\* \* \*

Telas's hunger weakened every ounce of strength, every muscle, every limb and organ. She leaned against the wall; her head flopped back on the concrete with labored breath, trying to calm the heart that jumped inside her chest with a slow thick and struggling pounding. She felt the cold rhythm of blood struggling to find all parts of her body.

Her eyes, wet and wide stared wildly over the room

*I should have fed. Should have kept my strength.*

She winced, baring her teeth, seething. Her veins on fire, burning, constricting, shooting pain to her brain.

*I'm drying up. Why, Mono, did you not hear me?*

She raised her hand, observing how the skin turned gray before her eyes. The veins swelled beneath the skin as if having a mind of their own, searching and begging for blood.

*I thought I had a few more days before this would happen.*

Vampires had gone five, even ten days before calcifying and turning to stone. She'd seen it before, a kind of vampire suicide for those who refused to take any more life. But this turn in events happening like this, it was too soon. Yes, she felt weak today but this was coming on all too quickly as if...

*Someone is doing it. Speeding up time.*

She forced a swallow, drawing in a narrow breath down her closing throat and her heart constricted, squeezing inside her chest. Her eyes now lost and dry, staring into blinding white light. She could hear her heart, pounding with a thick intermittent slam that echoed between her ears. Behind it a faint whisper hung in the room.

*Come and feed.*

"Sandy," she whispered. She could see the baby, lying asleep, listening to his peaceful heart and Sandy's voice behind it. Telas's thoughts were weak, too weak to project to Sandy. The light turned dark as her heart struggled. Pulsating veins longing for blood slithered up her neck. Like a human when being strangled, the pain and fear were immense, suffocating. Her hands shook and her stomach wrenched in agony.

*There's not enough time.*

Her feet kicked, straining for blood as the door unlocked. Telas's mouth salivated with the sweet scent of human blood.

"Telas," called Dr. Blum. He crouched by her side. "Telas, what's happened? You must feed at once."

Telas could not see the doctor. Her vision was steeped in darkness. His voice a distant whisper behind the flow of blood, like a thunderous river pounding through his veins.

"I'll get a human A-SAP." Dr. Blum took the radio off his belt.

Telas felt her heart stiffen. The organ transforming into a hallow stone. Instinctively she leapt onto Dr. Blum with every last bit of strength she could harvest. Sank her teeth into his neck and gulped a wallop of blood. That first stream of precious substance ignited life into her veins. Dr. Blum wriggled in her arms. Color returned to her skin as the darkness subsided to light. She suckled on his neck, not hearing Dr. Blum's cries and pleas. She'd never felt such a raging thirst before. She drank ferociously. Squeezed Dr. Blum in her arms tearing into his neck, ignoring the heartbeat that a second ago was pumping furiously, now subsided bringing death like a brush of wind against a dry leaf. Telas pulled her mouth from his neck.

The scene returned with a clear vision. Her eyes wide. She looked over Dr. Blum and over her own person. Blood all over her hands. Her chest. Pooling on the floor beneath them. Blum convulsed and flopped beneath her. She gripped the wound, squeezing to cease any more blood from leaving. He was dying. Dying by her hand and her folly. Dr. Blum was untouchable; those were her orders from Sanos when they first arrived, given from the Drac nine. She would be prosecuted for this action and the penalty would be death.

*I'm sorry, doctor.* He required blood to lift the heart and allow the veins to pump with renewed life. Telas tore into her wrist. Her teeth penetrating the vein. Except her plan was too late. Before she could reach her bloodied wrist to the doctor's mouth his heart stopped.

"No. C'mon, c'mon now. Take it." Her voice rushed and whining, desperate. Blood dripped from her wrist to his pale lips. "Take it, please," she cried.

No movement. Nothing. Telas watched as his eyes turned black.

And now there was no going back. Dr. Blum was deceased and by her doing.

The thought came in low, growing with a rage inside her mind. She saw the baby and feared for his life. Without her to protect him he would come under the thumb of Sanos.

"I'm sorry," she whispered.

The doctor was dead and Telas fought for a plan, searching for what to do. All she could think of was protecting the baby. Disposal of the body was now required. Should she be found out for this debacle Sanos would indeed detain her further. Time was now running out on her ability to maintain any sort of order and credibility. Of course there were other concerns with what she'd done. Like blame and cover up. What would she tell the others about Dr. Blum's whereabouts? What would she do with the baby? How would she continue her important work? Above all there was no way she would allow Sanos to even touch the child. She went to the open door and looked through.

*They're all gone.*

The room was quiet. Unnervingly quiet and she could hear her heart thumping, pounding nervous in her chest. This was her chance to dispose of Dr. Blum. She could figure the rest out after, but she desperately had to hide the body.

*Come on, Telas, think!*

The answer came.

*The pit.*

But how to get him there was the next concern. The pit was far, a mile or two down the tunnels. The pit was where they entered the camp, from any of several underground cities across the globe. A landing platform, large enough to house ships and a small army and in the center was the opening into the earth—the pit—where Dracs and Greys moved freely across the planet. She sprang into the lab, searching for a gurney to rush the body out and a sheet to cover Dr. Blum. She found both in a supply closet. She moved quickly, nervously lifting Dr. Blum onto the gurney. She covered the body with several blankets. The first was to soak up the blood. The second and third to hide the bloodied sheet from plain view.

She searched the room again, wheeling the gurney to the door.

*Hide your thoughts. Don't let them in.*

She breathed deeply, pushing the gurney through the door.

*Be inconspicuous. Hold steady but fast.*

She hurried down the hall to the pit; for the first time in all her life understanding what true fear felt like. The fear she had for her baby and what his future would hold if Sanos would claim the child.

## 11

**CAM KNEELED BY THE CHILDREN LYING** in the dark. Their breathing was heavy. Their chests jumped every so often.

*What've they done to them?*

He touched their heads. Hot. He remembered the order the soldiers were given not to inquire about the dark side of the enclosure, no matter what they heard or saw, to let it go. "But why?" he had asked at that time yet received no answer. Cam lifted a child's eyelid. His body jumped with the revelation. The pupil staring back at him, he'd seen it before, staring into the eyes of death when Titus gripped him in his arms. He pulled the lips back. The teeth were sharp as if someone had filed the teeth in perfect precision. Cam dropped his head. Closed his eyes.

*They're just kids, for God's sake. Children. Not some sadistic experiment.*

He thought about vampires, gathering every bit of information he'd ever heard, seen or read. They can't live in the sun. Dr. Blum and the pills. The treaty. Blum's experimenting on them, on all of them, everyone, turning men into mutes and children into…vampires.

He couldn't deny what was in front of him. Remembering what Phil said about the war. All of it was a farce. Lies and deceit. Our government is working with aliens. Every government is working with them. We're all slaves. Even us. The military. Are the Chinese and Russian soldiers aware of what's going on? Or are the Americans the only ones kept in the dark? The war had changed so quickly. One day they were fighting, the next the American government surrendered control.

*Maybe that was a part of the charade?*

He sucked back his tears, clenched his fists, and gnashed his teeth. What could he possibly do about this? These kids are vampires, and there's a good chance they won't survive sunrise. Even if they do, who's to say they won't feed on all of us with appetites befitting confused children.

His stomached turned, nauseous and lightheaded. *I made the right choice.* He scanned the perimeter. Turned to the night sky and the glint of stars that hung over head beyond the blood moon. A soft wind caressed his skin. *Right and wrong!* He glanced at the boys on the ground. *I'm going to need help. But who can I trust? No one! Have to though. The only way we can save anyone is to work together. But what do I say?*

He laughed. *This is insane.* He shook his head. *Phil, I hope you accomplish your mission. I don't see any way possible for me to accomplish mine.* He stood up. "I've doomed us to hell."

A flashlight clicked on from outside the fence. Cam's eyes squinted. He put his hand up, blocking the light. A Russian soldier spoke in broken English. "Who's that...soldier...disobeying a direct order."

Cam noticed the soldier's AR-15 pointed in his direction, the flashlight fastened to the gun. "American soldier," Cam hollered, raised both his arms. "American soldier...under orders...don't shoot." His hollering brought more soldiers.

"Cam?" a voice behind the light said. Cam recognized the voice as a confidant and fellow soldier, Corporal Grimes.

"Grimes, it's Cam. Tell him to stand down."

Grimes talked in Russian to the soldier who returned with a few short yet poignant words.

Grimes responded, returning his attention to Cam. "Where have you been? We received reports you went AWOL. Approach the fence."

Cam did as instructed. Hands in the air approaching the light. Whatever Grimes said to the Russian soldier didn't work. He was staring into a black hole of an AR15.

"Jesus, what happened to you?" Grimes said.

Cam remembered he was covered in blood. "I...I was attacked."

"Attacked?" Grimes said. "Who would attack you and why?"

"You wouldn't believe me," Cam whispered.

"Come again?"

Cam paused, searching for what to say, understanding how insane this situation was.

"I...um...well..."

The Russian, obviously in charge of the situation said something, loudly and profound. He was looking beyond Cam into the clearing. Grimes did the same.

Grimes jaw hung open. "What did you do to those kids?"

Cam's eyes widened. "Nothing...nothing at all. They were here when I came up." Realizing what the scene looked like, covered in blood with the four kids lying unresponsive on the ground. He responded quickly. "They're alive," Cam shouted. "Although maybe not for long."

Again, the Russian shouted an order. Grimes' voice dropped. "You've got to come out of there."

"How?" Cam said. "There's no opening...I checked every part of the fence, there's no way out other than the door back in."

"Climb over," Grimes said.

Cam surveyed the fence; it reached over twenty feet high. Looked back at the AR-15 pointed at his chest. The Russian hollered, stepping back. Cam climbed noticing a slew of soldiers watching him. He ascended quickly, draping his legs over the top. He descended slowly.

*Don't give them a reason to shoot.*

The Russian started shouting again, put the gun in Cam's back once his feet hit the floor.

"Ok, ok, ok, just don't shoot." Cam threw his hands in the air.

"Hands behind your back," Grimes said, and Cam obeyed, his wrists zip-tied quickly.

Again, Russian orders were given.

Grimes used his radio, "Dr. Blum, AWOL soldier has been detained." He glanced at Cam and winced when he saw his neck. "Dr. Blum..." he repeated. The Russian soldier saw the same puncture holes in Cam's neck. He reached to the wound, swiping Cam's neck to bring the wound to attention. Grimes bent his head. Talked into the radio again. "Dr. Blum?" He looked at Cam. "What happened to Dr. Blum?"

"I don't know. I haven't seen him."

"Your neck, Cameron. What happened to it? How'd you get such a wound?"

Cam stiffened, his thoughts racing. "I was bitten by..."

Grimes' eyes widened. Cam hesitated. "Bitten by what?" The Russian started shouting and jammed the gun against Cam's head.

"A vampire," Cam shouted. "I was bitten by a vampire."

"Impossible, vampires don't exist," Grimes shot back.

"Look at my neck, Corporal. Do you think I got like this by myself?"

Grimes hesitated, studying Cam's wound.

"Listen to me," Cam said. "There's so much more going on here than we know. We need to work together and get out of here."

"Listen to what you're saying, soldier. You've gone insane."

"Insane is what's happening here, Corporal. We need to get these people out of here and get out of here like now."

Grimes shook his head. "Ludicrous. This is ludicrous." He put the radio to his mouth. "Dr. Blum, come in." He waited. "Dr. Blum, where are you? We've detained the soldier. Dr. Blum, respond."

Silence. Again, Russian orders.

"Look at my neck, you've got to listen to me." Cam's plea brought commotion among the soldiers.

Grimes shook his head. Surveyed the growing number of soldiers surrounding them. His eyes narrowed. "Come with me." He gripped Cam's forearm, said something in Russian then led Cam towards the building. "We're going to wait to hear from Dr. Blum."

"There's no time for that."

"Why not?"

Cam shook his head. *Don't tell them about the bomb, it'll cause hysteria. Not yet.* "Go into the tunnels yourself; you'll find them there."

"Find who?"

"Vampires, Corporal. Fuckin' alien vampires, and Dr. Blum is with them. Jesus I can't tell you enough that we need to get these people and get out of here."

"We're not doing anything until we hear from Dr. Blum. Vampires don't exist, Cameron, that's insane."

"How do you explain my neck then?"

"Simple, you did it to yourself to concoct a story to hide what you've done."

"That's one hell of a story to make up. Why would I come up with such a story knowing what you'd say?"

Grimes paused. "Because you've lost your mind. That's the only rational explanation."

"Nothing about what's happened is rational, and nothing going on here is rational either, and you know it. We've had conversations about this and now that there's proof you won't accept it. We're all going to die, Corporal, unless we get out of here."

Grimes rushed Cam into the building and the soldiers resting all shot up from their cots. Grimes closed and locked the office door, shutting out the resting soldiers. The Russian behind them started talking into his radio, his voice hurried albeit commanding.

"Who is he talking to?"

"His superiors in Washington. That's protocol. The order we were given should something happen to Dr. Blum."

"Wonderful," Cam said. "Now we're all dead."

Grimes sat Cam down. "What does that mean? You know the protocol."

Cam shook his head. "So much is unseen." He looked at Grimes, now sitting on the desk. Cam pursed his lips and swallowed his breath. "Our superiors are not who we think. They're as much in line with these alien vampires as Dr. Blum is. Jesus, we need to get out of here, and you need to listen to me."

Grimes rolled his eyes, not meeting Cam's stare. "Alien vampires?" He shook his head.

Cam looked to the floor. "The short lady," he said.

"What? What short lady?"

His eyes narrowed, studying Grimes. "You know who I'm talking about. She retrieved the couple we caught, that lady in the hotel and her husband. She's an alien, and you know it."

Commotion behind the door where the soldiers were. Both Cam and Grimes turned to the door.

"You all know it too," Cam hollered. "And if he alerted

Washington, I guarantee we're all about to die. They're gonna come in here and kill all of us."

"Why would they do that, Cameron? It makes no sense." He turned his eyes to Cam who met his stare. Grimes' hands shook over his lap.

*He's scared. Nervous as all hell.*

"Think about it." Cam lowered his voice. "Their cover is blown, and you can't get in touch with Dr. Blum. Whatever has happened to him will come to their attention, and they won't have a bunch of soldiers running around with this information; it'll put a kink in their plan. If they haven't told us this information already, they don't want us to know."

Grimes shook his head. "Nobody knows anything. We haven't seen anything like you're describing. If anything, Cam, they'll be coming for you."

Cam looked to the floor.

"Is that it, soldier?"

"I guess so."

"Good," Grimes slipped off the desk, stood over Cam who shook his head. "I'll be back." He went to the door.

"You're making a huge mistake," Cam hollered. "We're all gonna die if we don't get out of here. I expected more from you, Corporal."

Grimes went through the doors.

"Fuck!" Cam said.

*Think of something!*

* * *

Dr. Blum's radio was lying on the floor in a pool of his blood. It had spun to the wall when Telas jumped on him. The soldier's calls went unanswered. Mono stood in the room, listening to the happening outside. The scene in the room revealed an apparent rationale over what had taken place; there was blood stained on the wall. And she could smell it too. The stink of the dead Dr. Blum.

*Unfortunate.* Not that Dr. Blum's death was cause for alarm; Mono possessed the ability to continue his work. But the humans would call for an inquiry and demand retribution. She'd seen it many times before. There are a few humans who were considered untouchable, and Dr. Blum was one of them. His work for all parties involved was considered paramount, and he always delivered. Had been since long before the war.

Telas would come under the humans' thumb, something Mono and her superiors would definitely not want. Although, considering the treaty and how close they were to the ultimate goal, no one would choose to rock the boat. They would deliver Telas to the humans. But Mono knew Telas was required, necessary for the baby's sake. And should Telas be delivered to the humans, control of the baby would be given to Sanos. And that, Mono knew, could not happen.

Of course, there was Sandy, but in order to be taught correctly, for Mono's purpose, Telas was required and Sanos was not up to the task. *He's gone mad on new blood. Not that he was psychologically stable before either. But now, he's become a liability. A large liability. A baby under his rule would be an abomination.* He was at most irresponsible, incapable of achieving any important task, his history proved it. *He's worse than humans. Like a child, the only thing he ever did right was to follow orders and now he's incapable of even handling simple tasks.*

It was best to close up shop and be done with this place. *But how?*

The radio crackled with static. The soldier on the other end declared they'd caught the AWOL soldier. Mono closed her eyes. *Simple enough. Our situation has been compromised by an American soldier who killed Dr. Blum. Rescue the important beings and desecrate the rest.*

It'll happen swiftly too as she's seen so many times before. The work and progress made in this camp over the years she could continue on her own, on a larger scale. Mono closed her eyes, seeing the rose quickly and prominently in her mind's eye. A second later wind whirled in the room. The blood was transformed, turning to dust, cleaning up what Telas had not, leaving no trace of Dr. Blum's desecration. Even the radio turned to dust. Mono looked over the room.

*Easy clean up. But where is Telas?*

Closed her eyes. Searching, feeling, sensing where Telas had gone with Dr. Blum's body. She locked in on Telas's movement towards the pit.

Mono smiled. *Clever girl!* Mono saw the pit. A grand and large opening in the tunnels that dropped deep into the earth, extending to all parts of the country through corridors and paths that allowed her species access to anywhere they desired. Large enough for space crafts to move freely without being seen. The element of surprise was always in their best interest. She could feel her people beneath the earth occupying cities as large as any above ground.

*We will all be home soon.*

She understood how close they were to initiating the next phase. Once the pills are deemed appropriate, the final phase into slavery would begin. Although the larger threat to the slave plan had not yet manifested, she knew it was inevitable. Her grey cohorts knew that much. And this baby, this mix of concocted Drac and human DNA was the centerpiece to the future conflict. The indigo trials would begin in the not so distant future.

*Act accordingly. As if you know nothing. We greys have a right to be proud.*

She arched her back, raised her shoulders and chin. *I will need the assistance of Mintaka, Alnitak and Alnilam.* The three witches, as Mono referred to them, were greys, although unlike Mono. The difference between them was shown to Mono shortly after their arrival when they had confided in Mono their own secret discourse and plan. And what they'd shown her of the future strengthened Mono's pride. Two possible futures. One brought ascension to Mono's people. The other: slavery. But Mono understood the minds of her grey superiors, choosing not to alert them with what she'd been shown. Superiors who'd become so blinded by Draconian lies, their lust for power hindered the ability to transcend. They would not take kindly to Mono's declaration. Knowing the future often comes with duress in the present, and Mono had to work with the three witches in secret.

Mono understood the baby would come. Recognized he had to be delivered specifically to Moth, the head of the Drac nine. *But he will have difficulties with raising the child. Unless…unless the energetic bond between mother and child could be broken.* Should such an event take place Moth would have no issue with future loyalty from the child. But severing the connection required the mother to give the child's heart over freely.

*There are methods, dire and harsh, that are necessary to persuade the mother or mothers to relinquish their bond.*

Although the witches may not approve of Mono's method. They were not on the side of torture. Their genetic code prevented violent behavior. Such behavior could only come from Mono. Her grey species were not as forgiving as the greys the witches had spawned from. If neither mother complied both would have to perish. Their bond would serve Mono's cause better if they were deceased.

She brought herself back, from the underground cities through the tunnels and to the pit to Telas, seeing through Telas's eyes as she approached the hole in the earth. Mono opened her eyes, back in the room. She understood the steps she must take to clean up as much of the mess as possible. Her first order of business was to contact her superiors so they can begin their arrival.

And then the mothers will be dealt with.

*In the harshest manner possible.* To sever the bond one or both would be required to die.

Mono's rational mind did consider another possibility.

*What if I am wrong?*

* * *

Orion studied Titus' body, crouched beside the corpse and head. The slit up the spine was direct and calculated causing the spine to weaken for the second slice that severed his head.

*The blades. He used the blades.*

He wasn't aware of any human who knew the sacred art. Not any who were living. He pondered other options, alternative possibilities for such a clean cut. But every possibility came back to the blades. Orion surveyed the blood beneath his feet. There were two colors, two shades of red one darker than the other. Drac blood was always lighter than human blood. It was in the chemical structure of Dracs that changed the compounds turning the blood a lighter shade.

*He was feeding? Where is the human body?*

Orion took Titus' head in his hands. Clenched his jaw, staring at the face of his cohort. A frozen stare of surprise looked back at him. Human blood stained the lips, teeth and chin. Surveying the neck brought the revelation of what he'd expected. The cut was clean and powerful slicing through the bone like a hot knife through warm butter, without restriction or resistance. Any human weaponry would have left resistance when cutting through Drac bone, much more dense than human bones.

*One of us?*

He couldn't discount the possibility that a Drac may have committed such a heinous crime. There was no other conclusion given the information available to him. Logic and rationale dictated the supposition. The "who" and the "why" were questions that required answers.

*Sanos? This would explain his behavior.*

Holding the head Orion glanced to the floor.

*What else could it be?*

All information led back to Sanos. Sanos who required the seven sleep; who became drunk on new blood and who tore those humans apart like a mad animal.

*There's no other explanation.*

Then something caught his eye, catching a glimpse of the dead eyes frozen in time. He bent his head, right then left, studying the dead eyes. His eyes narrowed.

*Old methods still work the best.*

He used his sharp fingernails to cut around the eye, lifting the eyelid away he removed the eyeball, dropping the head, investigating the back of the eye for a picture that reflected what Titus had seen before his death.

The human in Titus' grip had dark eyes, eyes that reflected a profile behind Titus. A picture frozen in time whose arm was raised above Titus' head.

*The first slice up his spine. The moment of Titus' death.*

Orion looked deep inside the reflective lens. No doubt it was a human. But not a soldier. Not one he'd ever seen before. The man's arm reflected the blade attached to his forearm. There was no emotion in the human's eyes, just a calm movement of knowing. Knowing exactly what he was doing. *Whoever it is he is still here, somewhere in here with us. But what would be the reason?*

*A stealth operation? Rebellion? Think, Orion, think!*

And Telas, where was Telas? Put away for insubordination. Now a human had the power of the blades, and he was clearly schooled in the art. Orion understood what protocol was when a Drac died. The body was to be cleaned and prepped for honoring followed by incineration. Ashes to ashes, dust to dust. Orion shook his head.

The next step was to honor the body and allow the family to pay respects. His people would need to be summoned to pick up the body, and an inquiry would begin. Sanos will need to be informed, and this revelation of human activity reported.

Orion gnashed his teeth. Shook his head. *Sanos is mad.*

Orion lacked faith in Sanos's ability to lead, considering his recent behavior. Considering his history. Orion had lost faith a long time ago. Telas had too. The reason their team was assigned to this forsaken outpost was an insult to their integrity.

*Once he's made aware of these events, he'll place blame on all of us. His team.*

*Everything in this outpost has turned into an outrage.*

Orion stood. *Why did you detain Telas? What had she done to cause such a reaction?* He understood Telas. Understood how she thought. Similar to himself. Orion concluded that Telas must have challenged Sanos on the new blood; there was no other explanation. But Dracs don't speculate.

*I have to speak to Telas before Sanos is made aware of this mess.*

But that action would clearly be deemed against protocol. The same for leaving the dead to lie and rot. Nonetheless he required answers, information to drive a clear decision. No one knows about Titus or that a human was the reason for his death.

*Lock up the room. Find Telas. Get a clear picture of what is happening. And in the interim...*

*Find the human who did this and bring him to justice! We require answers.*

He looked at the eyeball he was rolling between his fingers. Knelt down by the head and popped the eye back into the socket. Orion closed Titus' eyes, touched his head to Titus' forehead.

"Forgive me," he whispered, tightening his facial muscles. His eyes shot open. "To honor your death, I must do what is necessary." He gently placed the head on the floor. His eyes welled with tears that he refused to allow to fall. Kissed his fingers and touched the forehead.

"Your death will not be in vain."

# PART TWO

# FIRST THINGS FIRST, WE'RE GOING TO NEED MORE GUNS!

# 12

**SANOS'S CRAVING FOR NEW BLOOD DISTRACTED** rational thought. His mouth was dry, his throat constricted. When he closed his eyes, he could feel the sensation of new blood strengthen in his veins as if he'd just fed, but the sensation could not be followed to fruition. Something was missing, something that didn't connect, like a river that slammed into a dam with no means to connect to the water on the other side.

*More new blood is what you need.* This voice was his, although it seemed to come from the pills themselves. As if they called to him.

Depleted and wondering what course of action was required for him to feed on new blood, he sat on his bed, mulling over the many ways he could escape Dr. Blum's orders. Sanos snatched the severed hand from the floor. A minute amount of blood stained the wrist. He licked it.

*Not enough. Not nearly enough.*

He thought about ordering more humans to his chambers, but that privilege had passed. Dr. Blum would be informed of the order and, of course, would not allow it. More than likely the doctor was already at work, making changes to the mixture, the chemistry within the pills.

*The chemistry. There was a formula to Dr. Blum's genius.*

He tossed the hand and flopped back on the bed, staring at the ceiling.

*Get a grip, Sanos. You are weak and grow weaker with every thought. Think of your people feasting on this new blood, we would turn primitive. Think of what it has done to you already.*

*What you did to Telas!*

*You may lose your rank over this. Disgraced in the eyes of COR.*

(*No, they make you stronger.*) That voice again. The one from the pills.

He stood. "Cade," he hollered. His team waited in the hall for his orders.

Cade appeared in the door. "Yes, sir."

Sanos rolled his eyes, despising chain of command protocol verbiage. Once he enjoyed the respect, now it seemed tiresome and meaningless.

"None are to feed on new blood," Sanos ordered. "Dr. Blum has isolated a problem with the pills and is making necessary adjustments." He pursed his lips and forced a swallow down his constricted throat.

Cade stiffened then bowed.

Sanos paused hating what he'd said. *You appear weak in front of your subordinates!* The scowl in Cade's eyes confirmed his suspicion.

Sanos turned from Cade's stare, hands clamped behind his back. His eyes wandered from one severed body part to another, then to the blood-stained floor. His stomach constricted, his throat felt swollen and he fought to look away to the wall, his back to Cade.

"Bring Telas here, Cade. Give the order to the others not to feed. Let them stand guard in the corridor."

"Sir, yes, sir." His voice dropped and Sanos turned to his soldier.

"Something to say, Cade?"

Cade swallowed, his shoulders slumped, staring at the floor.

"Speak freely." Of all who were under Sanos's command, Cade had always been his most loyal subject. They saw eye-to-eye on all matters and in return Cade had quickly climbed the rank within the Sanos seven. He looked on Cade like a brother.

Cade looked to the wall, then forced himself to turn and meet Sanos's stare.

"The men thirst, Sanos. None have fed in over a day. If the pills are no good, how long will it take Dr. Blum to create new blood? We are Drac. Why do we bend to his will?"

His conviction brought pride to Sanos who stepped to Cade. Sanos understood the Drac dismay over COR's proclamation that essentially turned their people into slaves, at least in the eyes of Dracs. Having to take orders from humans was not ever what was intended. The Dracs lost faith in their superiors.

*Lost faith in me!* He took Cade's head in his hands, staring into his eyes.

"We will have our day again. There are happenings that will ensure our species hold on this planet is forever. To do so, certain events must take place. Not all are privy to these activities. We must stay in line. We must make sacrifices for the greater good. Do you understand, Cade?"

"I do." Cade looked on Sanos with a desperate stare. His face flushed, restricting and needing blood.

"But you still need to feed?"

Cade's eyes provided the answer. Sanos paused.

(*Allow them to feed. Look at your people. They are depleted and require blood.*)

Sanos lifted his chin, staring down on Cade. His men were dependent on him for survival. Every Drac was aware of the consequence of not feeding. His rank allowed Sanos to make decisions in the face of death. Protect Drac. By all costs protect Drac.

(*And then you too can feed. You should give the order. They are dying, Sanos. Can't you see?*)

*Yes, I can see.*

His eyes dropped, staring, lost in the thought of new blood.

"Sanos?"

(*Let them feed, Sanos. Even the Drac Nine can't discipline your actions when Drac lives are on the line.*)

He tried to swallow. His mouth and throat arid. He had to force his breath down his throat. His right eye twitched. He tasted new blood on his tongue. Felt the blood twist in his veins, clearing his thoughts.

(*The new blood makes us strong.*)

He looked at Cade. His subordinate. His friend. His brother. Drying up on the inside. Dying! The only means of Cade's survival is to feed on new blood.

(*And us. Yes. Don't forget us, too.*)

Sanos felt his body relax, his shoulders slowly dropped, jaw slackened. Even the mere thought of new blood brought a slight elation. The thought was a door to new blood. To power and strength.

To a world of ecstasy. He drew in a deep breath. A smug smile graced his lips when he exhaled. "You will feed before sunrise. All of you, I declare it, despite what Dr. Blum says. I will find a way."

"We have faith in you, Sanos. Please lead us," said Cade.

Sanos touched his forehead to Cade's. "Always, my friend. Always. I will find a way. Dr. Blum will meet his demise should he refuse us. We will feed on every human and take back our pride. In the name of Drac legend, I swear it."

Sanos felt Cade's shoulders ease.

"You and the others rest now. I will meet with Telas." Sanos released Cade, standing eye to eye. "And Dr. Blum."

* * *

The pit, a large and massive round opening, dropped down into the earth with no end in sight. The pit provided easy access to the camp from the multitude of underground cities across the United States. This pit in particular held no city beneath, used as an access portal over the last century for Dracs and greys to enter and oversee scientific experiments happening in the region without being seen by the citizens who lived in the area; an effort to cease unwanted attention drawn to the camp.

Telas moved swiftly to the pit guiding Dr. Blum's gurney as hurriedly as possible. She'd felt Mono's presence in her movements, bringing attention to the sinful deed she committed against Dr. Blum but drawing with it a sense that she was safe with Mono, despite Mono's resilience and abandonment of her hunger.

*I was too weak to reach her*, Telas convinced herself driving forward with the pit now in sight. She dismissed Mono's telepathy, blocking off her thoughts to outside interference. Mono has that ability to come in through the back door of the mind, slithering into thoughts like smoke filtering into vents, and Telas hoped she did not see the larger plan ahead.

*The baby.* Mono's worked for so long on the genetics experiment, and the baby was a prize discovery. He will need a mother, and Telas was the obvious choice over Sandy. Mono would never compromise the larger plan.

She came close to the pit, moving faster as she approached, her pace turning into a run pushing the gurney off the edge. She dropped to her knees, watching Dr. Blum's decent into the pit, feeling the heat from beneath rush across her face with a fierce wind. As she watched the gurney and body disappear below, she thought of Sandy and the baby.

Sandy appeared in her mind as if she were in the room with her. *Help us!* Telas heard Sandy's plea. Sensed the fear in Sandy's heart. Telas couldn't deny the sensation that tore through her veins. A connection like she'd never experienced, to protect Sandy and the baby, was all too overwhelming although instinctive.

*I must protect my feelings. For their sake!*

The ground beneath her began to rumble. The walls trembled. Telas looked everywhere. She'd felt this rumbling several times before, and it meant only one thing.

"They're coming?" she said pushing away from the edge to her feet. The rumbling ceased. Her expression turned to concern. Again, the shaking rumble.

*How? Why?*

The rumble died.

*Because I called them.*

Mono's voice stabbed in her mind and Telas turned, seeing Mono behind her. The question sprang from her lips, "Why?" But Telas already knew what this meant, that Mono was aware of Dr. Blum's demise.

*I did what was necessary,* Mono said telepathically. *This baby has brought weakness to you. A pathetic feebleness. Look at you, covering for your murder of Dr. Blum. Should COR find this information to be true, the baby will come under Sanos and that cannot happen. I've covered your actions, Telas. An American soldier will be blamed for Blum's death and Sanos will be tried for his lack of leadership. He had one simple order, to keep the doctor safe, now all has been compromised. His lack of leadership will come into question and he will lose all.*

The rumbling began again. Telas looked down into the pit, an attempt to avoid Mono's gaze into her mind. She couldn't help leaving herself open, these feelings and sensations were all new and difficult to comprehend. *Sandy!* Her eyes widened. Her body constricted.

"No longer required," Mono responded. "None here are required any longer. They come to eradicate this camp. There is no reason to leave any part of it. Loose ends do not bode well with COR, nor our human counterparts."

Telas shook her head, thinking of Sandy and what will be done to her and all in camp. Not that she cared much for the multitudes of human subjects above ground nor those imprisoned across multiple levels in the underground complex. However, with the pending arrival of COR all would be lost. Protocol was always to destroy any possible threat and save human survivors for feeding. Sandy would come under the control of Drac feeding, until her body was depleted, her veins abscessed until imminent death. The thought sank her heart.

"I find your reaction disturbing, Telas."

Telas turned to Mono who crept closer, her eyes wide, bulging.

Mono bent her head, staring as if she were seeing through Telas. Speaking telepathically, *I've protected you and the baby but my resolve in this situation will only go so far. The baby is my product. If necessary, I will eradicate your involvement. There is always another way. I need to know… will you adhere or no?*

Telas felt pressure in her skull. Mono's use of telepathy hindered her thoughts, crushing down on her brain. The pain like a knife twisted between her temples. Mono moved closer as Telas dropped to her knees, holding her temples in both hands.

*Yes or NO?!*

Mono was on top of her, igniting a thunderous wave of pain vibrating through Telas's body. Everything rattled around her, molding into the rumble of coming starships. Telas struggled to lift her head, her eyes bleeding, feeling her organs and bones being torn to pieces. She had no power over Mono's relentless ability.

*I will not ask again.*

The pain tore at her brain. Blood streamed from her ears. There was no other choice. "YES!" she screamed locking eyes with Mono. She was on the brink of death; any more pressure and her body would be torn. Blood ran from her nose across her lips and Mono's expression weakened. The rattling waves ceased, although the approaching rumble beneath the earth remained. Telas fell forward, catching herself with her hand as she gawked to bring air into her lungs.

"Now you understand true power." Mono moved from the gaping Telas as if warding off any possible physical threat. Telas crouched on the ground with whining cries emanating from her throat. Mono watched with a disgusted glare. "I question your loyalty...There is only one way to prove your allegiance. To us and to baby."

"Anything," Telas squealed, gathering breath into her lungs. She felt depleted, wounded and raw. "Anything you ask."

Mono smiled a conniving victorious grin. *Kill Sandy,* she said telepathically. *Before they arrive.*

Telas managed to force her head up, witnessing the rattling rumble of walls and ground. Her ears stung something awful disturbing senses and intuition. She looked on Mono defeated and unnerved.

*That is the only way to prove yourself. If it is not done before their arrival both you and Sandy will meet the same fate by my hand.*

Mono moved toward the corridor back to camp.

*You have thirty minutes. Be sure it is done.* She moved quickly as if skipping across wind. As Mono disappeared Telas clutched her stomach and head. Breathing hoarsely trying to catch her breath within gasping lungs that concealed squealing whines. Her thoughts were trapped within the mangling vibration Mono forced on her. *What did I agree to?* She wiped the blood from beneath her eyes as the rumbling ceased leaving a still quiet that allowed her thoughts to rattle in her skull. She thought of Sandy and baby, seeing them as clear as if they were in the room with her.

*Baby's heart calls.*

She thought of a thousand scenarios, and a billion reasons to take Sandy's life. Saw through baby's heart to Sandy's eyes, calling for her to come to them as Telas gathered herself to her feet. Another rumble shook the room and her head snapped to the pit that now seemed to breathe a horrid life of its own, calling like an impending doom for what she was about to do.

*Ordered to do.* She closed her eyes sensing the rumbling in her bones. *They will be arriving soon. And all will go to pieces.*

"I'm sorry Sandy," she whispered. *Sorry for what has happened and what is about to come.*

* * *

Phil braced himself on a ledge that rose high above the pit, crouching against the wall behind him. He'd come upon Telas wheeling Dr. Blum and followed, scaling up to the ledge when she entered the pit, a mounting ramp led to the ledge where he was able to observe Telas, using the rose to manipulate the air and carry her thoughts to him.

Just like Robyn had instructed.

And then the rumbling and Mono. He'd never witnessed such power. Mono made Dracs seem like a feeble child. He started piecing together Robyn's declarations and fears. Alien vampires were the nemesis, but there was something in the shadows even more sinister than he could imagine. He was sure Mono was it. He watched as Telas left the pit.

*Stay in the shadows until absolutely necessary. You have the element of surprise as an ally. Telas will lead the way to Sandy.* He thought of Cam and the children in the dark, now with the knowledge that more aliens were coming. Coming to destroy everything in the camp, kill every soldier and take off as if this place never existed.

*But why? Why do they still hide?*

Hearing Robyn's instruction. *When threatened with a common enemy, those who fought for so long will naturally fight together. They are so close to accomplishing what's taken centuries to plan, why stumble when you're so close to home? Why rock the boat when everything as it is has gone according to plan.*

He stood, watching Telas and proceeded with caution, following high above, coming out of the pit to the open corridor. He was amazed how big the underground was and wondered how long this particular underground complex had taken to build and how long ago it was created. It was like a small building or hospital beneath the earth. Phil had his share of underground alien cities and research compounds, but this particular compound was never identified nor was it on Robyn's map of the underground. He wondered why. Telas disappeared down a dark hall, and Phil followed far behind.

*Trust your instincts.* He felt fear rise in his heart. *So close. She'll lead me to Sandy.* His next task was to get Sandy out as quickly as possible. *One thing at a time...can't do anything until I've got her.*

Telas rounded a corner moving up a ramp towards the second floor. Phil picked up his pace, not wanting to let her out of his sight as a raging sound of clambering, hollers and banging rose from the hall Telas had entered.

*What is that?*

The sound rumbled in the hall growing louder as he approached. *Don't lose her.* He proceeded, rounding the corner where she had gone. A long hall lined with doors, the sounds coming from the rooms made by the prisoners locked within. Telas was far ahead now turning the corner out of the hall. Phil ran towards her, the slap of his feet covered by prisoner pleas. As he passed, he glanced through the doors' open windows. Human men locked away were alerted by Telas's movement.

"Let us out! Let us go! Help me! Get me outta here!"

The sound of fear escalated as he raced down the hall.

*"An American!"* one of them yelled, the revelation erupted into a hoard of screams and pleas and Phil's heart jumped. *Go!* He raced to the end of the hall then stopped, leaning against the wall as their voices and screams rose into a frantic frenzy.

"What kind of American are you? How can you leave us here, don't you know what they're doing? *PLLLLEEEEEEASSSSSEE!"*

Phil closed his eyes. Stay focused he told himself peering around the corner where Telas had turned. She was gone. Phil winced as the slamming on doors and walls turned thunderous. Phil shook his head, knowing there was not much he could do. He was losing Telas and releasing them would alert everyone to his presence.

*Sandy. Your mission is Sandy. Don't compromise the larger picture for a brief moment in time. Go Phil. Just GO!* He took the corner racing down the hall, putting distance between himself and their screams. His thoughts locked in on Telas.

\* \* \*

Orion was headed to the pit after hearing the oncoming starship-rumbling echo in the walls when he became alerted to a new thunderous sound. Heard screams emitting from the second-floor cellblock with pleas that called to an American. He could feel Telas too. The scent of her blood and skin lingered down the corridor where the shrieking came from.

*Obviously, they are not referring to Telas.* No one could mistake a Drac for a human. She's being followed, and the same coward who sliced up Titus is following. Orion had gone to Dr. Blum's laboratory to consult Telas with the information he'd gathered on Titus. The lab was barren, but the stink of death remained, and he followed the scent to the pit. He knew where the path before him led. Knew Telas was on her way to the medical ward where humans were brought for genetic experimentation. *Sanos must have released her.* Every once in a while, he did show a sliver of mercy for his team.

Orion considered an alternate path to the medical ward. No need to bring the humans back into a fury. No need to create unwanted attention. He wanted to bring Titus's executioner to justice, wanted to slice his head off as he did to Titus. Orion's anger swelled with the thought of destroying the gutless human. *Make him pay.* He searched for an alternate route to the ward, his thoughts running through a multitude of possibilities before securing his approach.

*Through the main corridor. I need to be quick. Very quick indeed.*

Orion dropped the cloak off his shoulders and gripped the handles in his palms. *And ready for combat!* He pressed down on both handles releasing the blades across his forearms, secured by the latch above the elbow on his black armor. He tightened his arms before racing into the main corridor.

# 13

CAM STRETCHED HIS WRISTS HOPING TO LOOSEN the zip ties with enough give to slip his hands through. Then the earth rumbled beneath his feet.

*The bomb?!* His heart jumped. *No chance, I set it right and if they did find it why set it off unless they tried to disarm it.* But the silence that followed solidified it wasn't the bomb. The rumble came again, and his feet trembled. He looked at Grimes, leaning against the wall by the doors, his eyes focused on the floor.

"You feel that?" said Cam but Grimes had no reply. "Somethin's coming."

He could see that Grimes was considering a multitude of possibilities, his eyes searching the room. The rumble was subtle, emitting from far down beneath the earth.

"Probably helicopters," Grimes said.

"Helicopters don't shake the ground from underneath." Cam's hurried tone revealed urgency.

"It's the area we're in. They're so far off the noise reflects in the ground."

"Sure, keep telling yourself that." He shook his head, frustrated. "Why would helicopters be headed here? Can't you see there's more going than we know?"

Grimes shook his head. "Stop, Cameron. Just stop. The Russians contacted their superiors and were told they were sending support. It's just helicopters or planes."

"Why would they do that?"

Grimes huffed as the shaking came again. "There's no communication from Dr. Blum, and that is their protocol."

"Why not go down themselves? Go down and see what I'm talking about."

Grimes shook his head and laughed. "What you're reporting is ludicrous. No one's buying your little farce. Look at you, blood all over you. You killed Blum yourself."

"Killed Blum..." He turned his eyes away. "That's right.... They're going to come in here and kill all of us. We need to get outta here and get outta here fast." He started yanking his wrists, jumping in the seat.

"Stand down!" Grimes ordered, pointing the AR15 at Cam. "Don't friggin' move in that seat."

"Go ahead and shoot," Cam hollered. "We're all dead anyway. Whatever sound that is can't be good." The rumbling grew louder and the expression on Grimes' face turned from certainty to fear. "Look at you, it's in your eyes that you believe me. Corporal, let me out, give me a fighting chance."

"And face a court martial...not happening."

Cam rolled his eyes. "Friggin' alien vampires, and he's worried about his career."

"Stop saying that. There's no such thing."

"Really? Like you know everything that exists in the universe?" He shrugged shaking his head. "Who the hell makes that up? This isn't some sick sci-fi novel," he hollered when Grimes sent the butt of his gun into Cam's temple. His vision blurred catching himself before falling out. His head throbbed with a sting thumping his skull.

"Now...shut...UP!"

The pain rang in his ears turning his stomach. He threw up over the floor, hunched over as far as the zip ties would allow, gagging and coughing. His eyes wet and sweat beaded his forehead. Cam spit a final wad of vomit.

"You done?" Grimes held his gun aiming at Cam's head as the ground trembled, igniting silence between them.

Cam leaned back attempting to regain his thoughts, his weary eyes catching a glimpse of the outside, where the children were. He jumped when he saw the face in the window, looking in on them, looking at them. The child, no more than ten, gawked with sunken green eyes, his mouth agape revealing a row of sharp teeth. Cam's jaw dropped.

"Think I'm lying, Corporal? Take a look in the window?" But Grimes didn't move. Not at first. The boy slammed on the window with both hands. The rattling glass caught Grimes' attention. His face dropped, stepping back, the AR15 now aimed at the boy.

"Don't shoot," Cam yelled. The child outside the window hissed, his expression one of pain and hunger and confusion. "He's just a kid!" Cam looked at Grimes as the pane of glass started to buckle.

"What do we do?" Grimes said, his hands shaking with uncertainty.

"How the hell would I know?"

The boy slammed on the glass. Grimes shot a quick nervous look at Cam. "There's more of them out there?" His voice jumped. "How many?"

Cam hesitated, in awe with what was happening. "S..seven," he said.

The boy stopped slamming and put his head to the window.

"How can he see in here, the windows are completely blacked out?"

Cam thought as the boy surveyed the window, studying the pane of glass as if assessing a way in. *The blood. My blood...all over me. He can smell it.*

"Not kids," Grimes whispered tightening his grip. "Not kids please." The boy glared at Cam with wide eyes.

"He can smell the blood on me. This is *not* good," Cam hollered. "I told you to listen to me…. For God's sake don't just stand there." He looked at Grimes who stood unmoving.

"That glass is two inches thick. There's no way he's coming through it." The boy stepped back. His mouth opened and closed as if he was getting used to the row of sharpened teeth, moving his head in a circle stretching his neck. "This is insane!"

"No shit," Cam said. They both stared, awestruck.

"That's what a vampire looks like?" Grimes said. "Looks more human than what I would have thought."

"That's the strangest part."

"What?"

"The vampire who attacked me looked different. Much different. And that kid was a prisoner when he first arrived. He was brought into the tunnels immediately. Do you remember?"

Grimes shook his head. "I don't."

Cam eyed Grimes. *Some Corporal.* "All of them in the fence were."

"Then how the hell are they vampires now?" Grimes' voice rose with a nervous tone.

The boy crouched beneath the window and started looking over the fence, his eyes searching. "How should I know? How are humans turned into vampires? I've never read a vampire book." The boy's neck stretched, eyeing the fence's height.

"He's gonna go for the fence," Grimes said. "He won't last more than a second once he's discovered."

"Better them than us."

Grimes shot Cam a skeptical stare, which Cam returned. "What do you know about them? How did you kill the one who attacked you?"

"I didn't," Cam blurted. Again another look from Grimes. Cam shook his head. "That's another story we don't have time for. But it was done quickly. I think their bodies are like ours. They die as easily as we do."

"So we can detain him?" asked Grimes.

Cam paused, thinking.

Grimes snarled, looked back at the boy. "I'm not killing kids if I can help it. No way. I've seen too many kids killed in this war already."

"It's worth a try but there's one thing we need to do first."

"What?"

"It'll help if you get this damn zip tie off." Grimes looked at him, and Cam cocked his head. "Just sayin." Grimes dropped his gun to his side, took a wire cutter from his side belt and clipped the zip tie.

Cam stood rubbing his wrists. "Shit," he said.

"What is it?" Grimes said securing the cutter to his belt.

The boy was headed to the fence. "He's gonna climb over."

"Shit is right." Grimes watched as the boy stood by the fence, staring up. "What do we do now?"

Cam paused. "Use your silencer and shoot the glass."

"What?" Grimes shook his head. "Why would we do that?"

"He's gonna climb that fence, and then they're all dead. Shoot the glass. The blood on me will bring him in here."

"Isn't that what we don't want?"

"They'll kill him and the others once he makes it over the fence. In here together we can detain him."

"And then?"

"Haven't thought that far."

"What if we can't?"

"We can, I know it." The boy grabbed the fence, ready to make the climb. "Shoot the damn glass now!"

Grimes pulled his side arm and silencer, connecting them with a quick and firm spin then shot the glass. The boy's head jolted to the broken window and he stopped scaling the fence dropping to the floor, staring.

"What's he doing? Why isn't he coming?" pleaded Grimes.

The boy stood stationary, surveying the open window then broke into a run towards them.

"Careful what you wish for."

"Wasn't this the plan?" Grimes said. The boy's pace quickened. Cam shrugged. "What?" Grimes stiffened. "Sit down," he ordered.

"Why?"

"Fresh bait." Grimes went to the window next to the open pane and crouched down. "Sit down," he ordered. "I'll grab him once he's in."

Cam shook his head taking the seat. "You friggin' better." The boy's approach was fast. Cam jumped when the boy mounted the pane, his eyes fixed on Cam with a confused stare. He dropped into the room with heavy breath. Cam noticed the change in his eyes, from confused to sinister, as the boy stepped towards him.

"Now's a good time, Corporal," Cam said, his body cringing as the boy approached. Grimes came up swiftly, grabbing the boy's wrists and kicking his feet for him to fall. The boy wriggled attempting to get free, growling and hissing beneath the force of Grimes' body weight. He zip-tied the boy's wrists.

"Calm down, boy. Calm down," Grimes said through a high-pitched saddened tone. "Help him up." They hoisted the wriggling hissing boy up sitting him down on the seat, and Grimes zip tied his ankles, maintaining eye contact, amazed how the boy's pupils changed, one iris green and elongated, the other dark and round. "What now," Grimes whispered.

Cam breathed staring at the boy whose whining and hissing morphed into a desperate low cry as he looked over the room with a fearful stare. Cam cocked his head, kneeling in front of the child who locked eyes with him. His innocent face reflected confusion and pain, mouth opening and closing.

Cam bent his head, staring at the boy. "I think he's hungry." The boy immediately nodded. Cam nodded too. "Yes," he said. "You're hungry?" The boy nodded feverishly.

"What now, Cam?"

Cam paused, thinking. A painful strain slithered across the boy's face. Cam cocked his eyebrows. "Well," he replied. "Let's get him some food."

\* \* \*

Lao, an Admiral in the Chinese army, looked over the building where the two American soldiers waited for further instructions. He sensed there was something more happening in that building. So much more happening everywhere in this camp. He studied the camp and all seemed fine except that nagging instinct that something was wrong, perhaps yet to come, kept squirming into his thoughts.

*That soldier they caught inside the wall. And those kids? What is the story with those kids? Why weren't we informed they were there?* That part of camp was kept in darkness with strict orders not to enter at any time. There was so much during the war he wanted to question, and current circumstances brought that same nagging inquiry, *What is really going on?*

The war had ended abruptly. After a decade of fighting the treaty was signed and delivered on a moment's notice. He received the order mid-battle to stand down. And all the fighting stopped. Literally stopped as if the bullets they'd fired dropped to the ground all at once. Within a few days he was on a plane headed to this camp with strict, cryptic orders. Perhaps everyone else felt it too, that nagging desperate feeling as if they were toy soldiers being played by the whim of a madman.

*And the American soldiers? Something's not right.* He would swear he heard an explosion, like glass blown out. He stopped outside the building doors and paused. Turned to see the camp and soldiers who tore into the ground, the noise deafening with bulldozers and excavators moving back and forth and dump trucks pulling away earth.

*Why the order to build a moat around the camp? Are they expecting an attack?* There were too many questions and too many unknowns.

## 14

**SANOS, STANDING IN DR. BLUM'S BARREN LAB,** knew what that rumble was. COR was coming but why? Who brought them here?

"This place stinks of death," he shouted looking over the room, his mouth watering with the faint smell of blood in his nostrils. The thought of new blood gripped him, constricting his movement as if it called to him.

(*There's always another way*)

"That blood is evil," he whispered but still the thought wouldn't let go as he locked eyes on Dr. Blum's computer with a thought he understood to be devious. *The formula is on the computer.*

His heart was jumping, his breathing shallow as he sat down by the computer. He looked over the room aware that COR was on their way. Knowing that the formula meant everything to them.

And I can have it for myself, he thought, now fixated, glaring at the computer screen.

(*All to ourselves. The formula is there, on that computer.*)

His eyes jolted over the names of each folder, each containing a date. *Most recent.* He found it and clicked the mouse to open the folder. He searched the room again with a paranoid gaze. All alone, no one was coming. He read the prompt on the monitor.

**Voice activation file secured. Dr. Blum, Speak Into the Microphone for Verification.**

Sanos slammed his fists on the desk. His hands trembling, fists clenched turning pale. He thought of racing above ground and feeding on every new blood human, running his tongue inside his cheek, across his teeth. His eyes glinted with rage glaring at the work area where the pills were manufactured. He jumped up, went to the machine, finding ten pills in a dish. He stared at the tiny blue pills, considering all possibilities.

*What would be the effect? These pills may be the last.*

*(Take them and see.)*

His heart raced as he took the pills in his hand, his throat closing thinking about taking them, staring at the tiny round blue concoctions in the middle of his sweaty palm.

(The blood makes us stronger. The pills will make us Gods.)

He looked over the room. Beads of sweat glistened above his lips. His knees started to shake.

*(And then they will have to listen. Listen or meet their demise.)*

Pathetic. This is pathetic. His hand trembling.

(Not pathetic. Necessary!)

"Dr. Blum, you're a true monster!" he whispered and swallowed one pill.

* * *

Mono raced to the genetics laboratory, thinking, pondering the many tasks she must complete before COR's arrival. Her concern was over the formula for new blood, the pills chemistry. If the files on Blum's computer were voice activated the formula would be lost with the exception of the humans who had taken the pills. *I can reverse engineer the formula if necessary or hack the secure file. There are ways around voice activation.* Mono knew how paranoid the doctor was about his work. High probability there were numerous firewalls in place to protect his files.

*Smart that human was.*

Blum's work was the reason he'd been given such protection, of course he would secure his files, to keep himself alive and necessary. The information on the formula would be the first required by COR once they arrive, and she would need to have this answer. It was imperative to how they would handle the humans above ground. As she propelled towards the lab she smiled thinking of how the soldiers were digging their own graves, trapping themselves in the camp with no possible escape. All we will need to do is drop their bodies into the ground and cover them up. At least those who aren't incinerated.

It will be a true show of power. *A necessary massacre!* She arrived at her destination, the genetics lab where she'd ordered the lab working greys, Mintaka, Alnitak and Alnilam, prior to Dr. Blum's death. The three witches attended to two human children grown deformed by experimentation. One child was about fifteen years old, his head swelled like a balloon, his brain showing through his skull. The EKG machine by his side bleeped intermittently as one of the greys mopped the sweat on his forehead with a thick washcloth. His eyes were closed and his mouth open. A second child, about nine years old, hissed and squealed pulling his restraints. A row of long sharp fangs hung from his mouth and as he bit down, they tore into his chin drawing blood that streamed down his neck.

"Mono," said one of the greys, her voice carried the same soft echo as Mono, inherent in the grey species. The other greys also turned to greet Mono. "This one is dying. It will not be long now, any minute."

Mono observed the teenager, his breathing close to non-existent.

"We will have to put this one down," said Mintaka regarding the nine-year-old. "Necessary death," she continued, "It's a shame not to." She looked on the child with an intent stare and his hissing and jumping calmed, his head drifting side to side, his mouth open emitting a low and soft painful moan.

Mono closed her eyes and bowed authorizing the extermination before addressing additional concerns. "I have contacted COR," she told them, and the three witches looked on her in unison. "Dr. Blum has perished, we will need to continue his work. Sanos's detainment is required. His lack of leadership has become a detriment. I have taken command of Telas but there is the possibility of the seven creating a disturbance. We are required to restrain any possible threat in such an occurrence. Should they not adhere to our demands, necessary actions must be taken." Mono gazed over her assistants with pride. "This is protocol, be swift and act as required."

"When is COR's arrival expected?" Alnitak and Alnilam asked.

"We deduced such an arrival when the ground began to shake," Mintaka added.

"They bring reinforcements for those above ground," said Mono. "Their arrival is soon, within a half hour's time. We must be swift in our deeds. Follow in."

Mintaka approached Mono as Alnitak injected a substance into the boy's IV, placing her palm to his forehead.

Mintaka inquired, "Mono, what of the children in the quarry? They have been our most successful trials. Should we retrieve them?"

Mono gazed at Mintaka. "COR will provide the answer," Mono replied. "Should their fate be to perish we have our documented exploration. Our work will continue, we are all aware of the necessity," she continued and raised her head to address the three witches, "For the Future!" She closed her eyes, dipping her chin to her chest.

"For the Future," repeated the witches, performing the same bow.

* * *

Sanos shook violently. He dropped to his knees. He felt change coming, unknown change that tore fear through his eyes. Every part of his body burned as if a fire were ignited in his blood, scorching his insides from his stomach and racing to his toes and scalp, kindling a scream that shook the room. The bones in his face swelled, his forehead bulged from his skull like large blistering bubbles then fell back again, deflated. His fingers tensed and curled, crackling and popping and stretching. His teeth swelled, tearing his gums with blood that pooled in his mouth. Sharp teeth morphed into long sharp fangs. He felt as if he was about to explode, gurgling on blood with a fear of death. His spine twisted and wrenched with a vibration that stretched from the base of his spine to his brain. His hands dropped to the floor as a squeal erupted in his throat spilling the blood that gurgled in his mouth. His eyes, wet with tears and blood, stretched in their sockets, protruding from the bone and burning, burning with heat as if from the sun.

Quadriceps contracted then swelled, his stomach twisted, base of his spine contracted, lifting his upper body in a painful jolt as a scream erupted from his throat. He dropped on his back, his legs beneath him, body folded. His pelvis thrashed, one, two, three times...*four*. Hip bones swelled, leg muscles popped. Eyes rolled behind his eyelids, stiff and wet, head shaking in short violent thrusts. Sanos turned his body, slow, slow, oh so slowly, so much pain, allowing his legs to stretch, a low labored whine seething over his lips. He felt his insides turn hollow, his blood thickened like liquid cement moving slow and painful in his veins to the heart that swelled in his chest with a sensation of continuous anguish.

And then, all the pain stopped. Calm and quiet greeted his eardrums.

He lay still, the screams and writhing done, hearing his breath, slow and calm. Sensing his heart, once pounding and straining, settle in his chest. His eyes, now pinned pupils inside bulging yellowish eyeballs, looked over the room with wide-eyed wonder.

"Amazing," he whispered sitting up. "I feel absolutely...unstoppable." He jumped to a crouch, a transformed and deformed Sanos, still recognizable yet so much more. Taller. Stronger. Nastier. The room seemed smaller through his new eyes and he could see vibrations moving inside the open air, as if witnessing the fluttering of atoms racing around him. He touched his tongue to his transformed fangs and smiled, stretching his back standing up, looking over the room, looking everywhere. He observed his hands. Fingers so long with nails so sharp.

He started to laugh. "Oh, Dr. Blum," he said, a glint in his eyes. "You are a genius."

# 15

SANDY WAS ABLE TO LOCK IN ON TELAS; she knew she was on her way to Sandy and the baby. Sandy noticed how the sensation grew stronger now that she had the baby in her arms. She'd followed her instincts to find the child, having gone from her bed into the corridors, sensing the baby call her to him, all the while holding a psychic connection to Telas. Sandy had also felt the pain and scorching organs that had gripped Telas under Mono's infliction when Sandy was walking through the halls. She had to hold the wall to keep from falling. She'd wanted to rest more than a few times. Nonetheless, she garnered the strength to continue.

"Momma's coming," she said in a soft loving tone, cradling the baby in her arms against the black Kevlar t-shirt she'd found in a drawer beside the bassinet. Sandy's dark cargo pants were in that drawer too, clean and folded, as if someone had anticipated her arrival. She felt at ease holding the baby and thinking of Telas. Ben had become a distant memory, faded far into the subconscious. She had tried to think of him but couldn't find the face or the emotion she held towards Ben for so long, since before the war. They'd suffered through the worst of all parental tragedy, losing Ben's son, Ares, when they did what most parents thought was the most appropriate decision. A decision that back fired and blew up in their face. She never expected to lose sight of Ben, not in all her life. But here she was, holding her baby, their baby, without even an inkling of thought to the baby's father. All she thought about was Telas. "That's right." She smiled at the baby touching her nose to his. "Here she comes."

The door opened as Sandy placed the baby in a bassinet. Telas was behind her. Sandy could feel her breath on the nape of her neck. "Isn't he beautiful, Telas?" Sandy said. "He's gonna do great things." Sandy caressed the baby's forehead. Telas gripped Sandy's shoulders. A nervous vibration ran through Sandy. Her hand froze.

"Do you still need to feed?" She felt Telas swallow as if holding back sadness filled with regret. The sensation constricted Sandy's stomach and breath. Wide eyes captured an overflow of fear. Not Sandy's fear. Telas's fear of dying and pain. She locked in on the baby, seeing beyond the child to a place under the trees by the ocean. "You're not going to do it, Telas," she said. "You're not going to kill me. You can't. It's not who you are."

She took Telas's hand from her shoulder and turned meeting her eye to eye, observing the defeated look of dread captivated in her eyes. Her skin stained with blood across ashen pale scaly skin. Sensed the nervous vibration coursing through her body. "Fight it," Sandy told her. She could see nothing more than a grim dark cloud in those eyes. Sandy tried to fight through it to capture a ray of hope. The baby started to wail, beginning as a low gruff whine that manifested to a screeching holler bringing tears to Sandy's eyes.

"Fight!" Sandy said through tears. *"Please!"*

Telas pursed her quivering lips looking down at her trembling hands. Sandy took Telas's hands in hers. She felt pain like an undeniable moment of death wrought with grief and finality. A black hole pulling her into its vortex of gravity, tearing at every part of her body and shredding her skin in a wallop of torment as a rumbling, a fierce whirlwind, spiraled her back to Telas's sunken eyes and the baby's ear-piercing cries.

"I can't," Telas said and tore into Sandy's neck.

* * *

Phil lost Telas in the dark corridors. The halls were like a maze that brought too many possibilities. He closed his eyes, thinking. Feeling his way to Sandy.

"Where are you?" he whispered, leaning against the wall as the lights flickered down the hall with a faint yellow glow. "Feel," he told himself. His heart was pounding in his throat. His thoughts filled with static that mounted his frustration. He swallowed his breath attempting to clear the static from his thoughts.

*Look into your heart.* Robyn's instruction. *There you will find the answers.*

He inhaled in through his nose pulling his navel inward, dropping the exhale over his lips. His heart calmed as the static cleared, and he felt Sandy's presence inside a wail of pain. "She's in trouble." His eyes twitched seeing Sandy under duress, although the path to her became clear. Phil opened his eyes. "Go right." He took off down the hall, following the trail to Sandy. *Left!* He could see clearly where to go as if riding a path to her.

*Close! Getting Closer.*

He heard Sandy's pounding heart growing stronger between his ears. *Just one more corner.* He took the corner as if he'd been shot from a cannon when his heart jumped, his feet slid to a stop. Not far down the hall stood Orion, blocking the hallway where Phil needed to go. The vampire's eyes glared at Phil, standing erect, arms by his side and Phil could see he wore the blades. Orion's face stiff. Phil took a few steps closer.

"This is the end for you," said Orion. He shook his head and stretched his finger in Phil's direction. "You will be no more."

Phil looked to the floor, cocked his head. *Times wasting away.* He shook his head. "No matter what," he said raising his eyes to meet Orion. "I'm getting down that hall."

Orion smiled. "Never." He stretched his arms, taking a fighting stance. "After I sever your head like you did to Titus, I'll reach into your corpse and pull out your heart to feed on."

Phil stepped closer, stretching his arms. "Damn vampires," he said. "Nothing more than devolved cockroaches, scattering in fear at the first sign of the light."

Orion threw his boot into Phil's chest. Phil reeled back, slammed on his back and slid across the floor. Orion dropped his arms. "Humans," he snarled. "So pathetic and weak. Nothing more than food..." he glared at Phil who pushed himself to his feet. "...for us cockroaches."

Phil spit a wad of blood to the floor. He gripped the handles in his palms and tightened his arms as he rushed at Orion who met Phil's blade with his own. As they fought, crossing blade to blade, Phil could hear Sandy's screams.

# 16

**WHEN MONO ARRIVED AT SANOS'S CHAMBERS** she and the witches were met by the remaining five, depleted yet standing proud in waiting for Sanos's return. Cade addressed Mono in a weakened tone.

"He's gone to speak with Dr. Blum. We await his return."

Mono shot back, "Dr. Blum is dead as a result of his incompetence."

Cade glared at Mono, his eyes narrowed. "How dare you speak of him…"

"I speak truth." Her tone was strong, a menacing echo and she looked over the Dracs, standing at attention. "Where are Orion and Titus?"

Cade swallowed, scowling at Mono. "Titus was not accounted for upon our awakening. Orion seeks him out."

"More incompetence. Very well then, we will find them." She looked at Mintaka, telepathically ordering her to find the two missing Dracs. Mintaka bowed leaving abruptly, gliding down the hall. Mono addressed the other vampires. "You will all follow in line with Alnitak and Alnilam. You are being detained until COR arrives. I will seek out Sanos myself."

"Detained?!" Cade said. "Under whose orders?" The other vampires stiffened, staring at Cade.

"Under my orders with approval from COR."

"We follow only Sanos, not you. If COR is coming, we will wait for them. Sanos will provide explanation for this tyranny."

Mono locked eyes with Cade. The wall behind him began to rumble. He clutched his head as his face winced in pain. "Do not dare question me," said Mono. A whimpering whine emitted from Cade's throat. Blood, pooled in his ears, started to drip down his jawline as he fell to his knees with a painful gasp. The rumbling grew louder, stronger, with waves of vibrating thunder.

"You're killing him!" Rygel hollered.

"Stand back," said Alnitak. Rygel looked at her. The stare in her eyes a warning to not suffer the same fate.

Blood ran from Cade's eyes, nose and mouth. He started to scream, his skin splitting, veins torn open. A pool of blood formed beneath him, blood dripping from every part of his body. Cade let out one final scream before his brain exploded, pieces of skull splattered across the wall as his body fell limp to the floor.

Mono breathed deeply. "Necessary deed," she whispered addressing Alnitak and Alnilam. "Secure them," she ordered. "Should any offer trouble, provide the same fate." The ladies bowed. "I go to await COR and attend unfinished business." Mono left the hall.

The vampires were awestruck. Quickly they were forced in line, one behind the other, paralyzed. Alnitak and Alnilam guided the Drac's to confinement.

* * *

Telas drank from Sandy's neck, the blood so sweet and delectable she felt at peace, listening to Sandy's fading heart. The baby's cries, once dulled became prominent, filling the room with a panicked high-pitched squeal. Sandy slammed on Telas's back, attempting to break free, but Telas gripped her closer, listening to the heart fade and sensing Sandy's strength leave her body.

Behind the squeal and faded heartbeat Telas locked in on Mono. The walls and ground started to rumble and shake as she saw Mono's eyes as if she were in the room. An understanding bow from Mono dropped into Telas's mind as Sandy's heart struggled for one more beat. This bow from Mono was what Telas waited for; the bow confirmed that Mono was aware that Sandy had completed her task in time. Telas pulled her jaw from Sandy's neck, holding her in an iron grasp. The walls shook as if an earthquake tore through the underground city, confirming to Telas COR was arriving in a moment's time, and she had achieved the deadline imposed by Mono. Carefully, within the rumbling and baby's wails, she guided Sandy's body to the floor; gently leaning her head back against the wall.

She touched Sandy's face with her fingernails, caressing the pale, bloodless skin and lips. "I'm sorry," she whispered, staring at Sandy, her eyes adoring and compassionate. "Some actions are necessary." Telas bit into her wrist, popping a vein and igniting a river of blood down her arm.

She forced her wrist over Sandy's lips.

* * *

Orion sliced across Phil's arm as the rumbling shook the walls around them. Phil winced but caught Orion's next strike sending his boot into Orion's sternum. His head dropped forward and, as Phil swiped for his neck, Orion caught the blade with his own igniting a fury of blade against blade. Phil caught Orion's hand, twisting his arm and sending his fist into Orion's jaw followed by an uppercut that brought his blade across Orion's chin. He tumbled back to the wall.

Orion touched his hand to his jaw, feeling the wound. Blood dripped off his fingers. He glared at Phil, his eyes referencing the shaking walls. Phil stood erect in a fighting stance, his face bulged and bruised from the many hits from Orion's fist. Blood dripped off his elbow. Orion had thought this fight would be quick, looking at the human who brought a fight he largely underestimated.

"My people arrive now," he said and stepped forward. "Time for this dance to end." He bowed then raced at Phil, blade against blade, swiping Phil's feet from under him. Phil dropped on his back to the floor. Orion slammed his boot into Phil's face, bursting his nose and cracking the back of his head against the cement but Phil popped up quickly catching Orion's blade with his own then sliced through Orion's leg above the knee. Orion hollered as Phil jumped to his feet, swiped his blade across Orion's teeth, severing the upper fangs. A painful hiss escaped Orion's throat, his hands immediately went to his mouth, and he stepped back. Phil tore his right blade up through Orion's body, sternum to chin. Orion's head jumped back then snapped forward. For a brief moment they locked eyes. A surprised gaze gripped Orion's stare. His intestines spilled to the floor and he dropped to his knees, falling forward.

Phil breathed through his mouth, his nose bloodied and swollen and his head scorching in pain. His thoughts shifted from another dead vampire back to his cause. "Now, where is Sandy?"

* * *

The pit quaked from the fast and close approaching disc shaped transports. Mono waited for their arrival with a satisfied stare after having locked in on Sandy's death, hearing the heartbeat cease within Telas's thoughts. A massive disc emerged from the pit, ninety feet in diameter and thirty feet high. Spinning violently the ship hovered above the opening. Mono moved closer. The ship shifted in mid air, mechanical arms dismounted. From the bottom and top two separate discs detached, one after the other, one ship turning into three. The main ship drew in the detached arms. All three ships hovered for a brief moment before landing. Ramps emerged from the two detached ships as their spinning wound down to a stop. Mono approached, gliding over the floor as the third and largest disk emitted a hiss of forced air and an opening emerged with a smooth mechanical hum, dropping a ramp to the ground.

A Drac emerged from the main ship, walking down the ramp. Behind him was another Drac, following close behind. Mono welcomed them both.

"Zeta," Mono said, addressing the Drac. "I am grateful for your presence." She bowed.

Zeta stood over six feet six inches tall. Although his frame was thick his slender shoulders were revealed beneath the red shawl wrapped around him. He didn't waste time with introductions. "COR is grateful for your service, Mono. They grow disturbed with the happenings here." He surveyed the room looking beyond Mono whose form dwarfed beneath Zeta. "Where is Sanos?"

"He hides within the corridors. We seek to locate him now including two under his command, Orion and Titus. Telas has accommodated all inquiries. She tends to our prize experiment, the human baby who holds Drac DNA. The others have been escorted under duress to seclusion. They wait your orders. Cade refused the inquiry. He was dealt with appropriately."

Zeta stiffened raising his chin. "And Dr. Blum?" He turned back to Mono. "What met his demise?"

"A soldier from the American Army. He had escorted human subjects to the lab, killing Dr. Blum prior to his departure.'

Zeta shook his head. "We will deal with those above ground quickly." He addressed the ships, waved his finger across his forehead as a 'go ahead, you have permission,' gesture. Perhaps this was discussed prior to arrival, Mono thought. The two smaller ships started to spin.

"There are the children," Mono said. "In the perimeter, waiting sunrise. Do you wish..."

"I wish nothing for them," Zeta scowled. "They will meet the same fate. When we leave this camp, nothing will remain of our presence here. Neither above nor below."

Mono bowed again. "As you wish."

"Dr. Blum's research, is it secure?"

"As requested and required, I've secured all files," she lied.

The spinning ships propelled up towards the ceiling where they halted, waiting with a slight hum. The ceiling moved. A large and round door retracted, creating an opening to the outside.

"You're a true dedication to the cause, Mono. COR will recognize your loyalty."

Again Mono bowed. "Grateful to be recognized."

"Provide escort to my Dracs. I wish to speak to them at once."

Mono with Zeta and his right-hand counterpart moved through the room as the ceiling completed its opening. The ships rumbled before ascending through.

"What of Sanos?" Mono inquired. "We feel he may be a threat. As you are aware, Zeta, he has been a rash on Drac pride for a long time. Will you bring him to justice?"

"Sanos will be dealt with accordingly. Should he refuse inquiry he will meet with the most dire consequence." Zeta addressed his right hand. "Saiph will secure him for our journey after we take consult with his remaining soldiers." Saiph, who hovered below Zeta's chin, was a mirror image of Zeta's appearance with the exception of the hieroglyphic tattoos that graced his countenance, drawn from his throat, across his face, surrounding his eyes and erected across his smooth elongated skull. His armor was a dark blood red. "Won't you, Saiph?"

Saiph bowed. "As you wish."

"Very well," Mono said. "I suggest the hunt begin in Dr. Blum's laboratory. Sanos was felt lastly within the lab."

"Take him swiftly, Saiph. I wish to leave this place as soon as possible. The rot of human flesh stains these walls. It turns my stomach."

"Of course, due diligence will allow us to return to COR quickly..." Mono declared, "With all necessary loose ends tried and true to the cause." Mono escorted them out of the pit, all the while a thought raged within. *Zeta, sending their number two to address such an issue is an insult.*

# 17

SANDY'S EYELIDS BLINKED WITH RAPID SUCCESSION as her veins swelled causing her heart to race and her eyes shot open. Her chest jumped, and a deep wallop of breath shot up her nostrils. She stared over the room with wide eyes, seeing past Telas who crouched in front of her.

"Amazing," Sandy whispered, seeing the room in a different light, like purity explained in her vision.

"Here, take my hand," Telas said, aiding Sandy to her feet whose survey of the room brought a refreshed air to the moment.

Her ears twitched. "I can hear bells in the silence." She bent her head, listening. She smiled. "Like wind chimes behind the light."

"You'll find many new observations. Both pure and…dark, like evil eyes glaring behind darkness."

"I don't see that," Sandy explained. "Just light." She paused. "The baby? I don't hear his cries."

"He sleeps. Sound and peaceful."

Sandy went to the bassinet. The baby was safe. She touched his forehead, caressing his skin as the memory of what happened drove into her mind like she was witnessing someone else's memory, disconnected from the emotional state. She saw herself drink from Telas's wrist. "Am I one of you now? A Drac? Isn't that how it works."

Telas grinned shaking her head. "No, that's just fiction."

"Oh," Sandy expressed, disappointed.

"But there are benefits, unfortunately they will subside once your body replaces the blood with your own."

Sandy stared adoringly at Telas. "Unless I drink again?"

Telas returned the stare. "Yes, unless you drink again."

Sandy returned her gaze to the baby. "A name," she whispered. "We must give him a name."

"What do you suggest?"

"Adam," Sandy said. "Seems appropriate. Your thoughts?"

Telas smiled. "Adam it is," she said softly.

"Adam!" Sandy repeated. Telas stiffened. "What fears do you have?"

Telas looked to the floor. "We must bring you and the baby to safety. There is a way out, through the tunnels. My people have arrived, and they will not be kind to find you alive. I will drive them away to hasten your escape."

"But we want to come with you."

Telas paused. "Unfortunate circumstances have arisen. I was ordered to take your life, when it's discovered that I've disobeyed..." she swallowed her breath. "They will not be kind in their treatment." Sandy shot Telas a bewildered stare. "The baby cannot come under Drac rule. He will be made into a monster, and that I cannot have."

"They'll kill you?" Sandy said. Her throat restricted as if saying the words meant Telas's demise was imminent. "Why did you not take my life in exchange for yours?"

"Because of the connection. I can't deny this sensation, it drives every action and thought I have." She stared into Sandy's eyes. "What I do know without a shadow of doubt is that the baby is best with you."

Sandy's eyes welled with tears. "You're leaving us?" she said. "Why don't you come with us? We are better with you."

Telas shook her head. "If they discover we are both gone they will lock in on my whereabouts putting you and the baby at risk. It is best for me to return to them...to stay their hand and help to hasten your escape. No matter what you feel, Sandy. No matter what you hear or see you must continue the cause. Get the baby to safety, raise him as your people require...give him your heart and he will do great things. Perhaps he is the conduit that brings our people to peace."

Sandy looked around the room. "Where do I go?" she asked.

"Before you were brought here you were on journey. What was your destination?"

Sandy thought of Phil and the hotel. "Atlanta," she said.

"Then you continue. The tunnels will bring you close. Atlanta is maybe a day's journey from the outskirts of the tunnel." Sandy nodded. "I must leave now," Telas said. There was a pause between them as Telas stepped to the bassinet.

"We will not see you again, will we?"

Telas caressed the baby's face. "You will not," she said on the brink of tears and she took her necklace off, handing it to Sandy. "Give him this," she said, placing the necklace in Sandy's palm. "When he is ready, please tell him what has happened here." Sandy gave a nod as Telas leaned into the baby, touching her head to his.

"There was a human I travelled with, Phil. He is here in the corridors with us. He will provide protection for safe passage. He seeks me out now. I can sense it."

Telas looked at Sandy. "Should he not arrive soon, you must go. Take the corridor and remain locked in on my thoughts, I will lead you in the right direction. Be sure to cover the baby once you reach the sunlight. We are not aware of the sun's impact on him. Understood?"

Sandy nodded as Telas went to the door, propping it open. Sandy was behind her and Telas turned abruptly touching her head to Sandy's. "In another life," Telas whispered. A moment later she was through the door, closing it behind her. Sandy stood with her hand on the closed door.

"God speed," she said. "God speed." She closed her eyes, clearing her thoughts. "Now," she said. "Let's get you secure...Adam."

* * *

The soldiers gathered above ground all stopped working. The buzz, hum and rumbling had grown louder. Almost deafening.

"Where is it coming from?"

"Be quiet. Listen."

"What is it?"

Lao stepped closer to the fence, assessing, locating where the sound originated. He crouched down, touching the earth. *It's coming from beneath.* He wondered how far the tunnels went. Are they big enough to house planes and helicopters?

Then the sound shifted, no more a rumbling beneath the earth. This new noise seemed like a door opening. The sound was faint but clear, a low mechanical hum that suddenly stopped. Lao stood looking beyond the enclosure.

*What is it?*

Lao snapped to the soldiers standing beside the moat. Looked at all of them, standing idle and confused. Saw the moat, circling around the camp then looked back to his men, witnessing their excitement and fear as a Russian soldier pointed beyond the enclosure, mouthing the words, *"What is that?"* Lao followed the man's hand. Beyond the enclosure a disc shaped vessel hovered in the night sky, framed within the blood red moon, as a second disc lifted from the ground joining the first. Lao's heart dropped.

"Arm yourselves," Lao screamed as the discs raced towards them, shooting light beams into the gathering. The fenced enclosure was the first to be incinerated as concrete shards exploded across the clearing. Lao started shooting but the force was relentless. Gunfire rang into the night sky, some soldiers started running, others shooting as explosions tore the earth. He saw soldiers incinerated by light beams, their bodies exploded into dust upon impact. He started shooting but the inexplicable movement of the discs confounded him. One second they stood still emitting a barrage of light beams and the next they were in another location, as if the discs defied the laws of physics.

An explosion dropped Lao to the ground, covering him in dirt and human dust. *Take cover.* He looked at the fence enclosure where they kept the experimented humans. A second later the enclosure was torn apart by light beams, explosions ripping through the fence, incinerating everything that lay within. Lao studied his surroundings. The ships had done their job, what had been a hoard of soldiers was now thinned to a few, running or shooting.

*Get under cover. Get out of sight.* He was sure the discs would land.

Standard protocol in military operations was to leave no trace of a massacre. Despite the current state of the world, alien spaceships would still cause a worldwide panic, and clean up would be imminent. When the discs firing settled to intermittent bursts of light beams, Lao made his move, towards what remained of the building. The front was crushed with blocks of concrete collapsed over the entrance. He looked for the discs' location finding the duo outside the moat Lao had ordered to be excavated, incinerating soldiers on the run.

*Go now! Now!* He darted to the building, climbing over torn concrete blocks.

# 18

WHEN PHIL ARRIVED AT THE DOOR to Sandy, he paused before turning the handle.

*Something's different.*

He heard Sandy calling him to the door but how? How was she able to lock in on him without any training on telepathy? He'd only begun teaching the rose and she didn't take to it, now she exhibited powers that had taken him years to learn and he still had so much more to discover. He wondered if it was a trick from another Drac, using Sandy to bring him out of the shadows and under their thumb.

*There's no certainty she is behind this door.* He gripped his handles. *Be on guard. Expect the unexpected.* The door propped open, and Sandy was behind it.

"We need to go," she said in a hurried voice and quickly went back into the room. Phil looked down the corridors before entering. "They'll be looking for us. We can escape through the tunnels."

She moved swiftly as Phil surveyed the room bracing himself for any trap that may jump out. When he looked back at Sandy, she was holding a baby, placing the child in a blanket she had tied behind her neck.

His jaw dropped.

"I don't have time to explain," Sandy said. "We've limited time and they'll be searching. We must go now."

Phil pointed to the blanket. "You were only six months pregnant. How...how is that possible?"

"They did it. They birthed the baby. Please, Phil, we don't have any time." She went to the door. "Are you ready?"

He stared at her, unmoving.

"Phil?" she said. "We have to go!" She was in the doorway, studying both directions and then was gone.

"What?" Phil whispered, shaking his head, thinking. *"Sandy?"* A second later, he followed her into the hall.

* * *

Cam, Grimes, and the boy heard the ships ascending from beneath. Cam and Grimes went to the broken window seeing the disc hovering in the night sky.

"I told you," Cam said as Grimes cocked his AR-15. "What're you doing? You don't stand a chance."

Cam turned to the boy, lethargic, his eyes rolling behind tired eyelids. Looked back at the disc, now there were two. "Shit!" He jumped over to the boy and clipped off the zip ties.

"Here they come," Grimes hollered.

"Get down!" Cam screamed running with the boy to the back of the building. "Grimes!" he yelled. The Corporal stepped away from the window as the first blasts of light beams raged through the enclosure, causing explosions that popped one after the other, racing at the window. Grimes took a few steps before jumping to the ground, sliding to the back. The windows exploded and the front of the building crumbled. Cam wrapped his arms over the boy, shielding him from dust and flying debris.

Gunfire, screams and more explosions erupted outside the building. They could see human bodies exploding into dust. "It's a massacre," Grimes hollered over the explosions and screams as the fence enclosure was torn to pieces.

"Jesus Christ!" Grimes shielded himself, his hands and arms covering his head.

And then the explosions stopped.

Cam looked over the broken concrete where he could see the outside and the discs across the moat, incinerating anyone who tried to run. Cam stood up for a better look.

"They'll come back around," Grimes said. "They'll sweep the perimeter for any survivors."

Cam thought and thought. Grimes was right, the aliens will look for survivors, and he was certain orders were given not to leave any human alive. Remaining above ground was futile; there was no place to hide. "We've got to get down," he said.

"Down? Down where? Down there? I'm not going down there with them. I'd rather take my chances up here than be food for a vampire."

Cam thought of Phil. Thought of the bomb. "It's our only chance. It's not us they'll be after, and they won't know we're down there." He went to the boy, crouched in front of him. "Are you ok?"

The boy nodded, coughing from the dust he was covered in.

"What?" Grimes said. "Who are they after?"

"Phil and the pregnant woman Sandy."

"Who the hell is Phil?"

Cam looked at Grimes. "Just trust me. I've been right about everything else. I'm right about this. I've been in those tunnels; I know them like the back of my hand. I'll get us out." He turned around, observing the scene outside seeing more soldiers' incinerations. "If we stay here, we don't stand a chance. We have to try."

He went to the boy, looking him over for any wounds when the concrete shifted, the feverish scuttling across the wreckage was paramount.

"Someone's coming," Grimes said standing abruptly, aiming his AR-15 at the concrete. Cam spun around; the concrete moved; someone or something was coming through. He eyed the 9MM holstered to Grimes's leg, jumped up, grabbed the gun and cocked it.

"Whatever you see," Cam said. "Shoot to kill."

\* \* \*

The remaining five under Sanos were frozen under a light beam that immobilized all possible movement. When Zeta followed Mono into the room their hearts jumped. Zeta crouched in the doorway to enter, Saiph behind him. Zeta held his arms out addressing them.

"The mighty army of Sanos so pleasantly held captive. Your leader missing." He dropped his arms. "*Disgraceful!*" his voice harsh and his menacing stare cut straight through them. Zeta circled around standing in the middle of the room. "I should have you all burned to ash."

"Three dead," Mintaka said, having just arrived, standing in the door. She glided into the room past Saiph who leaned against the wall. "Zeta," she said and bowed. Zeta returned the sentiment.

"Three?"

"Orion is no more, I located him on the third floor. Cut open from navel to throat, as similar a fate as Titus." Mintaka turned to Mono. "I located Titus in the armory, his head decapitated."

Zeta's face constricted. "By what means?"

"The blades," Mintaka answered. "Perhaps Sanos has lost all ability for morality."

"Sanos would never..." Rygel shouted. "He is dedicated to this team; he would not murder one of us."

Mono interjected. "Sanos rages with new blood, there is no telling what depths of madness they've brought him to." She glided to Zeta. "He must be dealt with in the harshest manner."

Zeta bowed, eyes closed. "Saiph will provide the necessary punishment."

"Is he up for challenge?" Mono inquired, eyeing Saiph.

"That's insanity," Rygel said. "We saw Sanos prior to his departure, there was no link or interjection indicating your claim."

Zeta turned to Rygel. "You deduce someone else is cutting up Drac." He laughed. "In what manner do you offer proof of this accusation? Who or what brings the blades other than Drac?"

Rygel paused.

"Answer!" Zeta hollered.

Rygel pursed his lips. "Human," he said, his answer resonating in Zeta, whose stare burned with rage. He approached Rygel.

"There is only one human who has ever learned the art and he is dead."

"Perhaps," Rygel answered. "But that has never been confirmed, only speculated."

"You dare question the authority of the nine? Sanos's rebellious antics turn your blood foul. Robyn Winter is dead as the nine proclaim. What you suggest is equal to blasphemy."

Rygel turned from Zeta's stare. "It's suggested because it is true. Sanos would not take the life of his people. The only deduction is that a human is among us, and this human is schooled in the sacred art."

"This Drac must be dealt with," Mono said. "He speaks blasphemy against COR."

Zeta did not hesitate, he cut Rygel's throat with his blade. Rygel's head flopped forward as blood spilled from his open throat, gurgling with a wallop of air bubbles. The light that had held him released the body, and Rygel dropped to the ground at Zeta's feet. He looked over the other Dracs. "Any more blasphemous proclamations?" No response, but Zeta saw the rage in their eyes. "Good," Zeta continued. "You will all be brought in front of COR to explain yourselves and what's happened here. You will be tried under your Captain Sanos. When one team member faces COR all the others stand in judgment with them." He turned to Mono. "Once the ships return have them boarded inside the detainment units."

"As you wish," Mono replied with a bow.

"Where is Telas?" Zeta asked. "You said she has been detained but she is not here."

"Telas tends to the child. She must not be detained. She will remain under my command until she stands before COR." Mono's proclamation was a direct insult to Zeta's authority. All in the room understood this.

Zeta looked over Mono, his body squirming beneath his cloak. His response quickly registered that Mono was indeed in charge. "Very well, Mono." And he bowed, something the other Dracs had not witnessed before. "Very well."

His submission to Mono's authority was indeed peculiar. The remaining four and Saiph had always believed the greys bowed to Drac. But now Zeta, a member of the elite nine, the highest order of Drac rule, bowed to a grey?

Zeta's jaw slackened, he clenched his fists, staring at his fellow Dracs through narrow eyes. He swallowed. "Bring Dr. Blum's files to me," he said to Mono. "They must be secured."

"Consider it done," Mono replied.

Zeta turned to Mintaka. "Deliver Titus and Orion here." He gestured to the remaining four. "They can prepare the bodies for burial prior to our leave. The sun will rise within a few hours; I wish to be done upon its ascent. I can already sense twilight is imminent."

Mintaka turned to Mono whose bow confirmed Zeta's directive.

Mono said to Zeta, "What of the human soldier who killed Dr. Blum? Do you wish for him to be detained as well?"

Zeta thought. "Is he among us?"

"No, he is above ground."

"Then he is dead. If not from the blasts he will be incinerated once they sweep for survivors. None above ground will remain. The Thorx have strict orders to leave this place in ashes."

"Excellent," Mono said, her eyes gleaming with certainty.

# 19

WHEN LAO SCUTTLED ACROSS THE CONCRETE DEBRIS both Cam and Grimes were about to squeeze their triggers. If he hadn't identified himself, they would have unloaded.

"Admiral Lao," he'd said, wriggling down the concrete. "Admiral Lao!" he repeated in a hurried hush and fearful tone. He'd mounted the concrete and scuttled across like a child chased by the town bully then dropped face first to the ground, using his arms to soften his fall. Grimes raced over, crouched beside him.

"Are you hurt?" Grimes asked.

Lao shook his head, breathing hoarse. "No direct hits, I'm fine." He snapped his head around. The ships outside descended with a quiet humming spin.

"They're coming," Cam said. Lao tuned around, noticed the boy sitting behind Cam. "They're going to sweep for survivors."

Grimes lifted Lao to his feet. "We're sitting ducks if we stay here," Grimes said. He took up his AR15. "Let's make a final stand. Kill as many as possible."

Cam shook his head. "We don't stand a chance. Who knows what monsters are coming out of that ship, and what weaponry they have."

"We're soldiers. We stand and fight."

Cam dropped his head. "We're humans in an alien war. We get out of here and take this boy to safety."

Lao looked at Cam like he was out of his mind. "Go where?" he asked. "Who is that boy? Where did he come from? I thought they took all children downstairs."

"Obviously there's a lot more going on than you know, Admiral. There's a camp in Atlanta. We take him there."

"How?" Grimes interjected. "They've killed everyone who tried to run. We have no choice but to fight."

"The elevator," Cam said. "We get downstairs and use the tunnels to get away."

Grimes stepped closer. "That elevator is more than likely destroyed, and who knows what's down there waiting." He shook his head. "No, there's no way we can make it."

"But making a final stand is your answer? I'll take my chances with him and the tunnels."

Behind them, outside, ramps descended from the discs. Cam went to the elevator door securing the 9MM behind his back then pushed the door with all his strength, forcing it open, until the doors slid apart. He used an AR15 to secure the doors from closing. He eyed the cable, secured to the ceiling above him, and disappearing into the darkness below.

"Cam?" Grimes said. Cam shot him a look. "Are you sure?"

Cam looked beyond Lao and Grimes and stepped forward. Outside, descending the ramps, were large, pale brown insect-looking creatures. Resembling seven feet tall crickets, their tentacles thumped down the ramps, forming a single file line. Cam's jaw dropped. "Friggin' alien war!" he said inciting stares from Lao and Grimes. He went to the boy whose head was leaning against the wall. "I'm not sure about anything anymore except that if we stay up here..." he lifted the boy to his feet, stared into his eyes. "You'll have to climb down. I'll be right with you. Follow behind me." Then turned back to his cohorts. "If we stay here, we are definitely dead. And so is this boy. Our best chance is in the tunnels." He reached into the elevator shaft and took hold of the cable, gripped it tight and pulled, testing its strength then turned back to Lao and Grimes. "Are you coming or not? If you're staying slide the doors closed."

Lao and Grimes looked at each other with uncertainty. They turned to the outside. One of those cricket looking things plunged its front right tentacle into the chest of a Russian soldier, forcing the human to the ground. The cricket screeched. A loud call and the other crickets started patrolling the perimeter. They locked eyes and nodded joining Cam and the boy.

"That's what I thought," Cam said. He looked at the boy. "Follow close behind me. I know it's scary but it won't take long. Hold the cable tight, wrap your ankles around it and slide down slowly. If something happens don't call out; whisper, and one of us will help you. Understood?" The boy nodded. "Once we reach the elevator drop down as lightly as possible." The boy nodded again.

Lao glared outside, those oversized crickets approached the building. "If we're gonnna do it, we need to do it now."

Cam looked outside seeing the same. Grimes was already on the cable when Cam turned back. "And he didn't want to come!" Cam shook his head, reached into the shaft and grabbed the cable. He looked at Lao before descending. "Help him on."

Lao nodded. His eyes widened. "Go!"

Cam took one last look at the boy then slid down the cable. Lao helped the boy who took the cable and slid down with ease leaving Lao the last to enter.

"Like descending into hell," he said in a faint tone. He took the cable in his hands and pulled himself into the shaft, turning so his torso leaned against the cable, wrapped his legs around it. Using the cable as support as he leaned to the door, gripping the gun holding the doors open. Took one final glance at the broken concrete. Cocked his head to the right, eyes narrow; it seemed like the concrete was melting. He shook his head, pulled the gun from the door, and wrapped it around his shoulder as the doors scraped closed. The shaft was in total darkness although he could hear movement down the cable. He reached for the flashlight on his belt, bracing himself. The light flickered on and he wedged it between his teeth, looking down. Grimes was already on top of the elevator and Cam and the boy were just about there. He slid down.

"Check the ceiling door," Grimes said to Cam when Lao reached the elevator. Cam kneeled, gripped the elevator's ceiling hatch.

"Where's that air coming from?" Lao said. He looked at the others, the flashlight now in his hand. "You feel that?" He lifted his hand; wind graced his fingers. He pointed the light towards the wall. Above their heads was a large shaft emitting forced air. Used the light on the other side where a second air tunnel was revealed. Both tunnels over seven feet high. "Where do they lead?" he whispered.

Cam gave up the elevator door. "Perfect," he said.

"You know where it leads?" Grimes asked.

Cam surveyed the holes, thinking. "Yes. They're used to bring in air from the outside. There's openings all through the tunnels." He turned to his comrades. "We can make it through to a safe distance. And stay out of sight."

Cam noticed immediate relief grace their eyes. Cam smiled. "Told ya," he said then huffed. "Make a final stand." He shook his head.

"How long?" Grimes asked ignoring Cam's antics.

"Well, no matter what, we've got to move fast and hopefully it's no more than a few hours." He looked at the boy who stood with the men staring at Cam.

"Why?" Lao asked

"Why a few hours?" Grimes added.

"The bomb explodes an hour after sunrise."

"Bomb? What bomb?"

"What're you talking about?"

Cam put his finger to his lips. "No need to worry, we'll be at a safe distance by then."

Lao and Grimes shot each other a concerned stare.

"Move fast," Cam said. "Just in case the path is longer than expected." He reached up finding the shaft's end and pulled himself up.

"This...isn't...good," Grimes said.

"He's crazy," Lao replied.

"The boy next." Cam reached down to the boy who took his wrists. He pulled the boy in with him. He looked at Lao and Grimes, still standing as if contemplating what they should do. "You coming or waiting for the bomb to explode? Or those things up there opening the elevator door? Which I'm sure they will." Cam cocked his eyebrows and disappeared down the shaft.

"Crazy like a fox, but..." Grimes said reaching his fingers to the shaft to pull himself up. "He's been right so far." Up he went, leaving Lao alone.

"I'm a long way from home," Lao whispered. He looked down, thinking. Thinking of home. His family. Not knowing. Not knowing anything about their whereabouts. He jumped when the elevator door thumped. Jumped up and pulled himself in, then leaned against the wall and breathed, catching his breath. Another thump, the scrape of metal doors opening. Took his 9MM from his leg holster and squeezed the gun between his palms. He heard screeching sounds reverberate in the elevator shaft. Looked back to his crew. Cam and the others had rounded a corner and were gone. Another screech. *What the hell are those things?* He moved his head back and forth.

*I hope I never find out!*

**SAIPH HAD LOCKED IN ON SANOS** several times, but each time his location slipped from Saiph's thought like a dream evading recollection. He wondered if Sanos was engaged in some kind of game, somehow knowing that Zeta had ordered Saiph to secure Sanos and not kill him. Sanos had to be taken alive; however, harmed would be fine to Zeta who revealed to Saiph prior to departure how the nine had grown leery of Sanos and his rebellious exploits.

"He's become a liability," Zeta had told him. "But there are questions the nine want answers to." Saiph had always displayed the utmost respect for Zeta, but what he said next rattled Saiph to the bone. "Sanos has angered the greys. We must show our allegiance. This order comes from those far, far away. From our home."

Saiph had so little information on their home planet. Dracs who resided on earth were born and bred on Earth as soldiers, living underground. None had ever seen their home planet. Home was as elusive to them as the human's notion of God. And no Drac had ever succumbed to grey. Not that he'd ever seen. He'd thought Zeta was acting with discretion in his response to the grey Mono. And then the shift. The shift in energy. The shift in Zeta. He took Rygel's life in response to Mono's declaration. The response turned Saiph's stomach.

Saiph sensed Drac pride swell in his chest and throat as he searched the fifth floor, down corridors, looked into rooms, and felt through his heart. But nothing! *There's nothing in these tunnels but foul-smelling humans.* The smell irritated him. *Don't they clean up their human feast?* He surveyed another room, the third in this corridor. Blood stained the walls from the human lying dead on the floor, dismembered with his intestines torn and tossed from the open gut. Three rooms with three dead humans. Follow the blood trail. *It must be Sanos.*

Even to him such a sight was foul. He believed feeding should be kept clean with no blood wasted. Whoever did this is a true monster. *Sanos! Is he truly as mad as they claim?*

A scream erupted down the corridor. Saiph constricted, pondering the exact location. These walls reverberated sound; the scream could have come from either direction. Again, the scream. Saiph looked up having located the source coming from down the corridor. As he passed each door, he was aware they were all open. Human death, a familiar stench, grew wild and frenzied with his approach. Dismembered human remains glinted in the corner of his eye as he advanced to the door where the screams were coming. He leaned against the wall outside the door. Squeezed his palms freeing the blades down his arms. He was about to go through the door when it smashed open, torn off its hinges and slammed against the opposite wall. Following the door's trajectory was a dismembered human, decapitated with its torso cut open. The body bounced off the wall and dropped to the floor with a thud.

Sanos sprang from the room, his feet bouncing off the wall where the door had been torn to pieces. He propelled to the opposite wall, twisted and turned then landed, his back to Saiph. He'd never seen such a massive Drac. Sanos was colossal, standing silent in the hall, creeping his head around towards Saiph.

He took one look at Sanos and knew immediately.

*This may be more difficult than I thought!*

* * *

When Sanos looked at Saiph, for the first time he knew that COR had arrived. This tattooed freak was sent to destroy. He saw inside Saiph, heard his heart jump, and his blood stiffen. Sanos licked the blood off his chin, turning to face Saiph, shaking his head.

"You should have stayed in Colorado," Sanos told him. "Nothing here but death and abominations."

Despite his transformation, Sanos felt a strange unsettling sensation bubble in his gut. With that last human he had to really tear into him to satisfy his desired effect. Even bouncing off the walls like he'd been doing required an unusual amount of strength. The simple fact that he never heard or sensed Saiph brought the revelation that the pill's effects were dwindling. How fast it would be gone he wasn't sure, nor did he know what would happen once the pill dissipated.

"You're a disgrace," Saiph said and stepped away from the wall. "The only abomination I see here is the one I'm looking at." Saiph shook his head. "What've you done to yourself?" He stood firm. "What manner of Drac does this to his food? Every room here is the same. Simply speaking, Sanos, you've lost your mind."

Sanos moved his head slowly back and forth, grinding his jaw. A taste like acid saturated the back of his throat as he sneered to push it away. "To myself?" he snarled and laughed. "We Dracs are the experiments under this..." his eyes turned to the ceiling. "Hellish lab. The nine care not for us. We've been thrown out like that human lying at your feet." His voice stuttered through a garbling of acid and blood. "*Research?!*" He spit. "Our people have turned us into rats for their research and prodding." He breathed hoarsely then shouted; "Don't think they won't do the same to you!"

Saiph glared at him. "Don't think I won't kill you here and now." He stretched his neck popping and cracking tendons and bone.

Sanos returned the stare. "Don't think I won't eat your heart."

He rushed at Saiph, blade grinding against blade, and seized Saiph's throat, tossing him backward against the wall. Saiph bounced back with a kick to Sanos's sternum, the force backing Sanos away. He came back with a blade that Sanos caught with his own. Sanos delivered a left hook across Saiph's jaw, his blade sliced across the back of his cheek. Sanos retaliated, sensing weakness, but Saiph was fast catching the next blade and stomped his boot across Sanos's right knee. Sanos bent to the floor then jumped with an uppercut, grabbed Saiph's head and crushed it face first into the wall. Saiph returned with an elbow to Sanos's chest, climbing the wall and jumping upside down behind Sanos, wrapping his arms around his throat and squeezed. Sanos slammed the back of his head into Saiph's face, felt Saiph release his throat with a grunt. Sanos sidestepped, took hold of Saiph's armor, spun around with him and tossed Saiph down the hall.

His body landed with a thud and slide, but he jumped up quickly, on guard again.

"Wretched fiend!" Sanos shouted pumping his fist into his leg, attempting to revive the damaged limb, still feeling the kick to the knee.

Saiph stood erect, unwavering. "You grow weaker by the second. I can sense it in your fury." He moved his head back and forth. "No matter what you do, Sanos, you will not win this fight."

"Impotent fool," Sanos raged. "Can't you see? You call yourself Drac, yet you stand by and allow your brethren to be treated like animals. Where's your rage in that?" Sanos jumped at him meeting blade to blade consecutively.

Saiph spun around slicing across Sanos's right shoulder, the blade cutting through his armor. Blood jutted from the wound, dropping Sanos's shoulder limp by his side.

Saiph approached with the stealth of a seasoned predator, sensing the weakness in his prey, registering the surprised stare in Sanos's eyes. Saiph lifted his arm, displaying his blade. "Upgrades," he said, "New steel provided by the home planet." His eyes lit up. "Cuts right through Drac armor."

Sanos huffed through labored breath, a low grunt wedged in the back of his throat. "Another blasphemy against our people." He stepped back, cautious, favoring his injured arm. Saiph continued his approach.

Sanos spun to his right to use his left arm for protection as Saiph escalated his attack. Sanos was able to ward him off. Three throws from Saiph's blade chinked against Sanos's blade. As the blood ran from his shoulder, Sanos's strength drained from his body. He hobbled backward and Saiph crushed his boot into his chest, dropping Sanos to the floor. His neck twitched and his head rocked against cement, bouncing off the hard concrete. His eyes dropped, seeing through eyelid slits, watching as Saiph came over him.

"All too easy," said Saiph.

And then, darkness.

\* \* \*

Saiph crouched beside the defeated unconscious Sanos. He tied his wrists and ankles with Drac metal handcuffs then wiped the blood from his nose. Touched the back of his cheek where Sanos had caught him, blood stained his fingertips. A groan erupted from Sanos's throat as his body started to change. Those long sharp fangs contracted, morphing to their original size. Even his frame contracted. Saiph's forehead crinkled, witnessing the transformation.

"Unnatural!" he said, studying Sanos, his body shrinking. Saiph shook his head, whispering, "What's become of you?"

Saiph stood, removing a small mechanical device from his belt and clicked the side button. On the surface Zeta was projected.

"Do you bring good news, Saiph?"

"Sanos has been secured."

"Excellent. Bring him and the others to the pit. I've requested our ships return so we may begin processes towards departure. All above ground have been wiped out."

Saiph paused, distracted by what he'd witnessed.

Zeta registered Saiph's expression. "What is it, Saiph?"

"Sanos," he said. "There's more than we know. He...he's changed form."

"Clarify please, Saiph."

"Hard to explain. He...he changed, in front of me, like a werewolf or shape shifter, I don't know how else to explain it. He looked one way and the next he changed form. I don't believe we should keep him with the others. There may be a residual effect."

Zeta tightened his jaw.

"Zeta?"

"Secure him alone for now. Report to me in the pit. We must inquire further."

"Acknowledged." Saiph clicked the machine and Zeta disappeared. He replaced the device on his belt, watching Sanos whose breathing turned shallow. His eyes seemed to shrink beneath his cheekbones. Saiph crouched down, held his hand over Sanos's pelvis, the Drac pulse registering health and balance.

*Weak!* "Like you're dying." His inquiry brought him to search Sanos, finding pills in a hidden pocket on his belt. He studied the blue pills. "Is this what they gave you?" he said, wishing Sanos could answer. "Nine pills." Saiph breathed deeply, closed his hand, gentle but firm around the pills. His head down, thinking, observing Sanos, his hand shook as he gritted his teeth. Saiph secured the pills inside his belt pocket. As he hoisted Sanos over his shoulder, he couldn't stop the thought,

*If they're poisoning Drac they must all die!*
*Grey and human alike.*

# 21

PHIL FOLLOWED SANDY WHO SEEMED TO GATHER more strength and endurance with every step. *Something's definitely off. And there's something she's not telling me.* He was amazed over how she knew every turn. Phil maintained a watchful eye and deft ear around every corner. He understood this wasn't a time to ask a billion questions, but trust was a needed commodity under such duress, and Sandy wasn't saying anything as if she was keeping secrets.

But even more, he felt disconnected, as if something was off within him. He couldn't shake the sensation that someone was locked in on him, creating static inside his thoughts.

Sandy looked at him. "This way," she whispered.

Phil followed. "How do you know all this?"

"Not now, Phil. I need your trust now, not your questions." She squatted down at the end of a hall that led off in two possible directions. She held the baby close, staring, and remaining as still and quiet as possible.

Phil gazed at her. *She's blocking me?* He dismissed the notion. *That's impossible.*

Sandy looked in both directions, and then at Phil. "This way," she said, popped up and went down the hall. Phil paused then started to follow, looking her over, how smooth she moved and how instinctive.

*Like someone whose locked in. Someone who…*

The revelation caught him. Phil stopped walking, looking hard at Sandy as the distance grew between them. The further the distance the easier he could think. Sandy looked for him over her shoulder; her hurried pace ceased.

"Phil?"

Phil twisted his neck, studying Sandy and that baby. "It's you," he said.

Sandy pursed her lips, as Phil looked her over, studying, prob-
ing, listening. Beneath his thoughts he heard another voice.

*You must hurry! There isn't much time before...*

"Before what?" Phil said. He listened with intention, bending
his head; his eyes open yet seeing nothing, lost in the thought of
hearing the voice again. Whoever it was, Sandy was with them. *Is
she compromised? Is that baby a farce to lead...*

*Before they find out I'm helping you*, the voice answered.

"Phil, please," Sandy said. "We must go." She stepped back.
"We're wasting time." The baby let out a small tiny cry. Sandy
kissed his forehead. Looked back at Phil. "Please!" She turned
around, continued that feverish parade, disappearing down a dark
hall.

Phil felt the voice leave with Sandy. *This is insane. What do I do?
This could be a trap. She trusts an alien vampire?*

The word Trust repeated when he took off towards Sandy. *Trust
in Sandy*, Robyn had told him. *All the way through to the end, trust
Sandy.*

* * *

Telas arrived at Dr. Blum's lab to meet with Mono as she'd
instructed. On her way in she had been locked in on Sandy's conscious mind, delivering the path to the tunnels, and hoping this person Phil was as trustworthy as Sandy explained. As she approached
Mono, she blocked her thoughts, pushing Sandy's travel as far from
conscious thought as possible. *Mono will see if I don't.*

She'd never been so nervous; her hands trembled, and she felt
her jaw tighten with an uneasy sensation constricting her gut.

"You're well fed, I see," Mono said. She stood in front of Dr.
Blum's computer, tracing through files at light speed.

Telas pursed her lips. "Fresh female blood is always delectable.
Women taste so much better than men."

"Female hormones offer a sweet fragrance in the blood, especially from a female who's just given birth. Helps the skin. See,
you're glowing."

Telas instinctively touched her cheek. The normal sandpaper-like Drac skin was smooth beneath her fingertips. She noticed Mono hadn't even so much as glanced in her direction. She quickly retracted her hand, shifting focus to Mono's work. She cleared her throat, looking over the computer and seeing Dr. Blum's personal files inside a folder marked, *The Future.* "How did you bypass the voice activation firewall?" Telas was staring at the monitor, trying to get a glimpse of the files Mono was speeding through, but they raced across the screen faster than she could register, only a title or single word managed to stick out.

**Opiate. Psychedelic. Psilocybin. AntiDepressive. AntiPsychotic. DNA.**

"I used his voice."

Mono's response registered a confused stare from Telas.

*Dr. Blum voice activation!*

Telas heard Dr. Blum's voice in her thoughts, as if he were standing next to her. "It's just vibrations, dear. Little nuances within wave frequencies inside a subtle vibrational depository sent directly to the computer's microphone. Speaking is merely a reproduction of our thoughts. Listen to your thoughts. Do you not hear your own voice?"

"Of course."

"There you have it."

Telas stiffened, waiting, sensing tension constrict her thoughts. "I should meet with COR," she said. "I've sensed their arrival. Who is it they've sent?"

"Zeta with his complement, Saiph. The humans above ground have been eradicated. Saiph has secured Sanos and the remaining in your clan wait for extradition. Our departure will be quick."

"What of the humans remaining in the catacombs?"

"Few will accompany us. Those who have showed progress and with whom we elect to continue our research. The others will serve to feed Zeta's Thorx army prior to departure. No sense in wasting food."

On any other day Telas would have agreed. Humans were food,

nothing more, but today she saw them in a new light. Not food but equals. The thought of humans being torn apart stabbed her heart with shame. *We've been fighting on the wrong side.* Her thought slipped and she immediately constricted, swallowing consciousness into a block of darkness. She turned her attention to the monitor.

**Gene Splicing. Cloning. Indigo Identification. Indigo Trials.**

"There it is." Mono moved closer to the monitor, her head moving slowly back and forth, taking in all the information with apt focus. Pictures of children, human children, beside personal descriptions jumped across the screen.

"Indigo trials?" Telas had never heard of such an experiment nor recalled the children depicted on the screen. "What are *Indigo Trials?*"

Silence. Mono's interest in the Indigo files was paramount, as if the information was of dire consequence. Telas had never seen Mono so focused, and she sensed excitement shivering in Mono's grey bones. Telas focused on the information, trying to keep up with Mono's quick attention but with little success. Despite the slowing of information, the files continued to race down the screen. A note from Dr. Blum concluded the folder.

*Immune to current testing. Subjects are not approachable at this time. Although non-threatening the advancement of protection from testing subjects must be broken before additional tests can be made.*

Mono stared at the screen, that excitement now gone. Now she seemed disappointed, angry and concerned, her eyes wide and glaring.

"Something wrong, Mono?"

Mono maintained her attention on the screen, punching a few keys on the keyboard, the last being Delete. The screen went dark before the computer and monitor dissipated, folding over on itself and crumbling to dust.

"But the files?"

"In here, dear." Mono said tapping her temple.

"Why not send the information through the cloud?"

Mono shook her head. "Some information should not be

stamped in time. Besides the information has already been received on the other side."

Telas understood that Mono was the catalyst for sending the information in real time to COR headquarters. There was no need for copying the information or maintaining the files in the cloud. Mono was the cloud.

"Now dear." Mono focused on Telas.

"Let's go and check on your baby."

## 22

**"MY MOST TRUSTED CONFIDANT RETURNS."** Zeta waited in the pit, greeting Saiph when he returned to provide intel concerning Sanos. Saiph bowed to Zeta, taking a knee.

"Sanos has been secured as requested."

"My most loyal subject. Saiph what troubles you? What have you discovered?"

"I found these on Sanos." He held his hand out revealing the pills in his palm. "I believe these are what brought the physical change in Sanos. Should this be true, we must accept the possibility that Drac experimentation is ongoing. Action to begin investigation is recommended."

Zeta looked over Saiph. "And you wish to lead the investigation?" Zeta felt the surge of Drac pride in his subject. A pride equal to his own when he was young and ambitious.

"In the name of Drac pride, yes."

Zeta closed his eyes. "Rise, Saiph." The ceiling opened and the disc ships descended into the pit. Zeta turned his attention to the ships, Saiph stood beside him. "In the name of SsaTa our people return unscathed." Zeta watched as the discs hovered projecting their ramps to the ground. Saiph stood by Zeta's side. The cricket army marched down the ramps standing guard along the ramp and ground outside the ship as the brown and large cricket in charge descended the ramp. Zeta went to greet him.

"Kee," Zeta addressed the large cricket. "Have all humans have been eradicated?"

Kee's voice was a garbled baritone that came not from his mouth but from his throat. "All above ground are no more."

Zeta stood face to face with Kee. He touched Kee's head, dipping his forehead to Kee's. "Triumphant and efficient, Kee. As always."

"Grant it, master." Kee returned Zeta's praise. "What are current wishes?"

Zeta turned, eyed Saiph who also waited instruction. "Direct orders from COR. Secure Sanos and his clan aboard ship," he ordered Saiph, then turned back to Kee. They walked together. "Leave the humans to stay and rot." He had not yet informed Mono of COR's order. He knew she would not be pleased leaving so many test subjects to perish.

"Necessary sacrifice to the larger cause," said Kee.

"Our hope is in Dr. Blum's research," Zeta continued. They walked past the anticipatory Saiph. "Should he have isolated the appropriate chemical we can all move to our final phase."

"All wait patiently, Zeta. A plan that has taken centuries..."

"Need not stumble so close to completion," Zeta concluded Kee's sentence, a proclamation commonly spoken within COR's elite. Zeta turned to Kee and reached his hand to his cheek. "You have done well. Rest now, our departure is soon." Zeta moved away from Kee.

"What of the soldiers, Zeta? It is best for them to feed after battle."

Zeta turned looking over the Thorx army. "Humans in the catacombs," he said to Kee. "Level three. Let those who fought feed, leave the Thorx from the main ship to stand guard with me."

Kee bowed. "Grateful for your mercy, Zeta." Zeta returned the bow and Kee went to address his soldiers.

Zeta could sense Saiph's anticipation, Saiph's eyes on him. Zeta addressed his right hand, locking eyes with him. "Upon arrival to COR provide your finding to the council. Request permission to investigate."

The disappointment was clear in Saiph's eyes, Zeta knew he wanted to begin his investigation now, not wait to return to COR for permission when Zeta had the power and authority to allow Saiph's inquiry to begin here in this moment. And Zeta was sure his first round of investigation would concern the greys.

"For now, secure the clan. Bring them aboard the ship. Secure them in the isolation containments."

Saiph stiffened but bowed before Zeta. "As you wish," he said. Zeta returned the bow and Saiph departed the pit as Zeta watched him.

*My heart bleeds.* He regretted bringing Saiph to this camp. Behind him Kee addressed the army marching out of the pit in single file. *COR will never allow your inquiry.*

"I must speak with Mono."

* * *

Above the pit, in the airshaft, Cam listened and watched as the Thorx soldiers made their way out.

"How many are in the catacombs?" Lao asked, kneeling beside Cam.

"Hundreds," Cam responded.

"Can we get there before them?" Grimes said.

Cam looked down then to the boy.

"Cam?" Grimes said.

Cam stood up, his head a foot below the ceiling, studying the shaft and its many twists and turns.

"Yes," Cam said and turned to face them. "But we must be quick."

## 23

**MONO WAS LISTENING, SENSING THE VIBRATIONS** Telas emitted. *Nervous, she is.* Mono was tired of the games the Dracs were engaged in. Like little children creating drama to make their lives seem more interesting, hiding the truth of their deeds as if everyone else were fooled by their treachery.

*None are ever completely obstructed unless there is something to hide.*

Mono studied Telas as they made their way to the medical ward to the baby. She was eerily quiet and the look in her eyes seemed blank, lost. Her hands, folded one inside the other, were trembling. Mono considered the possibility that Telas may have been affected adversely by the thunder Mono had impressed on her in the pit. Such a strong overpowering vibration often affects the central nervous system with a lasting impression.

And then there was the heartbeat. Mono had heard Sandy's dying heart. Felt it in the center of her mind dwindle to a hollow shell.

"What did you do with the body?" Mono asked noticing the sweat glistening on Telas's forehead.

"Dissolved," Telas said and cleared her throat. "Like Dr. Blum," she continued. "Thank you for the idea. The rose has more uses than I was aware of. We've always been taught its use in battle—as protection -- not cover up."

"Of course, dear. There's a lot Dracs are unaware of."

\* \* \*

Telas could sense Mono's skeptical nature attempting to grasp the thoughts behind the thought. She felt weak in her presence like a scolded child cowering under the shadow of an abusive parent as she fought to conceal Sandy's escape. *This is about to erupt.* Telas was able to conceal her thoughts by creating a dark room in her subconscious where the thought of Sandy's escape remained under a psychic lock and key. She refused all other thoughts that would normally be beaming at her a million miles an hour to enter that room. Considering the recent change of events and Mono's declaration over current circumstances, controlling every aspect of protocol and procedure to her linking, Telas knew she had to conceal Sandy's escape for as long as possible. Grey had always been a subordinate to Drac. Mono's display of power over Telas was, for all intents and purposes, completely unexpected, yet the power was undeniable. Telas had never experienced such raw power before. Never knew it existed until that moment with Mono. And the effect continued.

Telas felt feeble, weary and suffocated. She knew her body and her organs were weak and deteriorating. Even as she walked side by side with Mono, she sensed the hand of that power impressing upon her like a black cloud she couldn't avoid. She felt the sweat on her forehead and a pain in the center of her brain. Touched her nose and saw blood on her fingertips as her knees weakened. A single thought came to the front of her mind; *I'm not going to make it.*

# 24

THE REMAINING DRACS IN SANDS'S CLAN were preparing the dead for transport when Saiph entered. Knowing how these soldiers had died boiled his blood. Clearly the blades were involved considering the clean cuts through the bodies. Only Drac metal could make such clean slices.

"Are the dead prepared?" said Saiph.

None of the three answered, instead they continued, wrapping the dead in thick bandages. Saiph waited for a response.

"All but Cade," Jubal said.

"A fourth?" Saiph constricted, eyes narrow. "I was not informed of a fourth death by the blades."

Jubal completed the final wrap across Titus' neck before he answered. "Because he did not perish by the blade," Jubal shouted with tremors choking his voice. He touched Titus' head, dipping his forehead to the bandaged corpse.

Saiph was taken by the respect the clan showed for their brethren. "What has happened here?" he asked. His tone changed, more compassionate then demanding. "It appears madness has consumed this camp."

"Madness exists in the lies," Jubal said turning to face Saiph. His eyes red to the core, filled with tears. "Here, Dracs are treated less than human, subjected to scrutiny and experimentation." His jaw quivered, shouting his pleas and proclamations. "Where Drac cower before grey and human alike. Where we are tossed away *like dogs* and nothing is done." A single tear raced down his cheek. "Your own Zeta bends to the grey's hand." Moving his head back and forth, he pursed his lips. "Beseech your master to draw the wrath of Mono. You shall see for yourself the depths of persecution. The lies trickled from the band of COR down to the youngest Drac. Lies under duress turn to betrayal." He lifted his chin, standing proud among his brothers. "Our Cade fell under the wrath of grey.... Entreat your master of our claims. See if his eyes convince our truth to you."

Saiph understood what it meant to be a part of a clan. Knew all too well what the death of one meant to the others. His own clan had perished during the war performing black ops under the cover of the Chinese army. Saiph was the lone survivor after a tirade had erupted in lieu of a smooth operation, his own clansmen defying orders to back down. And here he was, confronted with events against his moral code. Yet betrayal came in many forms and confronting Zeta on such matters may prove more than he wanted to know. He stared at Jubal with a constricted countenance.

"Gather the dead," he said. "We leave now."

# 25

THE CATACOMBS, AS THEY WERE CALLED, consisted of the entire third floor, split in two sections with an overly wide hallway that cut through the center. On both sides, humans wasted away from starvation, locked inside large open quarters secured by a chain link fence that reached from floor to ceiling. Even when they were fed the food provided held a metallic taste, as if whatever meat they were given had been ground with oyster shells. And then there were the pills and a dark room where light was beamed into their eyes. The result was often consistent with a catatonic response.

Humans lay in their own excrement, sitting or standing, drooling with blank stares portraying that the pills indeed had a profound effect equal to a lobotomy. However, they were able to follow simple orders, falling in line when requested and walking single file, performing simple tasks such as cleaning, but only when commanded. They had no complaints, nor any real voice for that matter. Grunts and garbles were the primary form of communication.

And when Kee's army arrived on the third floor the sight of these humans was like an offering of rat meat. Nonetheless, there was no use in wasting food. Kee opened the gates with an expectation that the humans would run. No such occurrence came. They remained still, unmoving; even when Kee walked the hallway revealing himself, no such startled reaction had come.

A human, standing in front of the fence never so much as blinked when the door opened, as if there was no comprehension that the door had been opened and he could walk out. Nor did the other men raise so much as an eyebrow when Kee thrust his front leg into the man's chest, hoisting him from the cell to the hallway floor.

Kee applied his weight to the body, splitting the chest bone and puncturing the heart. He began to feed. Kee's species, the Thorx, were an unusual species of pet for Drac. Intelligent yet compliant like a mix between cat and dog. Their tough exterior a natural armor made of reinforced bone protecting their gentle interior organs, blood and cartilage. Their heads, including the small brain housed within a large elongated skull is a separate entity to the body. The brain does not require food to function, only oxygen, and as such the food drawn into the body has no effect on the mind. He gulped the man's organs, blood, and intestines through the foot plunged into the man's heart, burning the human's insides with a chemical injected into the body like acid dropped on food in order to turn the innards into easily digested liquid.

The drained man's skin turned grey and wrinkled. The bones were always the last to be taken up, ground into bits for easy passage into the Thorx body, leaving a deflated wrap of skin fuming with a putrid stench of smoke. Kee's team of twelve fed as well. No fight from the humans, just a Thorx feeding frenzy. Each human drained quickly, their deflated skin smoldering on the floor.

* * *

The stench wafted into the airshaft growing stronger with every step closer to the catacombs that Cam and his team hurried through.

"We're too late," Grimes called, the back of his throat salivated with acid that turned his stomach.

Cam stopped by a wall where he could go either left or right. The stank seemed the same in both directions.

"Cam!" Grimes called. "We're not going to make it in time."

"This way," the boy said, pointing to the right.

Cam shot him a look then stared down the right corridor. "How do you know?" He looked back at the boy who shrugged.

"I don't know how but I know it's this way. The smell is stronger in this direction."

Cam took a second to consider the boy's declaration before jutting off to the right.

"Cam?" Grimes said following him. "Is this even worth it?"

"Doesn't matter; we've got to try and save as many as we can."

"This coming from the guy who created a bomb to blow us all to pieces."

"Things have changed," Cam said. "I didn't know we could get outta here. Didn't know we had a place to go." Another crossroad but this time Cam didn't require the boy's nose to point the direction. He could see a waft of smoke ballooning into the shaft on the left. "We're here," Cam breathed. He turned to the team.

"What's your plan?" Lao asked with a sour snarl.

"No time for a plan. Just shoot to kill."

# 26

THE BABY STARTED CRYING, HIS WAILS echoing in the corridor. Sandy turned to her baby. "Shh, shh, it's okay," she told him caressing her fingers across his forehead. Her jaw trembled. She'd felt it a few seconds before, what the baby was feeling, pain in her knees and pain in her brain like a migraine with a vengeance.

"Does he need food?" Phil asked, a look of concern in his eyes.

The cry turned vicious and Sandy did nothing but stare.

"Sandy? Does he need to feed?"

Her vision wavered, feeling light-headed and sick to her stomach, Sandy fell back, caught by Phil who eased her to the floor against the wall. "Sandy?" he said, her head flopping to the right and left.

"Sandy, please. Tell me what to do."

Sandy's eyes drifted open, staring at Phil, her mouth open attempting to speak. "Yes," Phil said. He looked deep into her eyes. "Tell me what to do." He waited but received no response. Sandy's head flopped forward. Phil pushed her head back gently against the wall. "Sandy?" he hollered and slapped his hands in front of her eyes getting the response he needed as her heavy eyes opened. "Does he need to eat?"

Sandy nodded. "Yes," she said as her head fell to the right. The wailing now a constant thick drone.

Phil pushed her shoulders. "What does he eat, Sandy? Where's his food?" She drifted off again. "Sandy!" His voice shot her eyes open.

"Blood," she said losing consciousness.

"Blood." Phil mouthed the words. He looked at the crying baby, his lips trembling open revealing his sharp teeth. Phil winced at the sight of him. "Blood," he said and judging by the look of this baby it made sense but still he hesitated.

The baby's wails reached a fevered pitch.

Phil cut his arm with the blade, drawing blood down his forearm.

*"This better work."*

He turned his arm up keeping the blades away from the baby's face and dipped his arm to the baby's mouth. The cries ceased as the baby swallowed the salty thick fluid down his throat. Phil felt his blood draining from his arm, tickling and quivering his veins. His body shivered. "How much?" he said when the baby released his mouth, apparently satisfied, falling back into slumber. Phil looked at his arm, studying the tiny teeth marks around the wound, touching them with his free hand. "This gets stranger and stranger."

He caught Sandy's eyes, now wide open, staring at his arm and the blood that ran across his skin. She gripped his wrist above the blade, holding it with an iron grasp, twisting his arm closer to her lips.

"Sandy?" Phil said, tightening his arm.

Phil's eyes opened wide when Sandy clasped her mouth around his arm, gulping blood down her throat. In the prevailing silence Phil heard gunshots raging on the floor above.

* * *

When Saiph arrived at the pit with the remaining Sanos clan and wrapped bodies he escorted them onto the ship and into confinement. Once secured he then searched for Zeta. He had orders yet Jubal's words stung his mind. *Could it be true?* The flip in power disturbed him although he felt it himself, Zeta's cower in the presence of the grey Mono.

The question was why? Had Zeta been ordered by COR to heed Mono's direction? Considering all that was happening in this camp, Mono offered the necessary knowledge available to ascertain possible threats. It was widely known that greys held no capacity for lies or deception. They provided the perfect service to Dracs in this respect and were committed to the larger cause; turning humans into slaves through chemical modification and genetic engineering.

*And an endless supply of food.*

He found Zeta in a containment unit that pumped healing oxygen and allowed for a reprieve under the forced air brought below ground, sitting cross-legged, eyes closed in focused meditative concentration. In addition to the healing effects of oxygen, this particular confinement unit was made of Drac metal from their home planet serving as the ideal beacon to transmit and receive information without the possibility of said necessary information becoming skewed or adopted by outside interference.

No disruption was allowed when Zeta was in this unit. Saiph knew such a breach would be cause for dismissal from his current position. Such an outward display of disrespect was seen by COR as an ultimate betrayal. Some information was kept secret by COR, seen as privileged information only COR members were allowed. Saiph would not be receiving answers at this time. As he watched through a small window his master meditating, he couldn't help the thought that kept surfacing. *I'm being lied to.*

**CAM THOUGHT THE STENCH OF DEFLATED** human skin was the worst he'd ever experienced, until his bullet ripped into Kee's body. It was a direct hit; straight into what Cam surmised was the Thorx heart. The body crumbled and with it the remnants of Kee's feeding. Undigested human remains dripping with acid emptied over the floor. Kee's head lay on the ground, his eyes blinking.

"Nice shot," Grimes said. "Easier to kill than I anticipated."

Grimes jumped from the shaft into an open room outside the catacomb entrance as one of Kee's soldiers stepped away from feeding into the hall, assessing his fallen commander. Grimes raised his AR15 when the soldier locked eyes on him. His shot was on point— aimed between the eyes—except the bullet never hit its target. The Thorx soldier squealed something awful emitting a force field that disintegrated the bullet upon impact.

"Not good," Grimes said. Another high-pitched squeal as the Thorx slammed its tentacles, like flexing before a fight. "Not good at all."

The remaining Thorx soldiers filed into the hall, emitting high-pitched squeals one after the other like a row of dominos and with each squeal the Thorx shield was projected.

"Come back up," Cam shouted.

Grimes turned to Cam, then to the Thorx.

"Run," Grimes said. "They only saw me." He unloaded his clip. Like shooting blanks, the bullets evaporating through the Thorx shields. The Kee aliens formed a three in a row line of defense, beginning their approach and Grimes slammed in a fresh clip.

"Draw them out," Cam hollered.

Grimes looked up. Cam was holding a grenade.

"Is that going to work?"

Cam shrugged. "You got a better idea?"

Grimes turned to the Thorx, approaching with caution. "Guess not." He squeezed his trigger in intermittent blasts, moving back as they stepped forward. He glanced behind him. Another hall, smaller and in complete darkness. He triggered a few more shots as the Thorx marched out of the catacomb, continuing that same squeal one at a time, one squeal on the heels of the one before.

"Fuckin' loud." Cam watched as the first line of Thorx stepped forward beneath the airshaft. His eardrums on the brink of popping as he ducked down on his belly pulling the grenades pin and waiting. The second line passed beneath. Grimes stepped into the thin hall, shot a few more times and looked up, seeing the third Thorx line was past the shaft and watched as the grenade dropped. He ran to the end of the hall, stepped to the side. The explosion tore through the catacomb.

He waited for the smoke to clear before returning, assessing, listening for any squeals, seeing dead Thorx. Coming out of the hall he could see Cam's plan was successful. The Thorx were splattered into pieces. Chunks of human remains, and alien excrement covered the hall.

"Told ya," Cam said from the shaft.

Grimes looked up. "Are you coming down now?"

"Of course." Cam dropped from the shaft to the hall, smiling at Grimes then looked up. "I'll catch you," he said to the boy who dropped into Cam's arms. Lao followed.

"Friggin' stinks to high hell," Lao said, kneeling to assess any parts of the alien he could find, gathering a piece of bone that looked like it came from an alien leg.

"Let's see who's left," Cam said. He went into the catacomb, finding lines of smoking human skin covering the floor. Searching both sides of the catacomb, he saw three men, standing and staring.

"How many?" Grimes said.

Cam shook his head staring at the disgust before him then raised his hand showing three fingers.

"What? That's impossible." Grimes surveyed the clumps and piles of human remains at his feet, to the wall where coagulated blood and ground bones were plastered on the concrete. "Maybe not."

The boy joined Cam in the catacomb, pulling on his sleeve. "What?" Cam said with a frog in his throat. He couldn't take his eyes off the deflated human skin. The stench and rotting flesh walloped in his nostrils. "Epic fucking failure!" And the three men stood stiff, staring, unblinking, as if none of the carnage at their feet existed. As if waiting for him to speak. Their eyes black to the core and lost in strangled thought.

"We should get out of here ASAP," Grimes said. "There's no way to tell if anyone else is coming. We're like sitting ducks in a pond."

The boy yanked Cam's sleeve again. "Cameron," he said pointing at Kee's head.

"*What?*" Cam snapped and looked at the boy whose soft eyes revealed a glint of fear. Cam forced a smile. "I know," he said. He pursed his lips swallowing the frog in his throat. "I'm sorry."

The boy shook his head and pointed behind Cam to Kee's head. Cam turned. "He can't hurt you," he said turning back to the boy. But the boy shook his head again, this time with more urgency. "What is it?" He tried to understand what the boy was attempting to communicate, blinking with intention. Cam looked at Kee then back to the boy. Cocked his head, eyes narrow.

"Cam!" Grimes called. "It's time to go."

Cam looked at Grimes then turned back to Kee, noticing his blinking formed a pattern. "Morse code," he whispered then turned to the boy who nodded with wide eyes. "Morse code?" Cam nodded and the boy confirmed his finding with a rapid nod.

"Shit!"

Cam pulled his 9MM from his leg holster. "Fucker!" He shot Kee between the eyes, his skull exploding, and tiny pieces of skull, blood, and brains splattered across Cam. "Time to go." He holstered the 9MM.

"No shit," Grimes returned.

Lao looked up from his inspection of alien bone and blood. And then a loud bang, far away on the opposite side of the catacomb. Cam snapped his head to the sound, examining the hall. His eyes narrowed and he turned to the three men. "Follow me." On cue the three men formed a single file line. Again, the thump, like a crash into the ground rattling the floor.

"Something's coming," said Lao.

Cam looked down the hall then to the boy. "Get them in the shaft," he ordered then addressed the men. "Follow him," he pointed to the boy. "And hurry." He turned to Grimes and Lao. "Get back in the shaft."

More thumps, only louder. Whatever was coming was getting closer. Cam moved down the hall aiming his AR15 and moving towards the sound.

"Where are you going?" Grimes said.

"To see what the hell that is."

"Are you out of your mind?"

"Get everyone in the shaft. I'll be right behind you."

Lao went to the shaft.

"Where are you going?" Grimes said to him.

Lao glanced at Grimes. "Where do you think?" He lifted himself up.

"Of course." Grimes lifted the boy to Lao then turned to the three men with their blank stares. "What did they do to you?" The men moved their eyes to him. Grimes motioned for them to get up the shaft. Instead, they remained still, not understanding how to lift themselves up. "Jesus Christ!" He looked up at Lao then back to the men. "Grab his hand, he'll pull you up." They did as instructed.

"Dead weight," whispered Grimes. He looked back at Cam moving slowly down the hall. Again, the thud. "Let's go, Cam."

Lao lifted the last of the three men into the shaft. "You're next, Corporal."

Grimes turned to Lao then back to Cam. "Cam!"

"I'll be right there," Cam said.

Grimes shook his head. "This is ludicrous. Get over here."

But Cam kept moving, turning the corner into the dark hall.

TELAS COLLAPSED TO HER KNEES, her brain twisting, struggling to breathe she fell forward. Wheezing and garbling she attempted to move but all strength had dissipated. She was paralyzed, lying on the ground and staring trying to figure out what the hell was wrong with her.

"Perhaps you're dying," Mono responded to her fears, Telas's conscious thought of approaching death. "Oh dear, I may have pushed you a little too far in the pit. Sometimes I forget how weak Drac bodies are. Too much like the humans that feed you."

To this comment the three witches shared a compassionate and distasteful glance as if Mono's declaration was a personal insult.

Telas tried to move her arms but nothing moved other than the middle finger on her right hand, able to tap the floor beneath.

"So good," Mono said. "We can rule out total paralysis. At least for now, that may change soon." Mono jerked her head up, and Telas flipped over onto her back, continuing to tremble. Her body shuddering. The three witches observed her condition.

Inside a thought raged in Telas. *Shut down. Shut down now.* The greys appeared like bulbs of light covered in darkness. Mono reached her hand above Telas's eyes, and pain twisted to the center of her brain erupting into a high-pitched squeal that raged inside Telas's throat.

"She's attempting the dark," Mintaka warned.

"I can see," Mono responded, glaring at Telas, her head and shoulders moving like a snake.

"There is only one reason to reach the dark," Alnitak said, her thought completed by Alnilam, "To hide intention."

"Drac," Mono snickered. "So foolish." She placed her hand over Telas's sternum and squeezed her hand into a fist. Telas jumped, the pain brought her back to conscious awareness. "Fed the human your own blood, I see," Mono continued. Telas could feel Mono inside her mind, assessing, seeing her thoughts and memories, situations and events. "A useful Drac trick. And you're helping her escape. My, my, Telas, this is unexpected. Now we have to find the baby and Sandy." Mono dipped her head to the right and Telas felt Sandy's presence, tasted blood on her tongue followed by a relieving tingle in her stomach. "Most unexpected," Mono whispered and Telas tried to shut down the thought, to hide the connection to Sandy, searching for darkness.

"Perhaps she wants to die," Mintaka said looking to Alnitak and Alnilam for recognition. They both bowed in agreement.

"How noble," said Mono. "But it will not work. Telas is required; this link to Sandy is necessary. The human will listen to Telas, she will come willingly with baby." She squeezed again and Telas jolted up then back down, coughed blood over her lips. "We will use Telas to convince the mother to hand the child over. Once this is done neither mother will be needed. We can hand the child over to Moth of our own accord." Telas constricted, her chin rising.

*Shut...down.*

"We do not leave until the child is with us." She addressed Telas, her large oval eyes glaring into Telas's mind. "All you had to do was break the human mother's connection with the baby. All you had to do was deliver the baby to Moth by your own hand. Now we...*I* must take drastic measures." Mono moved her head back and forth as if a teacher scolding a student.

"But if she finds the dark? Should she shut down she will be no use to us. How will Sandy bring the baby then?" asked Mintaka.

"Zeta's oxygen chamber will restore her senses." Mono addressed the others. "Plus, she is receiving psychic nourishment from the human mother. Telas would otherwise be dead. I'm not sure how but I can sense it, this connection between Telas and Sandy is strong, as if they share the same mind. Once we confine her to the oxygen chamber the psychic nourishment will aid in Telas's restoration. We will bring her there now. In the interim, we shall have this place secured. All exits but one shall be closed. The pit the only way in or out. If needed the baby and human mother will come to us."

"The human mother will never hand over the child," the three witches said in unison.

"Much has been compromised. Perhaps we should show them the truth. Perhaps both can be spared, should they know the truth?" Mintaka, she glanced from Mono to Telas.

"They may give the child over if they know the truth. So much easier if the mother willingly breaks the connection. As is the case in point, in the end," added Alnitak and Alnilam.

Mono addressed the witches with an abrupt prideful tone: "There are powers of persuasion that have not been attempted with the mother. Leave it to me."

The witches constricted, all three together, as if they shared the same compassionate thought.

"The mother will give the child over. That is my purpose here." Then Mono's eyes glared into Telas. "Won't she...Telas?"

Mono's scowl resonated in Telas's falling eyes.

Mono stood. "To the chamber," she told the witches. "None are to leave until we have the child."

Telas searched within, closing off the windows and doors in her mind, slamming them shut, finding the dark place where no thought existed.

\* \* \*

Perhaps it was Phil's blood that returned Sandy to the safety camp. Maybe the mind needed to go there, back to the alternate reality, so very different yet all too familiar to present circumstance. But she was there, a passive observer to her and Ben's conversation. Watching the safety camp Sandy, sitting on a wooden pew in a renovated church that housed supplies and food. Buckets, boxes, and bins occupied the church; so many there was little room to navigate to the three rows of pews that remained. Stale wood, dust and neglect stained the air and Sandy sat, thinking, waiting for Ben whom she'd sent for through the grapevine that had become the most proficient means of communication between male and female camps. A small smile complemented the glint in her eyes, her hand on her stomach when the door opened ushering in a gust of cool autumn wind that stirred the stale neglect. Sandy turned, watching as Ben slowly and cautiously closed the door. Her eyes narrow with a wide smile.

"Hey baby," said Sandy with a soft tone. She always called him baby, a reverse nickname since Ben was a decade older.

He walked over, his finger to his lips, and sat beside Sandy.

"You feel it too?" she said referring to Ben's caution.

He leaned in and kissed her, his hand on her stomach. Kissed her with the passion and softness of desperate love. Touched his forehead to hers.

"Missed you so much," he said taking her hand in his leaning back in the pew. "So much I've got to tell you. So much that I've been hearing. Rumors are spreading Sandy." He smiled ear to ear, giddy, excited.

"What is it?" she said, her tone soft, loving.

"A treaty Sandy. They say we've signed a treaty. The war is over." He put his hand to her stomach. "We can go home soon."

He caught the skeptical stare in Sandy's eyes.

"What?" he huffed. "One of those feelings again?"

Ben had always been able to spot Sandy's *feelings*. Like a click in her stomach, instinctive, that changed her demeanor with a deer in headlights stare. Ben had always dismissed those feelings, Sandy's click in the stomach, to paranoia. They'd been together for twelve years after Ben had found Sandy living in a run-down abandoned mall, scared to death and starving. Many homeless refugees had taken up in that mall; which had become a weigh station to buy black market supplies. Ben had gone there after the death of his first wife, to secure formula for his first-born.

Sandy turned her eyes to the floor, escaping his stare.

"Sandy? Did you hear me, we can go home soon."

Her thoughts went to the guard standing on the wall with his arms crossed.

Ben took her chin in his hand and turned her eyes to his. "What is it?"

Sandy forced a smile. Her eyes met his and she shook her head. "Nothing," she said, not wanting to splinter his relief and excitement.

"We can rebuild," he said. "Create a new life."

Sandy's stare drifted. "Like a fairy tale," she said.

"Exactly. Like a fairy tale."

She turned to him; the promise in his eyes was comforting. That's why she wanted to see him, to feel that comfort and continue to wish, wish for this all to be over.

"All that's happened," she said. "All between us, and all that we've seen..." her voice trailed off. She rubbed her palms together. "Perhaps the baby is a part of the new beginning. A symbol that all things have changed for the better and after such a long journey we're finally on a path to freedom. A new beginning in a new world. A place we create for ourselves." She leaned forward; her hands gripped the pew.

"Exactly. Just like we've been waiting for." He wrapped his arm around her shoulders. "Doesn't that sound nice?"

She nodded. "It's all I want. All I dream of."

Sandy quieted, felt that click again and all she wanted was for it to go away. To leave her alone so she could live her life without want, need, or terror.

Ben sighed. "Have you told anyone about the baby?"

Sandy shook her head. "Definitely not."

"Why? I want to run and holler at the top of my lungs that we're having a baby. Why don't you want anyone to know?"

Tight and stiff lipped, she shook her head. "Not now. I just have...."

"One of your feelings?"

Sandy looked at him and nodded. "Yes, I do." She held back the tears.

"Ok," Ben said, and Sandy rested her head on his shoulder. "We won't say anything for now. It's just..." Turned his eyes away, hesitating. "I think what you're picking up on is that they're searching. At least, I think they are. For *what* I don't know but I heard they rounded up the fourth quadrant this morning. Started giving medical tests and asking questions." He stopped and looked, really truly looked at Sandy and her jaw quivered, bottom lip trembled. "I'm sure its nothing," he said. "Maybe they're just getting us ready to leave." He touched his head to hers. Kissed her forehead. "Good thing you're not showing. I hope they let us go before."

"Me too," she said, her eyes closed.

And then bells were ringing, and both snapped their heads to the door. They knew what it meant; an announcement was on its way and all in the camp were required to attend, congregating in the center where the four quadrants merged. Outside the church, people stirred as if a sudden relief had washed over them, talking, shouting...

*A treaty.*

*We've signed a treaty.*

*War is over.*

*We can go home.*

Sandy stiffened and Ben turned to her.

"It'll be all right," he said and smiled. He touched his head to hers. "Everything is gonna be all right."

And behind Ben's voice she heard Phil's guttural grunt. Tasted blood on her lips and tongue, swallowed down the throat. Eyes wide open. Phil was crouched in front of her.

Phil's blood tasted sweet on her tongue, turning her skin warm. She coughed on the final wallop of blood in her throat, and Phil pulled his arm away. She lapped her tongue across her lips and teeth as she looked at Adam, sleeping easy.

Phil moved away, pressing his hand over the wound on his arm. Sandy wondered what he was thinking. She couldn't lock in on his thoughts like before. Everything seemed dark, like she was normal once again, although looking at him he appeared distraught. *Obviously. How could he understand?*

"We should go," Phil said. "Time is running out." He turned to Sandy, offering his hand.

"You still wish to help us?" Sandy took his hand, standing close to him.

"What's happened is of no consequence to me. I was given a task of the highest priority. Robyn will decide what to do once that task is complete." Sandy stared at him, and Phil turned away, assessing their surroundings. "Is that," he paused, unable to hear that Drac voice in his head from before, "vampire still providing direction?"

Sandy registered the question. She hadn't noticed until then that Telas was not with her. She thought, locking in on the last bit of communication she received, remembering how Telas had informed Sandy she had to block her out. And then darkness. The connection lost. Sandy pointed, "This way," she lied and proceeded to move down the hall, trusting her instincts.

Phil moved his head to the right then left, listening and assessing for any possible threat. The corridor was quiet, and he noticed then that the gunfire from above had ceased. He turned to Sandy. "Does the path lead to the floor above?"

Sandy stopped, thinking, the connection had gone dark but she was able to reach back and remember the last direction Telas had given. "Yes," she said. "That's where we're headed now. " She turned to Phil. "Why?"

"When you were...out, I heard gunfire up there. Human gunfire. We are not alone down here. I helped an American soldier when I first arrived; there's a good chance he is up there and with other soldiers too. More than a few rounds were being fired. Question is, who won the battle and who is up there now?"

"And how many?" Sandy said. "If they're on our side they can help us, no?"

Phil paused looking at the baby and Sandy caught his gaze. "Oh. I see."

"People will be afraid," Phil explained. "They won't understand what's happened. I can't even comprehend the how behind all this."

"Then why continue?" she shot back.

Phil looked down then walked towards Sandy. "Is there another way?"

"Not that I know. You're scared yourself," she said.

He stiffened and shook his head. "I don't get scared. I do what's necessary. But here's another point. Whatever happened up there is over."

"Meaning?"

"A few possible scenarios. The humans won and, if so, our enemies will send more to take care of them, putting us in the middle of a human alien battle. Or the aliens won leaving the possibility they are still up there."

"Or?"

"The humans won and are headed for the tunnels."

"How would they know how to get out?"

"Cameron."

She shook her head. "Who?"

"The American. He told me the tunnels would get us out. If that's him up there, I'm sure that's where he's headed."

"So, we'll have more people to help us."

Phil shrugged. "Perhaps."

"A lot of possibilities and perhaps, but it's the only way so let's not stand here thinking it over." She turned and headed down the hall leaving Phil standing wearing a scowl.

"Crazy woman." He shook his head and headed off in Sandy's direction.

**MINTAKA ESCORTED TELAS INTO ZETA'S OXYGEN CHAMBER,** her body gliding, hovering a few feet above ground. Mintaka guided Telas to the floor, gentle and soft. Telas's eyes were opened wide yet revealed darkness where those emerald Drac eyes had been. *You'll return soon, Telas. Soon enough.* This connection between Telas and the human female intrigued the greys, which they dismissed as a side effect to the DNA procedure.

An effect they had not expected.

Mintaka touched Telas's stomach assessing any damage that may prolong her return to consciousness. Going into the dark meant complete shutdown of the mind, although the body continued to operate on instinct.

*Heart and lung damage. Kidney's operating at fifty percent.* She searched further, up to the head. *Oh, my how Mono tore your insides. Lesions on the brain, too. No wonder you're bleeding. Nothing that can't be dealt with medically. Naturally, you'll have difficulties the rest of your days. Seems she's shortened the life span considerably too.* She removed her hand, changing her focus to the wall where the oxygen controls were. *Let's give you the maximum dose.* The controls moved, rising to max level as the hiss of oxygen filled the room.

*See you soon.*

She moved through the door, which closed as she departed, moving through the ship to join Mono and her instructions to Zeta. They had taken up in one of the leisure rooms on the ship. Standing outside the door was Saiph, wearing an obvious stare that reported his disgust over taking orders from a grey.

* * *

Saiph couldn't stomach what was happening. Greys removing Zeta from his healing chambers for their own purpose. He wanted to slice them all to shreds or force them to replace the Drac clan held captive. He was tired of this complete turn of events and power. And what they were suggesting, using Telas to create a vampire human hybrid child burned him to his core. He didn't even have to think about it any longer. Sanos's Dracs were accurate in their assessment. This grey, Mono, killed their brother. What else have they done? What other acts of treason have they committed?

He had not been able to provide his findings to Zeta prior to the grey's disruption. As the door opened, Zeta rushed from the room and Saiph followed him, noticing the apparent frustration in his master's appearance, exiting the ship into the pit where the remaining Thorx army waited, standing in uniform solidarity.

"This situation is becoming useless the longer we stay here," Saiph said. Zeta stopped abruptly. His body trembling beneath his cloak.

Saiph cleared his throat. "Why do we allow this treatment of our brethren? It is clear the greys have engaged in treason at the highest level. I move for us to release the Dracs and secure the greys. We must restore order."

Zeta snapped, thrusting towards him and gripped Saiph's throat in his trembling hand, squeezing the air from his gullet. "Blasphemy," Zeta raged. "Do not question my authority. The greys will have their way, understood?"

Saiph nodded, and Zeta released his throat. He'd never seen his master act in such a way. There had always been respect and admiration, but these events brought all into question. The feel from Zeta's hand on his throat lingered as he stared at his master. Zeta turned away, as if ashamed.

"Secure Sanos," Zeta ordered. "Bring him here to join the others in containment."

Saiph swallowed hard. "What of Kee?" he asked. "Humans in the catacombs must be dealt with prior to departure."

Zeta nodded. "I've sent three lycan to dispatch them."

"Lycan?" Saiph thought of his pets.

"Yes," Zeta said, returning his eyes to Saiph. "Those putrid things you call pets. Why waste more Thorx when the lycan require food and can sniff out humans like no other. Their abilities will end any human threat. They'll seek and devour until all humans have been abolished."

"And if they fail?"

"Then you will find them." He stepped closer to Saiph. "No human is allowed to escape. Knowledge of our presence will cause rebellion not even our human counterparts will be able to stop. Not now. Times are different than they were. Lies and cover ups will no longer be as easy as they were before the war."

Saiph raised his chin in his master's close presence. "What is to become of the Drac Telas and this hybrid abomination the greys have created?"

"Telas will deliver the child to the greys. We are not to leave until the hybrid has been secured and on board."

He couldn't fathom why the child meant so much to the greys and Zeta. "And if she refuses?"

"Then she will die." Zeta walked away, his proclamation lingering. "Secure Sanos on board," he called to Saiph who watched his master re-enter the ship, his body stiff. Anger ran through every bone and muscle. He never would have considered the notion that welled inside him. Not ever before they arrived at this forsaken outpost. It seemed his world had turned upside down. *We're supposed to be fighting for our future. What kind of future are we creating with such abominations and declarations?* He understood the penalty for treason. The penalty was death. But death had become a viable option when considering living in a world where Dracs heeded the orders of grey and human alike.

*The baby means so much to the greys.* The thought of the child filled Saiph's heart with hate. But what could he do? Follow orders he did not agree with? *Not in any possible circumstance should this baby survive.* The thought of its existence shook Saiph to his core, begging the question; did he possess the strength to defy orders and destroy it?

## 30

**WHAT COULD IT POSSIBLY BE?** Cam thought, aiming his AR-15 in the dark. The thump continued. Louder and louder with his approach. *Something's definitely coming.* He clicked on the laser pointer attached to his weapon. The red glow reached down the hall, sweeping across the walls. Breathing heavy, his eyes darting from one wall to the next. And the noise grew, now like a scampering, like multiple feet slapping against the cement floor.

*This is stupid. Just get the hell outta here.*

And then the growl. Multiple growls followed by howls like wolves in a forest. He stopped, his hands trembling. *Now what the hell is that?* Another howl and Cam felt his stomach drop. *Time to go.* He ran back towards the shaft taking one final glance behind him, seeing the silhouette in the dark, running so fast it buckled against the wall but took off again running at him. Howling again as two more silhouettes followed behind.

*Fuckin' wolves.* Cam sprayed bullets down the hall. He must have hit one or two or even all three because a chocked back howl of pain erupted. *Go! Run! Friggin' run!* He darted off rounding the hall into the catacomb. Grimes waited in the hall, gun in hand.

"Get up! Get up! Get up!" Cam hollered.

Grimes shot a look in his direction, and his jaw dropped.

\* \* \*

They were right on top of Cam about to leap at him. Two wolves the size of bulls raced in his direction.

"Drop down," Grimes called holding his gun at Cam. "Drop down NOW!"

Cam slid across the floor, through human and Thorx blood, guts and bones. Grimes shot at the wolves, spraying bullets that tore through them. He hit the first one, the one that had been nipping at Cam's heels, point blank. The beast dropped to the floor, sliding in front of Cam. The second wolf leapt to the fence propelling itself over Cam and the other beast. Grimes stepped back, and the beast dropped to the ground then tore towards Grimes. Its howl was deafening, echoing in the catacomb. Fangs jutted from its mouth as it jumped at Grimes. He ignited a fury of bullets into the beast. Bullets from the shaft tore into the beast too. Lao shot from the shaft as the beast dropped lifeless at Grimes's feet.

Grimes backed off, holding his gun on the beast. Cam jumped up covered in blood. "Is it dead?" Grimes shouted. Cam poked the beast with the barrel of his gun. Shot a few bullets into its body. Shreds of blood, bone and flesh splattered from the body.

Cam looked at Grimes. "Just to be sure," he said. He moved from the beast towards Grimes, moving his head back and forth. "Good shooting."

Lao said something in Chinese.

"English, please," Cam said.

Lao shook his head. "Are you ready to go?"

Cam turned to the shaft. "Is the boy okay?"

"He's fine."

Cam nodded as Grimes crouched in front of the beast studying its features. Cam watched him. "See anything?"

Grimes looked at Cam. His face scrunched with an inquisitive stare. "Werewolves?"

Cam shrugged. "Who knows? Nothing we've ever seen. I mean, we got vampires, alien spaceships, friggin' blood sucking beetles or whatever those things are. That could be anything." He pointed to the wolf. "Why's it matter?"

Grimes stood. "Because, Cam. There's only one way to kill a werewolf."

"But look at it, it's not breathing. It's dead. Don't believe everything you read."

"Gentleman, lets argue later," Lao said. "Hand me your gun, I'll pull you up."

Cam raised his weapon to Lao. He looked at Grimes. "You first," he told him then looked back at Lao whose stare looked beyond Cam to the catacomb.

"What is it?" Cam said. "Lao?"

Lao shook his head. "You need to get up here now."

Cam followed his eyes. Down the hall was another wolf, standing on its hind legs. It reached close to seven feet tall and slammed its paws on the floor, igniting a roar from its snout. Cam's jaw dropped, his eyes wide. The wolf lying in the catacomb started to stir. "Shit!"

"I told you..." Grimes whined. "Only one way to kill a werewolf."

Cam snapped his head to Grimes. They both turned to the beast at his feet. It started to twitch. They looked at each other.

"Let's go, soldiers," Lao hollered reaching his hand to Cam. He took the hand, and Lao hoisted him up. The wolf at the end of the catacomb broke into a run as the two on the ground rose to their feet with a high-pitched howl. Grimes took Lao's hand as the beast jumped at him, barely missing his feet.

"Holy shit," hollered Grimes.

"Can they jump up here?" Lao hollered when the beast gripped the bottom of the shaft hoisting itself up, growling. Lao dropped back into the shaft, tore his 9MM from his leg and shot the wolf between the eyes, tearing a valley across its skull. The wolf dropped back landing with a heavy thud. The two other wolves were on their feet, circling the shaft opening.

"Go!" Lao hollered.

Cam looked at the boy. "Run," he told him pulling the three men to their feet. The boy took off down the shaft followed by the men who followed in line with the boy's quick pace, Cam and Grimes. Lao was the last to follow, looking back at the beast.

"Go right," Cam ordered the boy. He obeyed and they all followed, turning the corner.

Lao looked back. He saw the wolves' paws on the shaft.

\* \* \*

"You hear that?" Phil said; his eyes fixed on the ceiling.

"Of course," said Sandy. "Where's it coming from?"

"The air shaft."

He studied the possibility; all too sure it was Cam in the airshaft.

"What are you thinking?"

Phil turned to Sandy. "You lost connection with the vampire, haven't you?"

Sandy turned stiff. She never told Phil about losing Telas's connection. She couldn't describe what happened. The connection had gone dark. "Yes," she said, nodded then looked down at Adam.

Phil gazed at her and the baby. "Then we need to find a way out. Through the tunnels."

"And you think they know?"

"Cam does. He's been down here before. And there's strength in numbers." He went to the airshaft and jumped up, gripping the shaft's lip with both hands, pulling up, his chin just above the lip, assessing the shaft then dropped back down.

"You do realize they're shooting for a reason, right? There's something up there with them."

Phil shrugged. "Nothing I can't handle."

Sandy stiffened, cradling Adam closer to her chest.

"Stay close. Do what I say when I say it and don't hesitate." Sandy gave a quick nod. "Besides, I think I know what's up there and if I'm right..." He looked up at the shaft and a howl echoed through it. "I know I'm right."

"Right about what? What's in there?"

Phil gripped Sandy by the hips, hoisting her into the shaft, baby and all. "They won't know how to kill it." He jumped up into the shaft.

"It?" Sandy said, watching Phil move down the shaft, assessing their surroundings.

The growl came again. He turned to Sandy and cocked his eyebrows. "Only one way to kill a werewolf."

Sandy's heart dropped. She pursed her lips and whimpered, *"Werewolf?"*

## 31

TELAS FELT OXYGEN SLITHERING THROUGH HER BODY. Heard her own breathing, inhaling slow and steady, exhaling the same. Felt the floor beneath her back aware she was lying down. Saw in her mind's eye how the brain, heart, lungs and kidneys were healing, expanding like a blooming flower. Aware strength was returning, her consciousness rising, thinking clear. She could see the light in the room, although her eyes remained closed. Bulbs of warm light touched her eyelids.

Stay in the dark, she thought.

She knew Mono was about to enter the room. Knew she would use her power to transport Telas from the dark place. To find Sandy and Adam's location. Being in the dark meant complete shut down from the outside world, including Sandy and Adam. She had to restrict all connection to them, bury their thoughts deep in her mind. The more time she could allow to aid in their escape was paramount. Every second counted. The thought of Mono's power raced through her thoughts. She'd never felt a power so strong. Behind the thought existed pain, the agony she experienced in the pit. How her brain twisted igniting a river of blood from her nose, mouth and ears. And the impact the power had on the body, a lingering effect on the threshold of death. She wondered if she had the strength to endure another slaughter.

*But I have to.* The thought of Sandy under Mono's control and Adam's future should Mono break Sandy's will and take the baby existed as a conclusion Telas could not allow. *Not if I can help it.* She didn't notice it at first, but her eyes were wide open. The room now in focus and her heart jumped. *Go back. Find the dark and stay there.*

The door slid open and Telas felt tension constrict her limbs like a dark hand had wrapped her body in an iron squeeze. Struggling to breathe, suffocating, as she lifted off the floor as if an invisible rope connected to her stomach heaved her body with a painful tug, suspended midair. Her eyes wide watching as Mono glided in. Telas could feel it already, the pain inside churning within every drop of blood. Every blood vessel. Every organ. Twisting as if a handmade of pure steel cut through every inch of her existence. She felt sick, nauseous, like acid was boiling in her stomach, stained in the back of her throat.

Telas's eyes roamed over the room. Following Mono were the three greys, forming a circle around Telas. Mono floated closer, those large dark eyes impinging on her thoughts. Telas felt the weight of that stare pushing down on her forehead, across her eyes. Telas struggled, fighting, whining grunts in her throat, forcing her eyes to not look. But the strength was too much, she locked eyes with Mono, witnessing her reflection in those dark eyes, blood ran from her nose and ears streaming across her skin.

"My dear," said Mono in that soft and delicate echoing tone. She bent her head, staring through Telas. "This will not be gentle." Telas felt the pain subside. Felt her insides relax with a relief from pressure. "But it can be quick," Mono continued. "The baby is required, Telas. We know he's in here." Mono touched her finger to Telas's forehead. "We know Dracs can enter the dark." She moved her head back and forth. "Don't try it," she said. "Our patience has run thin." Telas managed to swallow the choke that gripped her throat. She felt sweat on her forehead. A warm sensation tingled her temples, turning hot then ignited into a burning fury. And she felt the squeeze turning over in her skull.

"No matter what you do, the baby will find his way to our arms. Save yourself in this moment. For when he does, he will need you to guide him."

Telas fought through the pain forcing her words between strangled breaths. "Under your rule, Mono. Like slaves." Her eyes narrowed, scrunched from the sting in the center of her brain as if a knife were being twisted in the skull. "Never will I allow such an existence for him."

Mono dipped her head closer, meeting Telas eye to eye. "Slaves you already are."

The pain swelled to a hurried fury. Telas's breathing now a shallow, constricted huff. Eyes fluttering, that knife continuously twisting, shooting anguish into the chest. Muffled grunts popped from her throat. She did all she could to hide what was inside. Fighting, she moved her head through a slaughter comprised with thunderous agonizing vibrations. She saw the greys with stiff eyes projecting into her mind, twisting and churning her insides at their whim. And then she saw light, white light like being blinded by a floodlight. Felt Mono's hand on her forehead. Behind the light she saw the catacomb and two humans entering with caution, their backs to Telas. Sandy and Phil as if they were in the room with them. Telas felt herself move, running towards Sandy like an apparition sneaking up on their prey. The back of Sandy's head, she raced to it, leaping into the mind. And Telas's intermittent grunts erupted in a heavy squawking scream.

"There," said Mono. "There they are."

* * *

Zeta heard the scream, confirmation the greys were tearing Telas apart. He knew torture was a part of war. How many he had tortured himself was beyond his scope of reasoning. *Saiph is right.* His right hand, his student had become his teacher. But there was so much Saiph did not know. Once a Drac became a member of COR the truth was discovered. Part of protocol for new members was a year in hiding. There were two reasons behind this rationale. The first to allow the truth to settle in. Zeta had heard how some members lost their minds under the duress of the truth. The year was spent preparing for service to the larger cause.

Isolation also weeded out any possible uprising or rebellion a Drac might engage in should the connection with their race not be broken. This was the second reason for the year in isolation. Disconnection! In order to serve the purpose, severing any and all connections between a COR member and their Drac counterparts was paramount. But the truth always hid in plain sight through a veil of denial thrown across Drac eyes, but the veil always allowed the truth to slip in when seeing with wide eyes. Denial became a necessary component to the cause. No Drac would continue to fight should they know the absolute truth. Such knowledge was crippling, and order was necessary. Their species depended on it.

*Order.* He walked silently in the pit. Order seems to have been broken in this place. He thought of Saiph and his treatment towards him, remembering when he had held such a strong connection to his race.

Another scream erupted from the ship. He wanted to run into the ship and stop the torture. Knowing he would not for the result would mean his life. And Saiph's. When one member is tried the others stand in judgment with them. Instead his body trembled, watching the ship, listening for another scream.

*Give them what they want, Telas. Stop fighting.*

He knew it was only a matter of time until Telas was broken. The greys were efficient in their ways of torture. He'd never seen anyone resist. Not even he was able to withstand their torment. A common practice during the year in isolation was grey torture; mind manipulation. Greys possessed the ability to break the connection Dracs felt with their species. The same reason why he wasn't helping Telas now, he couldn't. That part of his mind had been obliterated.

*They made us weak. Turned us into...humans!*

The humans in power were all Zeta knew of human existence. They turned his gut with disgust. Deserving of being food and nothing more. Any species that subjugates its own people...

*Does not deserve to inherit the future!*

And then conflict erupted in his thoughts. Zeta put his hand to his lips, thinking, *Is COR not the same?* He felt empty, hollowed out, and the thought that followed, a line of reasoning offered by isolation, shattered in his minds eye. His thoughts now gone, dissipated, and that hollow sensation reached to his brain.

Another scream screeched across the pit. Zeta turned to the Thorx soldiers standing guard. He felt their eyes on him, roaming. Sensed their judgment. They watched his every move. Zeta bowed, pacing.

He thought about Saiph.

And his blood boiled.

## 32

**THEY WERE TRAPPED.**

Cam had ordered them to take a right and once they rounded the corner, they hit a wall, no other way to turn, nowhere to go.

"What now?" said Grimes.

Cam looked in all directions. There was no other way out except going back in the same direction. Behind them a lycan slapped its paws against the cement. Its snarl echoed in the shaft, the thought of being torn apart as a final end to this journey did not sit well with him. None of them had any silver and, even if they got through, those things would still be after them.

"It's useless," Lao said. "We're trapped."

Cam looked at Lao, his eyes registered failure and loss. Saw the boy, huddled in the corner, holding his knees. Then to the men who mimicked the boy.

Two growls down the hall now. Cam walked up beside Grimes. The lycan were down the shaft, snarling and sniffing and growling beneath their breath.

"What're they doing?" Cam said. "They're not attacking?"

Grimes glared at the lycan. "Maybe they like to kill their prey slow," he offered a possible answer. "Take their time with us. Or maybe they're assessing our weapon situation. We did hurt them back there."

"Possible and likely," Cam said. "But we're going through them. It's our only choice."

Cam went to the boy, crouching in front him. "Stay behind and move fast," he told him, locking eyes with the boy. "If we don't make it you keep going. Understood?" The boy nodded. "Don't turn back. Just keep on. Get the hell outta here." He looked at Lao. "U okay?"

"Wonderful," he said, rolling his eyes. He walked over to Grimes.

Cam addressed the boy again. "Stay close to the wall," he said. "Once we start shooting, take off. Got it?" The boy gave a quick and frightened nod. Cam stood up, looking at the lycan. He went to Grimes and Lao. "What's the plan, gentlemen?"

"Shoot and keep shooting."

"Try not to waste ammo," said Lao. "When we get through, we'll need it to fight them off."

The lycan roared standing on all fours one beside the other.

"Where's the third?" Cam said.

"No sign of it. Could be hiding somewhere." Grimes swallowed his breath, wiped the sweat off his forehead. "Keep your wits about you."

"Silver bullets," Cam said. "If we make it, I'll never carry lead bullets again."

"Duly noted, soldier," said Grimes. He cocked his AR15 and the lycan roared again. Cam looked at the boy. "On your feet." The boy obeyed. The men followed.

"Start moving," Grimes said. "Let them make the first move." He took the first step and the lycan roared again, crouching down then jumped towards them, tearing down the shaft.

* * *

Phil heard the gunshots, escorting Sandy through the catacombs, the foul stench still lingering like smoke in the winter wind.

"What is that smell?" said Sandy. She saw the dead deflated human remains scattered across the floor. "Oh!"

"Watch your step," Phil said referencing the ground. "Blood is slippery."

Sandy looked at her feet. The ground was covered with human blood, skin and ground bones. A shattered skull beside her foot. Phil gestured for her to stand still. He went outside the catacomb. The airshaft was open. More gunfire. He looked to the wall seeing the controls to lock and open the gates to the catacombs. Then turned back to Sandy.

"What do you see?" she said, her voice soft. Phil went to her.

"They're up there. We haven't much time." He took Sandy's hand leading her beyond the fence.

"What're you doing?"

"You'll be safe here."

"Are you nuts? You're leaving us?"

Phil shook his head. "I'll be back. I can't take the chance of stray bullets or those lycan getting you. They can sniff out a baby, and there's nothing better than a baby meal to them."

Sandy looked at Adam. Phil led her to the corner closest to the fence, out of sight should anyone come down the corridor. "Stay here and don't move." He looked up. More gunfire. "This won't take too long."

Sandy's eyes widened. She held Adam tight, and Phil rushed out. He slammed the lock control and the fences started moving. Took one look at the airshaft and jumped up, pulling himself in.

# 33

WHEN SAIPH UNLOCKED THE DOOR to the chamber where he'd put Sanos he still did not have a plan. Wasn't sure what to do. The door slid open. Sanos was sleeping, his breathing shallow yet heavy. Sanos had come completely back to Drac form. No longer a monster. Saiph tapped his forehead, and Sanos's eyes drifted open.

"Get up," ordered Saiph. He walked the chamber. Watched the door close. Looked back at Sanos. His eyes were wide open and staring. He forced himself to sit up, leaning his head against the wall.

Saiph crouched in the corner, watching him. Sanos went to touch his forehead but his wrists were still bound. He grumbled under his breath. "Where are my men?"

"What do you care?"

Sanos moved his head and glared at Saiph. "Because they are my men."

Saiph snarled. "Men whom you allowed to be poked and prodded like dogs?" Sanos leaned back looking away. His body trembling. "Men whom you allowed to come under the thumb of a grey? And you a ninth. It's disgraceful what you've done here."

Sanos snapped his head to Saiph, snarling. "Foolish counterpart to Zeta." He moved his head back and forth, deep breath, stretched his back. "You know nothing. You're as much a slave as I."

Saiph stood, hovering over Sanos. "I want answers."

"Answers to what?" Sanos growled.

Saiph paused looking him over. "To what's happened here. To why you would allow your men to be subjected to experimentation. I want to know, Sanos...what could have possibly happened for you to turn your back on your brethren."

"For what purpose? You stand behind Zeta under false pretense. Why would I tell you anything?"

"Because," Saiph said, "I'm your one hope at redemption."

Sanos paused, staring at Saiph as a wide smile graced his lips. He started laughing. "Looks like the cat's *finally* coming out of the bag."

* * *

They broke Telas, penetrated the dark place, and gained control. Telas knew it too, lying there, suspended in midair, covered in blood. Her eyes looking. Looking at Mono and the other greys, completely at their mercy. Aware of their presence. Aware they were inside that special place in the mind that no one was allowed to go, nevertheless they were there. They were there, and Telas was not. Now she was cut off from the dark place.

Mono looked at the witches. "She's in the catacombs." Mono squeezed her fist mere inches above Telas's navel, shooting pain to her brain, and Telas coughed blood over her lips. "Baby is with her."

Mono's eyes closed. "And there's more." The witches moved closer.

"More?" said Mintaka who looked at the other greys. They all glanced at each other as if recognizing they all heard the same.

"A human," she said. "And he has the blades." She just about laughed. Would have laughed if greys ever did laugh. Instead she squeezed again, holding her tight fist trembling over Telas. Pain kept Telas from returning to the dark place, allowing Mono to slip in without resistance. And to stay.

"We decided correctly. Sealing off tunnel exits. That is where they are headed. And oh, look at this. He's left her alone!"

Alnitak and Alnilam locked eyes, saying together, "So foolish."

"Assume baby is with her?" Mintaka asked.

"Assume correctly."

"Where is the human male?" said Alnitak and Alnilam.

Another squeeze brought Sandy's thoughts to Mono. "More humans." Her revelation brought cautionary stares from all three greys. "He's gone to provide assistance to their escape."

"He requires passage to the tunnels," Mintaka said.

"Yes!" Mono answered.

"Because of the dark place," Alnitak and Alnilam continued. "Who is this human with the blades?"

Mono squeezed again. Telas's head dropped back, her chest raised as a painful groan rose in her throat. Mono searched, finding Sandy's thoughts. Phil flashed in her mind. The escape from the camp. The hotel. His lips moving but his words were quiet. Mono tipped her head. Searching. Inquiring. Seeing them in the hotel. Phil's lips revealed the name.

*Robyn Winter!*

Mono screamed, grabbing her skull. She stepped back, her brain twisting as if a knife had been plunged into her skull. "Can't be," she hollered. "Can't be true. *Can't be true.*" She covered her eyes. The witches locked eyes. Mono saw the scarred face of Robyn Winter. His emerald eyes staring as if he were in the room and watching their every move. Mono let go, released her hold on Telas, her hand shivering. She leaned over, drawing air down her throat, huffing and whining until the breath was calm. She stretched her neck, standing tall as a thick wallop of purple blood dripped from her non-existent nose across her top lip. "How is it possible?" Mono whined, scolding the witches. Robyn Winter had been a declared enemy to Mono's greys for centuries.

"If he's alive," Alnitak and Alnilam revealed, "Then there is one conclusion." They locked eyes. Their bodies relaxed as if some under the surface respite had brought relief.

Mintaka stiffened. Her voice constricted and hoarse. "Transcendence."

Mono touched her forehead, reeling, bringing herself back to the task at hand. "Preparations must be made." She gawked at the witches. "You've never spoken of Winter's involvement." She pursed her lips, ground her jaw. "I am not pleased."

"Transcendence hides within the Akashic Record," said Mintaka.

The witches spoke together, "We were not aware."

Mono wiped the blood from her nose, standing stiff, an angry vibration writhing off her skin.

Mintaka spoke first, "The enemy of our enemy is our friend, Mono."

"The human must be obtained," said Alnitak and Alnilam. "Should we send Zeta's counterpart to secure him?"

"No need," Mono said. She leaned into Telas focusing all the anger that had walloped and blindsided everything Mono had known in her grey lineage against Telas. Mono's greys always responded to such revelations with sheer telepathic torture. "He will follow the baby." Her eyes widened. "And she will come to us." Her hand hovering over Telas's navel. She squeezed her fist and the room rattled with a thunderous vibration. Telas constricted, her head snapped back as her chest jumped. And her scream tore through the ship as if Mono wanted Sandy to feel that pain too. There would be no reprieve. Mono's grip shook the ship with a fierce rumble, igniting a second even more ferocious scream.

Mono was not pleased. Not pleased indeed.

# 34

**THE LYCAN BACKED UP.** To the surprise of Cam and the others, the bullets must have had an impact. Or are they biding time for something else?

Knowing the bullets would only wound briefly; there was no reason to unload. Not until they jumped.

"Why are they not attacking?" said Grimes. The lycan snarled and snapped but did not leap.

Cam kept his gun on them. Glaring. He looked at the boy then back to lycan. They were looking at him. Like they waited for his command. "I think it's the boy," he said. "Keep moving."

They moved closer. Step by step. Guns pointed. Lycan growling.

"It's like they're confused." Lao looked at the boy. Heavy breath. He pointed his rifle at the boy, and the beasts growled.

"What're you doing?" Cam shouted.

"It *is* the boy." Lao said. "Why would they be protecting him?" He withdrew his weapon, aiming at the lycan.

Cam and Grimes locked eyes.

"Because," Cam said, "He's a vampire."

The beasts snarled, huddled close to each other, sniffing. One took off in the opposite direction. The other blocked their entrance down the hall.

* * *

The information was conflicting. First Sandy heard Telas's voice telling her to continue on and to be fast. To get out. Then the voice changed, but it was still Telas. Calling her. Wanting Sandy to join her in the pit. That she'd found a better way out. To come immediately before the window of opportunity vanished.

Sandy searched the fence. She was locked in with no possible way out. *I can't.* She sent the thought hoping her plea would reach Telas. She looked down on Adam, sleeping snug next to his mother.

She thought of Phil. *He'd never allow me to go.* The thought then came. She tried it before, paralyzed on the bed after they took the baby. Unable to move, she tried the rose but couldn't bring the power to fruition.

*I've got to try.* "Telas needs us with her," she said to Adam. Looked around the room. The floor covered with human skin. Some on top of each other, lined in thick heaps, deflated but there were so many of them. Their eyeballs missing. No teeth. No bones, only skin. And the smell clung to the air. Looking at the dead skin the smell was even more putrid. A reminder that these carcasses had once contained life. The stench corroded organs, blood and veins. She thought of sitting to relax her body before attempting the rose. *Not happening.* She closed her eyes trying to find that place in her mind. Trying to see the rose. To bring it out into the open. To feel it, as Phil had explained.

Tried to forget where she was.

*See the rose. See beyond it.* She brought the picture into her thought. The rose outside the fence. Prominent. She traced every curve, every lapel, circling into its center. Felt the connection in the center of her mind, manipulating the space between herself and the projection. Sensing the light envelope her body. Seeing the fence begin to disintegrate.

And then a scream. Telas screamed inside Sandy's mind. She lost the connection as her heart jumped. Her eyes shot open.

"Telas!" Sandy mumbled.

There was a hole in the fence, but she lost the vision, lost the power. Felt it filter from her body and was gone. Tears welled in her eyes. "I'm sorry, Telas." She choked back the cry. Frustration welled in her throat.

And then a growl as a lycan emerged in the hall, slapping its paws on the ground. Sniffing and snarling. Sandy caught its eyes. Black to the core surrounded by a deep pale yellow that turned almost empathetic. Sandy cocked her head, watching this beast climb to its hind feet hovering above her then its claws swiped the hole in the fence tearing it apart.

Sandy felt a release. Her body fell loose. The beast dropped to all fours, staring. And then the beast bowed.

* * *

Phil heard the snarls and growls. He broke into a run hoping the beasts hadn't devoured Cam and whoever he was in the shaft with. There's so much they don't know. So much they don't understand. Things that have been hiding in plain sight for centuries. Even longer, as Robyn had always taught. Beneath the surface another world existed. Maybe we weren't ready. Maybe denial has its benefits. Ignorance is bliss they say. But ignorance allows the enemy time to develop and implement their plan.

Another snarl. Slapping paws against cement. But closer. Much closer. *It's coming this way.* The shaft was dark, but he could see it coming. Hear it and smell it. That foul stench of werewolf body and hair wafting through the shaft.

He stopped, peering into the darkness that revealed two pale yellow eyes.

*Clever beast!*

He gripped the handles in his palms. Tightened his body, staring down the beast. It stepped from the darkness. Roared at him, slapping its paws.

"C'mon," Phil roared back. The beast stood on hind legs, towering in the shaft seven feet high. It clenched its paws then roared again. Phil moved his head back and forth. "No matter what," he said. "I'm getting through." He bowed taking up his fighting stance. "Your move!"

The beast took a few steps back. Stretched its neck and roared at Phil. He didn't waver nor move. Holding steadfast glaring at the beast. "Werewolves," he said. "Always flexing and barking." He tipped his head. "You gonna bite or stand there?"

The beast broke into a run, tearing at Phil. "About time." He ran at the beast. *They always jump.* It roared again. Phil timed the beast's leap, dropping to the ground as it jumped at him, sliding across the floor and driving his blade across its body, from the throat down, splitting the beast's skin and bones, then jumped to his feet. The beast squealed dropping on the ground. Its insides emptied into a pool of blood and intestines. It let out a final whimper, attempting to get up, to rise to its feet but flopped down with a thud, unmoving. It ceased movement. Dead in a pool of blood!

Phil closed his eyes and bowed.

When he turned, a second set of yellow eyes greeted him. Jumped on him, taking his head in its paws. Slamming him against the wall then tossed Phil into the corridor; he jumped up, his back to the beast that slashed its claws across his shoulder, tearing flesh and bone. Phil hollered and winced, stumbled and fell face first.

Quickly he rolled over, trying to regain his wits as the beast growled a long sinister howl. Phil's shoulder dropped, weak and draining blood. Managed to get to his feet. The beast was behind him, slammed into him and he flew forward. Crashed against the ground and slid to the dead werewolf. Phil's head weary. His eyelids heavy. Struggling to breathe.

The beast snarled. Took slow steps towards him.

# 35

**"WHERE DID IT GO?" CAM SAID.** The beast blocking their way took off. They all exchanged confused stares.

"Who cares?" Grimes said. "Let's get outta here."

Cam looked at the boy. Then the men huddled close to the boy. He heard a growl somewhere down the corridor in the darkness. Cam turned, staring down the hall. "Phil?" he said under his breath.

"That guy?" said Lao.

Cam looked at his AR-15. Pulled out his clip. About half full. Slammed the clip back in. Took a look at the boy. "Get them out of here," he told him. The boy nodded and Cam took off, down the hall after the beast.

"Where are you going?" Grimes hollered. "Are you out of your mind?"

But Cam didn't respond. He had a debt to repay.

* * *

His left shoulder swelled, throbbing and pulsating as blood jutted from the wound. The beast was approaching, assessing Phil's weakness. It moved to the side, to Phil's unwounded side.

The beast howled at him. Phil could sense the beast's heart was jumping. It licked its lips. Its long tongue lapped across its teeth and jaw. Phil forced himself up, favoring his left arm. Feeling weary. His loss of blood was turning his skin pale.

Phil attacked the beast, attempting to swipe his blade across its snout, hoping to catch any part of its body. But the beast snapped at him, tossing him against the opposite wall. The back of his head slammed, his neck snapped. The beast stood tall, growling and snarling. It tightened its claws and raged a howl at Phil, its final howl before tearing into him. Phil fell to his knees. He couldn't feel his left arm, lying limp at his side. The beast stepped to the side. Its eyes opened wide.

*Got to get closer.* He swallowed his labored breath. His heart thumping like a rabbit in his chest. He thought of Sandy. Thought of the baby. How will they make it? *Can't let it happen.*

The beast circled him. Dropped to all fours.

*This is it.*

The beast jumped as a hail of bullets tore into it. Its momentum thrown to the wall. Phil jumped, spinning, catching the beast's throat with his blade. He felt dizzy and dropped to the floor. He saw Cam at the end of the corridor. Rifle in hand. The beast choked on its blood, grasping at its throat, garbling. Its large body fell dead between Cam and Phil, hitting the ground with a slumped heavy thud. And then a screeching howl erupted, echoing through the shaft. Phil's eyes widened. The howl came from the catacomb.

"*Sandy!?*"

\* \* \*

She mounted the beast with a nervous hush, cradling Adam. The beast sniffed and snarled. Gunshots from the airshaft and she wondered about Phil. *Would he survive?* The beast turned and howled.

Sandy felt Telas. In pain. On the brink of death. "We must go," she told the beast. It sniffed, raising its giant snout towards the airshaft, then bared its teeth, growling. Sandy saw Phil in the airshaft, staring at her. Blood ran down his arm. He looked weak and pale. His sunken eyes revealed betrayal.

"I'm sorry," she whispered. She gripped the wolf's fur, the thick abrasive mane that ran across the beast's spine. Took one last look at Phil. She gave a slow nod. Her eyes closed as if to say thank you. Then she tugged the mane as if it were the reins guiding the beast. The lycan leapt down the catacomb, turning the corner and was gone.

\* \* \*

Phil couldn't believe what he witnessed. *Sandy with a lycan?* And they took off in the opposite direction. Back towards the pit. He dropped down to his knees. The pain in his arm immense and throbbing. He felt weak. Blood drained from his face.

"You okay?" Cam stood behind him.

Phil flopped back, leaning against the wall, slid down carefully and slowly. With a heavy struggling breath, he pursed his lips and forced air down his throat. His right arm trembled, reaching behind his back, squeezing his thick fingers into his belt. He gripped a small vial between his fingers. Breathed deeply. Squeezed the bottle's contents over his wound. His face constricted. A grunt and wince. The medicine healed on contact, sealing the wound. He could feel it, tightening around his arm, although the pain remained.

Cam took a knee in front of him. "That was the girl you were looking for?"

Phil nodded. "Yes," he said through a painful grunt.

Cam bent his head, eyes wide, thinking. "Why?" he said. "Why would she leave like that?"

"It's complicated," said Phil, studying Cam. Noticing his answer didn't register. "Has to do with the baby." Phil observed the catacomb from the corner of his eyes.

"Baby?" Cam asked. "There's a baby?"

Phil turned to him. "She was pregnant when we arrived. They took the baby from the womb."

"Oh," Cam said, his eyes narrowed, then shook his head. "What?"

"Like I said, complicated."

"You're telling me." Cam offered his hand helping Phil to his feet.

"How are they dead?" said Grimes. The rest of the crew behind him. Grimes poked the dead lycan with his rifle.

Phil noticed the crew for the first time. "Dipped in silver," he said referencing his blade.

Grimes cocked his head. "Only one way to kill a werewolf."

Cam turned to Phil. "What's your plan?"

"They'll take her to the pit." Phil surveyed the airshaft, looking left then right then locked eyes with Cam. "I can get there from here?"

Cam nodded. "Yes," he said. "But... they're all down there. UFOs, cricket blood sucking creatures, and who knows what else." He shook his head. "The odds are not on your side."

Phil paused, thinking. Looking over Cam and the others. Seeing the boy and the men who stood close behind him. "On the second floor there's another corridor with humans held captive."

Lao stiffened, listening to Phil. He stepped closer.

Phil turned to Cam. "Can you get them out with you?"

"Distraction?" Lao, he cocked his head. "But then they'll be on us. We don't have the ammunition to risk it."

"Then we go down fighting," Cam shot back eyeing the crew. He turned to Phil. "I'll get them." Then to Lao and Grimes. "You get the boy and these men out. I'll meet you at the tunnels end."

"Split up?" said Grimes. "You know there's safety in numbers. We should stay together."

"How many are there?" Cam asked Phil.

"Not sure. Twenty maybe."

"Are they coherent?"

Phil's brow curled, puzzled.

"Like those men there..." Cam gestured to the men standing behind the boy. "They're incapacitated. They did something to them. These men can only follow orders; they haven't spoken a word since we found them."

Phil cocked his head. "The others were quite verbal." Phil noticed the boy, gestured to him. "Is he all who's left from the wall?"

Cam clenched his jaw, gritted his teeth and nodded. "Yes," he said, then continued, "Everything above is completely gone. Every-one and everything." He pursed his lips and swallowed. "They've got a small army down there." He stared at Phil. "You're walking into a possible catastrophe."

Phil surveyed his arm, the medicine tightening around his wound. The blood had stopped. The wound sealed. He could sense the feel of his arm again. Stretched the limb above his head. "Which way?" he asked.

Cam pointed to the left, down the airshaft. "Just follow it down. It'll take you to the pit. You'll be able to see everything from there."

"Okay." Phil went to the boy. Took his chin in his hand. He forced a smile. "Trust your instincts," he told him. His statement brought confused stares from Grimes and Lao. The boy nodded.

Cam stepped to Phil. "Is she worth it?"

Phil dropped his head then eyed Cam.

"Guess so," Cam said.

"After you get the others out, don't look back. Just go. I'll find you. Head to Atlanta. Ask for Robyn Winter. Tell him what you've seen here."

"How can we trust them? What guarantee do we have that they won't ambush us?" Lao asked.

Phil looked at him. "You're human," he said. "They'll see you coming from miles away. They'll find you. All you have to do is enter Atlanta." Phil turned to leave.

Lao stepped forward. "Are they able to provide passage to China?" His voice shaking, desperate.

Phil turned to Lao, seeing desperation in his eyes. Cleared his throat. "We lost communication with our people in China before the treaty was signed. I'm not sure...but if anyone knows how to get you home, it's Robyn." He studied Lao who dropped his head. "You'll make it to him. Good luck." He addressed all of them. "Good luck indeed."

"Phil," Cam said stepping closer. "You know we don't have much time. Sun's coming up soon."

"That's why you've got to move fast. There's no telling what could happen. Get them out and go. Get out of the tunnel, and don't look back."

Phil and Cam exchanged knowing stares.

"Thank you," said Cam "For everything."

Phil returned with a quick nod, a slight bow then took off down the airshaft.

"He's as good as dead," Grimes said. "There's no way he can fight all of them." He turned shaking his head. "No way at all."

Cam ignored the statement, watching Phil disappear. "Ya know, Corporal...I've noticed you're a bit negative."

Grimes shook his head. "Friggin' aliens everywhere, and I'm negative." He took up his AR-15. "Ok, Cameron," he said. "How do we get out of here?"

Cam turned to him. Looked at the boy, the men and Lao. "First things first," he said. "We're going to need more guns."

# PART THREE

# AND-HERE-
# WE-GO!

# 36

"LET'S TEST THAT RESOLVE OF YOURS..." said Saiph, crouched down against the wall and scowling at Sanos. He took a pill from his belt; placed it on the floor away from Sanos's reach. "Leave things to fate...so to speak."

Sanos's jaw tightened. His throat bulged forcing his breath down his throat, staring wide-eyed at the pill in front of him.

"See how much you truly want your revenge." Saiph stood looking down on Sanos who took his eyes off the pill, returning Saiph's gaze.

"You're not going to release me?"

Saiph moved his head back and forth. "No. I'll give you a fighting chance, but personally speaking you turn my stomach. What you've allowed to happen to your people. They trusted you, and you tossed them off like lab rats." He went to leave, knowing that once he walked out the door there was no turning back. Disobeying a direct order, and what he was about to do...there will be heavy implications for him and his master. But he'd become sick with the entire scenario. There was one thing left to do, even if it meant death, which he was sure it would, either here or once he was taken up by COR. Death for Zeta too, who would not go down without a fight.

"You understand though?" Sanos said. "The implications? The path you're about to take? You know where it leads?"

Saiph turned to him. "All I know is that the baby must not leave this forsaken place. Whether what you're saying is true or not, that child is a disgrace to all Drac. It must not live to see the light of day."

Sanos pursed his lips. "What will you do?"

"Release your men. No Drac who's suffered such a fate should have to face death without the chance to fight for their freedom. Then I'll seek out the child. No matter where it takes me, no matter what I must endure, I will not stop until that child has been wiped out of existence."

"That may require killing Drac," Sanos said. "Neither Telas nor your master will allow it."

"If they are as blind and corrupt as you proclaim, then they will perish as well."

"They'll ostracize you. All Drac will deem you a traitor. Your legacy will be written in the Drac archives as such. An example of mutiny."

"That's merely semantics, Sanos. We all die. Die knowing you've made a stand against tyranny. A soldier's death is served riches in the netherworld."

Sanos shook his head, huffed and said, "Sure, Saiph." He met Saiph's eyes. "Everything is a lie."

Saiph stiffened. "Be as bold, Sanos, to see the truth behind the lie. There is always truth at the core. It's the lies that hide the truth."

Sanos turned from Saiph. His voice low and defeated. "We are nothing more than simple holograms in a twisted mind." He bared his teeth and jerked his wrists twice, testing his restraints. "At the whim of a madman. It doesn't matter what we do when the creator has already plotted our actions. All else is self-indulgence discovered to give entertainment to sensation. Like a writer who allows his characters to think, knowing that in the next chapter that life will disappear...disappear and be gone like a sick joke."

"Shared pain, Sanos. Creation is a gift to the masses."

Sanos leaned his head to the wall. "But a game played under the thumb. Bending to the insatiable appetite of omnipresence. All has been written. It only matters which story we take into our arms. Which mind allows us to thrive. Every being wishes to prosper, the light is never enough. It's merely a part of the lie that's been streamed into a state of consciousness, covering truth to be revealed within. A lie that continues in a never-ending cycle. Like a trap door leading back to ignorance." He looked at Saiph. "Think of the lies told before the war. Think of how history has defined these humans. History stripped down and rewritten with intention for the writer's benefit. Do you think we are immune? All is simple fodder to feed the larger mind. The truth hides in plain sight. This is the way and the way encapsulates the reach of fiends."

"Minds within the one mind, that is all, Sanos."

Sanos laughed. "You don't believe a word I said, do you?"

"I think you took too many of those pills. Your mind is warped."

"Trust your eyes, Saiph. Trust your instincts. That's where you'll find the truth."

Saiph opened the door. Looked back at Sanos. "Stay and rot," he told him. "For all I care your story comes to an end soon. We Dracs are the future. We make our own."

"If the future is full of darkness, yes, you are correct."

No response. Saiph walked from the room. The door closed behind him. He never so much as offered a glance back.

# 37

**MONO TURNED TO THE WITCHES. TELAS** hovered midair beneath Mono's hand. "She comes," said Mono.

"Will she hand the child over willingly?" asked Mintaka.

Mono searched Sandy's thoughts. "She will not," her voice just above a whisper. Her eyes closed, continuing to rifle through Sandy's reflections.

Alnitak and Alnilam exchanged stares. "It's best the child be handed over freely."

Mintaka shared their sentiment. "Yes," she said. "It will circumvent so many years of programming should the mother relieve duty of the child."

Mono quivered taking in a scene from Sandy's memory. She clenched her fist. The action brought a groan from the now unconscious Telas. "The connection between these two is strong," she said. "It will be difficult to break."

Mono continued to search, moving her head back and forth as if scanning pictures and thoughts, scenes and circumstances, dismissing those that did not serve her purpose. Searching and gathering information.

"We will offer riches," Mono said. "Humans are always privy to status. Treat her like a queen," she continued earning glares and gazes from the witches. "The illusion will keep her married to us. The child will listen. So much easier to conform. Old tricks," Mono said. "Such an offering can happen quickly. We have the technology here on the ship."

"What of this one?" Mintaka said. She referred to Telas.

"Death closes on her," Mono replied. "Her resolve is unique for a Drac. A change that will require further exploration."

"Much to do," Mintaka added.

"Have you secured her, Mono?" asked Alnitak and Alnilam.

"Yes," Mono said. "Telas answers to me now. Sandy approaches. Prepare the ship as discussed. I will take Telas to meet Sandy."

The three witches bowed. They floated from the room. Mono released her hold on Telas. She dropped to the floor with a thud. Her eyes shot open and she winced. Her eyes revealed confusion as she looked over the room. She pinched the bridge of her blood-covered nose. Weary, she clambered to her knees, attempting to maintain balance. Her body trembled, movement disproportionate as if every slow undertaking contained pain. Her hands shook. Her head wavered back and forth.

She vomited over the floor. Telas slumped over. Her eyes wet. She coughed and gagged. Mono moved her head back and forth. "Putrid," she said. "Putrid and foul, Telas."

Telas wavered, looking over the room, looking for Mono. She flopped back. Staring, moving her head to see.

"Sandy approaches," Mono told her. "We will have the child soon." She put her hand on Telas's shoulder. "You are dying, Telas. Truly only a matter of time. The slow struggling beat of your heart. Your organs rotting. Disintegrating. Polluting the body with toxicity. Do you feel it?" she asked. "Do you know you're about to die, Telas?"

Telas started to wheeze, the oxygen brought into her lungs restricted. Like breathing through a straw. "Yes," she managed to say, squeezing the word over her lips.

Mono smiled. "Good," she said. "Good, Telas."

Telas's head floated back and forth, her eyes like wet slits. She dropped her head back, leaning against Mono.

"You do not have to choose death, Telas. I can bring you back to health. It is in my power to do so." She touched Telas's temples, holding her head. "But you must offer the child to us. You know as well as I only one parent needs to provide the offering. Do so now, and I will spare Sandy and yourself. You may live a long life of luxury. Raising the child." She forced Telas's head back. Stretching the bones and tendons, choking the throat, to meet her eyes with her own. "Your one and only chance, Telas." She squeezed her temples.

Moved her head closer, their eyes a centimeter from the other. "You must answer, Yes or NO!"

Telas grumbled, her throat stretched and choking. Forcing the answer from the throat, to her lips. "Never."

Mono snapped Telas's head forward. "I thought as such. Dracs and humans. So similar yet so different." She gripped the back of Telas's neck and shoulders. "I do give Dracs an upper hand over humans when it comes to honor. But humans are easier to break. I doubt your Sandy will have the same resolve." She felt Telas drop forward, her head down, unmoving. Mono tipped her head, looking over Telas. "Out again. Oh dear, but you are required. Your presence will put Sandy at ease. Come, Telas..." Mono put her hand to the back of Telas's head, the other on her forehead. She squeezed. A black mist enveloped Telas's skull between Mono's hands. Telas's body shook. Her eyes rolled to the back of her head. Her lips quivered. "There we go. Into the darkness. Do you see the translucent wavering around you? Do you sense the dread? Severing your conscious thought from the body." The black mist fluttered inside Telas's eyes. Like a snake slithering around its prey circling those emerald pupils. "You'll adhere to my commands now. Your body will be in my control."

Mono laughed. "I'll even have you kill Sandy. Maybe drain her blood like I told you. Such deaths are always exciting to witness." The black mist was close to consuming Telas's eyes. "Good-bye, Telas," Mono said when the black mist covered the eyeballs. "Enjoy the little time you have left in bondage."

Telas's eyes were jet black, like metallic blinders had covered the eyes. Mono released her hands. "Rise," she said. Telas obeyed. "Good, dear." The door opened and Mono floated to it. "Stay close," Mono said. "I'll provide instruction as needed."

Telas followed Mono to the pit, where they waited for Sandy.

* * *

Sandy balanced herself, holding the lycan's mane with one hand and securing Adam with the other. *She wants me to flee?*

The thought had come in fast disappearing a moment after. Sandy knew Telas was in pain, sending signals to flee than to return to the pit. The lycan was offered for safe and quick passage. Now as they came to the pit's entrance, she pulled back on the mane, and the lycan stopped.

She wondered about Phil. Knowing he would be in attendance, somewhere in the pit. Phil was not the type to run or to give in, even though the odds were not in his favor. *Nor mine!* The ships and Thorx standing guard in the pit seemed like plastic soldiers in a child's imagination.

Sandy dismounted the lycan, glaring into the pit. She looked to Adam, caressing his forehead. "Good baby," she said. "Good, good baby."

They want Adam, Telas had said. They won't stop until he is with them.

Except the next thought challenged the notion. They're killing me. If you don't come I am doomed.

It was a command Sandy could not fight. She felt her body move as if someone else was in control of her body. She knew returning would be best. She could save Telas and keep Adam. *What does it matter, now, as long as we are in control? What does any of this truly matter? To live is to live. And what existence would we have with Phil and rebellion. No life to live at all.*

*No. It's better this way. Better with Telas.*

She held Adam close as she stepped towards the pit. The lycan moved by her side. She could feel her body, gliding to the pit. Heard her thoughts, rattling in her skull. Conflicting messages. But one message rang most prominent. *I must protect it.* She felt the heat from the pit rise in her nostrils. Her skin pale and damp with perspiration. What she'd heard from Telas before the dark had come had emerged from Telas's core and was not something she'd thought, said or felt but derived from basic instinct.

*We can defeat them...together.*

## 38

SAIPH WAITED OUTSIDE ZETA'S PRIVATE CHAMBERS; a mercury built oval room on one of the ships. Mercury was a conductor allowing for telepathic communication over a large area. He was communicating with COR, providing information on the current state of events. Part of Zeta's responsibility was to keep COR informed and up to date. Something Saiph anticipated. *Got to look in his eyes.*

He would have preferred to be a fly on the wall while Zeta communicated with COR. Had his master become aware of Saiph's plan? Did he anticipate what Saiph was about to do? The connection he felt to Zeta was strong, had been in the years he'd followed him. Taking on the role of COR member counterpart was considered a high honor, climbing the ranks into COR lore as he'd always wished. But in his time with Zeta he'd come upon what would become a familiar sensation. That COR was hiding a secret. Manipulating Dracs to serve personal interests. An act he had considered to be uniquely human.

Dracs should be held to a higher standard, such masters of the universe should not behave in this manner. No secrets should be kept from our species. One Drac for all. Any deterrent from this philosophy should be considered treason. He could have laughed at this notion, considering his current plan. But treason is in the eye of the beholder. History will judge my actions depending on which side writes the story.

The door slid open. Zeta emerged, walking a hurried anticipation.

"Master, I bring bad news," Saiph said following Zeta. "Sanos has evaded us. He's escaped."

Zeta stopped, turned to Saiph. "How?" Zeta asked. "You secured him with Drac steel?"

"Of course."

Zeta stepped closer. "No Drac has ever escaped from such steel." His eyes narrowed. Saiph felt Zeta's inquiry. His skeptical and questioning probe.

"Perhaps we've underestimated him."

Zeta was quiet, thinking, looking over Saiph.

"Should you provide COR with the update?"

Zeta looked back to his chamber. "I've already provided the necessary details. It's of no consequence." He stepped to Saiph. His hands on his shoulders. "You will seek him out, Saiph." They locked eyes and Saiph felt a sliver of uneasiness jolt down his body. "Kill him," Zeta said. "He's caused enough misfortune."

Saiph raised his chin. "Should he not stand in front of COR?"

Zeta moved his head back and forth. He squeezed Saiph's shoulders then turned from him. "No," he said. "COR will declare him insane and call for his execution. We will save them time to focus their efforts on more pressing matters."

"Pressing matters?" Saiph inquired.

Zeta clasped his hands behind his back. He nodded. "COR is in receipt of Dr. Blum's research." He stepped from Saiph who followed behind. "It appears that the doctor was close, very close to achieving his required task, but there are effects we did not anticipate. It will take time to set right the unanticipated."

"But we were so close."

Zeta stopped walking. His eyes glinted as he gave a quick nod. "So close we could taste it, like human blood on our lips." He looked up as if he could see through the ship, outside the cave and above the earth into the stars. His gaze returned to meet Saiph. "Take Sanos, Saiph. Be done quickly and make sure of it. I want to know for certain he is dead before we depart. Knowing his taste for human blood I'm sure he's following the scent of the lycan."

"Lycan?" Saiph said. "Have they not returned?"

Zeta shook his head. "Only one." He turned his back to Saiph, moving to the ship's ramp towards the pit.

"How is that possible? My lycan are efficient."

"I anticipated their demise, Saiph," Zeta said. "You could ask your surviving pet." They came to the ramp where Zeta stopped.

He turned to Saiph. "He's with the greys," he laughed. "Torturing that human girl."

"She's here?" Saiph's eyes lit up. "The one with the child?"

"Don't look so anticipatory, Saiph. It doesn't suit you. The greys require the baby. For their purposes their job is much easier should the human dissolve the instinctive connection with the child. She must hand it over willingly."

"Where are they?" Saiph said.

Zeta paused. He turned to the pit and gestured to the ship outside. "In there," Zeta said. "They are all in there."

*She came freely? Why?* He turned to Zeta. "Telas?"

"With the greys," Zeta said. "She works with them now."

Saiph understood what that meant. Telas was under their control and more than likely, not willingly either. His blood boiled. "I move to strike?" he said with immediate regret. His declaration meant he requested putting a stop to the greys current dealing, to maintain order among Dracs in an effort to free one of their own. In spite of any larger advancement, the life of one Drac was considered as sacred as all Dracs'.

Zeta's face turned to a scowl. "You will not!"

"Master, the greys insult us. Why do we bend to them?"

"It is a COR matter and of no consequence to you."

"A Drac is under their rule and manipulation. It's a consequence to all of us."

Zeta stepped to Saiph. "You will end this inquiry now. I'll not have direct disobedience. Not from you, Saiph. Not ever." His eyes narrowed, barreling down on Saiph. "Understood?" His voice hoarse.

*He'll put you in containment.* Saiph's face constricted as he clenched his jaw. He bowed. "Of course," he said and stepped back.

Zeta lowered his chin staring down on Saiph. He offered his hand, which Saiph took, kissing the top of his hand. "Stand proud," Zeta said. He met Saiph's eyes. "Your loyalty will be rewarded. In time you, too, will discover the *why* behind the questions you seek. Allow time to unfold before your eyes. Trust in COR and our agenda, and you will be proud of your race with all that you see."

Saiph relented. He couldn't stand being in Zeta's presence any longer. "Yes, Zeta. I fold to your discretion." And he bowed again.

"Seek Sanos," Zeta said. "Follow the scent of your pets and bring his body to me." He walked down the ramp.

"And the surviving humans?" Saiph asked, remaining on the ship, watching Zeta descend.

"Their time runs short," said Zeta. "We've sealed all exits. There is no possible means for escape. Once the air runs out, they'll tear each other apart." He stopped at the bottom of the ramp, looking over the pit. "A fitting end to this cemetery."

Saiph watched as Zeta made his way into the pit, towards the Thorx army standing guard and waiting his instruction. "Your pets," Saiph said under his breath, referring to Zeta's favor to the Thorx. "You treat all better than your people." His disgust turned his gut, thinking of his lycan. How could they have perished? There was one simple answer. The humans had silver. More important, the humans were prepared with silver. But to his knowledge any human threat not under Drac control had perished a long time ago. But the evidence was undeniable. Something or someone had survived.

And they were here in this camp.

* * *

Cam entered the site of his confrontation with Titus. The storage area was also filled with weaponry. Guns, ammo, grenades. Since the plan had changed having a full arsenal at their disposal was paramount.

"You knew this was here the whole time?" Grimes said.

"We didn't need it until now. Considering what we've seen so far, yeah, who knows what else is coming down the hall."

Grimes pointed to the blood-stained floor. "That you?"

Cam looked down. "Yeah, I..." his voice trailed off. *Where's the dead vampire?*

"Something wrong?" Grimes said.

*They took the body?* Cam's eyes darted through the room. No sign of Titus.

"Cam?" Grimes said. Cam looked at him. "You ok?"

"Yeah," he said. He swallowed. "The body's not here."

Grimes went to survey the weaponry. Handing Lao full clips, grenades, and handguns.

*The ship.* Maybe they retained the body. He caught the boy's eye, looking him over. Did they find it, hidden in Titus' body? Couldn't have. High probability they would attempt to disarm it.

"Here," Grimes said, handing Cam a clip. Cam took it and the others Grimes handed him. "Grenades?" Grimes asked. He turned to Cam.

"Of course," he replied. Grimes passed a few grenades to him. "What's the significance?"

Cam cocked his head.

"The body," Grimes said. "What's it matter that it's not here?"

"Nothing," Cam said, not thinking about it, the answer just came. *Why don't you tell them?*

"You sure?" Grimes looked hard at him, his stare stone cold. The others looked too.

"Of course," Cam answered. "You better go." Cam provided the necessary directions through the tunnels. There was roughly a mile travel to the end, coming out of the earth by way of what would look like a cave dwelling to anyone on the outside. With an illusion of course, used to ward off any inquiring and adventurous minds. Should someone wish to explore the tunnel they'd be met with a constructed rock wall capable of opening from the other side. Cam told them about the controls for opening the wall, essentially allowing them out of the tunnels.

*If they make it. If any of us make it. I may have killed off any possible hope for escape. And with that body not here, the detonator is in their control. Hopefully they leave it alone and we can all get out of here.*

*But Phil is headed to the pit.* Cam shook his head, breathed deeply, gnashing his teeth. *You're making a mountain out of a molehill.*

But the thought kept nagging at him. Even when he gave his good luck and God speed to his cohorts, that nagging feeling stayed with him.

*I may have damned us all to hell.*

* * *

The pill was out of reach. Sanos kept trying. His restraints were designed for Dracs; not even the rose could destroy them. He pushed and pulled, kicked and yanked for that damn blue pill. Frustration mounted. He wanted out. Out of these restraints so he could reap havoc on the greys. Everything Saiph had said was accurate. He was a disgrace to his species, having sold them out for experimentation without even so much as a question to COR or warning to his men.

*And now my men are dead.* He thought of Orion and Titus, thought of Rygel and Cade. All dead, and he did nothing to stop it. Sure, the pills turned him into a monster, but still there was no excuse. He should have known better. And now this, losing to Saiph, his remaining men imprisoned, and Telas, that child. She was as corrupt as himself. Maybe even more. What was happening in this outpost was blasphemy, and he participated, he was a part of it. *Disgraceful!*

He reached again, using all his power, all his frustration and anger. But the restraints held. I'm going to die in here. The ships will leave, the humans gone. No way to feed, no way to escape. A slow fitting death for betrayal. He thought of Mono, her large black eyes glaring at him as if she were in the room with him. The thought enraged him. He yanked and pulled again, half standing attempting to use every ounce of strength he could garner.

If I could just…

The thought hit him like a pounding in his brain. Move the pill. *Once it's swallowed I'll have the power to break free.* He knew the pill provided this power, turning a Drac into something else. A monster! But a monster with power. Stronger and otherworldly. These restraints don't even exist within the realm of the pill.

*I require focus, extreme focus.*

He closed his eyes. *Let go of the pain. Breathe out the frustration. All that exists is the pill. Right there. Right behind the rose.* He saw the pill in the center of his mind. Saw it turn to powder, lifting from the floor as if carried by a controlled wind. A wind he controlled.

Sanos opened his mouth and felt the powder on his tongue.

# 39

**"WHY ARE YOUR EYES LIKE THAT?"** Sandy asked Telas. She had to admit; despite all she'd witnessed in the short time she'd become aware of aliens here on earth, Telas looked especially creepy with those black metallic eyeballs. When she was first received in the pit, Telas's eyes were not metallic black, they reflected her normal eyes, but with a smear around them, like an illusion that bent the light around her eyes. An illusion Sandy now recognized from when she had first arrived, standing in the foyer with Ben when Mono had come off the elevator. That same illusionary film had masked Mono's alien features from human sight.

They'd taken the baby from her. The two little greys had whisked away with him. Not willingly of course, Telas assured her he would be fine and, despite the apparent new appearance, Sandy believed her. Then they escorted her aboard a ship and brought her into a circular room with walls Sandy was sure was made of crystals. The glint of light caressing off the walls was mesmerizing. They held a still quietness and serenity Sandy had not felt since before the war.

She felt at peace in the room, sitting on silk pillows and blankets like an heiress or queen.

"Just sit, my dear," Telas said. Her tone of voice had changed too, now monotone and lacking emotion. More matter of fact than anything Sandy could describe.

A second later Mono entered the room. Sandy's heart dropped upon seeing her. She expected torture. She expected Telas to help her, to send a signal, a thought with emotion. But Telas appeared robotic, as if following commands Sandy was unaware of. Mono stayed behind Telas. She was so small it was difficult for Sandy to even see her behind Telas's tall stature.

Telas ruffled sheets and fluffed pillows. "So, you're comfortable," she said.

"Comfortable for what?" Sandy asked over quivering lips. She eyed Mono every time Telas would lean forward or crouch down tending to Sandy's comfort. She was staring, standing, no, floating in space, watching Telas complete the task. Telas fluffed the pillow behind Sandy. "Lie down, dear."

Sandy sat looking Telas over, then back to Mono. Both waited for her to obey. Quiet.

"Lie down," Telas repeated.

Sandy looked to Mono who watched her with a stare equal to malicious intent. She looked back at Telas. "Where's Adam?" she said.

The voice that answered was not Telas. No mouth moved. But she heard Mono speak, her voice dropped inside her brain like a heavy stone plunged in the sea with waves that spread in circles to her inner ears. "He's in good hands, dear. Safe. Safer with us than any place on earth." A pause as if Mono was choosing her words. "We thank you for handing him over freely." Sandy noticed Telas froze in response to Mono's statement.

Sandy glared at Mono, her response floated off her lips instinctively. "I didn't," she said.

Mono just about jumped, gliding close to her. "You will!"

Sandy couldn't take her eyes off Mono. It seemed like the air was bent in between them. Like she could see the atoms, every tiny one, making up the space from Sandy's nose to Mono's eyes, constrict, turn in the opposite direction, then begin to move again. The room's air turned thick in Sandy's lungs. She swallowed her breath, forcing the air into struggling lungs. She started to wheeze.

"What's happening?" Sandy said, her heart jumped, body tensed.

"You're about to lose consciousness," Mono again. "We've changed the air in the room to elicit this reaction."

Sandy held her breath. Her head floating, light-headed and straining for air. The crystals sparkled across the wall like a wave. Her breathing turned heavy, unable to withhold the air any longer.

"It's not your conscious mind we wish to communicate with," Mono said. Sandy began hyperventilating, her mouth agape struggling to bring the thick air into her lungs. "It's your subconscious where our answer resides."

Sandy looked at Telas, her head throbbing and heavy. Flushed skin, blotched red and pale. "Go with it," Telas said. "Let it take you." She eased Sandy back on the pillow, cradling her head like a baby, hovering over her. "You'll be fine, dear."

Sandy gripped Telas's cloak. Her hand heavy yet so tightly constricted.

*Feels like I'm dying.*

"Don't do this." Sandy said to Telas, staring into those black eyes.

Mono floated to the wall, her hand hovering above the crystals, which ignited into glows of red then orange then yellow. She felt her brain wrench in her skull, an immense pain that dropped her head back. Colors of green, blue, and indigo filled the room, overtaking all her eyes could see. Except for the eyes. Telas's black eyes reflected the light. She gripped tighter Telas's cloak. "Please!" she pleaded, mesmerized by black eyes that now appeared as one. A large black oval enveloped in violet.

"It is like dying, dear."

The voice faded as white filled the room, washing away the black oval.

"But only of your conscious self."

All she could see was white. Light everywhere. And she could breathe easy.

* * *

The remaining members in Sanos's clan felt their restraints release. The force field that held them had vanished, leaving them standing. They shared an inquisitive stare when the chamber door opened.

"Sanos?" Moya said. But the Drac standing in the doorway was not Sanos. Saiph entered the chamber, the door closed behind him.

"You?" Jubal said. "Why?"

"I have my reasons."

"You understand the repercussions of this action?" Kaidan looked at Saiph.

"I do," he said. "As unnecessary as it has become."

"We'll be hunted. Living on rats on a desolate planet," Moya said. "COR will never allow this." He referred to his fellow clan.

"COR will have us dissolved," said Jubal. "And the truth will die with us."

Kaidan stepped to Saiph. "You understand where this will lead? Once word of this action is received by fellow Dracs they'll call for an inquiry."

Saiph gave a quick nod. "An inquiry they will attempt to dissuade from happening. But any Drac already questioning COR will have reason to persist."

"Civil War will begin," Jubal intervened. "At such a time too."

Kaidan locked eyes with Saiph. "Zeta," he said. "He would not allow you to do this." No response. "You've betrayed him?"

"My master has betrayed Dracs," Saiph shot back.

Jubal eyed Saiph. "You don't plan on leaving this outpost, do you?"

Saiph stiffened. "The sun rises soon. We've entered twilight. There is no safety for Dracs on the open terrain. This ship is empty for now."

"You want us to take the ship for cover?" Moya said.

"I do."

"But once we start up the engine, all outside the ship will know...," Jubal explained. "They'll shoot us down before we even get close to the surface."

Saiph shook his head.

"How can you be so sure?"

"Because they will be distracted." His eyes met with Jubal. "Your escape is required. Find other Dracs with similar interests. Seek the truth. No Drac should live under the control of another species. What we've become," he moved his head back and forth, "I do not wish to be. What I do today I do for all Dracs, so that we may take our place in the universe with pride." He went to leave.

"Wait," Jubal said. Saiph turned to him. He held his hand out. "We found this inside Titus." The detonator in his palm was small, but one look at it and Saiph knew the destruction it would cause. Saiph looked at him. "It's set to go off soon."

"You planned to sacrifice?" Saiph asked.

Jubal nodded. "To destroy the greys. And to send a message. We secured the detonator during Titus' burial preparations. We surmised the bomb is in the supplies area. There's enough explosives in there to decimate this entire outpost."

Saiph glared at the detonator. He took it from Jubal's hand. "Human?" he asked.

"The human who killed Titus must've added this to his insult. It can't be disarmed; there are too many traps that will escalate the timer."

"Should it be escalated how long until detonation?" Saiph asked, observing the detonator.

"Maybe ten minutes. Maybe less. Depends on how close to zero time is left."

He clasped the detonator. "I'll tear a hole through that human and stuff this into his bowels. No human will leave this place. No grey either." He looked at Jubal, Moya and Kaidan. "Do not let this act go without cause. No other ship is allowed to leave. All here will not survive. Remember what you see here. Let the sacrifice bring freedom."

They looked on Saiph sensing the kinship. Knowing the rebellion had begun, and it started with Saiph. They bowed to him. "Remain here until the fighting begins. Tear apart the other ships before you leave. They won't expect it. And then make your way out, hide, and use your power to gather similar minds. They'll believe you have all perished. Bide your time wisely and resurface once the time is right. Your existence will prove COR's outrage and damnation."

"Noted," Jubal said.

Moya stepped closer to Saiph. "What of Sanos?" he asked.

"Sanos?" Saiph clenched his jaw. "I have a feeling he'll be making an appearance. His fate is now in his hands. Let us see what he does for redemption."

* * *

Phil watched from the airshaft. All was quiet, like the calm before the storm. The ships hovered in their place. Thorx soldiers waited for orders. No sign of Sandy nor the child. Even the lycan was gone. Zeta emerged from a ship. Phil watched as he paused as if addressing someone on the ramp, and then he went to address the Thorx.

"Who's hiding inside?" Phil said following Zeta's movements. *Maybe Sandy?* Then the third ship started to spin in place, detaching from the ramp, which continued to stand in place. This also took Zeta's attention. Light beamed from the ship's windows, and a grey glided down the ramp. Not the same grey from the pit. Phil could tell by this grey's differently shaped skull. The circumference was larger, wider and denser than the grey he'd seen with the Drac. And she was taller. She approached Zeta.

Phil crouched down, attempting to get a better look in the spinning ship. The grey who took Zeta's time did not seem pleased. *Sandy! They're trying to break her.* He bent his head, thinking.

*Trust Sandy, all the way to the end.* He heard Robyn's instruction. But this scenario seemed appalling. Robyn never mentioned these events. Then again, he always talked in a cryptic way. Robyn had taught Phil everything about so many alien species his head spun. And Phil's own encounters proved he was spot on with every confrontation. How to kill them. How to block your thoughts so they couldn't gain access. *Once they've gotten in your head, you're done for,* Robyn had said.

He searched the pit, looking for any possible alternate entrance. His eyes roaming over the walls and ceiling finding another airshaft, across the pit, on top of the ships and Thorx army. But how to get on that ship proved an impossible task. *Even if I do get on how do I get her off and out of here before that bomb explodes? Thorx are easy, it's the others that'll prove difficult. And then there are the greys. They will not be easy, not with the power they possess.*

*Coming down to the wire, it'll come.* He headed through the airshaft. *The answer will present itself. Once Cam releases those prisoners these Dracs will send the Thorx Army, possibly any remaining Dracs too. Cam will get out I know it. I can feel his freedom is imminent. They won't follow Cam to the outside, there's too much to risk at this point in their plan. And that's all the distraction I'll need. If it works, hopefully, all will be well.*

*Most important, I hope Sandy can hold out against the greys.*

Phil's thoughts returned to the first time he met Robyn. He was four then but in those four years Phil had experienced the worst of human suffering. Not that he knew it then, the torture and horror he'd endured were all normal, in line with the theory that normal was what you witnessed every day. Not that he understood then that there was so much more to life, such beauty, and that thing with the heart...yes, it was called love. An emotion he'd held until that time for one person, his mother, associating the profound sensation to her alone once he learned the definition of love.

If only Robyn had arrived to rescue the four-year-old Phil from the island a day before, he could have saved Phil's mother, Alena, before she was selected for dismissal, sent away to be cut from ear to ear. Filleted like a deer under a hunter's knife. Such was the fate of all who were bred on that horrid island. Thank the heavens for Robyn Winter. Thank the Gods for love.

## 40

**CAM GRIPPED THE LEVER IN HIS PALM.** He performed one last search through the corridor, listening for any possible footsteps. All was quiet. He pulled the lever unlocking the cell doors that propped open on cue. No alarm. Nothing to cause a distraction for Phil. Perhaps it's a silent alarm, Cam thought.

He waited, craning his head left then right, wondering if there was anyone in those rooms. The long moment he had to wait before anyone stepped out seemed to last a century.

One by one they emerged, slow, caution held in their eyes. Cam put his finger to his lips. He waved them over. The crowd of men and boys were emaciated. They shuffled over to Cam. Understanding to keep quiet they provided gratitude in hush tones. Ten of them, seven men and three boys who couldn't have been older than sixteen, surrounded him. Their faces thin, bodies frail, with hair that thinned revealing thick overgrown skulls. Their hands were small but with long bony fingers.

Cam had seen the effect starvation had on the body. Had seen it all during his time in the war, even before the war had begun, when he was young and serving his country abroad. But this seemed different. And then the smell hit him. A foul body odor that rifled off thin skin and tattered clothes. He couldn't help the thought or the sensation, but something was indeterminately wrong with these people. *What did they do to them?* Cam kept shushing them; a simple mannerism used to ward off his thoughts because anything he would say in this moment would not be good. Then the paranoia started to rage. They were scared, some of them shaking.

"We're getting out of here," Cam whispered. His eyes darted from one to the other. "Follow close. Help each other."

"Do you know what they've been doing to us?" one of the men said.

Cam paused looking the man over, his gaze sympathetic. He shook his head. "No," he answered. "But it's over now. Let's be swift and move as fast as possible."

"Are they coming?" another said. "I think they're coming. Oh no, if they find us..." he started walking back to his cell. "If they find us. If they find us. If they find us." His voice started to rise. Cam pushed through the others to get to him.

"Sir," Cam said. "Sir, this is a rescue so they can't do any more to you." He gripped the man's sleeve. The arm like a thin fragile stick came off in Cam's hand without the need for force, igniting a scream that echoed in the corridor. Blood rushed from the severed limb. The man's scream continued. The amount of blood that drained from his shoulder was equal to the scream that seemed to heighten as more blood rushed out. He dropped to his knees. Fell forward with a flop that smacked his forehead with a bounce and small rattle. His scream abruptly stopped.

Cam held the arm up. His eyes wide drawing a confused stare. He dropped the limb and stepped away from the pool of blood growing wide on the floor. Looked back at the men, all-staring with wide large eyes. They huddled close together, glaring at the body and blood, although unmoving. Cam mouthed, *What the fuck.* Having no clue what to do he kneeled down and checked for a pulse, knowing the man was dead but felt he had to do something.

"He's dead," one of them said. His mouth agape. He looked back and shouted, "He's dead," to the group as if relaying a message to a larger crowd. The others repeated, "He's dead!"

Cam shook his head. *Strange.* He turned to the small group. All they did was stand and stare. *Get a grip. Bring it together.* And then he saw the smoke rise from the blood on the ground. The group looked on like children at a theme park, mesmerized and in awe. The blood was disintegrating, smoldering as if burning as the smoke also faded and was gone. *What did they do to them, indeed?*

He stood up, gripping his AR15 on his shoulder. "Any more surprises?"

They turned to him. The man answered. "Don't you know what they've been doing to us?"

Cam shook his head. "No," he said. "I wasn't given that information."

"Well, sir," the man said. "You'll find we're full of surprises."

"Hopefully pleasant," Cam said.

"Indeed."

Cam shook his head, attempting to clear his mind. He closed his eyes and took a deep breath. *Is this even worth it?* As he opened his eyes, he saw them as the men they were, tortured and paranoid and frightened half to death. *More than half, almost completely.* He stepped to them, and they all took a step back. Cam scowled. "We can dispense with the pleasantries for now. We've limited time to get out of here."

"We will follow," the man said.

Cam stiffened. "Good," he huffed. "Follow along please, single file."

They shared confused stares.

"One behind the other," Cam explained, and they all gave a quick nod with a smirking smile as if they got it. He moved to the end of the hall, the man who'd been speaking stood behind Cam and the others followed behind him.

Cam opened his mouth to speak but the group spoke his words, "Keep quiet. Move fast." Perplexed and now unnerved, Cam looked over the group. Their stares, those large sunken dark eyes stared innocently.

Cam said, "Let's just..."

His words completed by the group, "Get you all outta here."

* * *

Something was wrong, Grimes knew. He couldn't stop the feeling that Cam was hiding something. He led them down the tunnels, amazed how easy it was. There was no one coming. Did they allow them to go or...they don't need to follow us?

He looked at the boy, walking hurriedly with the three men almost latched to him. Lao followed behind them. He looked nervous too. Either he shared the same sentiment about Cam, or he was waiting for something unseen to claw out from the walls. Maybe both. Cam had said he hid the bomb but not *where* he hid the detonator. And he was definitely freaked out about that body.

He shook his head, thinking, traveling down the dimly lit corridor.

"Look," the boy said. He pointed ahead. Grimes stopped. They all stopped. Up ahead the corridor dropped into darkness. "I think this is the end."

Grimes looked at the boy then back into darkness, squinting to see further. He gripped his rifle. "Stay here," he told them and walked cautiously. It was difficult to place in the darkness, but the wall was there. A makeshift rock wall.

"Is that it?" Lao said.

"Appears so," said Grimes, surveying the wall. He reached his hand out. Felt like rock. *Is he sure this is a door?*

"He said there's controls," Lao looked at the boy. "Spread out, let see what we can find."

There was a relief in the moment. Beyond the wall was freedom, at least freedom from current circumstance. Despite all that has happened, getting out of here meant the world. And the world had changed for sure. Grimes ran his hand over the wall's edge, hoping something would give way.

"Got it," Lao said. Lights turned on illuminating the corridor. Grimes turned around. The area was huge. Lao stood in an oval control center on the far wall, lined with computers, monitors and a hoard of buttons and controls. He was looking over the controls when Grimes approached.

"Any controls for the wall?" he asked.

Lao shook his head. "None. At least none of these mention the wall specifically."

Grimes bent his head. "Maybe try the computer?" he said. "There's got to be a way to open it." Lao sat down, in front of one of the large monitors embedded in the control center.

That uneasy feeling came flooding back, and Grimes gripped his rifle. It was too quiet. He kept thinking something was coming.

Maybe another one of those werewolves or those...whatever they hell they are, headed towards them now. Biding its time before jumping from the darkness to put an end to this rescue and escape mission. "Any luck?"

Lao scoffed. "This thing is still turning on. It's ancient, probably been here since the 1950s."

"Wonderful," Grimes said chewing the inside of his cheek. "Friggin' aliens everywhere, and we're dealing with an ancient relic."

"Here it is," Lao said. He just about jumped in his seat pressing closer to the monitor. But what reflected back was not a computer screen. The image reflected a clear picture of the moon. His jaw dropped. His eyes wide. "You may want to take a look at this."

"Can you open the wall or not?" Grimes shot back, then noticed Lao's expression. "What is it?"

Lao locked eyes with him. "See for yourself," he said, moving away from the screen as Grimes walked around the control center entering from the side. He shouldered his AR15 as he came upon the monitor. His jaw dropped. On the screen was the moon, a clear picture. And there was more, much more. A large spaceship hovered above the moon. From it several smaller ships made their way to the moon's surface, some returning from the surface to the ship.

"Is that," Grimes pointed to the screen, "happening now?" He looked at Lao.

"I assume so."

"Assume. Don't assume. Is it or isn't it?"

Lao glared at him. "How am I supposed to know that?"

"True."

"I mean, I don't think it's a recording or anything. When the monitor came on the image was there. I think it's a monitor for a telescope."

"What're they doing?"

"Again, how am I supposed to know? Looks to me like their occupying the moon for..."

"An invasion?"

"Possible."

Grimes bent his head, thinking. "Can you get a closer look?"

Lao searched the screen, the keyboard below it, buttons and controls on both sides. Grimes closed his eyes. "I can't believe this?"

"Why can't you?" Lao said, punching keys on the keyboard. "After all we've seen this doesn't come as a surprise."

"True." He looked at the boy, sitting with the three men. They seemed to huddle close to the boy.

"Got it," Lao said.

Grimes's eyes darted to the screen. The moon growing large on the monitor, zooming in to the moon's surface where the ships were landing and people in space suits bobbed across the surface. Some of them human, some looked like greys, working together. They were drilling. Drilling colossal holes in the moon.

"Get a better look at those holes," Grimes said. Lao punched a few keys and the moon expanded, focused on one of the holes. In the image he could see the pointed tip protruding from the hole. "Is that what I think it is?" he said, pointing to the screen.

Lao tipped his head, taking in the view.

"Nuclear?" Grimes said.

"I do believe you are right, Corporal."

"They're arming the moon with nuclear weapons! Why? They're gonna bomb us from the moon; that makes no sense."

Lao chewed his lip, thinking. "Maybe it's not for us," he said.

"What?"

Lao sat back. "Maybe they're preparing. Turning the moon into a battle station." His proclamation took time to register. "Maybe they expect someone else arriving."

Grimes glared at the screen. The ships, the bombs, the holes, the men in spacesuits bobbing across the moon's surface. What Lao had said made sense. There was no need to plant nuclear weapons on the moon to destroy the earth, there were many already on the planet to perform that Armageddon. "I do believe you are right," Grimes said, his voice low and shallow. The picture scanned across the holes. Of all of them, only one housed the nuclear warhead. He looked again at the boy. "Let's just find the controls to get us out of here. We've got our own bomb to deal with."

Lao pushed his seat close to the monitor. "Duly noted, Corporal."

Grimes went to search the wall again. The thought of the moon as a battle station stayed with him. Who's coming? What other alien races could be out there headed to earth? *Put it away Grimes. Focus on the task at hand. We haven't much time.* He knew the sun was on the brink of rising, its power shedding light on the outside world. And then he found it. The control panel was covered with what looked like rock, blending into the wall. "Got it," he called, and Lao stood up. The boy looked over, the men huddled next to him. Grimes flipped the rock panel. Two buttons were beneath, one red one green. "Yes," he huffed and pushed the button. His sense of relief quickly turned to frustration.

The wall didn't move.

* * *

"That damn grey," Zeta said. He referred to Mintaka who provided information received from the human mother, along with an order. He boarded the third ship to complete his task, wanting nothing more than to get off this base camp and back to the comfort of COR. For the first time in a long while, he felt alone. Like when he spent a year in solitude. Loneliness can be maddening after a while, but the madness relented into comfort, after the truth was accepted.

That disconnection programming weighed heavy. He thought of Saiph as he trampled through the ship, slipping into a hall covered in darkness. Saiph's loyalty to Dracs blinded him from even attempting to understand there was a larger cause involved. A cause he'd been involved with first hand. A cause that was slowly coming to fruition, as expected. And the cause turned his stomach. What his people will have to endure on their way to triumph. *But Dracs have historically endured much, much more.* He placed his hand to the door he'd come upon. His hand was scanned, and the door propped open. He entered the room. Inside was a cage. In the cage stood a human whose black eyes shimmered in Zeta's vision.

The man was large, standing close to eight feet tall. He had to crouch down under the roof, which was too short to hold him. His features were thick and massive, his hands the size of baseball gloves, and his head, more like a thick square than round, with thinning black hair that dropped just above the eyes. He stood, crouched and hunched over, staring at Zeta who held a penlight in the giant's direction. The glow of white light illuminated the dark room.

Zeta said, "We've come to a crossroad." The giant attempted to reach for the light, but his hand was held captive by the cage. Zeta stepped closer. "The greys require a human. A human schooled in the sacred art. He's killed many Dracs and won't come willingly." The giant gaped as if informing Zeta he understood. "You are to find him. Bring him back here so we may prepare him for reconditioning." The giant turned from Zeta, looking to the ground. "He has the blades," Zeta said, and the giant looked up. "And there are others who will try to protect him." Zeta moved his head back and forth. "You will not compromise. Kill them all if you must but bring this human here." Zeta unlocked the cage, sliding the door open without effort. The giant watching the door as it clicked in place, and now he was in an arm's reach of Zeta.

Zeta held the light to his eyes. A light the giant could not take his eyes off of. "They are at the end of the tunnel, but they are confined to its reserve. You must go, Perseus. Find the human who dons the blades. Bring him here." Zeta moved the light in between his own eyes. The giant followed the light. "Bring him here." Perseus nodded. He looked beyond Zeta, beyond the room. Then back to Zeta. "Go!" Zeta said. A second later, Perseus jumped from the room and was gone.

Zeta clicked off the light, leaving himself in darkness. His green eyes glimmered.

"Now, where has Saiph gone to?"

## 41

SANDY WAS SURROUNDED BY LUSH BILLOWING green landscapes. Herself a queen among immortals. She lay on a bed of roses, her eyes drifting open to what she would expect the Garden of Eden to look like. The expanse of greenery seemed to go on forever. Behind her a waterfall dropped into a pristine crystal-clear body of water. Birds flew from tree to tree, peacefully tending to their daily duties.

In the distance a baby's cries rose above the landscape. Not a furious cry but a simple whimper as if Adam had required food that was immediately provided. The hush of his cry replaced with the silent spring of waterfall and wind. Sandy stood taking in the view with miraculous intrigue. Her eyes wide and dazzled. She felt peace but peace with a bobbing trepidation that this scene would not last. And she wanted it to last forever.

"Hello," she hollered. Her voice echoed off the rolling hills in the distance. She searched the landscape, finding a deer and its doe drinking from the water that received life from the waterfall. "Hello," she called again, and the deer lifted their heads to gaze in her direction. *How did I get here* was the question that dropped in the center of her brain dissipating in the same moment the question had been presented. She stepped back, and the wind rushed across the edges of her skin, her hair brushed by its decadence. Closed her eyes for a brief moment, feeling the warmth of the sun.

Her gaze caught a glimmer in the waterfall. A rainbow graced the lake at the point of entrance as if calling her over. She stepped to it, gliding across the greenery, and the waterfall with its pond seemed to meet her halfway. The water was clear, crystal clear. She could see all the way to the bottom where caverns and caves waited exploration. Seemingly bottomless with gentle species of rainbow-colored fish taking advantage of a life spent without defeat or predators. *Harmony.* She dipped her hands into the water and sipped from her cupped hands. She covered her face with water, brushed fingers through her hair, and splashed the back of her neck. Beads of water dripped from her chin. The water was cool, quenching thirst with a simple touch of its wholesome purity on the tip of her tongue.

Her reflection in the water wavered into focus. Her skin shone in the water, glowing with a hint of gold. Her hair cascaded to her shoulders in curls that brought remembrance of childhood. She wore jewels of red, green, and blue that glimmered under the sun and complemented the silk crimson dress she was wearing. Her image brought a smile filled with joy. Except the reflected smile did not match. Sharp fangs gleamed back at her from the water. She reached her hand to her mouth and touched her thumb to her teeth. Sharp like a razor. Her eyes darted right to left as she ran her thumb across her teeth. All were sharp like the reflection revealed. A butterfly landed on her hand as if its purpose was to erase any and all trepidation. Its wings were golden brown with red inkblot stained circles. Sandy raised the butterfly to eye level. She could hear the flapping from its fluttering wings.

Birds cooed and chirped in the distance, first on her right then to her left. Back and forth they talked, and their avian songs filled the scene. Sandy smiled and laughed. She could sense the song in her chest like a gentle vibration that ignited a feeling of peace. Sandy turned to the blue sky, allowing the butterfly to continue its exploration. She turned her gaze to the butterfly watching as it fluttered to a purple flower protruding from a rock on the opposite side of the pond.

*What is this place?*

She tried to remember how she arrived, how she came to this serene scene, but her thoughts subsided every time the answer graced the tip of her tongue, the tip of her mind. She tried to catch the thoughts but like the butterfly's wings they fluttered from consciousness, taken on the wings of the wind to places unknown. She laughed again, this time over the inability to remember. *How you got here matters not, only that you'd arrived.*

Sandy closed her eyes, not to think but to sense the peace that existed all around her. To feel that peace in the wind that brushed across her hair, tingled her skin and filled her heart. Beneath the wind a strange occurrence erupted. She heard whispers as if someone commanded the wind to blow and the butterfly to flutter. Low murmurs, inconceivable words and Sandy wondered if they truly did exist. If they were real. If any of this were real. She leaned her head forward attempting to capture a word with clarity.

*Telas!* Sandy heard. **Telas!** And a brief second later, *Telas!*

Sandy nodded as if understanding the instruction. Her distraction trifled by laughter from the edge of the pond where the waterfall dropped. She saw Telas sitting with her knees up. Resting on her legs was a baby. "Adam," Sandy said and now she heard the baby's laughter. Adam's baby noises and laughter rose to touch the sky. Sandy went to them. Telas doted on the child, touching her finger to his belly creating laughter among them.

"Here's Mommy," Telas said stretching her finger to his rib. "Yes, here's Mommy."

Sandy quickened her pace, excited. She wanted to be with them. To be a part of them. She glided behind Telas. "See, here's Mommy," Telas said and Sandy's jaw dropped. The baby was covered in blood, Telas too. Her body tensed, appalled at the scene. "No need for concern," Telas said. "We were both hungry." Telas turned to Sandy and Sandy cringed. Her eyes were metallic black. Sandy saw herself in those eyes, covered in blood, sweat and soot. Her hair, matted, seemed to be pulled by the wind. The baby's laughter ceased drawing Sandy's attention. The baby watched her with a sour expression. He started to cry, his screams blood curdling.

"What did you do?" Telas screamed at Sandy.

Sandy straightened her back, staring, confused. "Why is he screaming like that?" she asked, frightened.

"It's you," Telas raged. "He doesn't want you."

\* \* \*

Phil reached the end of the airshaft. He peered down into the pit. No change in the scene. One of the ships continued to spin with a crystal white light gleaming from within. The other ships hovered calmly in place, outside the ramps were the Thorx standing in attention. All else was quiet.

He was plotting his way into the ship glimmering with light when Zeta exited one of the ships. As if on cue Saiph trampled down the ramp of the middle ship. He glared at the ship where Sandy and the greys were. His concentration was interrupted by Zeta who stood watching before calling him over. They walked toward the pit, meeting face to face.

Phil crouched down, listening. His eyes roaming over the pit. Saiph and Zeta's conversation was unintelligible from his high distance. And they were walking further away, around the pit to the opposite side of the opening. He found the exit to the outside world in the ceiling high above the pit. The opening, from what Phil could see, gleamed with shimmering stars about to lose the cover of darkness in the pending twilight. *Sunrise!* Phil knew that should the opening not be closed the sun would beam its rays into the pit and be done with the Dracs who posed a threat to his mission. *But they're not that stupid.* As if they heard his thoughts the opening started to close. Phil watched as the closing hole shut out twilight. And the air turned thick and hot in the airshaft.

He shook his head, standing. "I'm gonna have to run through every one of them. I don't see any other way."

*And times running out.*

"Either they break Sandy and it's over or that bomb goes off and we're all dead." Robyn had taught Phil about the influence the greys had over others. That all it took was a word, the answer to their question to a parent who had been offered delicacies and riches in exchange for lives for which they were able to do with as they pleased. It was an age-old custom that churned acid in the back of Phil's throat: parents handing over their children for personal success and fame. Parents have a cosmic hold on their children, a hold that remains until the child possessed knowledge of choice. When a parent gave in and offered their children the receiving party was able to do with the child as they saw fit. And with the pending trials on the cusp of watering and coming to fruition, the greys did all they could for as long as they could to corrupt the lives of as many human children as possible. But if the parent did not give the child over under their own free will, or if they were coerced or threatened, the hold on their children remained unbroken. It was cosmic law.

Phil gripped his handles and braced himself for the fall when he was taken by a peculiar scene. His vision wavering. He cocked his head and beheld two eyes gleaming white, staring at him from the ceiling. It was a Drac for sure, although this particular Drac was different, very different indeed. Its teeth were long and protruded from its mouth. Its body was massive, large and thick, and it reached its long and thick finger to its lips.

*Ssshhhhhhhhhhh*, its voice appeared in Phil's mind. And then it smiled at him. And looked down on Zeta and Saiph.

# 42

"DON'T SHOOT," CAM HOLLERED. HE DRIFTED out of the darkness into the light, those strange men on his heels.

"Cam," Grimes hollered. "Over here."

Cam rushed over to meet the Corporal who continued to try and force the wall open. Lao stood up looking over the people Cam had arrived with, his face scrunched as he studied them, perplexed.

"What is it?" Cam said surveying the wall.

"It won't open," Grimes replied. His voice nervous.

"Got it," Cam said. He holstered his rifle over his shoulder. "Did you try to override the controls?"

Grimes motioned to the control panel on the wall, torn from the wall with the wires hanging from it. "Shit," Cam said. "What about a grenade? Blow this thing off its hinges."

Grimes shook his head. "Can't do it," he said.

Cam eyes were wide while looking over the wall. "Why not?"

"Look around you. The walls are made from a synthetic polymer. Any blast will tear through this place like an atomic bomb."

Cam studied his surroundings. Grimes was correct. A grenade blast would rip through the tunnel with amplified firepower. Cam chewed his lip, thinking. He turned to Lao who continued to glare at the men Cam had arrived with.

"What about the computers?" Cam pointed to the area where Lao was.

"These computers have no control over the wall," Lao said. "The controls have to be in one central station."

"Where?" Cam said.

Lao glared at him. "I don't know." Cam dropped his shoulders. "I assume they're somewhere inside."

"The pit?" Cam said.

"Again, I don't know."

"Not good."

"No shit," Grimes said pushing on the wall. His palms slipped as he breathed heavy. His head against the wall.

"Save your strength," Cam said.

"For what?" Grimes hollered. "We're all going to die in here."

"How about shooting the controls? Try to shoot a hole through it."

Grimes shook his head. "Can't. I tried. The bullets ricochet off the wall."

Cam tensed, locked eyes with Grimes. He could see how hope was fading from the Corporal. "How much time do we have?" Grimes asked.

Cam surveyed the top of the wall. "Less than an hour."

"Maybe we should go back. Get back up the airshaft and up the elevator. Maybe they're gone."

Cam looked everyone over. "It'll take too long," he said. "With everyone here. We'll run out of time fast. Real fast." He ran his tongue inside his mouth.

"Ideas are appreciated," Grimes said. "What're you thinking?"

Cam cocked his head. Turned to Grimes. "Well," he began. "On the other side of this wall is freedom..."

"Something like that."

"Freedom from this place and a fighting chance at least."

"Ok. So how do we open it?"

Cam looked at Lao. "Does that computer show any schematics? A map of the tunnels? Something that'll tell us where the master controls are?" Cam went to Lao.

"Let's see." Lao punched a few keys studying the monitor that glimmered back at him. The screen changing with every punched key. "Here it is." He looked at Cam who returned his stare then leaned over to take in the image on the screen.

Cam shook his head. "The pit," he said. "How did I know?"

Lao shrugged. "You tell me."

Cam cocked his eyebrows. He turned to Grimes who was staring at the men Cam had arrived with. Their eyes glared back at him. His jaw dropped.

"Corporal?" Cam said. Grimes raised his eyes to him. "I'll get it open," he said.

"You're leaving?" Grimes said.

"Seems like the only way. We haven't come this far to hit a roadblock. I'll get it open. Just be ready. Once that wall opens get everyone out." He swallowed the lump in his throat. "Don't look back," he told Grimes. "Just go. Head to Atlanta."

Cam went to the boy.

"Where in Atlanta?" Grimes said. "We have no idea who those people are and they don't know us from Adam. How do we know they won't be hostile?"

"We don't," Cam said. "But it's your only chance."

The boy looked at Cam who dropped to his knees eye level with him. "Seems they've taken a liking to you," Cam said referring to the men who clung to the boy. He forced a smile. "I don't know what to say," he huffed then paused, looking away. He removed his uniform, stretching it over his head. A green t-shirt saturated with sweat clung to his skin. He stretched his uniform over the boy's head. "For when you reach the sun," he said. Locked eyes with the boy and forced a smile. "We don't know the reaction you'll have."

The boy reached his hands to Cams temples. They locked eyes. "Thank you," the boy said. Cam stiffened as the boy reached his arms around him resting his chin on Cam's shoulder. He whispered, "You'll be back." Cam held the boy tight, as if this could be the last time he'd see him.

"I know it," the boy said. "You'll make it back."

* * *

The cries were relentless. Sandy did all she could to comfort the furious baby. Telas stood behind her and Sandy could sense her anger.

"Maybe he's hungry," Sandy said. She looked up to Telas. "Would you like to take the honor?"

Telas looked back with a stare revealing disgust. She moved her head back and forth. "What good are you?" she said. "Can't even feed him. He's not human, he's a Drac like his mother." Sandy's jaw dropped. "Give him up, he's no good with you. Here, let me take him. I'll show you."

Telas took the baby from Sandy and the cries stopped. Sandy looked away.

"See, he's fine with me. He needs a Drac to raise him. Not you. You're his food not his kin."

Sandy gazed at the green expanse beyond the water. "Why do you say such things?" she whispered.

"We should have kept your father," Telas said talking to the baby. "At least he would realize he *can't* take care of you. At least he would do the right thing and give you over."

*Where is Ben?* She tried to remember, to locate Ben in her thoughts, in her memories. She couldn't recall what had happened to him. Couldn't recall how she got to this place. How or why she was sitting by the water? She thought and thought but there was something missing. Some memory she couldn't tap into that would tell her where she was. Everything seemed synthetic, as if nothing here were real. She eyed the water and then the waterfall and beyond to the blue sky above it. Looked back at the waterfall and how it emptied into the pond. Water pounding into water. But there was a part missing. Something that did not sit right with the scene. A flaw in the landscape.

"Are you willing to give him over?" Telas asked. "He's better off with me. Don't you agree?"

Sandy's stomach turned. No answer came. She looked down at the water.

"Sandy?" Telas said. "Do –You — Agree?"

Sandy turned her gaze to the blue sky that glimmered like a rolling wave sparkling with white light. The glimmer did not fit the scene, seemed out of place. *Why would the sky do that?* Bulbs of white light shimmered in her eyes. The light was familiar. White light. Where had she seen such light before?

"Do you agree, Sandy?" Telas's voice dulled to a low hush.

The blue sky turned dark with rage.

"No," Sandy said. "I do not agree."

# 43

**WHEN ZETA MET WITH SAIPH, HE NOTICED** the strain in his Saiph's eyes. *There's mutiny in that stare. Mutiny and guilt.*

Saiph held his cloak closed around his throat as he approached Zeta.

"I send you to destroy Sanos and instead you speak to prisoners?" Zeta scowled at Saiph.

Saiph stopped a few feet from Zeta. "Much has come to pass," Saiph said. "All has changed."

Zeta clenched his jaw looking over Saiph with imminent disgust. Betrayal was not dealt with frequently among Dracs, especially at such a high ranking as Zeta possessed. Saiph's actions would reflect largely negative on Zeta's ability to lead, possibly ending in a loss of his power unless the situation could be dismantled quickly.

He knew what he must do. Killing Saiph was the only way he could preserve any dignity.

"You intend to bring your findings to COR," Zeta said.

"No," Saiph answered quickly. "That part is not in my hands."

Zeta gestured to the ship where the Dracs were held. "Them," he said. He laughed. "Foolish children. COR will dismantle all of you once word of this mutiny has graced their ears."

"COR will be required to listen. To consider what has happened and the injustices brought to Dracs. We must not trust the greys. Their interests are in conflict with our own."

"Foolish boy you are, Saiph. COR will bury all you have to say and exile you all into the stars, to drift alone, hungry and cold until you tear each other apart."

"Not me, Zeta. Not me."

"How noble." Zeta shook his head. "How truly noble." Zeta removed his cloak. "I must not allow any of you to leave if this is your plot. All betrayal must be dealt with in the most extreme manner."

Saiph bowed. "You do what you must."

"Truly disappointing, Saiph. I was hoping you would have more insight. Betrayal is a coward's way. Accepting the truth and standing up for it, that is what makes heroes."

"No," Saiph said. "That is what turns the dreams of youth into regret."

"Your plight is to listen and obey. Not create doubt and upheaval among your people."

"My purpose is to fight for Dracs, something you've lost sight of. Caught under the thumb of greys. That child they created must not leave this place."

Zeta laughed again. "You plan on confronting greys. My my, Saiph, how foolish you have become."

Saiph turned to the ceiling. "Only one fool here, Zeta. And it is not who you stare at now."

Zeta followed Saiph's gaze. His eyes widened by what he witnessed.

* * *

Sanos smiled at Zeta. He dropped into the pit fifty yards from where Zeta and Saiph were standing. He stood erect, stretching his shoulders. His chin raised and eyes gleamed watching Zeta's jaw drop.

"Abomination," Zeta huffed.

"Spare me, Zeta." Sanos growled under his breath, stretching his jaw. Saliva dripped off his chin. "We've grown tired of your politics."

Across the pit the Thorx stiffened, erecting themselves to prepare for battle under Zeta's command.

Sanos dipped his head, snarling at Zeta. "Your Thorx only work on unsuspecting humans. You should have brought a more formidable opponent."

Zeta moved his head back and forth. "I have," he said, turning to Saiph.

Saiph narrowed his eyes. Took two steps back while shaking his head. "This is your fight. I will not interfere."

Sanos laughed watching the interaction. "All alone, Zeta. All alone."

Zeta snarled at Saiph. "So be it then...Saiph."

* * *

"Vampires," Phil said. "Always so over dramatic." He studied his options. The ship that held Sandy continued to spin with gleams of light. Looked at the Thorx. No concern with them. *They go down easy. Well, not that easy. Keep your eye on your back.* No chance in slipping through unnoticed, the pit was a wide-open space with too many eyes roaming. And time is running down. He shook his head. *Only one way to go!* He gripped his handles, standing erect. "Time to join the party."

Phil dropped into the pit, landing on his feet with a subtle bounce. The Thorx next to him squealed and flinched. Phil spun like a propeller slicing at the Thorx. Its severed legs dropped to the floor, the elongated body torn open splattering bile across the air. He sliced through the neck, popping its head off. Phil sliced through the head in midair, cutting it in half, the equal parts dropping to the floor by Phil's feet as he ceased spinning, crouched down with his arm extended to the Dracs. Piercing screeches and loud whining cries erupted from the remaining Thorx like bats signaling for help. Phil scowled at the Dracs across the pit.

"The human!" Saiph said stepping closer to the pit.

"Well, well," Sanos snarled. "Seems all are in attendance." He eyed Zeta. "What to do? What to do?"

Phil watched, waiting for the roar on the brink of Zeta's tongue.

"Kill them!" Zeta shrieked. "My Thorx..." He signaled to the Thorx referencing Saiph and Sanos. "Kill them all!"

The Thorx slammed their tentacles and screeched.

Phil caught their movement in the corner of his eye as he whispered under his breath, "And — here — we — go."

* * *

Saiph's heart jumped. The human was here, presenting himself for battle. He licked his lips, surveying the pit, looking for a faster way across.

"A human," Zeta scowled behind him.

"With the blades," Saiph said, watching as Phil tore into Thorx like paper. "He's here for the human girl and baby."

"How can it be?"

"Because you don't listen to your brethren," Saiph answered glancing back at Zeta.

Zeta glowered at Saiph. "What's your plan now?"

Saiph looked up then turned to Zeta. "It doesn't matter, Zeta," he said. "You'll be dead all too soon."

Sanos leapt towards Zeta who caught Sanos's blade with his own, ducking down as Sanos flipped over and dropped to his feet. The Thorx army closed in on Phil. The closest to him snapped its tentacle towards him. Phil sliced through it, side stepping to his left and the tentacle dropped. Phil spun round slicing across the neck and dropping the Thorx's head. Saiph pulled a wire off his belt, pulled it far out and tossed it to the ceiling where the clamp tore into rock securing Saiph as he jumped across the pit landing on the opposite side, slamming his hand against his belt releasing the wire.

A Thorx soldier threw its feeding tentacle at his chest, but was met with Saiph's blade. He cut off the tentacle, slicing through the Thorx head. More Thorx came at him, surrounding Saiph. He looked right then left. Every Thorx was in the pit. He looked at Phil, tearing into the Thorx. He wanted that human. *This is wasting my time!* Four Thorx surrounded him. Saiph cut through them, spinning with both blades stretched out slicing through their heads. More Thorx were behind them.

And Saiph whistled.

* * *

Zeta looked on Sanos. Never before had he seen such a Drac and for a brief moment he sided with Saiph. What appeared before him was an abomination. *This is what they're doing to us?*

"Yes, Zeta," Sanos snarled. "This is what your precious masters are doing to us."

*He caught my thought?* Zeta lowered his chin, peering at Sanos through narrow eyelids. Sanos stretched his arms to his sides. His blades glimmered in the light. He gently rocked back and forth, waiting, anticipating. "Your move!" he said.

Zeta moved his head back and forth. "Children," he snarled. He raised his right hand, stiffened his back, standing erect, reaching his hand towards Sanos, palm up. "Always need to be taught a lesson."

Sanos snickered, leaping at him. Zeta stepped forward, his arms stretched in front of him. His hands together, his forefingers and thumbs connected, formed a triangle as his blade handles stretched with his forefinger and thumbs, emitting a dark glow and sound frequency, a vibration that erupted from the formed triangle, rippling towards Sanos, slamming into his chest and throwing him onto his back. Zeta tensed his hands and the dark glow and vibration strengthened. Sanos smacked the back of his head, which bounced off the concrete only to be tossed further across the ground.

Zeta snarled at him. "I've always found it dull and unwitty... the uniform rebellion of youth." He lifted Sanos, enveloping his body within the dark glow squeezing him. "The rebellion of youth turns to obedience in maturity." He squeezed Sanos whose seething whimpers turned to guttural grunts. "Rebellion is tolerable when the instigator is naïve." Sanos's skin started to rip, his veins tearing open writhing up his neck. "But rebellion from those with higher knowledge, Sanos...is inexcusable." Blood poured from Sanos's neck like a gateway had opened. His eyes rolled to the back of his skull. "No need for concern, Sanos," Zeta laughed. "I'll make this as painful as possible."

He tossed Sanos face first to the ground. His protruding fangs snapped, broken to pieces, cutting his lips and chin igniting streams of blood across his jaw. Zeta tossed Sanos towards the pit then released his hold. Zeta bent his head snarling at him. Sanos spit blood and pieces of teeth.

"And as long," Zeta said, "as my time will allow."

# 44

CAM HEARD SCREECHES ECHO THROUGH THE AIRSHAFT. *Those things again.* He rushed towards the pit. Thinking of Phil. Thinking of Grimes and the crew, waiting for him to get that friggin' wall open. Thinking of the bomb and how he wished he hadn't rigged the damn thing without a fail-safe. A few hours ago, he'd wanted the world to blow sky high, now all he wanted was to get the hell out of the tunnels and get as many to safety as possible.

*There's a long journey ahead if we do get out of here. But first, we have to get out of here.*

He arrived at the end of the airshaft leading to the pit and peered through the vents. Yes, those things again. Many of them too. Phil seemed to slice through them like paper. *What's this? Friggin' alien vampires.* Some tatted-to-the-hairline vampire looked like he was wrestling with those things like Phil. Maybe he's after Phil. *No idea what's happening.* Two vampires battling it out, closer to him. And there's the control panel, just below the vent. And one of the ships is spinning with a fury. *What's that light?*

He pulled the clip from the AR15, checked it to be sure where he stood. His problem was with the vent. How could he get rid of the vent without anyone taking notice of it clanging and clanking down to the floor? The purpose is to get to the control panel before he was seen. Who knows what these aliens have hiding under their sleeve? Cam ran over the possibilities. Think fast! He peeked through the vent following the control panel, following the path to the right of the panel that led down a ramp back into the underground compound. Traced the many twists and turns the airshaft took, remembering a second level exit where he could get out unseen and sneak into the pit.

"And hopefully they don't take notice." Cam pursed his lips swallowing his breath. It was hot down here in the pit, the temperature close to twenty degrees higher than anywhere else. Sweat beaded on his lip and trickled down from his temples, disturbing the dried blood and soot that covered his skin. The heated air was thick. "I can do it. Got to do it. There's no other choice."

* * *

"We can't stay here," Grimes told Lao, leaning against the control desk where Lao continued his inquiry into the moon. Lao looked at him with a crossed glare.

"Where do you wish to go?"

Grimes shook his head. "No clue but we can't stay here. It's like we're waiting to be blown to pieces. There's got to be another way out."

"You heard Cam, there is no other way out other than the way we came, and that's useless. There's no way we're getting out of there with everyone up that elevator shaft. Cam will get the wall open."

Grimes huffed, shaking his head. "How are you so calm?"

"Disposition."

"Don't philosophize with me please, I'm not in the mood."

"You asked."

"My mistake." He dropped his gaze and shook his head. Looked at the boy and the men by his side. Looked at the others Cam had brought with him. *Is this what waiting around to die is like?*

Lao looked back at the monitor, and Grimes looked at him.

"Any more news from outer space?"

"It's amazing."

Grimes cocked an eyebrow. "Amazing?"

"Yes. The things that go on without our knowledge. I mean, look at us, we're soldiers fighting World War Three on American soil and while this is all going on, the same countries at war on earth are building and hiding nuclear bombs on the moon. And covering them up too."

"Cover up?"

"Exactly. Each warhead is encased in a radioactive shielding cell. It's the material they're using to hold the bombs."

"Why?"

"Considering what we've witnessed here in this compound, I'm sure there's a ton more we don't know. Think about it, when you woke up this morning, aliens did not exist. Now, not only do they exist there's multiple species and they're right here, on our own planet." He shook his head. "Alien conspiracy theories and cover ups have now become the norm. What else is out there? Why build bombs on the moon?"

"To provide a surprise defensive attack."

"Yeah!" Lao huffed. "Against who?"

Grimes shrugged. "No clue."

"Better question is, also considering what's happening, are these bombs for an alien race who's our ally? Meaning mine and yours. Quite obvious at this point we can't trust anyone in our own governments."

"I don't get it."

Lao closed his eyes, shook his head and dropped his shoulders. "The people. The citizens of the world who thought we were fighting a war for the people...we were pawns, all of us. Killing each other for what? Think about what Dr. Blum's pills were doing to your own people, and all ordered by the government. They're turning people into mindless barbarians." He motioned to the boy and other victims. "Look at the result. It's obvious this experimentation has a purpose behind it. Maybe the aliens these nuclear war heads are for mean to stop what is happening here."

"Peaceful aliens? I don't think so."

"Why not? It makes sense there would be peaceful aliens just like there are peaceful humans. Look at the countries and parts of the world that refused to take part in the war." He moved his head back and forth. "Everything changed," he said. "Nothing feels real anymore. I just want to get home to my family."

Grimes could see Lao was holding back his emotions. He felt like crying himself. He thought about the war, looking over Lao, and how a month ago he would have put a bullet between his eyes to save himself and only a day ago he was following Lao's orders and standing by while elderly Americans were lined up in a shooting gallery. Told to stand down by his own government as an effort to build cohesion with the other countries. How he wanted to spray bullets at everyone who took a shot at them. Cam said that guy Phil told him the war was a ruse meant for population control and should that be true, the powers that be achieved their goal. More than two thirds of the world's population had perished during the war. And he was sure there was more to come since most Americans were now confined to camps that had been built as a refuge for American citizens to find safety during the war. *America, land of the slaves, home of the depraved.*

He caught a scurry in the corner of his eye. It was the boy. He backed up against the wall where he sat. His eyes wide, body tense, head cocked, peering down the hall.

Grimes cocked his head. "You okay?" he called to him, holding his rifle high. "Boy," he called receiving the attention he expected. "What is it?" The boy's eyes glinted with fear. He stretched his finger towards the hall where they entered, beyond where the light dissipated, and the darkness took hold.

"The...there's something coming."

Grimes followed the boy's finger. Nothing but darkness. He looked back at the boy who continued staring. Grimes dropped his rifle towards the darkness and took a few steps closer. He squinted, trying to see what was coming, looking for a silhouette. A shape, a tentacle, a friggin' werewolf barreling through the darkness. Nothing. Whatever was disturbing the boy was waiting, assessing them and the situation. But there was nothing in the corridor he could see. Looking eye level, all he saw was black.

"I think your imagination's running away with you, boy." He dropped his rifle.

"No," the boy called. "There's definitely something in there."

*  *  *

The humans reeked of fear. Perseus studied them from the darkness, the light they stood under provided the perfect cover and he could see everything. The one who aimed his rifle at him was armed to the eyeballs. The other he couldn't tell too much about other than his emotions were running high.

And then there was that boy and the others huddled around him. He could feel their shivers and constricted thoughts. But the boy, the boy knew Perseus was here. Now he understood Zeta's urgency. They were getting away with his kin, holding them captive, and that was something Perseus could not allow.

He analyzed his attack concluding the best method was to rush at them. Those bullets will hurt so he'll have to be quick. That one closest, take him out first.

Perseus snarled, backing up, far into the tunnel and took off, barreling towards the light.

# 45

PHIL SLICED THE LEG OFF ANOTHER THORX, flipping over its limp body, bouncing and jumping, blade out and splitting the skull off the next Thorx. He caught Saiph battling his own Thorx. They surrounded him, holding him close to the pit's edge. Across the pit Zeta continued to thrash Sanos. He'll prove difficult, Phil concluded. *But none are immune to death.*

His attention shifted to the three Thorx behind him who slammed their tentacles into the concrete to make their presence known. Phil shook his head, snarled and jumped, drawing his blade across their throats in one flash swipe. Landed on his feet and crouched down, knees bent when Saiph whistled. Eyes narrow. *Why the whistle?* Another Thorx came barreling towards him, screeching and squealing.

*Again, why the whistle?*

Phil leapt at the Thorx, slamming his boot up across its chin, flipped his body then came down with his blade slicing down the Thorx head. But the Thorx behind him slammed its tentacle into his back. Phil's chest jumped. The Thorx raised him up. His protective gear stopped the tentacle from penetrating his skin. The Thorx tossed Phil ferociously. He slammed into a wall, the rock and concrete splitting his skull, and he dropped to the ground with a thud.

His face winced, vision blurred. He shook his head trying reset and focus. His back burned. Acid from the tentacle, he thought. The pain gnawed at his spine. *Get it off, get it off.* He tore at his gear, unfastening the clamps holding the gear in place and his armor dropped. Smoke rose from the opening where the tentacle had entered, the acid disintegrating his armor. His attention snapped to the vicious growl that erupted over the pit.

The lycan jumped into the Thorx in front of Saiph, the beast apparently protecting him. *As if he needs protection.*

*No, it's a distraction.* He watched as the Lycan stood on its hind legs and roared at the Thorx. Phil stepped forward locking eyes with Saiph. The lycan tearing at the Thorx who rushed at the beast.

And Saiph barreled towards Phil.

\* \* \*

Sanos had enough of Zeta. His power was unexpected but not all-powerful. And he despised Zeta's little speeches. *It's time to shut him up...permanently.* His veins swelled with a nauseating pain, and his chest and arms seeped blood. His face was beet red, blood dropped from his teeth, and his mouth swelled through his gums with an acidic throbbing.

He thought of his men, what few were remaining. Somewhere on board one of the ships. Thought of Zeta and COR and what they'll do to them. *All because of me! Because I was weak.*

He climbed to his feet.

"Still some fight left, Sanos?" Zeta snarled.

Sanos eyed Zeta through narrow eyelids, his breathing labored and his throat hoarse. He felt his insides rotting. His right leg twitched and felt heavy like lead had been dropped into the bone. Sanos seethed through his teeth as the pain surged to his skull. He gripped the handles in his palms. "Until you're dead and buried, Zeta, my strength will remain."

"Purpose, Sanos?" Zeta moved his head back and forth. "I've no time for petty insurgencies."

He unleashed his power, igniting the vibration from the triangle formed by his fingers. Sanos slammed his arms together; blades towards Zeta and the power that erupted from his arms met Zeta's vibration. The two forces collided with heavy resistance. Sanos and Zeta struggled to overcome the other's intensity. Zeta took a step towards Sanos, barreling his vibration on top of him forcing Sanos to drop to one knee. Zeta's force inching closer to Sanos. And Zeta took another step closer.

"No concern, Sanos," Zeta snarled. "The end is here."

\* \* \*

"We've got to help him," Jubal told the others. They were watching the battle in the pit from the ship. Their focus on Sanos and Zeta. "Dracs don't sit when our leader fights for us."

Kaidan eyed Jubal and gave a quick nod. "Agreed."

Moya stepped towards them. "What about the human with the blades?"

Jubal addressed him. "Saiph will dismantle him. Zeta is strong. We must attack together."

Kaidan added, "Give Sanos a reprieve to replenish his strength."

"And take him down," Moya said.

"Together!"

* * *

Phil caught Saiph's blade with his. Saiph's boot slammed into his chest pummeling Phil back crashing into a wall where he dropped to his knees. His back writhed in agony. Not only did the crash jolt pain up his spine, the Thorx acid burned his skin, growing and widening across his back.

Saiph was on the prowl. Arms stretched, hunched over, eyeing his prey. Behind him his lycan tore at the Thorx attempting to surround the beast. He watched as Zeta forced himself over Sanos. And three more Dracs emerged from a ship, spreading out across the pit. He breathed deep, sensing the blood gurgle in his throat.

"You're dying, human," Saiph said scowling at Phil. "All will end for you soon enough. The gentle black of death will greet your eyes and you will be no more." Saiph stepped closer, cautious. "By my blade you will meet your end."

Phil snarled at Saiph. "All you vampires know how to do is talk. Once my blade tears open your throat, I'll watch as you garble your words, Drac."

He leapt at Saiph. Blade to blade, ignited steel sparks of white and blue. Phil jumped over Saiph, slicing down his shoulder. Saiph quickly turned catching Phil's blow across his neck. Phil connected his fist across Saiph's jaw. An upper cut splattered blood from his nose as Saiph reeled back. Phil quickly took a few steps, jumped and slammed a second fist across Saiph's cheekbone. He dropped to his knee but bounced back quickly catching Phil's blade. Jumped to his feet. Blade against blade.

Phil clenched Saiph's shoulders with both hands and slammed his forehead into Saiph's bloodied nose, dropping him to his back. A quick step forward while swiping his left blade towards Saiph's head only to be met by Saiph's blade. Saiph swiped Phil's legs from under him. Phil dropped backwards, slamming onto his back but bridged quickly with his palms. Phil flipped back to his feet. Saiph jumped, backing up. He glowered at Phil. The human whose resolve stood before him, his arms stiff, his eyes scowling at Saiph.

* * *

Mintaka glided into the crystal room where her fellow greys surrounded Sandy with Telas standing over her, her eyes metallic black. Mintaka had been tending to the child, kept secure and away from the mother to help break the maternal connection. Her attention had been disturbed by the fighting in the pit. She addressed the greys.

"A battle ensues," she told them. The others gave her audience. "Drac rebellion against Zeta. And the human is here."

"He's here for her…" said Alnitak and Alnilam. "And the child." The witches turned to Mono.

"We may choose to leave now," Mintaka said. "If the human wins this battle, he may cause us concern. We do not possess your ability," she said to Mono. "Our greys do not possess the gift for attack...only defense."

Mono addressed them, her eyes wide, scowling. "We continue with our inquiry," she said. She reached her hand toward Telas, fingers stretched and tense, then clenched a moment later in a tight fist. Her power erupting in Telas's skull reflected by the painful constriction writhing across Telas's visage.

Mintaka, Alnitak and Alnilam shared concerned stares.

# 46

**GRIMES STIFFENED. SOMETHING MOVED INSIDE THE DARKNESS.** He stepped back. "I do believe you're right, boy," he said under his breath.

Lao stood as Grimes clenched his rifle. His eyes scrunched. The movement was quick, like a wallop tearing through the tunnel. His jaw dropped when the giant barreled into the light.

Grimes squeezed his finger igniting bullets that seemed to disappear as the giant propelled, jumping onto the wall, up the ceiling and jumped feet first into Grimes. His bullets circling the giant never found its target. Grimes was tossed back from the blow, hard against the floor as Lao shot at the giant with his 9MM. But the giant was fast, its massive hand swatted the gun from Lao's hand, taking his throat in the giant's mitt and raising him off his feet then tossed Lao across the room.

The giant roared at the boy and men huddled on the floor.

* * *

Cam thought about the boy as he gazed into the pit, crouched down against the wall. The control panel not too far away, just a slip into the pit and he'd be there. He peeked around the wall and watched as the lycan tore into Thorx. He couldn't see Phil from his position but hoped he remained alive.

And then there was that sound, like a screeching reverberation that walloped and fluttered in his eardrums, coming from that alien vampire. The one who appeared as if he maintained some sort of vampire status Cam was unaware of, whose vibration emitting from his fingers dropped that...that...*friggin' vampire mutation* to his knees. All were distracted. *It's now or never.* He crept around the corner to the control desk, crouched down with the hope of not being discovered.

He hid behind the long half-moon desk with three monitors. Cam searched the desk on his knees to avoid disclosure. His eyes darted across the desk. There seemed to be a billion buttons, switches and controls. Cam pursed his lips. *Think!* He focused on the central monitor. The screen was black. The keyboard was set inside the desk below the monitor. He punched the return key. And the monitor gleamed with life.

* * *

Sanos eyed Zeta's approach. With each step closer his sound wave grew heavier, stronger, barreling down on him. He felt weak under the vibration. His eardrums had already popped, blood running down the side of his neck. The thunderous sound dulled to a light roaring wind but the power continued to hold strong. He felt his insides depleting. Wasn't sure how much more he could take. How much more his body could sustain before he lost all ability to function.

Zeta stepped closer forcing the vibration down onto Sanos. His skin continued to tear, splitting down his veins. The back of his eyeballs burned and his vision blurred. His brain twisted with excruciating pain. Blood dripped from his eyes. Sanos, weak and feeble, released his power, and his own combatting vibration ceased. His guard dropped, and Zeta's power ascended upon him with relentless ferocity.

Death, Sanos thought. It's not that bad.

* * *

Zeta was seconds from delivering Sanos into the netherworld when he glimpsed a shadow in the corner of his eye. The vampire Moya was barreling towards him in midflight, about to strike down with his blade across Zeta's neck.

Zeta quickly shifted his vibration toward Moya, turning up the volume through a quick reaction, tightening his fingers and catching Moya as he descended with a roar that turned to a fading squeal once caught within the vibration. His body disintegrated with its descent. Every vein, every artery split, tore open and burst. And

Moya's remains dropped to the ground, whisked away like ashes in a hurricane.

"FOOL!" Zeta barked at the remains before snapping his neck around. Jubal and Kaidan stood on opposite sides of him, arms stretched tight with the blades ready. Both looked at Moya's remains, then to Zeta. He moved his head back and forth. "You are all fools, look at all around you. This is blasphemy."

"Only if it's what you believe," Jubal hollered rushing at him. Zeta caught his blade with his own when Kaidan attacked but Zeta caught him in the vibration from his free hand, sending him flying to the ground with a crash.

Zeta threw his free arm against Jubal's blade. One after the other, slamming down hard as Jubal backed up under the weight of his force. Zeta snarled at him thrashing as steel sparks raged from their blades. Kaidan scurried to his feet running at Zeta who spun around swiping at him catching blade against blade with long swoops of his arms. Kaidan backed up. The force was strong, like strength brought on from rage. The force backed him up and Jubal went at Zeta who sent his boot into his chest, lifted him up with his vibration. Spun around with his blade slicing through Kaidan's neck, his bones severed with a smooth and forceful swipe. Satisfied, he turned to Jubal, apt focus and control, contracting his arms, turning up the vibration. Jubal's skin beginning to split. Kaidan's head rolled to a stop by Sanos. The decapitated body dropped falling forward with a thud, blood jutting from the severed neck.

"Killing young foolish vampires is easier than sucking on the bones of humans," Zeta said to Jubal, holding him in isolation, his feet dangling above the floor, blood dripping from his torn veins and skin. An agonizing scream rose from his throat.

And Sanos's eyes opened.

* * *

Saiph scowled at the human in front of him. His resolve equaled his own. But he was weak. Saiph could sense strength leaving him. Even as Phil stood before him, poised and ready to continue he knew this human was hanging on by a thread. *But an injured animal is ever more a threat.*

He stepped with caution towards Phil. Arms stretched wide as he circled the human who mirrored his movements. Behind the human Saiph's lycan tore into Thorx. His beast ripped through them like paper. Thorx squeals and screeches raged inside the pit. Lycan roars accompanied them. And across the pit, Zeta ripped apart the Dracs. *I told them to stay on the ship.* And whatever hope Saiph had in Sanos's ability to dismantle Zeta had gone. He knew his battle with his master was forthcoming, a battle he'd hoped to avoid but was now inescapable. But the human was first. He required a quick death for Saiph had tired of the human and there were more pressing matters to be dealt with.

He locked eyes with the human. Saiph had heard in rumors and whispers over the years about a human who carried the blades. A human who lived in the shadows. A human who was trained by Robyn Winter. But there was never any proof of such an existence. No one had ever come forward who'd battled with such a being. No survivors at least. The story had become a myth. A human with the blades was scoffed at as there was no way a human could learn the art, and the infamous Robyn Winter was dead. Had been for a very long time. But this human was proof that the myth was true. And Robyn Winter was alive. Somehow, somewhere, he was alive, and the proof was snarling in front of him. And he had to admit, the human was damn good.

"You gonna keep circling, Drac? Or are you gonna bite?"

Saiph smiled. An instinctive reaction. Behind the laugh he felt a tremble of fear. A sensation he did not like. He rushed at Phil. Sparks raged off the connecting blades. Phil stepped forward backing Saiph up as they dueled, blade against blade. Saiph planted his feet. His left blade caught Phil's. Saiph forced Phil's arm down. And he saw his chance, his shot at Phil's throat by way of Phil's injured left arm. Saiph threw his free blade at Phil's throat. But before it landed, before he tore into the human's windpipe, Phil leapt over Saiph slicing his blade across Saiph's shoulder, ducked and rolled as Saiph swiped at air with his strong arm. His shoulder stung something awful. He saw blood pool around his shoulder, seeping through his armor. Phil had caught him perfectly, in that vulnerable part of his armor that connected the sleeve to the shoulder. Saiph gritted his teeth.

And in front of him stood the human, ready to deliver more of the same.

* * *

Cam rushed through screen after screen. Every so often he looked up at the battle raging not too far from where he was, hoping none of them noticed him. The monitor reflected DOS programming, green text on a black screen. His eyes roamed across the text, moving from screen to screen. Enter. Enter. Enter. Enter. His head moved ever so slightly with every new screen, reading over headers and bits of information before passing over to the next screen until the word bounced back at him. Tunnel Security and Controls. He paused. "Yes," he whispered. And pushed Enter. The screen changed and Cam's jaw dropped.

"What the fuck?" He shook his head. The screen was no longer in English. What glowed on the monitor was a language he'd never seen before.

# 47

SANDY NOTICED HOW THE SCENE GLIMMERED like a crystal shimmer that waved across the landscape changing the scene. Where once there had been light was no more. The scene was dark with overcast black clouds carried on the heels of a thunderous wind that quickly garnered immense strength.

And the baby's cries were relentless. And Telas was even more relentless. Her nagging degrading remarks kept coming. "You're useless. Give up the baby. Give me permission, and I'll raise him as he should be, a Drac. Not a human. Humans are weak." And the most prevalent degrading remark, "Give him over, and you can stay here like a queen."

Sandy may have given in were in not for the eyes. Telas's eyes remained black to the core. Standing with the baby in her arms, trying desperately to calm his cries. "He won't stop crying because of you. Because he wants to be with me, and yet you refuse his basic needs." Sandy squinted in the wind sitting by the water. A nagging foreboding twisted in her gut. *This is wrong. This is all wrong.*

She searched her thoughts. Searched her memory but there was nothing. Nothing to tell her how or why she'd come to this place. This lake and waterfall. It seemed like she'd always been here. With Telas. With the baby. She couldn't even remember giving birth or being pregnant. Had no recollection of the war and base camps and....Ben and Phil. And that nagging feeling kept walloping into her throat like nausea grips the palette, poisoning thought with a sense of foreboding. Telas sat next to her.

"Here, take him," Telas said. "If you won't give him to me, then take him."

Sandy looked at her. Those black eyes shimmered as if the wind were inside them. She looked down at the screaming baby in Telas's arms. His eyes were also black. She looked back at Telas. She was saying something, but her voice was mute as Sandy searched her eyes. Looking at what those eyes reflected. She did not see the landscape. She saw herself. Stretched out, lying down, behind her a range of gleaming crystals. Telas moved her head and the scene reflected the movement and Sandy's eyes narrowed, looking, observing, peculiar. She saw Mono reflected in Telas's eyes. She looked at Telas's arms and hands in the reflection. The cries continued but there was no baby in her arms. She looked back at Telas then at the landscape. The wind was crashing against the trees, sending ripples through the water. Tree limbs bent under the weight of the wind.

Across the water she saw it. One single rose seemed to reach toward her. She studied the rose. Bright red petals supported by a thick stem that reached into the earth. She felt the answers to her questions resided inside the rose. She didn't notice that Telas was no longer beside her. Behind the rose the scene changed with that same glimmer. She saw light behind the rose. Bright white light reflected from a wall of crystals. And someone was speaking, muffled words in the wind.

She kept her focus on the rose. Behind it the wall became prevalent in her periphery. The scene changed, glimmering between landscape and wall. Sandy saw the greys. Saw Telas standing over her. *I'm lying down. In a room. On a ship.*

Memories flooded her thoughts. Aliens. The camp. Ben. Vampires. Phil. Like flashes of lightning the memories pumped in her thoughts behind the rose. Telas. Lycan. The pit. Her eyelids fluttered. She saw Telas standing over her. Behind Telas the white light began to dim. She saw the room, the wall covered in crystals. Felt herself spinning. *No, the ship is spinning.* And those muffled words turned coherent.

"There should be no loose ends."

"She won't relent."

"There is another way."

"Prepare for departure. We leave now."

"Without the others?"

"Yes."

Sandy may have been dizzy, but she did all she could to hear what was happening around her.

"And the mother?"

The question seemed to float inside the room. Sandy's eyelids were heavy, her eyes dry and tired. She turned on her side, and her head spun. She closed her eyes trying to stop that spinning dizzy sensation. The question was asked again, "And the mother?"

The answer dropped like an anvil in Sandy's brain. She recognized the voice now. It was Mono who answered.

"Both will die." The statement was followed with a pause. "Neither will give up the child. We cannot allow loose ends. The hold is too strong. Both must die."

* * *

Perseus snarled at the boy, his fury resolving into calm under the boy's presence. The boy approached the giant.

"It's okay," the boy said. "It's okay."

Grimes drifted awake, watching the scene. The giant seemed to calm with the boy. He took out his 9MM. Perseus growled at him but the boy shouted, "No." The boy shook his head. "He's not gonna hurt us."

"Not gonna hurt us?"

"Put the gun down, Corporal," the boy ordered, and Grimes cocked his eyebrows.

"Why?" Grimes whispered.

The boy approached Perseus who dropped to his knees. "He's just scared."

"Scared? Of us? I find that hard to believe."

"Not of us," the boy said. "Right?" The boy touched Perseus' head. "No more," he told him. "No more. You're safe here. No more. No more at all."

Perseus growled and snarled. He looked on the boy with a frightful grimace.

Lao walked cautiously behind the boy.

"It's okay," the boy repeated.

"How are you doing that?" Lao asked eliciting a snarled stare from Perseus.

"He's one of us," the boy said. "Another experiment for their benefit. Tortured by them." The boy moved his head back and forth. "No more," he said. He touched his forehead to Perseus.

Lao and Grimes locked eyes. They both shrugged. Grimes stood, walked towards the boy and Perseus snarled at him. "Can you tell your giant I mean no harm? Please?"

"He's protecting me. He'll be good. He will."

Grimes approached, cautious, glaring at the giant.

Lao said, "Is there any way possible you can convince him to force that wall open?"

* * *

Jubal was on the brink of death. His body covered in blood that seeped from his veins and splitting flesh. His eyes rolled to the back of his head and he felt his insides disintegrating.

"Look at me," Zeta snarled.

Jubal forced himself to look at Zeta. Blood covered his eyes with a silken crimson glow. The look in Zeta's eyes revealed unrelenting madness. A thin conniving smile spread across his lips.

Zeta lifted his chin. "Now the end comes for you," he snarled. "And the black abyss of death will welcome you."

Jubal's brain swelled inside his skull. Blood rushed in thick streams down his nose, ears, and mouth. The vibration strengthened, forcing a wrenching scream from his lungs. Then, a massive movement blurred behind Zeta. The movement came in fast, a large black blur that dropped with a heavy thud. And Jubal dropped to the ground. The vibration ceased. The hold on him relinquished. But still the pain continued, lying limp on the concrete. He saw Zeta. A surprised and constricted gaze graced his countenance. Blood trickled from the center of his throat. His head slid off his neck and dropped to the floor. Behind him stood Sanos. And Zeta's body slumped forward. Jubal could see Sanos, standing erect over the body, blood dripping off his blade.

# 48

PHIL THREW HIS BOOT INTO SAIPH'S CHEST. Saiph stumbled back. Smacked his head against the ground. He jumped up quickly, and Phil shook his head. *Damn vampire won't stay down.*

Behind them a Thorx plunged its tentacle into the lycan's back forcing the beast head-first into the ground as the Thorx acid went to work. The lycan howled and squealed. Two more Thorx thrust their tentacles into the lycan body. Their tentacles pumping as the lycan squirmed beneath them.

"Looks like your pet just met its fate," Phil said to Saiph who stood erect. Phil could see his anger, torn across his bloodied face.

Saiph snarled at Phil, his lycan howling and squealing behind him. "He'll just have to tear you apart in oblivion."

"C'mon!" Phil raged and they rushed at each other with a fierce exchange of steel against steel. Saiph kicked Phil's kneecap. Followed with a roundhouse kick that crashed across his jaw and Phil reeled back stumbling but caught himself before losing his balance. Saiph rushed at him. Blade against blade. Saiph sliced Phil's shoulder with a clean cut. Phil winced as Saiph dropped down spinning and sliced Phil's leg above the knee.

Phil grabbed his leg and blood seeped through his fingers. Fell back awkward, dropped down with a heavy thud on his tailbone. Saiph kicked his face, and blood spewed from his nose and mouth. The back of his head smacked the ground. His vision blurred. Pain jolted to his brain. He felt himself losing consciousness. Saw darkness as his eyelids sagged. But Phil snapped his eyes open.

*Don't go out! Don't go!*

Blood streamed from his arm and leg. Stinging pain writhed across his body. Every part of him had gone numb with pain. His awareness was reinvigorated by the ship that held Sandy. It seemed to change. The spinning remained the same but the light that emanated from within stopped abruptly. Did they break Sandy? Phil thought seeing past Saiph to the ship. Saiph noticed the change too. His head turned to the ship.

Phil sensed a rush of urgency. *Is that ship about to leave?* And then the smell hit him. The lycan skin lay on the ground bubbling and steaming. He heard the screech. The Thorx thrusting its tentacle at him. Phil moved quickly slicing the tentacle before it entered his chest. He jumped up slicing through its head and looked up. The two remaining Thorx attacked Saiph. But the ship. The ship emitted a sound reflecting a release of power. Then the ship hummed. Phil knew what these sounds were. The ship was about to leave.

With Sandy still inside.

\* \* \*

Sanos held Jubal. "Stay with me," Sanos told him. Jubal's body covered in blood that continued to gush from his veins. "I'll bring you to the oxygen chamber." He went to pick up Jubal, but the sudden movement caused Jubal to yelp in pain.

Jubal opened his eyes, looking over Sanos. He reached his hand to him touching his cheek. "Glad you came back," he said then coughed, blood spilling over his lips. His eyes closed, and his body fell limp. And Sanos snarled, holding his subordinate dead in his arms.

\* \* \*

Cam rushed through every screen he could find. But they all contained a language he was not familiar with. He pushed keys. Flicked buttons on the dashboard. His attention caught by a snarling and raging Sanos.

And the ship that appeared to be leaving.

\* \* \*

Mono waited for the greys to leave before addressing Telas who remained under Mono's spell. Sandy coughing, gagging, hacking. Mono had instructed the greys to power up the ship for departure and secure the baby for transport. Mono released Telas and saw her eyes return to normal. Mono glided over to Sandy, hovering in front of her eyeing Telas's reformation.

"We can't allow both to remain," Mono told Telas. She placed her hand over Sandy emitting pain throughout her body and Sandy constricted, screeching in agony.

"Leave her be," Telas said. But Mono squeezed her fist, and Sandy reacted again, her body convulsing and contracting. Telas hollered at Mono, "I said leave her be!"

Mono's eyes flickered at Telas. She released Sandy, bent her head and glared at Telas. "Do you wish a soldier's death? I do agree you've earned that much."

Telas looked over Sandy. Her eyes filled with tears.

"How sweet," Mono said. "This union of Drac and human...I've waited so long to witness. The child will provide what is necessary. All else is paltry. The future is what remains most important."

* * *

Telas locked eyes with Mono. She moved her head back and forth. "But you'll never see it." She touched Sandy's ankle before Mono's wallop of pain drove into her skull. She hunched over, and Mono threw her against the wall where she fell to her knees, clutching the sides of her head, her eyes bleeding. Screaming. Being torn apart. Mono reached to Telas's forehead.

*Hold on!* Telas felt everything inside her twist and squirm. *Hold on!* She saw Sandy sit up, and Telas clenched Mono's hand as she eyed Sandy in the corner of her eye. Sandy's eyes were wide, watching Telas and Mono. Telas shook and trembled but she held Mono's hand with an iron grip.

*Now, Sandy!*

She projected her voice into Sandy's mind. *Now!*

Mono's eyes changed then. What once had contained certainty now reflected fear. She tried to force her hand from Telas's grip but Telas held on using every ounce of strength she could find. She wasn't fighting for her life. She was fighting for another.

* * *

Sandy understood what to do. Understood what it meant. Telas would not survive this ordeal. But her sacrifice was for the child. Sandy had received a download of information when Telas touched Sandy's ankle; the information dropped into Sandy's consciousness as if the knowledge had always been there.

Sandy achingly stood, mesmerized by what she witnessed. A rose, that same rose that was in the garden, was prominent and unwavering. She could see it. The rose looked back at Sandy, gleaming in the center of Telas's eyes. Sandy took two steps and reached out her hand, gripping Mono's skull in her palm. And Telas smiled. The room whirled, thundering as Mono contracted, tried desperately to pull her hand free.

"Into oblivion, Mono. We go together!" Telas shrieked.

Their skin tore and split. Bones shattered into dust. The final scream coming from both Telas and Mono filled the room, the ship, and thrashed into the pit. Sandy felt Mono's skull split beneath her hand. And both were torn into tiny pieces that fluttered like ash, disintegrating in the next moment and were no more.

Sandy dropped to her knees with a heavy labored breath. One last piece of ash drifted in front of her. It gleamed with light, shined in Sandy's pupil, then disappeared. The ground where Telas had been was stained with blood. But that too dissipated, as if some wind had come into the room to wipe it clear. And Sandy let out a quick stuttered cry. Telas was gone.

She felt the ship move. Looked around the room.

*Where's Adam?*

And then white vapor showered into the room from the walls. And the ship lifted off the ground. And Sandy's eyelids began to close.

* * *

Saiph cut the head off the last Thorx when the ship lifted into the air over his shoulder. *No way that ship leaves.* But the ship was too high and too fast with no possible method to stop its flight. Except!

*Ignite the bomb. Turn this whole place into ashes.*

He reached for the most secure place on his belt. The place where he hid the detonator.

* * *

Phil's heart dropped, watching the ship rise. Like watching his dreams dissipate in front of him, reaching out to grab them except they've gone before his fingers had a chance to close. His attention snapped to Saiph, holding a device and snarling at the ship. Phil recognized it immediately.

*He has the detonator.*

Phil's next move was pure instinct. He ran at Saiph, his eyes locked on the detonator in Saiph's hand. The detonator held between both thumbs and forefingers.

"From the heart of Drac, I stab at thee." Saiph's voice a low triumphant growl.

The ship spun overhead, and Saiph's eyes snapped towards Phil who leapt at Saiph, his boots leading the charge, connecting with Saiph's chest and propelling him back towards the pit. Phil dropped to the ground, and Saiph plummeted through the pit's opening, the detonator tossed from his hands, spiraling into the earth below. Phil went to the edge. Below was a straight drop that went on for miles with no end to be seen other than a cloud of billowing smoke with a dull pinkish and yellow glow. He watched as Saiph dropped, becoming smaller with every second, plunging into the cloud miles below.

Phil pushed himself to his feet, his entire body shaking and stinging with pain.

And the ship raced overhead, spiraling down into the pit and was gone. And Phil's heart with it.

* * *

The scene dropped Cam's jaw. Watching Phil as the ship dived out of sight, and the look in his eyes, that defeated blank stare. It seemed like Phil had just died. At least that part of him that carried his pride on his sleeve.

But Cam wasn't the only one watching the scene. Sanos was watching too. He roared at Phil standing across the pit. Sanos stretched his arms, clenched the handles in his palms. Phil looked up. His expression changed. Hate revealed in those eyes.

# 49

PERSEUS GROWLED. FORCING THE WALL OPEN. Metal breaking, being torn apart, popping wires and bolts and clamps.

"He's gonna get it," Grimes said. "C'mon." He went to the wall, pushing. He could feel the wall easing in their hands. Grimes looked back at everyone. "C'MON!" he hollered. Lao went to the wall with the boy and all others followed behind them.

Perseus huffed and snarled.

"PUSH!" Grimes called. "PUSH!"

The wall opened, no more than an inch, but the air that rushed in from the outside was cool relieving the tunnel's thick cloud of heat.

"It's moving," Lao said.

Perseus shook his head violently and roared forcing the wall to open. Metal pops and snaps whisked across their ears. And Perseus took a step back then thrust himself at the wall. His massive thick hands gripping the beveled rock, grunting and hollering as the wall slid open, the locks popped off their hinges.

And the tunnel became consumed with sound. A high-pitched alarm on the heels of a mechanical voice.

*System Breach! System Breach! City Self Destruct Activated!*

Grimes and Lao locked eyes.

"Go!" Grimes called. He forced the boy out first and all followed. Perseus behind them who gathered a few of the slower movers in his arms. All followed tearing out of the tunnel. The deafening alarm and mechanical voice faded as they ran up an incline to the outside. The boy with Cam's shirt over his head led the charge into the sun.

And the ground beneath them started to quake.

\* \* \*

The alarm was ear piercing. The ceiling began to crumble. Pieces of metal and rock dropped to the ground. Sanos looked above. The door in the ceiling opened. Sanos knew how the self-destruct responded. Knew what was coming. Knew that ceiling would remain open for a few minutes. The self-destruct allowed for anyone caught inside to find escape. He eyed one of the remaining two ships. Then turned to Phil. He wanted to slice the human into pieces but knew there was not a moment's time to engage in combat. The entire city would plummet into the earth once the self-destruct was complete.

He leapt across the pit landing on his feet and immediately turned to Phil.

Another time, he thought, staring at the human, his lips curled, snarling as rock and debris fell from the ceiling in between them. If you get out of here. *If!*

He jumped and bounced towards the ship, propelled up the ramp that retracted after he was on board. A moment later the ship roared into a whirling spin.

\* \* \*

Cam searched the monitor. The language remained as before, but the screen revealed where the breach had come from.

"They got it open," he said and could have laughed if it weren't for current circumstances. The ground beneath him quaked and rumbled as he watched the ship with Sanos propel up through the ceiling. Watched Phil enter the last ship. Cam fired his rifle to catch Phil's attention. The alarm combined with falling rock and metal allowed no such attention to be given.

"Shit!" Cam looked up as a piece of ceiling came crashing down towards him. "SHIT!" He jumped from the control desk slamming against the ground and rolling. Jumped to his feet and ran to the pit watching as the ship began to spin and the ramp retract.

"He knows how to fly that thing?" He started to flail his arms.

\* \* \*

Phil saw Cam on the other side of the pit. System controls alerted him to the ceilings closure. He ground his teeth as he clenched his jaw; fit a metal halo over his head with two prongs that reached over his temples. The screen in front of him lit up like dominos with a pumping sound that circled the room as Phil pushed his hands inside a metal box on the panel in front of him. The screens provided a clear panoramic view from the outside. The ship roared over the pit where he released the ramp with a simple thought.

Watched as Cam jumped onto the ramp and ran into the ship. Phil retracted the ramp and Cam sprinted into the cockpit.

"Strap in!" Phil ordered. His voice rushed.

"Of course. Of course," Cam acknowledged in a hurried tone. He was in his seat and strapped in as if all were accomplished in unison.

The window Phil looked through glimmered. **WARNING** it buzzed in red letters. **Object Approaching.** The screen revealed that the ceiling had broken and a large piece of rock and metal was spiraling down on top of the ship.

Phil hands were steady, his thoughts projected on the screen in front of him as the ship turned on a dime dipping to a ninety-degree angle into the pit. The falling ceiling plummeted into the earth as Phil guided the ship away from the pit, the roof over them breaking and falling apart. Cam's eyes were wide. The ship was fast. He knew the exterior was spinning however the cockpit was stable.

Massive round and thick beams reached into the roof from somewhere down below. They looked like neurons in a brain with dendrites that clasped into the roof. Flickers and bolts of electricity sparked up the synapse electrifying the dendrites. Phil guided the ship, weaving around plummeting pieces of roof.

"Why's it collapsing?" Cam hollered and for the first time turned to Phil, noticing how bloody and wounded he was. And that scowl in his eyes. How intent those eyes were.

"The self-destruct," Phil said. "Everything will fall into the earth. Everything that was will plummet down."

"Like a sink hole."

"Exactly. But the self-destruct won't leave a hole. It'll cover up the hole with a hundred feet of earth."

"Like it was never there."

Phil nodded.

"Where does it go?"

"Down," Phil said. "Far, far down. But it'll incinerate before reaching a final destination."

"Which is?"

Phil shot Cam a stare and Cam understood what was behind that look. *Shut up!*

The ship roared forward, weaving between neurons. Cam bent his head, as if to see what had happened to the pit. And he could see. See the pit. The underground city falling into the earth. It was as if the ship's spin created one long round window. He could see everywhere, from all angles.

He looked back at Phil. His arm where Saiph had sliced him continued to bleed.

"You're wounded," Cam said.

Phil didn't look at him. "I know," he said.

Obviously, Cam thought. He's not up for chitchat. He told himself to shut up.

Phil's eyes narrowed. On the window screen a path was set. Phil looked up and Cam followed his eyes. The earth opened above them and the ship roared into it changing directions and spinning, twisting and propelled into the opening. Out into the sun and wasteland that was now American soil.

# 50

**"IS SHE SECURE?" MINTAKA SAID TO ALNITAK** and Alnilam upon their return. Mintaka guided the ship through the earth. But the scene did not reflect the pinkish clouds from the pit. As they flew the scene became dark gray and black. The ship moved smoothly through the neurons and dendrites. The darkness illuminated with blue and white flickers of electricity that pumped slowly up the neuron to the dendrites, the branch like web that reached and clamped into the ceiling.

Alnitak and Alnilam answered, "Yes. The human has been secured. Primed for reconditioning."

"And the child? Is he as expected?"

"He presents with the appropriate traits. Only maturity will provide the answers we all seek."

Mintaka paused before a response was made. "And Mono?"

"Gone," they answered.

Mintaka lowered her eyes. In the distance a festival of lights could be seen, glimmering and buzzing with life. An underground city the size of which would rival the state of Texas. The city lights reflected in Mintaka's wide eyes as she turned her gaze to the city. The ship flew undisturbed and alone in the darkness.

"Only time will tell," Mintaka said. "And time is all we have."

\* \* \*

Grimes and crew waited under the hot morning sun, having witnessed the camp collapse into the earth and quickly covered with rock and soil. What had been teeming with life and death was now a memory and myth. Grimes and Lao talked among themselves. No water. No food. And a host of refugees they had no clue how to progress with.

The boy stood under the sunlight, Cam's uniform by his feet, quiet and unmoving. The others sat, huddled together. Perseus sat alone watching the boy.

"Cam said Atlanta," Grimes said to Lao. "That guy too, Phil. Said to look for someone named Robyn Winter."

"If he even exists." Lao responded. He gestured to the refugees. "Getting to Atlanta will be a challenge."

Grimes nodded. "Of course, but we have no other options. Obviously, we're in the dark here. Not sure about you but Atlanta's worth the risk because I'm not contacting my superiors. That ship has obviously sailed."

Lao pursed his lips. His eyes reflected agreement. "How far is Atlanta?"

Grimes was about to answer when they heard what sounded like a whirlwind of hovering thunder. Lao looked over Grimes' shoulder and saw an approaching alien ship. The others turned too. Perseus stood and the boy opened his eyes. The ship raced towards them, turned abruptly away, twisted and turned then headed straight for them. Grimes stepped forward, tracking the ship's movement.

"Where did it come from?" Grimes said.

"Where do any of them come from?" said Lao. He turned to the refugees. There was nowhere to go. Nowhere to run or hide. The ship will incinerate them. He remembered the men he'd been with. Remembered how they were incinerated into ashes and dust. He drew his rifle. Grimes did the same.

"No," the boy hollered as the ship roared at them.

"Are you crazy?" Grimes said. "Do you know what those things can do?"

"It's not them," the boy said. "It's Cameron."

The ship stopped, hovered a moment then descended. A ramp projected from the ship to the earth. A moment later Cam appeared on the ramp. Arms stretched wide, he cocked his head and said, "Need a ride?"

And Grimes and Lao lowered their weapons. For the first time in a long while they felt relief.

## 51

**WHEN SANDY AWAKENED, THE DREAM SHE'D BEEN** entrenched in remained like a thick cloud she couldn't wipe clear. Back in the safety camp Ben's voice, fearful and nervous, raged across the camp:

*Ruuuunnnn Sandy!*

Ben's order echoed in Sandy's ears. Her heart thumping, heavy panicked breath, hiding in the church where she'd met Ben two days earlier, before the camp had erupted in a frenzy. The camp gates and doors had been opened that morning, ushering in the very soldiers they had been hiding from: the Chinese and Russian military. American soldiers stood idle when orders and declarations were given to those in the camp. Mass hysteria resulted in a small uprising, quickly quieted by bullets and death. People in the camp were forced in line, told to take pills (for medical reasons), asked questions, personal questions about the past, where they came from, who their family was. Sandy had lied after three women were escorted away on account of pregnancy. But this morning her stomach showed, and she knew, she knew she had to find Ben. Had to find a way to escape together. An American soldier had warned the refugees about the sinister experiments he'd witnessed first-hand. And Sandy believed him, felt that click in her stomach.

And now she was hiding, hiding in the church, knowing they were coming, searching for her. Beads of sweat cascaded from her temples and forehead, her hair matted with sweat, her heart pounding in a panicked rush, wishing the sun would go to sleep so she could hide under the cover of darkness. She thought about Ben. What were they doing with him? How had they retaliated when he'd lunged at them to help Sandy escape? But how could she escape? They were confined, locked inside a wall that had turned into a prison.

Outside the church, hurried words spoken in Chinese followed by a Russian tongue. She could see silhouettes beyond the stained-glass windows. They were coming and fear shuddered through her bones, constricting her veins, skipping heartbeats. She backed up as if to hide further. As if she could disappear with a single thought and not be discovered. She should have told Ben about the click. Should have been more up front with her instincts. But she had wanted it all to end, all the carnage, the fear, and the war. Tricked herself into believing all was well and would end as such. After years in the camp, she could taste freedom and wanted it so badly she played the fool to her thoughts. Now this, another spiraling turn for the worse. She wanted Ben, her confidant, her companion. The person who rescued her, who always made her feel safe no matter what had happened. Life without Ben was a life she had never imagined.

The door bumped. Locked, although she knew that would not keep them out. They were coming in and there was nothing she could do to stop them.

Sandy stepped back and a hand clasped across her mouth, strong, unwavering. An arm wrapped around her arms and torso and she was locked within an embrace. Eyes wide and a whimper escaped her throat, her scream stifled by the hand clamped across her lips. Breath on her neck, warm across her ear.

And the voice, soft but strong, whispered…

"My name is Phil. I mean you no harm." Sandy jumped attempting to break free, but his grip was like iron, now even stronger, tighter, his bones like steel. "Look at what is happening out there… see with wide eyes, accept a simple fact…" Sandy could feel his head move to the other side of hers. "You have two choices, go with them and die…or…come with me…if you want to live."

Sandy felt the baby kick, saw her eyes dart to her stomach when the scene dissipated, phased out in a haze of red. Behind the red film was a man full of rage. An insatiable appetite for inflicting pain reflected in his eyes. When he snarled his sharp teeth were prominent. His thirst was for blood. Human blood. And when he prayed, he did so with bowed head to a being that stood over him with a rage that reflected in the man's eyes. This being, tall and massive, with yellow reptilian eyes, seemed to snarl at Sandy, as if it knew she dreamed of him. Those eyes remained, chiseled in Sandy's thoughts, in-between sleep and waking, her eyelids fluttering. The dream dissipated.

She was lying down, inside a white, oval shaped room lined with medical gurneys. The walls were made of a material she'd never seen. Oxygen pumped through vents into the room, she could feel it in her lungs. Sandy raised her arms. She was clean and dressed in a white tunic that stretched below the knees. All was quiet. The room empty. The walls a reflective metal. And she felt calm as if worry and concern had no place in this room with no windows. Sandy moved from the bed, her bare feet touching the cold pristine floor that glimmered under the reflection from the lights in the ceiling. She walked slowly to the wall, turning her head from one side then the other, observing her reflection. Her hair was finely curled, pristine and now blonde. She noticed how her skin glowed. Walking closer, her nose close to the reflective metal, searching her eyes, now wide and staring. Witnessing the change in her eyes, green irises with a touch of black stained inside the pupil.

And she grinned at her reflection.

She had no concern where she was. Somehow, she knew. She knew, and she felt calm. Complacent with knowing she was safe. She went to the door, touched her hand to the palm registry and it slid open. The hallway was dark like the night sky under the reflection of the full moon. To her left the hallway dipped into total darkness. To her right the hall snaked to a wide round opening with a waist high wall. Beyond the opening lights glimmered in the distance with sounds that reflected flute music and an intermingling buzz like listening to a teeming city full of life. She went to the wall, leaning her arms on top of it as she beheld the city that stretched well beyond what her eyes could see. Aircraft moved through the city like a futuristic highway. Scores of buildings stretched for miles with connected ramps, like arteries, revealed living creatures traveling to and from. The smell was clean, and the city reflected such: pristine and every so often it gleamed as if the city itself were divine.

A slight wind graced her skin. And Sandy closed her eyes allowing the wind to place her mind at ease.

*The future. It seems absolutely beautiful.*

\* \* \*

The ship spiraled toward a decimated Atlanta. Buildings half torn to pieces continued to stand. Some were reduced to debris and dust reflected in Phil's eyes. The ship flew past Atlanta towards the outskirts and into the woods where Phil dipped the ship down towards a small mountain and what appeared to be a rock wall. He flew the ship towards the wall and the rock glimmered as he flew through the hologram into a dark cave. He eyed a three-dimensional circle on the screen and a spotlight lit the darkness. The ship moved smoothly yet slowly through it.

Cam entered the cockpit and took a seat. He was quiet while taking in the scene outside the ship. After a while he said to Phil, "Robyn Winter?" to which Phil answered by pursing his lips with a slight nod.

Phil did not appear at all okay. At least to Cam who understood what it felt like to win the battle but lose the war. His mission had been to bring Sandy here, to this cave, to meet with Robyn Winter. Instead she had spiraled off in an alien ship taken to who knows where. But Cam was grateful for him. And grateful to be in this cave with him. He owed Phil a debt of gratitude. Maybe even more.

"How will they know?" Cam asked. "How will they know you're flying this thing and not them?"

"He will know," Phil said. His voice low and abrupt. Cam then noticed his wounds had healed. Not completely but they stopped bleeding and had been sealed shut.

The ship moved so slowly Cam thought for a moment that Phil was searching the perimeter. Maybe making sure they weren't being followed. The thought occurred to him that the scene seemed like an underwater excavation.

"How are the troops?" Phil asked.

"Bruised, confused and overloaded."

"I'm sure. It must be a lot to take in."

"That it is." Cam rested his head against his seat. "Reality is a strange concept to comprehend." He could have broken into tears at that moment, but he fought every gag in his throat. "Total mind fuck."

Phil was silent. He gave a slight nod.

"Was it the same for you?" Cam asked. "When you were told about...all this?"

Phil did not respond at first as if he was contemplating how to respond or did not want to. His answer came in that same hushed tone, "I was born into it," he answered.

Cam furrowed his brow and looked off to his right, away from Phil's eye. His mind raced with so many possibilities. So many questions. The events over the last twenty-four hours intermittent blips between those questions. He started piecing together a timeline concerning the war when an obvious revelation dawned on him. Phil's war must have been waging for much longer than his.

"Robyn Winter too?" Cam asked looking back at Phil. "Was he also born into it?"

Phil slowly shook his head. "He is from the time before the war. Before the collapse and upheaval. What we refer to as the *Dark Veil*."

'Oh,' Cam mouthed and shrugged his shoulders as if he knew what Phil was referring to. He chewed his lip, thinking. Again going back to the timeline, he was itching to understand. *Before the war.* Cam had no recollection of that time. Although he was born in that period, he was too young to remember and have memories of that time. Which means this Robyn Winter must be somewhere in his fifties.

"He's relatively young then," Cam said. "This Robyn Winter?"

Phil smiled. There was even a slight laugh behind the smile. Cam cocked his brow again. He wasn't expecting that response.

"Give it *time* Cameron. All answers in time." Phil shot him a quick stare. And for the first time Cam felt that the man was actually human. "Don't try to get it all in at once. It'll drive you insane."

*I think I'm already there.* He took a breath to calm himself. "Just one more question?" he asked.

Phil eyed a three-dimensional rectangle on the window and the screen lit up with schematics for the cave they were in. Arteries seemed to stretch on for miles into what appeared to be more caves. More areas that could be housing more human beings. More refugees. A circle outlined in red bleeped on the screen. Cam was sure the circle represented the ship that now stopped its approach, hovering inside the cave.

Phil eased back in his seat. "Sure," he said. "One more question. Just know that...from my experience, every answer has another question behind it."

Cam clenched his jaw and nodded. "Understood."

"But go ahead," Phil told him. "Ask away."

Cam shrugged. His eyes focused on the darkness outside the ship. "That woman...Sandy. Why is she so important?"

Phil guided the ship down, releasing the ramp as the ship descended. Cam waited for his answer.

"She's an indigo," Phil responded. "Her child too."

*He's right. Every answer has another question behind it.*

# 52

PHIL LED THE CREW INTO THE CAVE, the once dark area beamed with light when they departed the ship.

*Electricity. Down here? How's that possible.*

There were more ships. Cam counted nine ships scattered across the large open area. Several land cruisers and three pods he presumed were used for travelling under water. They looked like mini submarines.

"This way," Phil said. He led them to another rock wall, flipped open an eye level control panel disguised as a rock. Phil widened his eyes as the control panel lit up and a red beam reached toward his eyes, scanning his pupil. A second later the wall opened, scraping across the floor, revealing another large opening twice the size of the cave. Carved into the rock were what looked like rows and columns of small bedrooms. A bonfire was lit in the center, the ceiling towering high above. Cam stretched his neck, scanning the ceiling.

*Must be a hundred feet high.*

To Cam's right he could see a water reserve being fed from somewhere behind the cave. And there were people. Lots of people. He didn't know if he should feel relieved or frightened by his accompanying guest list. Not one person roaming the cave appeared to be alien. There were children too. Scores of children running and playing. Laughing and happy.

Happy, Cam observed. *I haven't seen a happy child in…*

He didn't finish the thought. He wanted every child he'd seen during the war to be here. *This place seems like a sleep away camp.* And the adults were working. Moving crates of food and buckets of water from one place to another. Working together.

"Are you from up above?"

Cam looked behind him where a group of these…*cave children….* surrounded the boy who wore Cam's shirt with pride, the sleeves bunched up above his elbow. The boy shot Cam a stare and Cam shrugged. Cam noticed something different about the cave children. Their eyes were larger than normal. Their heads too, and oddly peculiar were the two protruding lumps on the bottom back of the child's skull, like two thick nubs.

The boy pursed his lips. He looked scared. Maybe afraid to show his teeth, or fangs or whatever they are. The boy answered, nodding, "Yes."

"Wow," one of the kids said.

"You must be very brave," said another.

"Can we see your teeth?" asked again another.

The boy looked at Cam, but it was Phil who answered.

"Annison," Phil raised his voice and all the children turned to him. Phil moved his head back and forth. "That question may make him feel...a little unwelcome."

The girl, Annison, looked back at Phil, smiled from ear to ear and nodded. Her hair was blonde but thin. She looked back at the boy.

"Do you want to play tag? It's a lot of fun."

The boy seemed overwhelmed, afraid.

"It's okay," Annison said. "You're perfectly safe here. What's your name?"

The boy's face scrunched, confused. He looked at Cam.

"Cameron," he said. "I like that name."

"Me too," Annison said. She smiled and touched the boy. "Tag," she said. "You're it."

Cam smiled. The boy, now Cameron, did too. Cam had thought he'd never smile again, considering all that had happened. But he did, and it felt good to smile. Cam noticed Lao and Grimes observing the cave, their eyes wide with wonder. The refugees behind them, the people they rescued, wide eyed and staring. And the giant. The kids went to him and started playing. When Cam looked back at Phil, he was speaking quietly with someone who carried a concerned yet inquisitive stare. Their conversation was muffled and incoherent. The man was thin but not malnourished thin. Skinny bones thin. He wore baggy cargo pants and a tight thin shirt. It seemed that everyone in the cave wore the same although in various colors. Cam was able to catch the last part of the conversation.

"They'll be perfectly safe," the man said.

Phil was staring at the refugees and how the kids were now swinging from Perseus's arms who laughed with them, seeming to enjoy this new role.

"We have to be sure," the man said.

Phil gave the ok with a quick nod.

The man put his hand on Phil's shoulder.

"Are *you* okay?"

Phil locked eyes with him. He nodded. "Yes," he said. "A few cuts and slices but they're all fine now."

He released Phil's shoulder. "That's not what I meant."

Phil returned his gaze and mouthed *I know.*

He closed his eyes briefly, scrunched his face pursing his lips. "Understood," he said.

Phil looked back at Cam. Waved to Cam, Grimes and Lao. "Follow me," he said. He led them to the end of the cave where another wall opened into a large dark hallway. Lao and Grimes followed close behind Phil. Cam stood still, looked back into the cave, observing how the person Phil had been talking with went to address the refugees.

"Circle around, gentlemen," he told them. And without hesitation they obeyed. He was holding something in his hand that looked like a pen. "Look here," he said.

The flash of light popped inside the cave like an old bulb flash from a camera. Cam bit his lip, looking down, drew in a deep breath then went to join Phil.

Phil led them through the short hallway to another rock wall and placed his hand on a control panel. Another red light, scanning his palm and fingers. The wall opened. Dimly lit the round circular room was mostly barren. Roughly fifty feet away several men and women were conversing, standing in a circle around a hologram that reflected what looked like an underwater city under construction. Those mini submarines Cam had seen in the cave were moving through the construction site. Cam counted nine people, humans, standing around the hologram, five women and four men. They were dressed in similar versions of Phil's former armor. Or whatever you'd call it. The one he'd taken off when that Thorx jutted its tentacle and spilled acid over it. They were engaged in conversation when they entered. Phil stood back as if waiting for them to finish.

"How long?" one of the women asked. Her question answered by one of the men.

"Another ten, maybe twelve years. Enough time to become operational before the complete attack is initiated. We do have time. But not much."

One of the women responded. "The indigo gene grows stronger with each generation. Twelve years may prove difficult to account for all."

A third female continued. "Should there be any who remain at that time. The unholy human and Draconian union has already eradicated so many who have shown promise. The pure indigos have yet to be identified. The union's decimation over the last ten generations has altered the pure gene. With the growing insurgence and unions hold on those above ground, there is no telling if any indigos will remain in twelve years or if the pure gene will manifest."

"I surmise the pure indigos are among us. And a few who've yet to be born," said one of the men.

"What brings your conclusion?" asked the woman who had previously talked.

The man answered, "Because the Arcturian nine *are* coming. The Akashic Record indicates the indigo trials will begin prior to their arrival. It is inevitable. The pure indigos must be identified... and provided protection until the Arcturian arrival." He turned his head up, as if gazing through the ceiling then turned back to the hologram. "As far as the underwater compound, the Arcturian's physical arrival," he pointed to the hologram, "will provide the necessary tools to complete construction."

"Should the union's plan not decimate them upon that arrival. And let us not forget, the Arcturians are bound by cosmic law. Should the union's hold on the human masses continue, by the time they arrive our own species may hand over the planet to Draconian rule with a simple wave of a reptilian hand," the man who stood with his back to Phil and the others said. He shook his head. "Even if we manage to alter this plan, the union continues with its alternate decimation." He pushed a button on the waist high desk in front of him. This desk circled the hologram and each person in front of it had the same set of controls. The hologram changed to the moon.

Lao stepped forward. It was the same scene he'd seen on the monitor with an addition that he'd not seen before. A space station now appeared close to the moon.

The same person continued. "Its construction rivals our own with no telling if our underwater compound will survive a nuclear holocaust. We must consider an alternative location. All is coming to fruition as predicted. The Akashic Record continues to reflect said prediction." He pushed another button. The hologram now reflected Mars. "The same for the Mars colony. Nuclear upheaval has once again decimated the planet. The nine cannot land on Mars. The nuclear cloud is locked in its orbit. Any ship that attempts to land on the surface will be annihilated. They will require an alternate station to launch from."

They all paused. One of the women broke the silence.

"Perhaps one of the larger asteroids in the twelfth planet belt." She pushed a button on her controls. Mars was reduced in size, now it showed the asteroid belt between Mars and Jupiter. "The asteroids contain the needed elements to complete construction."

One of the men was shaking his head. "A disturbance in the belt may dislodge the asteroid from its orbit."

"Perhaps. But it may be the only choice we have," the woman answered.

"And risk a cataclysmic event prior to our security?" said another, one of the females who had not yet spoken.

The response came not from any of the nine around the hologram, but a voice in the darkness beyond the hologram.

"The nine are aware of the implication." The voice was heavy and thick. Reflecting age and wisdom. This person walked from the shadows on the opposite side of the room, into the light. Rust colored cargo pants dropped to his ankles, a black Kevlar shirt tightly wrapped around him. A thin frame although his hands and arms gave off the impression likened to immense strength. His skull was smooth, however his face and the rest of his body was scarred as if he'd been caught in a fire and burned from eye to toe. And his eyes. They reflected a gelatinous milky white with no pupils or iris. Cam scrunched his brow, looking over the young male.

Phil stepped forward. "Robyn," he whispered.

He seemed to glide over to the nine. "They are also aware of the shimmer in the record. They leave their fate *to* the record." He addressed the nine. "They proceed as required of them, as always."

It was the female, the one whose question Robyn had responded to, who addressed him first. "But, Robyn, without their safe arrival all is lost. Not even the indigos will be able to stop the union's plan."

Robyn paused. He held his chin high. His head moving side to side. "The record will always balance itself. That is its purpose. The Arcturians know this more than any. Should the record require their dissolution, they will accept it as such."

"But the galactic response will be devastating should such an event transpire. We must not allow it."

"That is your lot," Robyn said. "It is only in your time. The record will always balance the equation."

The others stood with bent chins, as if they all contemplated the same thought.

"Let us put this to rest for now. We have visitors to tend to." He addressed Phil who went to him, his head bowed.

"My love," he said. "You fought gallantly." Robyn put his forehead to Phil's.

Cam noticed, beyond any doubt, that Robyn Winter was younger than Phil. Although his eyes, those milky white eyes, seemed centuries old.

"The rose is your ally," Robyn told him. "Not the physical."

Phil released his forehead. "But the rose evades me."

Robyn shook his head. "No. *You* evade you."

Phil considered this statement then nodded in agreement. He regained his composure, standing tall. Cam noticed he was taller than Robyn. "My stay is brief. Both child and mother have fallen under their grace. And…" He paused as if he was about to confess some great revelation. "The child was birthed in the camp. His DNA! Robyn…" Phil pursed his lips forcing a swallow. "They may have isolated the necessary component in the child."

One of the male nine responded. "If that is true…" He turned to the others. "Then the future spirals into peril. The pure indigos will face a dire threat. Robyn…what course of action do we take with this revelation?"

Robyn addressed them. "Phil knows this answer."

Phil paused, addressing the panel of nine. "I'll find her," he said. "And the child. I swear to it."

"He has to," a female nine said. Cam was watching Robyn's reaction. His complexion seemed to change. While he had appeared young before now his countenance reflected withered age. Cam thought Robyn did not agree with this course of action. Even more, he felt Robyn's presence. *Actually* felt it. And the presence was familiar. He thought that Robyn regarded him with a connection that seemed old and ethereal. The female continued. "We must not allow the child's maturity to occur within the union."

The others agreed.

"Do you know where they've been taken?" a male nine asked.

"I do not," Phil answered. "But the ship we've confiscated will be able to direct me to their location."

"Very well," said a female nine. "You have our confidence. Proceed as you must."

"Thank you," Phil said with a bow. He then addressed his associates. "These men have fought with equal valor. Please provide them with their wishes."

The female nine who provided Phil with his continuance spoke first. "Please step forward. We are in your debt. How can we be of service?"

They all stepped forward. Lao was the first to speak. And as he did Cam noticed how Robyn had taken Phil by the elbow. He heard the first part of what Robyn said to him, "You may not like what you find…"

But his voice trailed off when Lao addressed the nine; his voice cracked and desperate.

"I wish to go home," he said.

As if the nine had anticipated Lao's request, the hologram changed. Represented was Beijing. Its decimation was evident in the hologram. Lao's eyes went wide, his mouth agape, beholding the destruction and the image of a massive hovering spaceship. It was one of the females who said, "Your Gods have already revealed themselves to those not secured within reprogramming camps. We expect the same coming for us, here on American soil."

## 53

MINTAKA GLIDED THROUGH THE HALL WITH ADAM cradled in her arms. The circular hall illuminated with small rectangular lights placed in columns. Their bluish glow tainted Mintaka's grey skin, reflected in those large dark eyes. The baby, calm when she first gathered him in her arms, was becoming restless. A reaction she had anticipated.

The round door slid open upon her entrance. Inside the room two Dracs stood in front of a hologram. The Drac on Mintaka's right, Jayda, was short in stature with a massive frame. His thick skull like that of a bull, although his energy was gentle, his eyes revealed a soft stare. The second, Moth, was tall and thin, his skull elongated like a thick eggshell with spotted red scales and a face that reflected both the sinister snarl of alien vampires with a rugged skin likened to something close to human. His nose flattened in a forever sneer, dark purple lips covered those vampire teeth. Moth is the head of the elite Drac Nine, his power immeasurable and uncontested. To Mintaka he did not look pleased. The being reflected in the hologram was a reptilian. Its voice was harsh and garbled, addressing the Dracs. Mintaka froze and the baby squirmed in her arms. The hologram disappeared but Mintaka's eyes continued to search the area where the hologram had been.

"The child," said Jayda. The baby's restlessness continued. He began to squirm and kick with ferocity. Jayda gathered the baby in his arms. "His training begins today," he said to Moth who regarded the child with a stare of disgust. The child started to cry, grunting in Jayda's arms.

"Take that thing away," Moth sneered. Jayda regarded Moth with a fearful stare then bowed. The baby's cries wailing as Jayda disappeared down a long hall on the far end of the room.

When the baby and Jayda were gone, Moth said, "Is your maturity assessment accurate, Mintaka?"

"Mono informed us of the revelation. Maturity is the only way to be sure the gene will manifest appropriately."

Moth turned away, his hands clamped behind his back, thinking.

"Moth," Mintaka said a moment later. "What will be done with the mother?"

Moth turned to Mintaka. "I'll take care of it. The matter is of no consequence."

"The human will return to find her."

"If he has survived. On all accounts the camp has been destroyed. We have received no communications that indicate any possible survival." He paused. The glare in his eyes changed, his head bent, snarling. "There are other matters we must discuss, Mintaka."

Mintaka raised her chin. "Such as?"

Moth took a seat, sitting close to the table in the room's center. He locked eyes with Mintaka. "Dr. Blum's research," he said. "It seems he isolated the necessary formula. We must implement Phase Three. Begin mass reconditioning."

* * *

"After what they said, are you sure you want to return?" Cam asked Lao. They were standing in the cave, surrounded by ships.

"My family," Lao said. "I have to know what happened to them."

Cam looked to the ground and paused. Turned his eyes back to Lao. "Understood," he said. He gestured to the ship Lao was about to board. "Anti-gravity?"

Lao nodded. "They said we will be in China within a few hours." Grimes and the boy Cameron along with Annison and the giant entered the cave. Lao referenced them. "Are you sure you want to take on their responsibility?"

Cam turned to Grimes and crew. He looked at the boy who had taken his name. "Purpose," he said. He looked back at Lao. "They said the experiment will cause a psychic link, and the Dracs will be able to isolate his whereabouts and find this cave."

"That also means wherever you go they'll find you too."

"I know," he said. "But I can't leave him alone in the wild. If that's my burden to carry, I hope one day he will be worth it. Until he learns to guard his thoughts, as they say he will, he will need protection."

Lao raised his brow. "Understood."

"Perhaps one day our paths will cross again."

"Perhaps." Lao offered his hand. "Until then God Speed, Cam."

Cam took his hand. "God Speed."

Lao turned to Grimes, closed his eyes and bowed. The Corporal did the same. Lao boarded the ship and Cam joined Grimes.

"I hope he finds what he's looking for," Grimes said.

Cam looked back at the ship. "He will."

"What of our savior?" Grimes asked. Cam turned as Grimes cleared his throat. "Is he still going after the woman?"

"He is."

"It's suicide," Grimes said. "From what they say, there's no way he can win."

"A little faith," Cam offered. "After what he did in that camp, I think he can do just about anything."

Grimes pursed his lips. Gave a quick nod. "We better go," he said. "If we're going to make the next stop before nightfall."

Phil entered the cave, wearing new white armor that shined under the light, when Lao's ship powered on with a whistle likened to forced air. "Get them on board," Cam said. "I'll be with you in a second."

"Gotcha," said Grimes. He looked at Phil and gave an apprecia-tive nod that Phil returned.

"Are you all set?" Phil said to Cam.

"As set as can be expected."

There was a momentary silence between them. It was Cam who broke the silence. "Are you sure this is what you want to do?" Cam asked. "You heard what Robyn said. And by yourself? Don't you think you'll need assistance?"

Phil shook his head. "I work better alone. Besides, you've got your own concerns." He put his hand on Cam's shoulder. "All is well. But we both have our mission. Our paths were meant to cross. If for only briefly."

Cam gestured to the ship they'd escaped in. "Do you think they're tracking it?"

"Possible," Phil said.

Cam nodded. The term, *suicide mission* stained his thoughts. He locked eyes with Phil. "I hope you find what you're looking for."

"Such a notion is inevitable. Sometimes what we seek is different than what we find although what we need. What is required."

"Straight from Robyn's lips."

Phil nodded. "You better go."

Cam wanted to say thank you. Thank you for everything. Not just saving my life but saving all of us. For giving us the opportunity to continue. If it weren't for Phil everyone in his caravan would be dead. And maybe Phil would have accomplished his mission. But he couldn't get the words out. He felt if he had it would mean one conclusion. He wouldn't see Phil again.

The fixed stare in Cam's eye told Phil all he needed to know. Cam offered his hand and Phil took it. "See you on the other side," said Phil.

"Good luck," Cam told him, Phil offered the same then went towards his ship, Cam watching him.

"Phil," Cam shouted. Phil turned and Cam paused, searching for something to say. He didn't want to see him go, for whatever reason. Perhaps to find a relatable consistency, other than war, death and carnage he said, "I hear you have a wife and child."

"And one on the way," Phil responded.

Cam nodded. "Well, god speed to them as well."

Phil responded with a tight and grateful nod. He boarded the ship.

"Let's go, soldier," Grimes hollered.

Cam turned his head, brow furrowed. "Ya know something, Corporal?"

He relaxed his shoulders, letting go, walking over to Grimes. "Your ego's big enough to fill a dump truck," Cam said, shaking his head.

"Well, I'm still your superior officer," said Grimes.

Cam laughed. "Sure, Corporal. Sure!" He turned back, observing Phil's ship.

"Let it go," Grimes said. "Let it go."

"I know," Cam agreed, taking in one last view of Phil's ship. Drew in a shallow breath and clenched his jaw. "Is everyone on board?"

Grimes' eyes narrowed, "Seriously?"

Cam shook his head, rolled his eyes. "Whatever, Corporal!" he breathed. "Seems like we've got a long road ahead of us," he whispered, as if talking to himself. Then met Grimes' eyes with his own. Put his hand on Grimes' shoulder and offered a smile. "There's no telling what we're gonna find down the road."

# 54

"**DO YOU LIKE WHAT YOU SEE?**" said a voice behind Sandy. She'd been looking over the city for what seemed like an eternity. Mintaka had come to her, informing Sandy a Drac representative would be along soon. That she had no reason to fear the Dracs. They were in her debt for what she'd done for Telas.

Sandy turned to the voice behind her. A male Drac.

He stepped closer. "Moth," he said with a slight bow. "How is it you were able to leave the infirmary?" His eyes narrowed.

Sandy bent her head, brow furrowed. "I...I put my hand to the door," she said and shrugged. "It just opened." She forced a smile.

Moth pursed his lips, gave a slight nod then stepped closer. "Is there anything we can do...to make your stay with us more comfortable?"

"My child," she said. "Where is Adam?"

The look on Moth's face turned to heavy concern. "My lady," he said, moving his head back and forth. "Did Mintaka not share with you..."

Sandy paused before saying, "Share?" She felt a rush of nerves flush across her face.

"My lady, I am so sorry, the baby...he expired on the ship."

Sandy's jaw dropped. "How?"

Moth stepped closer. "By your own hand." His sad smile sent a shiver down Sandy's spine. Her body constricted, shaking her head, staring deep into Moth's eyes, into his soul. Thought she saw a glimmer in those eyes, like a shimmer in the truth, as though he were lying.

"Impossible," Sandy said in a fury. She turned from Moth shaking her head. "Can't be," she said. Moth stepped closer. "Why didn't you tell me?" she whispered, thinking of Telas.

"When a Drac is disintegrated the way Telas was, the psychic link to your child was severed. A Drac baby cannot live without the mother. It is a condition of our lineage. The baby was lost in that moment."

Tears welled in Sandy's eyes.

"So sorry, my lady." He placed his hand on her shoulder.

Sandy cringed, overwhelmed with grief, crying.

"So, so sorry." He forced Sandy into his embrace, his arms like an iron grip.

Sandy was weeping. Moth squeezed her tight yet gentle. Sandy felt a click in her stomach. As if a strong connection had either been severed...or became prominent. She saw Telas then, in her mind's eye. Telas holding the baby, somewhere in oblivion. Sandy's hands trembled, her stomach wrenched, shuddering in Moth's embrace. Unable to move.

"How is it possible? I can still feel him." She constricted, her jaw tight.

And Moth bared his teeth.

Sank his fangs into Sandy's neck.

* * *

*Sometimes we must let go,* Robyn's words in Phil's mind. Phil watched as Cam and Grimes powered up their vehicle. A land cruiser that ran on solar power. Phil took his seat in the alien ship then fit the metal halo over his head.

*You might not like what you find,* Robyn had told him. *We will find another way. Forcing our will never ends well.*

Phil powered up his ship. A blinking blue light flashed on the control panel. Phil couldn't accept what Robyn had said. The way Phil saw it his mission was put off briefly, not permanently. *Follow it through to the end,* he told Robyn. *Follow Sandy, all the way to the end.* Robyn's own words used against him.

Robyn had furrowed his brow when he replied, "Did it not end?"

"I'll find them," Phil had declared.

Robyn responded, "To that end there is no doubt."

Phil eyed the blue light.

"But at what cost?" Robyn had asked.

The ships monitor lit up.

"My life, if necessary," was Phil's response.

On the screen was the third ship from the pit.

"Eagerly given," Robyn said.

Phil had stiffened over Robyn's comment. "*Freely* given," Phil responded. "For the sake of our species, of course I would lay down for it."

Sanos appeared on the monitor. His eyes staring through Phil. He bared his teeth in a sickly grin. The word *recording* flashed on the screen bottom. Sanos began to speak: "To the human who bested Saiph, a challenge to you. I have the whereabouts of the human female you seek." Sanos snickered. "Now that I have your attention, I challenge thee come find me. My location…has been sent with this transmission."

His image paused. The transmission ended. Phil glared at Sanos.

"Such things are nothing more than ego," Robyn had said. "Besides, there is another child we must secure. And train. I was hoping we could do that together."

The monitor changed from Sanos to the location of his ship. A question then appeared on the screen: Chart course to CR115: YES NO

Phil chewed his lip looking out into the cave. He watched as Cam's cruiser hummed out of the cave followed by the anti-gravity vessel headed to China.

"Plenty of time to train young Ares," Phil had told Robyn. He'd put his hand on Robyn's shoulder. "I will be back," he told him. "You can count on it."

But Robyn did not respond.

Phil turned to the monitor and to the question on the screen. There was a brief hesitation before he eyed the word YES and the monitor jumped to life, charting a course to CR115.

*Course obtained,* a mechanical voice instructed. *Be ready for lift off.*

Phil drew in a deep breath, whispering…

"And — here — we — go!"

# Author Note and Acknowledgments

*The Rose* started as a short story, a kind of prequel to the *Indigo Trials*, a novel I had been writing at the time but, like most stories, the characters in *The Rose* took on a life of their own. They had a story they wanted to tell and refused to relent from my thoughts and visions. As I kept writing, a short story turned into—at least in my mind at the time—a novella, then it kept moving, progressing, and eventually developed into a full length novel for which I was certain would require at least two volumes to tell the story as it should be told. Yes, Vol. II has been plotted and diligent notes have been taken to develop what will be the continuation of this first novel.

The story is a culmination of various novel ideas I've had over the past decade, all of which developed simultaneously like the cells of a fetus come together to breed an unborn child within a mother's womb. The first idea came from a hard science fiction novel (no title had been decided on but the blades came from this story), second, a dystopian World War 3 conspiracy novel (originally titled Celestial Silence which was a novel about a man who falls asleep in heaven and wakes up in a nightmare); the third is a novel I was developing that revolved around the collapse of society that led to World War 3 (main character in this novel is Robyn Winter, *hint, hint, wink, wink*). Personally speaking I do enjoy a good conspiracy theory and have developed a few of my own over the years. Coupled with my love of science fiction, action and adventure, *The Rose* reached into my brain, sank its talons into a heart of passion and gave my spirit purpose. I've been writing all my life but never have I had more fun with a book than I had writing *The Rose*.

The title comes from a meditation practice used by alchemists. I happened to come across an old email from a trusted source in alchemy that detailed the meditation and what it was used for: namely protection from dark energy and dark influence. And I thought to myself, "Self, that would be a really cool method to use in a science fiction battle."

My first thank you goes to the novel and its many cast of characters. Sanos, Phil, Sandy, Telas, Mono, the witches, Cameron, Robyn, and Saiph, you are all forever etched in my mind and I thank you for the time we've spent so far. I'm way too excited to see where you all take this story, it is yours, have at it. Second thank you goes to Pink Floyd and Led Zeppelin, namely the songs *Shine On You Crazy Diamond* and *Kashmir*. I struggled with choosing which song to include in the beginning quotes and I hope I chose wisely. These two songs carried me through the writing process and put an exclamation point on the mood I was hoping to harness within the novel. Music has always helped set the tone of my novels, and has had great and persistent influence in all I've ever done, so I'm more than proud to have brought these two iconic rock bands along for the ride.

To my editor, Judy at Goddessfish Promotions I am forever grateful to have found you. Not only did you take a passion filled slam of ideas and turned those ideas into a coherent novel, you gave me a great lesson in editing. There's an old adage "Give a man a fish and you've fed him for the day. Teach a man to fish and you've fed him for a lifetime." Thank you for teaching me how to edit, a practice I now welcome and have fallen in love with.

To my son Dominick, for whom this novel is dedicated. The two of us reading and editing *The Rose* has become one of my most precious memories. Your excitement and love of the characters and story remains in my mind forever. I thank you for sharing the experience with me. Nothing makes me more proud than knowing the story blew your socks off. Dom, my harshest critic, this one is for you.

To Alicia Gard, Anthony Alleva, Michael Paup, and Vanessa Petrillo, thank you for beta reading, your influence and input raised the bar on this novel, I am grateful to you all.

With that being said, a special thank you to my wife, Lisa, who, for some reason (I think its that whole love forever thing) puts up with my antics, insecurities, and eccentricities and continues to stick around. You are the light in my dark tunnel. To my daughter, Bre'Anne who owns my heart, thank you for believing. And to my boys, my men, my twins, Leo and Santino, who looked on me with wide fearful eyes when I told them I was writing a book about alien vampires. There is nothing to fear.

To my publisher, Quill and Birch, thank you for taking a chance on an indie writer. To Cherie Fox the cover designer, you took my vision and hit the nail on the head, thank you. To The Book Couple, Gary and Carol Rosenberg, thank you for putting the pieces together and turning out a professional novel.

And to you, dear reader, a novel that's never read is a waste of a world, thank you for breathing life into *The Rose*; the cast of characters welcomes your passion. My firm belief is that great projects are achieved through collaboration, so it is from the bottom of my heart that I thank you all. And to the world of Indie Authors and Indie Publishing, we're all coming out, guns blazing, and ready for battle. In the great words of Phil, "And Here We Go!"

~ PD Alleva
Boca Raton, Florida
May 2020

Made in the USA
Monee, IL
13 October 2020